LAST OF THE
TALONS

LAST OF THE
TALONS

SOPHIE KIM

Entangled Publishing, LLC
644 Shrewsbury Commons Ave., STE 181
Shrewsbury, PA 17361
rights@entangledpublishing.com

Entangled Teen is an imprint of Entangled Publishing, LLC.

Visit our website at www.entangledpublishing.com.

Edited by Jen Bouvier and Stacy Abrams
Cover design and interior graphics by Elizabeth Turner Stokes
Cover illustration by Ashley Mackenzie
Interior design by Toni Kerr

ISBN 978-1-64937-280-2
Ebook ISBN 978-1-64937-297-0

Manufactured in the United States of America

First Edition September 2022

10 9 8 7 6 5 4 3 2 1

an imprint of Entangled Publishing LLC

*For those of us who have wanted to see ourselves
in a story like this for so long,
and for my family, who have encouraged
me every step of the way…
This book is for you..*

AUTHOR'S NOTE

One of mythology's many beauties is that the stories are ripe for reinterpretations and retellings that reignite interest in traditional tales stemming back to ancient times. Stories such as these are meant to be passed on—either orally or in writing—throughout the ages. They are to be immortal, indestructible, tales that live and breathe throughout the many centuries the world has since undergone. Retellings keep these stories alive, anchoring them to the modern world even as the danger of fading into obscurity tugs at their every word.

It was therefore irksome to me that Korean mythology was largely dismissed in the world of retellings. Korean mythology brims with a wonderful assortment of magic, romance, betrayal, philosophy, and political intrigue tying in true events of Korean history with fantastical elements such as Yong (dragons) and Gwisin (ghosts)...yet it was often cast aside, just as non-stereotypical Korean characters were often cast aside in favor of the opposite.

Growing up, I rarely saw characters who looked like me and were not crammed into the stereotypical role of "geeky best friend." There was nothing I wanted more than to see myself as a snarky assassin, a swashbuckling pirate, or a fearless warrior...and yet I never did. It would have been empowering for me to pick up a book brimming with both Korean mythology and Korean representation, to see Korean gods and goddesses instead of the same old stereotypes that litter both the pages of books and the screens of Hollywood.

Bringing that empowerment to other readers was a large motive of mine when I began to write *Last of the Talons*.

Yet before setting pen to page, a vast amount of research went into fully understanding and appreciating the original lore of Korean mythology, as well as the cultural narratives behind it. I felt that it was exceptionally important for me to ensure that this manuscript—while being a new twist on the original legends—was still written by an author who wholly understood and appreciated the origins of her culture's stories. The Kingdom of Sunpo and the hidden realm of Gyeulcheon are entirely fictional, but the mythology within both stems from centuries of Korean history and tradition (with the exception, of course, being the Pied Piper element of this novel. That original fairy tale originates from the German town of Hamelin).

Last of the Talons is not intended to be a guide to traditional Korean mythology. This book is a retelling, and as such, there are a variety of spins on the original stories. As an example, the original Tale of Manpasikjeok (also known as A Black Jade Belt and the Flute to Calm Ten Thousand Waves) is quite different from the tale utilized in this novel. The original myth finds its roots during the reign of the Silla Dynasty's 31st sovereign—Emperor Sinmun (681–692). While the magical flute was never used by a sarcastic and sensual Dokkaebi emperor, Manpasikjeok (만파식적) was gifted to Emperor Sinmun by a sea dragon, and the story is still rich with a magnificent mysticality.

This book also contains creative spins on beings such as the Korean pantheon, Dokkaebi, Imugi, and Gwisin—as well as the underworld realm of Jeoseung. If you would like to learn more about their original forms, I recommend purchasing a copy of *Korean Myths and Folk Legends* by Hwang Pae-gang and translated by Han Young-hie, as well as visiting folkency.nfm.go.kr, where a variety of resources relating to both Korean mythology and traditional culture may be found.

Last of the Talons is a love letter to the stories of my heritage as much as it is a love letter to readers who have wanted to see themselves represented in a book like this. I hope, from the bottom of my heart, that you enjoy it.

Fondly,

Sophie Kim

At Entangled, we want our readers to be well-informed. If you would like to know if this book contains any elements that might be of concern for you, please check the back of the book for details.

CHAPTER ONE

The Temple of Ruin has been abandoned for centuries, but it's an unspoken rule that nobody enters the looming pagoda.

There are legends of dark, dreadful *things* lurking within its depths—fanged creatures that lunge out of shadows and drag unsuspecting mortals down into the nightmarish underworld below.

And the gods do not lift a finger to help them.

Yet my lips still whisper a prayer as I eye the damned temple that Konrarnd Kalmin has deemed our mark for a midnight heist.

I am not surprised when there is no answer.

They abandoned us centuries ago, those gods, growing bored of the realm's human trifles. They are not here now. None of them are. Not even the Dokkaebi look upon this kingdom tonight.

I am alone. Completely and utterly alone, as always.

Though considering who I'm stealing from… I wince. My loneliness is, for once, a rather large blessing.

My stomach tightens with nerves as I adjust my position on

the roof of the dingy wooden complex that neighbors the temple. Its scarlet color gleams tauntingly under the light of the night's half-hearted moon.

Bloodred pillars and a swirling, ink-black finial reach toward the growing storm clouds up above, determined to blot out the already-faint stars that hover over the decrepit kingdom of Sunpo.

I've snuck through almost every crevice of the Eastern Continent's dilapidated territory, every tavern and pleasure hall, every manor and slum in the four sectors. And if I hadn't, Sang or the twins had described it to me.

But neither Sang nor the twins had ever been in *there.*

Nibbling on my bottom lip, I check my suit to ensure that my single knife is sheathed at my waist. It is. I glance down at the sloping tiled roof before me with narrowed eyes and make my best effort to transform my clammy apprehension into stone-cold resolve.

For Eunbi.

I launch into action, sprinting across the ragged tiles in a rapid blur. An icy wind whips my face raw as I launch myself into open air. For a beautiful moment, I savor the feeling of utter weightlessness before my stomach drops and I'm crashing downdowndown*down…*

The pagoda's roof approaches me in a blur of crimson.

I land in a crouch, with one hand gripping a curved red roof tile and the other stretched out behind me.

My left leg, scarred and ruined from the merciless bite of a blade, screams in pain from the sudden impact. I do my best to ignore it, quelling a groan as I focus on adjusting my position to glance at the pagoda's bracket below. It's about fifteen feet underneath a dip in the red roof. *Easy.*

My boots hit the ground with a soft thud. Another jump, and I'm on the balustrade below. A moment later, I swing myself over the railing-like structure onto the awaiting wooden floor and land with a soft exhale of relief.

There's no time to waste, though.

The window I'm planning to enter through, and Kalmin's precious prize, are waiting. I touch the glass with a gloved finger and run my tongue across my front teeth. The window is certainly small, but just large enough for me to squirm through.

Hopefully.

In a swift, sure movement, I slam my gloved fist into the glass, expecting it to give way completely. Yet it only cracks, a thick sliver running down the center of the square panel.

My jaw tightens.

I've never had trouble breaking as thin a glass as this, but a year of working for Kalmin, malnourished and mistreated, has left me weakened.

And angry.

As red-hot fury heats my blood, I slam the hilt of my dagger into the window with a rough growl. The glass shatters into a storm of shards.

"Finally," I mutter and glare at the now-open entrance of the Temple of Ruin as I brush shattered glass from my hair. I peer into the inky darkness.

It's not hard to believe that the Temple of Ruin was once the place of worship dedicated to the Pied Piper—the infamous goblin who, after the gods' abandonment of our world for another, once reigned over the Three Kingdoms of the Eastern Continent as emperor of both mortals and Dokkaebi alike.

And from whom I'm now stealing.

Wonderful.

I hiss a profanity as I grip the upper windowsill and slide my legs through. I may not be able to see it, but surely there'll be a floor below. I push myself from the ledge with a slight shift of my arms.

The temple is filled with a series of barking curses as I

realize that there certainly *is* a floor…just thirty feet below. I tumble through the darkness, barely managing to twist my body into a position that thankfully results in my *not* cracking my head open.

Landing on the ground and flipping myself forward on impact to soften the blow, I envision running Konrarnd Kalmin through with a particularly large sword. Godsdamn him to the depths of Jeoseung for sending me here. Godsdamn him for taking so much from me and expecting to receive pretty little prizes in return.

A burst of agony slices through my bad leg as I struggle to my feet and fish my lighter from the pocket of my stealth suit. With a hiss, it ignites, but the flickering flame barely manages to illuminate the space.

The Temple of Ruin is nothing like I expected it to be.

I anticipated a palace within the pagoda, complete with twisting, winding stairs and richly furnished rooms, haunted with whispering shadows and air thick with a sense of sinister foreboding.

Instead, I take in a simple, spacious room like that of a studio. To my dismay, it's empty—save for a thick coating of snow-like dust that now covers my suit and a small black chest in the center of the room.

There are no signs of any wailing Gwisin. No ghosts here— nothing but silence and that odd little trunk accompany me. I fight back an incredulous laugh.

The infamous Temple of Ruin is nothing more than an empty room. If anything, this temple is glaringly obvious proof that the Dokkaebi pay very little attention to the one territory they still possess. And why should they? The immortals have better things with which to occupy themselves in their own pocket realm of Gyeulcheon.

I limp my way over to the chest, in which I'm certain lies this tapestry that Kalmin so desperately desires. I blow a heavy layer of dust off the box and fight back a sneeze as the thick powder rises into the air in a cloud of white.

There is a black lock, engraved with small silver markings in a language that I don't immediately recognize. Perhaps it is the Old Language, from the time of the gods. The lock itself seems simple enough—I've picked hundreds, probably thousands, of locks before. This will be no different.

Yet I hesitate.

Stealing from the Dokkaebi...

I wonder, grimly, if I will face the wrath of the Pied Piper after this. If he will lure me away with his enchanted flute as he's done to so many mortals and slaughter me in his hidden realm. A sick sort of satisfaction creeps its way into my chest.

If the Pied Piper comes after me, I shall take an immense delight in explaining that it was Konrarnd Kalmin who sent me to the Temple of Ruin, Kalmin and his little gang of Blackbloods.

If I go down, so do they.

I smile as I jimmy the narrow tip of my blade into the trunk's keyhole. I move the blade farther into the lock, my brows furrowing in slight concentration. *Right...about...here.*

My grin grows. There we are.

The trunk unlocks with a satisfying *click.*

Slowly, I open the chest.

And realize, as my light bathes over its contents, why, exactly, the tapestry was deemed such a bother.

It is magnificent.

Washed in the glow of my flame, it shines in starbursts of vivid colors. Interwoven with threads of string, small, gleaming jewels are nestled between each stitch. Thousands of them.

I suck in a sharp breath.

With a trembling hand, I heft the tapestry out of its resting place. It must weigh the same as a small child, but judging from the number of folds, it's no bigger than a small welcome mat, and just barely as wide.

The jewels bite into my gloved fingers, slicing through the thick, padded fabric with frightening ease. My heart races. *"Gods,"* I breathe.

These jewels are from Gyeulcheon, *their* realm, which is hidden by Dokkaebi magic. Even the jewels from the Southern Continent's kingdom of Oktari—renowned for its precious stones—do not compare to this.

Touching the jewels sends a rush of giddiness through my body and summons the image of a curly haired, gap-toothed girl with dancing eyes and an infectious laugh. *Eunbi.*

I wonder how dire the consequences would be if I take the tapestry for myself and run. Perhaps I would be able to buy out the men stationed on the Yaepak Mountains with the jewels... but no. Kalmin would give the order for his cronies to murder my sister long before I'd make it to her mountaintop school.

My throat constricts as I tuck the tapestry under one arm, quelling my fantasies of a life of freedom lived alongside my little sister. I shut the now-empty chest with a *thud* that echoes through the derelict temple.

Kalmin wants his treasure.

And so he'll get it. Just like always.

When the moon follows me home through the darkened streets of Sunpo, I can almost swear that Dalnim, its dark-haired goddess, is watching me.

CHAPTER TWO

"Beautiful," Kalmin breathes, a razor-sharp grin splitting his lips as he stands back from his mahogany desk, on which he has laid out the vibrant tapestry.

Next to him, his second-in-command, Asina, sends me a cold glance, but even she cannot hide the awe on her angular face.

As I allow my gaze to drift down to the tapestry, I realize that I've been too preoccupied with the thrill of thievery to wonder what image the carefully interwoven stitches and treasures creates. When I take it in, my eyes widen slightly, and I struggle for the rest of my face to remain impassive.

The tapestry depicts a garden dappled by light and patches of glimmering blue. In between colorful flowers and blades of grass, an orange snake unfurls its body, its eyes a pair of glossy gemstones. The cloudless sky enwraps a white bird in its embrace and silver stones form small crescent moons that cast an ethereal glow onto the garden below.

I loosen a breath. Kalmin, for once, is right. The tapestry is beautiful. Gorgeous, really.

I suspect that I would be content to gaze at it forever. *Could it be Hallakkungi's garden?* In the stories, the flower god's garden is described as lush and alive—I begin to smile, imagining Hallakkungi standing among the lotuses and chrysanthemums.

I'm only vaguely aware that Kalmin is talking. His voice is muffled and muted, like he's underwater. Despite my better instincts, I ignore him as my gaze swims with those small, beautiful stones and those mesmerizing rays of soft, welcoming moonlight.

Crack.

A burst of pain sends me reeling, a white-hot burn ripping its way across my cheek as I stumble backward. A second later, I raise a hand to my smarting cheek and spit onto the floor in pure fury.

Asina, that godsdamned bitch, has slapped me.

A snarl tears through my curled lips, but the slim, bald woman is infuriatingly unaffected. Her wide, fishlike eyes are cold with disgust, and her right hand still hovers in the air, poised to strike again.

"I suggest that you pay attention," she says in a tone of haughty satisfaction.

I straighten myself in one fluid motion—only to stop in my tracks as Kalmin hurls a look of warning in my direction.

Konrarnd Kalmin is ruthless. Violent. His hair is the color of rust, his skin the color of freshly fallen snow. His eyes remind me, horrifyingly, of a snake's—they're a dark, murky green and constantly slit in a sly, calculating look.

Gods, give me strength. It takes every ounce of my self-control to restrain myself from shrinking under his sharp attention, to remind myself that this man is dangerous beyond belief—even to an assassin like me.

It is said that he was born in the Northern Continent's brutally icy kingdom of Brigvalla to a well-off family thirty years ago. It's also said that he came into the world bearing a knife, with which the minutes-old Kalmin took his mother's life, then his father's, and finally, the midwife's.

During simpler times, I always scoffed at that story. But now, after meeting Kalmin, after working for him… Well. I can easily see how that tale was born.

"Were you ignoring me?" he purrs, tilting his head. My back molars ache as I clench my jaw, trembling.

I hear his voice every day, but I still cannot ignore the way he makes a mockery out of the continent's language. Where his words should be melodious, undulating with expression, they are flat and jerky. It's clear he takes a sick pleasure in mauling our language, its rhythms. In the grand scheme of things, perhaps it's a small offense. But it still makes my blood rise to my face and burn like fire.

Bastard, I think.

"Answer me." His pointedly butchered words suddenly become as sharp as a whetted blade, so at odds with the sickly sweet croon they were just a moment before. "Were you ignoring me, Shin Lina?" The caustic bite to his question warns me to proceed with caution.

My nails dig into the palms of my hands, surely forming vicious half-moon indents. "No," I grind out.

"Ah-ah-ah," Kalmin tuts, arching a delicate brow. "It's not your place to tell lies. You understand that, don't you?" He tilts his head, those snake eyes glittering an unforgiving green. "Tell me who you are."

I shake from the effort of restraining myself from marring that snow-white face as those bloodred lips form the words I refuse to say.

"You're the Reaper. Sunpo's finest assassin. And my most impressive heist." Kalmin smiles, and it's a cold, dead thing.

A silence so sharp it could cut glass tears through the room. My heart stops as my mind snags on that last claim, that last title…

Heist. The whole world freezes on its rotation as I see *red* at that word.

Red, because that was the color I saw back at the Talons' manor the night after everything—*everything* went so unbelievably wrong. The color seeping from those bodies, the bodies of my gang, my *family*. Red, because that was the last color I saw before a rag—heavy and sodden with the bitter smell of a sedative—was roughly shoved against my face and the world went so very, very dark.

It is an effort to keep still, to refrain from leaping across that glossy ebony desk and jeopardize everything I have left.

My entire body quivers with the effort from containing the violence churning within it. Kalmin exchanges an amused look with Asina.

That look snaps something inside me.

I can do it.

I can fling myself across the small expanse of polished wood between us and claw at his face, his chest, until he bleeds the same red as the Talons did that night. I bare my teeth, tensing, allowing my hand to drift toward my dagger…before I remember Eunbi and freeze.

Eunbi, with her chubby freckled face and bright, sparrowlike eyes.

Eunbi, with her love of sticky candies and a laugh that sounds like the tinkling of bell chimes.

Eunbi. My Eunbi. Innocent and sweet, untouched by bloodlust. A child still, small and sensitive, with her whole life ahead of her.

With a chance to become somebody I never got to be.

"Let's behave ourselves, shall we?" Kalmin slowly makes his way around the desk. "You'll be meeting with one of my Oktarian buyers in the Fingertrap tomorrow to give him his share of the jewels in exchange for the money. If he refuses, kill him." I can feel Kalmin's gaze seeking mine. It leaves a damp film on my skin. "If he hesitates, kill him. If he tries to give you anything less than the agreed amount—"

"Let me guess," I interrupt icily, glowering at the ever-watchful moon through the window. I wonder if Dalnim can hear my steady stream of prayers, even though she abandoned the mortal realm's moon long ago. "Kill him."

"I can always find other profitable buyers. The Oktarians hunger for more stones, and they possess the means to retrieve them. These, these are Dokkaebi treasures. I will not accept any less than what they are worth." Kalmin taps a gemstone with a quick, sharp rap. "Even you seem fond of this tapestry." Something in his voice makes my stomach drop. Whatever's coming next—it can't be good. "I'll let you be the one to tear it up. You have that dagger of yours, don't you?"

Tear it up? I furrow my brow in confusion. *But why…? Oh.*

The beautiful garden, the painstakingly small stitches of shocking color, is not what these men want. These Oktarian buyers want the materials, not the art.

"Do it yourself," I jeer, forcing every bit of indolent arrogance I have left into each and every word. "I am occupied for the rest of the night." *It isn't enough*, I think, as Asina rolls her eyes in exasperation.

Or—perhaps it is too much.

Kalmin stiffens as he examines a gnawed cuticle. "Lina, Lina," he warns, cruel laughter tingeing my name, "if the jewels are not separated from the threads, I will be unable to receive my money. And if I don't get my money, things will turn out quite badly for you. And your sister." Although the threat is one used often, my stomach still drops. He gestures to his desk. "See that it is done by the time the sun rises." The snake cuts his eyes to Asina. "Watch her," he adds.

It's a small delight that she looks immensely peeved.

Sending Asina a saccharine smile, I decide that I will take a very, *very* long time to dismantle the tapestry.

Hours later, my hands ache, and my vision is bleary from painstakingly cutting through the threads to free the sparkling treasures.

Asina had nearly nodded off in her spot in Kalmin's chair but quickly came to, and is now scowling at me as the faint beginnings of morning sun trickle in through the window.

There were hundreds of gemstones within the tapestry, all of which now sit atop a pile of shredded thread. Destroying the garden, tearing apart the sunset-orange snake, made my chest tighten and my heart ache. It felt wrong, so utterly wrong, but what other choice did I have?

I will not sacrifice my sister's life for a tapestry.

Finally finished, I rise to my feet from where I have been kneeling on the floor. It's an effort to find my voice after the hours of disuse. "I'm done," I rasp to Asina, and I don't bother to wait for a response before stalking out the door.

Brash, a little voice of rationality warns as I stride through the Blackbloods' base, but I ignore it. The sun is up, and I'm done playing games.

I expect Asina to storm after me, demanding that I clean up my scraps, but she doesn't. I'm uninterrupted as I make my way through the building that has been my prison for a year now.

The cramped hallways are lined with murals stolen from every museum within the continent, priceless paintings hanging lopsided on chipped walls. A crooked chandelier casts a shimmer of light on me as I walk toward the door half hidden underneath a flight of uneven stairs.

As I enter my pathetic excuse for a room, ignoring the heavily tattooed Blackblood guard stationed a few feet away from my door, I shuck the boots off my sore feet. I don't know who had this room before me. There must have been somebody, as the Blackbloods take hostages all the time.

The "bedroom" is glaringly empty, save for the tattered blanket on the floor, a crate full of clothes, and a bucket of murky water I'm allotted for face-washing. There is also a small mirror on the wall, chipped and cracked from years of use.

I don't look in the mirror as I peel off my tunic. The smudged glass holds nothing that I'd like to see—only an image of filth and hunger, guilt and desperation incarnate.

Instead, I turn my back to the godsdamned thing and try to ignore the fact that I can count my ribs. I try to ignore the greasy, dirty feeling of my waist-length hair as I undo the black braid with fatigued hands.

As I splash the bucket's cold water onto my face, I feel the ridges of my face—sharp and sallow and gaunt—underneath my fingertips. Starvation has made my pointed nose even more defined, and my cheekbones protrude from my face, uncomfortably bony.

It wasn't always like this.

I wasn't always like this.

A year ago, I was strong and fit, my tanned skin toned and muscular. Although I was lean, I'd had curves, and in all the right places. I was able to sprint for miles on end without stopping, disarm a man three times my size in one move, and have him lying prone on the ground in the next.

Of course, there were things I wanted to change about myself back then. My small height, for example. I also hated my nose itself—the tip's curve is unseemly; it points up too much. It's a trivial thing, but one that incessantly bothered me all the same.

Now I am a stranger, a malnourished and frail girl with deep, dark circles under her eyes. The change isn't just from lack of food. It is from everything else...the loss, the grief, and most of all, the *guilt*.

The guilt that gnaws on my bones every minute of every day, never fading, never ceasing. Never.

Not bothering to remove any other articles of clothing, I collapse onto my tiny cot with a groan from the mattress. My left leg is sore and strained from the exertion, and I massage the puckered skin with a grimace. The pain is always there but is now even worse from the exertion of my mission.

But it's a pain that I deserve. An injury that I deserve.

Slowly it fades, leaving behind only the usual dull ache, and I close my eyes.

And just when my toes have dipped into the shores of sleep...

As it does every night, the Thought enters my mind.

I stiffen as a cold sweat pools underneath my arms and beads its way across my clammy forehead.

It is a vile, twisted thing that takes satisfaction in worming its way through the crevices in my brain, trailing a stream of sticky black oil in its wake.

I don't bother to fight it. Never do, even though I know what is coming.

I just grip my ragged blanket in a death-tight embrace and wait.

What would they think of you? the Thought hisses, every rasping word dripping with accusation. *Filthy, filthy traitor. Your fault. Your fault. They lie buried in the silt, and still you breathe the city air, helping guide the hand of the monster who slaughtered them. Sick, twisted, vile, wretched thing...*

I choke as the Thought winds its way around my lungs, laughing deviously as it *pulls*, tighter and tighter until I can't breathe, can't do anything but claw at my throat and struggle for even just a sip of air, hot tears burning as they drip down my cheeks, tremors shaking my body...

Sang, the Thought whispers. *Chara. Yoonho. Chryse. Sang. Chara. Yoonho. Chryse...*

The spots of darkness dancing across my vision begin to coagulate. I go limp, even as my lungs scream for air.

Sang... Chara... Yoonho... Chrysssss...

With a final hiss, the Thought seeps away to whatever inner corner of my mind it slithered from. It leaves nothing behind but the faint echo of a low, grating laugh.

I gulp down shaking breaths of air, pressing my face into my hands as I shudder. Sometimes the Thought brings me visions, visions of the dead Talons standing in a world of misty darkness where nothing grows—the Underworld, Jeoseung. Sometimes I see them as Gwisin, blurred and translucent human bodies, nothing but flickering echoes of lives once lived. Other times it pushes me through memories with forceful hands, laughing as I sob.

The Thought comes in that early stage of sleep when I teeter on the edge of consciousness and blissful oblivion. It has now for the past year. There is nothing I can do to escape it, not when it's a manifestation of my own guilt.

Not when the piercing, burning knife of self-hatred is forever embedded in my chest.

CHAPTER THREE

After a measly two hours of sleep, I stand in the middle of Sunpo's marketplace in the Fingertrap. It's the kingdom's commercial sector, only a short distance from the Coin Yard—the wealthy district where the Blackbloods' giwajip lies.

A heavy black satchel is slung over my right shoulder as I lean against the cold stone of an alleyway wall and watch the goings-on of the early-morning market. Women dressed in hanboks ranging from fine and silken to worn and shabby are careful not to let their slippers touch the dirty puddles on the street. Men wearing paeraengi—hats made of thick strips of bamboo—lead donkeys carrying baskets of fish through the ambling crowd.

The mackerels and salmon come from Fishtown in the eastern part of Sunpo, known for its harbors atop the Yongwangguk Sea. Sunpo has no shortage of fish—since we're blocked off from the other two kingdoms by the Yaepak Mountain Range, we've been forced to make a living off the one natural resource this armpit of a kingdom supplies. I watch the fishermen closely and scour their windburned faces, but none of them meet the description of the person I'm searching for.

According to Kalmin, I'm looking for a man of about fifty with graying hair and a drooping mustache—as if that doesn't describe half of Sunpo's population, and undoubtedly Oktari's as well.

As I wait, I fiddle with my one remaining cigarette—the very last of the pack that was in the hidden pocket of my stealth suit a year ago, when I was first captured.

Ever since he realized what the spark of introducing me to smoking halji ignited, Sang warned me of the danger of inhaling those gray, ashy fumes, but...

Sang isn't here now, is he?

Now seems to be as good of a time for a smoke as any.

I crave the inhale of ash and dust, the biting bitterness of the halji leaves, with every fiber of my being. I put the cigarette between my teeth and fish around for my lighter. And scowl because...

"It's bad for you, Lina," Sang's voice cautions, and I can almost sense him, *feel* him next to me like he was that night on the roof. "You need to stop."

I still remember what I did next. I rolled my eyes, blowing a puff of smoke in his face. "Hypocrite. You smoke what? Twelve a day? This is nothing."

Sang's face darkened. "I'm not proud of it. And I shouldn't have given you that first roll."

I leaned back onto the tiles of the roof, watching Sang carefully.

His face was bright under Dalnim's moonlight, his chestnut curls falling into his face. His hands, scarred from years of spy work and weaponry, sat in his lap as he twisted his fingers into his palms, a nervous habit that rarely showed itself.

"I'm worried about you, L," Sang said quietly. "You're a living, barely breathing smokestack... If I had known, I wouldn't have offered…" He trailed off. A moment of silence stretched out between us, the two Talons. The assassin and the spy.

"Don't worry about me," I finally said. "I'm fine." It was true, more or less. Contrary to Sang's dramatic metaphor, my lungs were clear, my breathing easy.

For now, a little voice in the back of my mind warned. I ignored it.

"I don't believe you. You're young. Sometimes, I think…" He swallowed hard. "Sometimes I think you're too young to be the Reaper."

The words rang in my ears, and I went still. "You're only three years older than me, Sang." I rolled my next words around on my tongue, then spit them out like bullets from my favorite pistol. "And you didn't think I was too young four months ago."

A tangle of silken white sheets. Sang's hand covering my own.

A bottle of champagne on the bedside table next to two glasses, one overturned, dribbling droplets of pale gold onto the clothes scattered on the floor below.

Sang blinked in surprise and, quite possibly, admittance. Because four months ago… "I told you that was a mistake." He avoided my gaze, turning his eyes to the moon. Its light did little to hide the regret painted on his face.

I wondered if Dalnim was watching us from above, if the moon goddess was watching my heart fracture in my chest over and over and over again.

I made myself crack a coy smile. "A fun mistake."

Pale pink bloomed on Sang's cheeks. "Stop smoking, Lina. Please. If something happens to your health, I can't bear knowing I handed you that first one." Sang closed his eyes. "Please."

I fell silent. Looking at him made my heart hurt.

It wasn't that I loved him…like that. I told myself I didn't care, but to call it a mistake *meant* something. Meant that he regretted the night of champagne and silk sheets. Regretted the way he had kissed my forehead at the end of it, his breath hot on my skin.

It hadn't been my first time. But still, it had happened. And I had liked it.

It was just that, apparently, he hadn't.

A mistake, he'd called it.

"I'll stop if you stop," I finally said on the rooftop after a long while. I didn't bother to look at his pained expression before sliding off the roof, landing on the ground neatly, and disappearing into the night.

I don't know how long Sang sat there afterward. Staring at Dalnim's moon.

I didn't want to know.

And now I never will.

Still leaning against the wall of the alley, I shove the cigarette back into my pocket.

I'll save it, I decide. Save it for when I need a smoke so desperately that it feels as if ants are crawling up my throat.

I shut out the thoughts of Sang and instead observe the marketplace.

Vendors lean over their cluttered counters, waving their goods animatedly to shoppers, who can barely move two feet without bumping into one another.

"Fruit from the kingdom of Bonseyo!" a man hollers, naming one of the other two kingdoms while waving a persimmon in the air. "Persimmons and apple pears from the famous Bonseyo orchards!" The fruit is so ripe, so perfect, that I wonder if Jacheongbi herself blessed Bonseyo's crops. My mouth waters.

It's rare that Sunpo receives any trade from Bonseyo—the kingdom at the very tip of the Eastern Continent usually disregards our dingy southern kingdom, especially since passage here requires fare across the Yongwangguk Sea or taking the perilous paths atop the Yaepak Mountains. Besides, Bonseyo is typically too caught up in its own politics to even remember us; its royal family struggles to control the inner turmoil of their dynasty.

But Bonseyo has sent fruit today, and I can't help but suspect that it was in return for Sunpon criminals' help in the less...legal aspects of smoothing out disputes within the royal Jeon family.

"Seashells from the Yongwangguk Sea!" another vendor hollers. "Dried and salted seaweed! Dried mackerel!"

"Furs from the Wyusan Wilderness! Fine and thick, bound to keep you warm!" Trade with Wyusan, while still somewhat rare, is consistent enough for their goods to arrive in the marketplace. The inhabitants of Wyusan are surly and rough—they'll make the passage over the mountains or atop the sea once every six moons or so if it means more coin.

"Meat from the Wyusan Wilderness! Large cuts, delicious and preserved!"

With still no sign of a mustachioed man, my gaze snags on a small stall squeezed in between a Wyusan pelt stand and a floral booth. The counter brims with an assortment of still-steaming pastries, each one glistening appealingly under the morning sun.

The woman behind the counter is preoccupied with smiling prettily at the Wyusanian pelt dealer, who bites into a jam-filled pastry with a roguish grin.

My stomach rumbles, and my mouth waters.

Yoonho, knowing my love of sweets, used to make sure that a platter of pastries was left out for my breakfast, alongside a glass of sparkling lychee juice. Chara and Chryse were always jealous, and secretly, I'd taken an immature satisfaction in their envy. I might not have had the twins' long legs or perfect noses, but I did have five glazed sugar rolls just begging to be bitten into.

Before I know what I'm doing, I'm peeling myself off the alley wall and weaving my way into the market, nimbly dodging laughing men already drunk on cheap rice wine and gaggles of rouge-heavy women linked arm in arm.

It takes almost no effort for my fingers to close around a pastry sticky with sugar and slip back into the crowd, my mouth filling with the sweet, flaky dough.

It's been ages since I ate something other than stale rice, spoiled vegetables, or dried strings of chewy fish. I shove another bite into my mouth, my eyes filling with hot tears as I huddle against the alley's wall. As crystals of sugar scrape against my teeth, the pastry reminds me of what it was like to be something other than this sick, twisted traitor.

Something…human.

"My goodness," a nasally voice notes dryly, and I startle. "Does Kalmin even remember to feed his little wenches?"

I jolt to my feet, whipping my dagger out of its sheath.

The man in front of me just snorts wetly and itches at his receding chin with a stubby finger.

Graying hair, a long and drooping mustache…and an Oktarian accent. Where my syllables are long and curling in my mouth, his are brisk and rapid. Quickly, I collect myself.

"Took you long enough," I snap, taking another bite of my pastry, dagger unwavering. "I've been here for nearly half the day."

"It's not even midday," the Oktarian man protests, frowning. "Besides, I have traveled farther. The journey from Oktari is quite…" He sees that I don't particularly give a damn and clears his throat. "The jewels, if you will."

"Payment first." I polish off the pastry and wipe the remnants on my pants, fighting the urge to lick the sweet glaze and crumbs from my fingers. *After this*, I tell myself, *I'll be passing by the pastry stand again. And again. And again.*

The man scoffs. "How do I know you won't make off with my gems?" He pauses, scratching at his chin once more. "How do I know that Kalmin was even able to breach the Temple of Ruin? How do I know that bag of yours isn't empty?"

Rolling my eyes, I unzip a portion of the satchel, letting the man peer at a hint of the vibrant gemstones. Then, with a yank, I zip the bag back up and narrow my eyes. "Payment *first*," I demand in a voice that makes the man flinch. Steely and ice-cold, it's the tone of the Reaper, Murderess of Sunpo.

I chose the name years ago, in honor of the legendary Jeoseung Saja, beings who reaped the souls of the living and delivered them to Yeomra, God of Death. I like to think that I bear a resemblance to them. I would not know, though—the Jeoseung Saja disappeared with the gods, leaving people like me to continue their former occupation.

The buyer quickly withdraws a crisp cheque from his pocket and hands it to me. I look it over, careful to keep my expression bored at the sum, despite the large numbers. Warily, I focus on the finer details.

The man's name is Doi Arata, and he made out the cheque to Konrarnd Kalmin in Sunpo's currency—the yeokun—as promised. I tuck the piece of parchment into my suit and toss the satchel at Arata's feet. He scrambles to the ground with a rabid sort of eagerness, his greedy hands closing around the straps. His fingers tighten as he grins. I watch him with utter distaste.

"Enjoy your rocks," I say in revulsion, my black boots stomping dangerously close to Arata's fingers as I stalk past, glad to be rid of the heavy bag. There are three more waiting for me back at the Blackbloods' compound, but I refuse to worry about that now.

Instead, I once again join the crowd bustling through the marketplace. I can spare a few precious moments to filch another pastry or two. I dodge a woman precariously balancing a barrel of dry rice above her head, but a shower of the grains still rains down onto the crown of my head. I brush them out impatiently as a girl around my own age stumbles into me, clearly drunk and brandishing a bottle of strong-smelling liquid.

"Sorry," the girl slurs, making to saunter off.

But I grab her wrist. Hard. "Give me back my lighter," I say softly. Dangerously.

Her eyes widen in fear.

I cock my head and wait. *Petty pickpockets.*

I didn't miss the way the girl's hand dove into my pocket and certainly didn't miss that the smell of the drink is contained only to the bottle with not a tinge on her breath when she speaks.

The girl, wincing from my grip, hands back the lighter with a sullen expression. I pluck it from her grasp and shove it into the pocket of my pants. But I don't let go—not yet.

"Word of advice," I murmur as I tighten my fingers around her wrist. "Don't hesitate before pulling out the item. That's how you get caught. The Fingertrap is called such for a reason." I release my hold on her, and she stares at me for a brief moment before darting away with a fearful backward glance. I watch her go and shake my head in a mixture of pity and scorn.

I was that girl once, filching yeokun from passersby, hunting for the money in bustling crowds. But never was I so clumsy. That girl will be caught one day, and by a person much less forgiving than I am.

I make my rounds at the marketplace quickly. The baker is still flirting with the poacher, who looks as if he is on his third or fourth jam pastry. Neither notice as I sweep two more sugar rolls from the display.

Biting into a flaky pastry with considerable satisfaction, I leave the marketplace and decide to climb a nearby roof to finish my stolen treats. My feet dangle off the edge as I watch the tiny people below *ooh* and *ahh* over vendors' wares. A warm feeling lights up the inside of my chest. For a moment, I cannot place it. But then… *Oh.*

I am *happy.*

Or at least feeling some semblance of it.

Instantly, my throat tightens, and that flicker of comforting warmth gutters away and leaves a hollow coldness in its place.

I do not deserve happiness, do not deserve the sugar rolls I was so excited about just moments before. Suddenly, they are too heavy in my hands. The glaze sticky on my fingers like blood. My vision blurs as the reality of my situation hits me.

I am on a roof, eating sugar rolls.

My friends are dead, their bodies dumped into the sludgy water of Habaek's River on the outskirts of Sunpo, just north of the Boneburrow.

I went there once, to beg Habaek the River God to return them to me.

He did not.

Bile burns my throat, and my vision tunnels, swimming dangerously as I struggle to breathe. I dig my fingers into the pastries and scramble to my feet.

I shouldn't have them. I don't deserve to have them.

With a hoarse grunt, I draw my arm back and hurl the pastries into the air, my heart pounding like a war drum.

That is when the Dokkaebi appears.

CHAPTER FOUR

t happens with a ripple.

A ripple around me, as if the air is water and somebody has skipped a stone across its sleek blue surface. I feel the hairs on the back of my neck rise as my eyes fix on the roof of the hanok across from my perch, where the air is moving.

Moving.

My breath suddenly feels too thin, yet at the same time too heavy.

The atmosphere is thick with a strange, foreign scent that is not at all unpleasant. It's almost the scent of dark licorice candies…and sweet, yet spiced, plum blossoms.

Frozen to my spot, I watch as the air undulates one last time before it parts…to reveal a shadowed figure, who steps onto the rooftop from what looks like an endless corridor of darkness. With a low hum, the ripples stop, but the smell of licorice and plum lingers.

My brain cannot make sense of the figure that stands on the roof opposite mine.

Will not make sense of the fact that my pastries, which I

hurled toward the sky moments before, now hover above the figure's outstretched hands. I gape as they plop, one by one, into the awaiting palms.

One word jolts through my mind, as hot and burning as a shock of lightning.

Dokkaebi.

My mouth goes dry. *Impossible.* The immortals never visit Sunpo…unless to lure citizens to Gyeulcheon.

And that is the work of only the Pied Piper.

My hand flies to my dagger.

Shit. Shit, shit, shit, *shit.* I want to scream to the heavens and beg for the gods to answer me, to protect me, to shield me from this creature.

Seokga, I think pleadingly, wishing that the trickster god would deign to listen. *Please. Save me. Teach me a trick, a trick to escape…*

But he will not. I know that.

I glance down to the street, and my blood turns to ice. Nobody below sees what's happening on the two roofs, too preoccupied with purchasing trifles and trinkets.

I am alone.

As always.

I can feel the Dokkaebi's eyes on me. Their gaze feels… curious. Amused. But beneath it all, there's an undercurrent of darker emotions.

Wariness. Animosity. Wrath.

The shadows covering the figure on the roof shiver and recede, seeping into the tiles of the roof below their feet like black ink, before disappearing completely.

There is a Dokkaebi across from me.

A Dokkaebi who is looking directly at me as he bites into a sugar roll.

Pure, undiluted terror finally plunges its icy blade into my chest and jerks me out of my daze of shock.

My first thought is that he resembles a marble statue.

His face is all chiseled angles, his frame long and lean. Even from my position on the opposite rooftop, I can make out the curves and slopes of the hard, toned chest that peeks from beneath his clothing—a long, flowing black robe cinched at the waist with a silver ribbon and embroidered with floral patterns mirrored on his black baji pants.

His long, dark hair doesn't have a single midnight strand out of place as it falls to his chest. Parts of him, I suppose, could look mundane, like his tan skin and his glittering silver earrings. But those pointed ears could never pass as human. And his eyes...

They are fox eyes, sly and angular, and they burn a vicious silver as they sear into my own. And yet, even with the complete lack of humanity within those swirling silver depths...he is the most beautiful creature I have ever seen.

My breath catches in my throat.

Slowly, the Dokkaebi considers the sugar rolls in his hands. I watch him with an uneven heartbeat as my fingers slowly drift to the sheathed dagger at my waist. Hopefully, I won't have to attempt to use it against him.

But why is he here?

"These," the Dokkaebi says, taking another bite of the sugar roll and chewing contemplatively, "what are they called?" His voice is soft, almost velvety, but I don't miss the lethal undercurrent. He arches an eyebrow as he stares quizzically at the pastries.

"Is it routine for your people to pop onto rooftops out of nowhere?" The words tumble forth before I can fully think them through.

The Dokkaebi chuckles under his breath, and his bloodred lips curve into a devastatingly gorgeous smile as he looks at me underneath thick, dark lashes. "Is it routine for your people to hurl perfectly good food off rooftops?"

Something stirs in my broken, bleeding heart as that silver gaze fixates on me and glitters with a clear invitation to taunt, to tease. "A Sunpo tradition. It's said to bring good luck."

"Is that so?" If those laughing eyes are any indication, it's clear that he sees right through my bullshit, but I hold his gaze — more out of stubbornness than courage. I will not be the first to look away.

Doing my best to ignore the foolishly uneven thudding against my chest, I narrow my eyes at him. "What, exactly, are you looking at?"

The ghost of a laugh flickers through the air. "Nothing." He pauses, his face flashing with something that causes me to blanch and instantly regret my sharp tongue. But a moment later, whatever sparked in his gaze has been extinguished. Only idle amusement remains. "I must have the wrong roof."

I gape at him incredulously. "The wrong roof," I repeat flatly. "The *wrong roof*?"

"Indeed." The barest hint of a smirk delicately curls itself around the Dokkaebi's lips. "Farewell," he says casually, *too* casually for what is undoubtedly a thousand-year-old immortal who has no inkling of what a sugar roll is.

I hold my breath, anticipation beading sweat on the nape of my neck as I watch the creature for any sign of malice, any sign of ill will…but none comes. His smirk only grows, and in a swift, graceful motion, he tosses my pastries into the open air. And then, before I can do so much as blink, there is another ripple, another rush of licorice and plum and shadow…

And he is gone.

The two pastries the Dokkaebi has left behind hover in the air for a split second before tumbling down to the unsuspecting marketplace far, far below.

Impossible. Fucking *impossible*.

I stagger backward, collapsing to my knees, reeling as I nearly lose balance.

A Dokkaebi.

In Sunpo.

Talking to me.

This isn't possible. This *can't* be possible. There must be another explanation.

I rub my face with shaking hands.

Either a Dokkaebi truly appeared and carried out a pastry-oriented conversation with me, or I hallucinated. The latter is much more believable, I decide as I make my way off the roof with wobbling legs and a dull roaring in my ears.

But I can almost smell that dark licorice and spiced plum again, lingering atop the sour and putrid scents that blanket Sunpo's streets in a suffocating embrace. It almost seems to grow stronger with every step I take. I shudder, overcome with an inescapable chill despite the heat of the summer day.

The fragrance only strengthens as I unsteadily weave my way through the city's slumping wooden chogajips, the thatched roofs of the homes in danger of caving in completely. Handfuls of women cluster atop the uneven decks of their homes, exchanging the day's gossip in hushed whispers behind wrinkled hands.

The difference between the other sectors of Sunpo and the Coin Yard is remarkable. Its architecture differs from all the other small hanok buildings within the kingdom. The Blackbloods' base is a giwajip—a larger house with a tiled roof constructed for the upper class—and it's gated, set apart from the rest of the city. It's impressive even for the Coin Yard, and at least five times the height of the sector's other buildings. Of course, it's nothing compared to the Talons' old fort.

The Blackbloods' giwajip lacks the sophistication of the old, abandoned palace on the opposite side of the kingdom—just on the outskirts of Fishtown, near the salty Yongwangguk Sea. Lacks the impressive flight of white stone stairs, the glossy black columns underneath the curved emerald roofs. Lacks the willow tree garden, the burbling koi pond brimming with iridescent color, and the echoes of perpetual laughter—music of life, and of love.

That palace was a place of mischief and malice, of dancing and drinking, where thieves and spies and cold-blooded killers laughed as they raised bottles of wine to their lips and shouted in victory… *"Long live the Talons! Long live the damned!"*

Now, though, our home is abandoned—the garden swallowed whole by famished weeds, the willow trees drooping underneath their own weight against the dead, dried grass. Only Gwisin, spirits of the departed, inhabit the halls.

My stomach tightens. Grief claws at my heart, gouges that useless organ with nails as sharp as knives.

My vision blurs with hot tears as I approach the black stone wall, barely noticing the Blackblood who guards the entryway. I do notice, however, when a hard, swift blow slams into my stomach.

I gasp and lurch backward into the street, the air rushing out of me with enough force that I gag, one hand flying to my throat and the other to my dagger.

"You *bitch*," the Blackblood roars down at me. "You *fucking bitch*!" His fists rear back in another attack as he screams, bringing his knuckles down—

My body spurs into motion even as my brain struggles to catch up. *What did I do?* I dodge his punch, rolling to the side, the cobblestones of the street bruising my arms before I haul myself up.

"Where is he?" the man roars, a vein bulging on his forehead as he shoves me back to the ground, my knees cracking in protest as they hit the rough stone ground hard. "Where the fuck is he?"

I snarl as he lands a blow across my jaw, then spit out hot blood and leap to my feet, slashing my dagger through the air. The Blackblood pulls back as I slash my knife again, blood trickling down my chin. "Where is *who*?" I demand.

"Don't lie, *Talon*," the Blackblood hisses. "Don't fucking lie."

I smile a shit-eating grin with bloodstained teeth and cock my head. "You Blackblood grunts are all the same," I purr. "Use your words. *Tell* me what's wrong, little boy."

The Blackblood breathes heavily, hatred contorting his face as he draws his own dagger from the black leather sheath at his side. *"Bitch,"* he spits—and then he's rushing at me again, silver blade flashing through the air.

I spit blood back onto the ground as he draws closer.

Fine. He wants to play rough—so we'll play rough. I whisper a quick prayer to Yeomra, God of Death and Ruler of Jeoseung. It is him I sometimes imagine standing behind me, guiding my every move with pale, bloodstained fingers. With his name on my tongue, strength pulls my muscles taut and twists my lips into a sneer.

When the Blackblood is a hairsbreadth away from me, I move like Yoonho taught me—like a viper, quick and deadly.

In two swift motions, I have him surprised and pinned against the wall, my dagger pressed to his throat. I laugh cruelly under my breath, smiling again as I let the dagger bite into his skin, watching as blood beads against the blade. "I'll ask once more," I say quietly, pressing farther into his neck. "Where. Is. *Who?*"

I watch carefully as the Blackblood licks his lips nervously, all traces of aggression trickling away into nothingness. But before any words can emerge, something cold and sharp is poking into the small of my back. I go taut, my heart pounding.

"Drop your dagger," Asina hisses in my ear, her breath hot against my skin.

Mouth dry, I slowly slacken my grip on the dagger.

"Now."

I let my weapon tumble to the ground. The Blackblood spits on my boots as he shoves past me.

Asina grabs my right shoulder. "Kalmin's office. Go."

CHAPTER FIVE

The inside of the giwajip is utter chaos.

Blackbloods huddle together in groups, their voices loud and grating as they wildly point and gesture, weapons flashing through the air.

But I don't have time to gawk as Asina drags me past the throngs of gang members and shoves me into Kalmin's empty office, slamming the door shut.

Her eyes flash as she storms toward me, her hand wrapping around my throat, then she throws me to the ground. I grit my teeth as she crouches over me, dagger unwavering.

I look at the legs of Kalmin's desk through watering eyes.

It's only then that I realize that Konrarnd Kalmin is notably absent from his own office.

"Where is Kalmin?" I ask slowly.

A beat of suffocating silence. And then… "Gone," Asina spits.

Gone. The word echoes through the room. *Gone.*

A smile tugs at my cracked, split lips. Oh, this is good. Too, too good.

"What *sort* of gone? Lost? Kidnapped?" I pause, my grin

growing. *"Dead?"*

Asina snarls.

"My condolences," I croon, a laugh burbling up in my aching throat. "My *sincerest* condolences, Asina—"

"The others think that *you* did it. I didn't tell them otherwise," Asina spits with wicked glee.

My smile falters. "Did *what*?"

Asina pauses, and I think I see something like fear flash across her face.

A terrible sense of foreboding, of knowledge, begins to uncoil in my stomach.

"Where is he." It isn't really a question as I keep my eyes on the dagger still leveled at my throat. "Where is Kalmin."

She says nothing, but her gaze burns through me. I wonder, as I stiffen on the ground, if she's finally decided to kill me. If the Blackbloods think that I did...whatever's been done to Kalmin, then there is no excuse for Asina not to slit my throat here and now.

I hold my breath, regretting my former snark.

Shit.

Shit.

Asina finally responds, her tone cold and clipped. "He was taken."

I exhale in one fell swoop. "Taken by who?"

"Not who," Asina hisses back, "but by *what*." Ice freezes over my bloodstream. Despite her furious exterior, I can tell that Asina is *scared*.

Out of nowhere, a horrifyingly vivid image of the silver-eyed Dokkaebi from the rooftop flashes across my mind's eye. *No. No. I imagined him.*

I imagined *him.*

Right?

"He took him. Right from his bed. I was there; I saw all of

it." Fury contorts her features before she hauls me up from the ground. Her nails dig into my skin as she drags me back through the doorway.

I close my eyes.

Queasiness is threatening to overcome me from the sharp, jostling movements as Asina hauls me through hallway after hallway. Only when everything falls still and silent do I crack open a bleary eye.

We're in a bedroom.

And I realize, slowly, that it must be Kalmin's.

Various framed paintings of nude women sprawled in compromising positions hang lopsidedly along the room's wooden walls. Rumpled clothes are strewn across the floor, as are three empty bottles of rice wine. On the bed is a sea of messy sheets, still containing the scent of musk that's only slightly drowned out by an overwhelmingly pungent cologne.

But there's another scent, another underlying smell that lingers beneath layers of cheap perfumes. My stomach curls in dread. Because that's the smell of licorice and plum blossoms...

Oh gods.

Oh gods, oh gods, oh gods, oh gods.

"Do you know what appeared at the foot of this bed? What materialized out of thin air and took him? Do you *understand* what has Kalmin?" Asina pants wildly. "Do you, girl?"

"No," I croak, simply to piss the woman off.

It works.

On shaking legs, Asina stalks to the bed, her typically cold eyes bright and frantic.

And dangerous.

"We were in bed," she grinds out, gesturing to the sheets with the dagger. The silver metal flashes through the air in jerky, sharp arcs. "The air started moving. *Moving.* And then *he* appeared. The Pied Piper."

I stiffen, blood draining from my face.

"Kalmin didn't even try to fight. I didn't, either. Because the moment he raised that flute to his lips, it was over. He took him. He took Kalmin." Asina is breathing heavily, her pupils so dilated that the entire irises seem to be a shade of black found only in the night. "*You.* You broke into that building; you stole the Dokkaebi's jewels. And you'll die for it, you fucking Talon."

I snarl in outrage, even as my breakfast rises in my throat. *The Pied Piper. Oh gods.* "You and your master *sent* me into the Temple of Ruin knowing that those rocks belonged to the Dokkaebi. I'm blameless."

"*Damn* your insolence," Asina snaps, her face whitening. There is a blur of motion and a flash of steel. I barely have time to drop to the ground before Asina's blade whizzes by my head, embedding itself in the wall with a *thunk*.

I shoot to my feet as Asina speeds toward me, a rush of rampant fury. I block a punch with my forearm and hook my leg around Asina's ankle to send her to the floor with a crash that rattles the picture frames.

"I had nothing," I pant as Asina rises, "to do with this. Kalmin got what was coming to him."

"You had *everything* to do with this." Asina delivers an uppercut that clips me in the jaw, sending me stumbling back. A split second later, her heavy boot connects with my stomach. I groan, and one of Kalmin's prized paintings crashes to the floor as I'm thrown to the ground. My vision swims, and Asina bares her teeth, her fingers curling into a fist.

Two blows. Three.

Blood begins to fill my mouth. The room reels.

Four. Five.

She's going to kill me.

Six. Seven.

My vision darkens as a mercilessly hot, burning pain bursts

through my body.

She's going to kill me. I consider this revelation hollowly. *She's really going to kill me.*

Eight. Nine.

I close my eyes and wait for the final blow. For my soul to wander down to the dark realm of Jeoseung and cross the Seocheongang River, leaving the world of the living behind forever—for my body to be nothing but a lifeless heap on Kalmin's floor.

I want to say a prayer, but I can't move my mouth, my lips. It's over.

If the gods are merciful, it will be quick.

But—

Fight back, a voice snarls, and it's not my own, not Asina's either. *Fight back.*

My eyes fly open. Because that voice is *Yoonho's*, harsh and gravelly. I would know it anywhere.

Fight back.

Asina draws her fist.

Fighting through the pain that threatens to overtake me, I roll to my side before staggering to my feet.

The Reaper of Sunpo does not fall, Yoonho whispers. *Death does not die, and neither will you, Shin Lina.*

It is the mantra that the Talons created for me when I was young and trembling with fear at the knowledge of what they expected me to do.

It is the saying that I used to whisper to myself as I slashed throats in the darkest of nights.

It was the motto of my childhood, before I found the ability to kill and fight without so much as batting an eye.

Slowly, I raise my gaze to Asina, holding hers for a moment.

And then I erupt.

CHAPTER SIX

thumb the hilt of Asina's dagger as I stand above her and point it at her pale, exposed throat. Blood dribbles down my chin. My right eye is swollen shut, limiting my vision, and I can feel a wicked set of bruises tightening my jaw and cheekbones. Everything—*everything*—hurts.

But I won.

Death does not die, and neither will you, Shin Lina.

Yoonho's voice is gone now, leaving me with nothing but a dull roaring in my head.

But I must think about what this means. What strings I need to pull to survive. I'm in a compound full of Blackbloods who believe I harmed their leader. I am outnumbered one to one hundred.

I almost scoff. If I had planned a hit against Konrarnd Kalmin, it would not have been a kidnapping. It would have been an agonizing murder. But that's beside the point now.

Thought after thought, calculation after calculation, flits through my mind.

The Piper spirited Kalmin away to Gyeulcheon in retribution

for the stolen tapestry. At least, that's what I assume happened. And I'm betting my life—and Eunbi's—on it.

I run my tongue over my bloodstained teeth before carefully choosing my words. "Kalmin isn't dead. If the Pied Piper truly took him, then he's still alive. In Gyeulcheon."

"Isn't dead *yet*," Asina corrects me, her breathing uneven from both exertion and hatred. "The Dokkaebi will kill him."

"You don't know that," I reply evenly. "If the Piper wanted to kill him, why not just murder him in bed? He had his chance; he forfeited it. The Pied Piper took Kalmin with him. Alive."

The Piper. I held a conversation with that godsdamned Dokkaebi just this morning.

Wrong roof, he said. But was it?

I'm the one who stole the tapestry. If the Pied Piper knows that Kalmin ordered the art to be stolen from the Temple of Ruin, then he must know that I stole it. And yet the Pied Piper did not abduct me. He visited me. But why?

The words fly into my head almost immediately.

Mouse Trap.

My mouth goes dry.

It's a tactic that nearly every gang uses, one that employs bait to lure a target. I have participated in countless Mouse Traps over the years, and I am participating in one right now.

As the mouse.

The Pied Piper is trying to trap me by stealing Kalmin. Because Asina is right—I stole the jewels. I caused this. I broke into his temple, and the Piper *knows*.

He's luring me out. Because he thinks that I will rescue Kalmin.

I nearly laugh.

The Piper thinks that Kalmin is my beloved leader, and I his faithful lapdog. He doesn't know that I despise Kalmin with every molecule of my being and am *glad* that the bastard has been dragged off to Gyeulcheon. He doesn't know that I am forever a Talon.

So the Dokkaebi wants to punish me for stealing the tapestry.

I bite back a curse. There was only one item within the temple—the tapestry. To hope that its disappearance would go unnoticed was a mistake with devastating consequences. Swallowing hard, I struggle to steady myself. I must be the picture of composure if I want to leave this compound alive.

Because there is only one way for me to do that.

"I stole the tapestry," I grind out, knowing very well that my next words will forever determine my fate. My stomach twists as I lower the dagger. "I'll retrieve Kalmin."

Asina's gaze narrows. She wets her lips as she watches me carefully, fishy eyes scanning the sincerity I have summoned to the surface of my face.

"I will journey to Gyeulcheon," I continue hoarsely. "I will retrieve our master from the Dokkaebi emperor."

As the words leave my mouth, I can see the inner gears turning in Asina's head. It's clear that she wants Kalmin back— as clear as day. It's also clear that although she yearns for the safety of her lord and lover, she is unwilling to venture into the realm of the Dokkaebi herself. Unwilling to confront death and demand Kalmin's return.

"Thirty days," she finally says through a thin mouth. "I will give you thirty days to do as you claim. But I want to have collateral, Reaper."

Collateral.

There is only one thing that can be, for there is only one thing I have left to lose. I stiffen.

Asina smiles blandly. "You have a sister, don't you? A sister on the mountaintops? Yaepak Mountain Academy, if I remember correctly."

Eunbi. As sweet as sugar, as innocent as a baby dove.

"Bring Kalmin to me in thirty days," Asina says, tilting her head as her gaze bores into mine, "or I will bring *you* your sister's head."

No.

I flinch as a cold sweat dampens my body. Silently, I send a prayer to the gods who never answer this world. To Gameunjang, the goddess of luck and destiny. Of fate. *Please. Not Eunbi. I will do anything. I will give anything.*

Asina is still watching me, and she looks pleased. Like she knows that I am screaming for the help of the absent deities.

Like much of Sunpo, Asina is not religious. The gods have gone to another world—and what is out of sight, for many, is immediately out of mind. Most do not pray to the gods, most have forgotten them entirely.

I have not.

I still speak to them, hoping that somehow, someday, they will hear me from their world in the clouds.

No doubt Asina takes satisfaction in watching the prayers of the few who still hope for the return of the divinities go unanswered.

"Thirty days, Shin Lina. Thirty days. And if you try to grab your sister and run…" She clucks her tongue. "Well. Let us say that I will enjoy bestowing the consequences upon you."

"I will not fail," I whisper, clenching my fists. My fingernails dig into the palms of my hands. "I will retrieve Konrarnd Kalmin. I swear it on the gods."

Asina just laughs, cruel and cold.

. . .

My tongue knows the taste of a lie well.

A lie tastes like burnt sugar.

It tastes of a hint of honeyed sweetness that quickly disappears, leaving only a lingering tingle of bitterness in its wake.

The taste of my lie is strong in my mouth as I limp away from the Blackbloods' giwajip, every step shooting pain up my limbs.

I hold on to consciousness with everything in me as I push the door open and step onto the cobblestoned street outside, my breathing shallow, my left leg threatening to buckle under me.

My dagger still lies where I was forced to discard it earlier. The dull metal hardly gleams underneath the fading evening sun. I grit my teeth as I retrieve it, jamming it into the sheath at my waist.

Thirty days.

I roll my eyes and hold in a disgusted snort as I begin to limp down the street. The Blackbloods are more oblivious than I ever realized. It's almost pitiful.

Of course I'm going to grab my sister and run.

I'll kill all those men in the process, too. And I will savor it.

As if I'll *ever* place my life in jeopardy for Konrarnd Kalmin of my own free will. As if I'll *ever* leave Eunbi on the mountaintop, surrounded by the Blackbloods, when I have a single, precious chance to spirit her away to safety. To create a new life for us, away from this godsdamned kingdom. Away from the brutality, away from the bloodshed.

Eunbi is small, and young—so very, very young, barely past the cusp of early childhood. She has known enough grief in her lifetime, and I have tried desperately since to shield her from the rest of the world's cruelties. To protect the innocence she still possesses, the remains of a child's sweet naiveté. To give her a life different than the one I lead, a life that is luxurious in its simplicity. Its safety.

She is my one remaining tie to a life like that, and the thought that even after all I've done, death will knock on her door this soon enrages me enough that my vision swims. My baby sister, my best friend, with her chiming laugh and crinkled nose.

The Pied Piper is a foolish bastard if he thinks I'll fall for his little Mouse Trap. He can kill Kalmin, for all I care. In fact, I hope he does.

And I hope he takes his sweet, sweet time doing it.

The streets are darkening now, the shade of the night sweeping across the kingdom and casting the world in a cold gloom. I pause where I am on the street and slowly turn in the direction of the Blackbloods' headquarters. It is now just barely visible, the dark wall hardly perceptible in the falling dusk.

I raise my hand in a vulgar gesture, triumph and grief searing my blood.

Dalnim's moon emerges at that moment, and it casts a glow of white light over me as I stand on the street, seething at the place where I have endured so much suffering—so much torture, so many tears, so many sleepless nights haunted by *their* voices that still ring in my ears even after a year of silence.

In this moment, it almost seems as if they stand beside me, translucent underneath the star-dotted sky. I take a shuddering breath, my arms falling back to my sides. A gust of cold wind brushes against my skin, lingering over my bruised fingers.

My lower lip trembles as a knot constricts my throat, and the Thought uncoils from its hidden crevice in my mind, slithering from its hiding hole with a wicked smile.

The Talons' presence next to me seems to dissipate into nothingness, leaving me cold and trembling and alone with only the Thought for company.

One breath in. One breath out.

Isn't Konrarnd Kalmin yours to kill? the Thought muses. *Yours to reap? After all, after everything... His death by your hands is the only way that you'll be able to atone for your sins.*

Only when you dirty your hands with his blood will they truly be clean.

"Leave," I grit out, falling to my knees, a jolt of pain spreading up my leg as I hit the ground with a heavy thud. "Eunbi. I need to get to Eunbi—" My words ring on the empty street, echoing, but it's too late.

I'm tumbling through time, through flashes of smiles and laughter, through snippets of conversations long finished.

"Sometimes I think you're too young to be the Reaper..." I catch a glimpse of Sang's dark, long-lashed eyes as I fall.

"Lina!" Eunbi is running toward me, her untamable black curls bouncing with every step. She is four years old again—four and chubby, her tiny feet pattering across the glossy floor of the palace. In her grubby hand, she holds a dagger. *"Look what I have, look what I have!"*

I hear my own voice reply, in both dismay and horror. *"Stop! Eunbi—stop. Where did you get that?"*

"Yoonho gave it to me," she replies petulantly, cradling the knife lovingly. *"As a present."*

"As a present—" My incredulous voice drifts away, quickly replaced by a sweeter cadence. Chara.

"Lina, my darling, seduction is an art."

"A craft," Chryse adds as their faces swim into view, red lips pursed in contemplation, deep emerald eyes glittering. *"Not for the fainthearted. You'll be a natural, though, my love. Sang won't be able to resist you."*

I'm falling faster now, gaining speed with every tear that slips down my cheeks. I close my eyes, blocking out their faces as their words pummel me, barely audible with the speed at which they tear through the air.

"I know you would never let anything happen to this gang. Not over your dead body—" Sang...

"Promise me, Lina. Promise me that you will lead—" That gruff voice. Harsh, yet warm. Yoonho.

Oh gods.

I scream as I plummet through these memories, these nightmares...

Another voice cuts through my fall, sly and sweet. It rips me out of my memories, shoving me back onto the Sunpo street, where I grab my stomach in pain as sobs wrench out of me.

Kalmin's voice echoes in my ears, and I press a hand to my mouth as bile scorches my throat. *"Well, Shin Lina. You are my inheritance."*

I groan, pressing my forehead to the cold ground.

Sang. Chara. Yoonho. Chryse.

They're dead, they're *gone,* but I'm still here. Still here with my utterly worthless life, my hands coated in their blood.

"I'm sorry," I sob into the street. "I'm so sorry." Meaningless words. They are ash in my mouth.

Silence answers me.

The Thought departs with a final, satisfied laugh.

Trembling, my eyes swollen and my vision blurred, I drag myself upright to my knees and wipe my nose on the sleeve of my tunic. My other hand dives into the pocket of my pants and closes around my last cigarette and my lighter. I have been saving it, saving it for when I *need* that bitter, ashy inhale to cloud my lungs. And I need the halji's bitter bite—need it *now*, to chase away the grief, the guilt. Need it to give me enough strength to climb to my feet and rush to Eunbi. To shield her in my arms from this violent kingdom, protect her with the barriers of my bones and flesh and blood.

The cigarette is halfway to my mouth when a soft, wicked laugh is carried to my ears by a cold wind that dances through the night.

I go rigid.

The air that brushes through my hair is heavy with the scent of licorice and plum blossoms. As it curls around my neck, my blood turns to ice.

It's him.

My pulse hammers in my throat as I shoot to my feet, replacing my precious cigarette with my dagger, leveling it at a pair of wickedly gleaming eyes as I twist around and meet the glittering gaze of the Dokkaebi from this morning.

"Hello, Lina," the Pied Piper purrs.

CHAPTER SEVEN

One moment, I am standing on the street, my body crouched low in anticipation of an attack. The next, I am pressed against the Piper's chest.

For a brief second, I'm unable to do anything but gape as cold hands fold me into a lover's embrace, and as the frigid metal of his rings kisses the heat of my exposed skin. Somehow, my dagger has found its way back into its sheath at my side—and I'm unable to reach for it, inescapably pinned against the Dokkaebi.

As a blue flame dances in the Piper's glare, I'm reminded of the whispers that the Emperor of Dokkaebi is the only being who possesses the ability to summon a flame of indigo. To summon Dokkaebi fire, so white-hot that it is as cold as a bitter winter, and ten times as biting.

For a moment, I think he plans to summon that flame, to wield it against me…but the burning fire in his gaze quickly recedes, replaced by cold amusement. "I suggest that you close your eyes, little thief," he says in a feather-soft whisper that caresses the side of my cheek.

It's the feeling of his breath against my skin that jerks me from my reverie of terror, flooding my body with scorching adrenaline and boiling hatred. "*I* suggest you let go of me," I snarl from behind gritted teeth before lifting myself up on my tiptoes, jerking my head back the way Yoonho taught me, and slamming my forehead against his hard enough that I see stars. A normal man would stumble backward, disoriented and weakened, leaving an opening for me to gain the upper hand and disembowel him in a few quick movements.

But as a dizzying pain racks my head, the Pied Piper merely chuckles, not at all fazed by my attack. If anything, he seems amused as I gasp weakly for breath. Dokkaebi heads, it seems, are infuriatingly resistant to blunt trauma.

A warm, wet trickle slowly makes its way down my forehead.

"And what exactly," I hear him whisper mockingly, "was that supposed to accomplish?" One of his fingers, cold with rings, slowly brushes away the droplet of blood. I can *feel* him silently laughing at me as I choke out a vicious curse—

But then the ground seems to drop beneath our feet, and we are falling—falling, falling, falling through shadows and darkness.

A scream of pure terror erupts from my lips, answered by a soft, wicked laugh as we jolt from side to side, forever tumbling through the eternal night.

Through returning vision, I glimpse flashes of Sunpo speeding by through the darkness.

The marketplace, the dingy taverns, pleasure halls, and the Blackbloods' giwajip... But then they are gone, replaced by a blinding light and a rush of heat that sends me gasping.

My boots hit ground.

Solid ground.

The impact is hard enough that it sends a wave of sickness through my body, but I shove it down as my eyes adjust to the quickly fading burst of white light—and to the Dokkaebi looking down at me, glimmers of amusement dancing across his fine features.

I swallow hard.

There is no use trying to deny that this Dokkaebi is as beautiful as he was this morning on the rooftop. His golden skin, his inky black hair, the cheekbones that could have been carved by the gods themselves… All of it is gorgeous in a way that only an inhuman can be.

I remind myself that it is very probable that this beautiful creature is about to kill me.

Red lips curve into a sly, sleek smile as I strain to break free from his arms.

A moment later, I crash to the floor as the bastard abruptly releases me, his smile quickly replaced by a look of pure boredom. My heart drops and my head throbs as my eyes meet the vast, high ceiling looming over me.

Flecks of gold dapple a dark sky. Dragons with ruby scales swim through dozens of moons, their taloned toes brushing against storm clouds. Fighting back awe, I turn my gaze to the rest of the room.

Black columns line the expanse of the room, surrounding the marble floor on which I sprawl. A silver carpet weaves its way to a throne raised on a dais. My eyes linger on the throne the longest. It's made out of dark thorns woven together and twisted into a seat.

My blood runs cold a split second later.

Next to the throne, in a glass case, is a flute.

Long, narrow, and a rich black, the flute is nearly as stunning as its owner. Delicate swirls of silver glint as they wrap in tendrils around the pipe, as if they are choking the slender neck of the instrument. Danger seems to throb through the air as I stare at the flute, entranced by its beauty.

This is the flute that the Dokkaebi emperor wields as a weapon, the flute that I have heard of, but never seen.

This is the flute that lures men and women from their beds in the middle of the night, leaving them vacant-eyed and hollow as they walk through the twisting Sunpo streets, following a haunting melody underneath an ink-black sky. Following the Pied Piper to his realm, *this* realm, where they surely meet some terrible fate.

This is the Pied Piper's flute.

"Beautiful, isn't it?" I didn't see the Pied Piper move, but he now lounges listlessly on the throne, amused as he follows my gaze. His ring-embellished fingers curl around a crystal glass of what appears to be black wine. He takes a sip, the liquid leaving a glossy stain on his lips. Something glitters in his eyes as he licks the stain away. "It was my father's flute, and his father's before him. Manpasikjeok. The Flute to Calm Ten Thousand Waves."

My lips continue to move of their own accord, even as a dull roaring fills my ears. "Only ten thousand?" I drag myself to my feet, careful not to put too much weight on my bad leg. The fall has not been good for it—spikes of sharp pain are shooting up its length. I grit my teeth and do my best to ignore it.

"You ask the oddest questions." The Dokkaebi raises a brow. "But perhaps it is because you are ill. You look unwell. Quite different from this morning." He pauses as he delicately sips again at his wine. "You also have a rather large bruise blossoming on your forehead. However did that get there?"

I fight the urge to massage my aching forehead. "If you are going to kill me, I would rather you do it without the small talk."

"So brash. And much too eager." He traces the rim of his glass with a slender finger. I watch as it circles around and around. "No, Shin Lina. I do not plan on killing you."

I blink slowly. "Why have you taken me, if not to kill me?"

The Pied Piper chuckles and leans forward. "Why, you're the Reaper of Sunpo. Word of your...*exploits*...has made its way here in the form of whispers that a wrathful spirit has deemed Sunpo's souls ripe for the reaping. Killing you, little thief, would be an awful waste of talent."

I struggle to grasp his meaning. All I can manage to think is that I am in Gyeulcheon. *Gyeulcheon.*

How did this happen? my mind chants. *How did this happen, how did this happen, how did this happen, howdidthishappenhowdidthishappenhowdidthishappen...*

The Piper cocks his head. "I would like to ask you some questions, Reaper. And I would like, very much, for you to answer them."

I release a too-shaky breath. Questions—not killing.

Not yet, anyway.

I clench my fingers around the hilt of my dagger. This is too good to be true. Something is wrong. Very, very wrong.

"The scarlet-haired is your boss."

"That is hardly a question." I hastily snap my mouth shut as the Piper's eyes darken to a storm-cloud gray. I bite my lip hard. This is no place for smart-assery. "Konrarnd Kalmin is my boss. Yes."

His brows furrow slightly. "And yet you despise him."

I freeze. *How does he—?*

"You did not fall for my little trick," he explains, waving a hand aimlessly. His rings flash underneath the light of the chandelier. "Imagine my surprise and disappointment, Shin Lina, when you did not play with me." The corners of his mouth tilt downward into what is almost a petulant pout.

"You mean fall for your bait."

"Semantics." The Pied Piper raises a shoulder in a shrug. "I suspect that you were not planning on coming to retrieve the scarlet-haired. You are not fond of him. And I now suspect that he returns the sentiment." He runs a hand across his chin in contemplation.

I slowly incline my head in a nod.

The Pied Piper's expression is inscrutable. "It is he who ordered you to steal my tapestry."

I nod again, this time fervently. "Yes. Yes, he ordered me to steal it. He desired the jewels, he's in the Oktarian jewel trade, he's greedy, he's—" I'm silenced by a sharp look.

"This is not a test of his character. And you will not escape my judgment by pinning blame on *him*. What I do find interesting, though, is where you were planning to run instead. There is something that you want very much, and it is not here in Gyeulcheon. It is somewhere else entirely, isn't it?"

Eunbi. I hold my breath.

"I watched you on the street," the Dokkaebi continues, sending hot humiliation creeping up the sides of my neck. I fight back a flinch at the knowledge that he saw me in those moments when the Thought had me entirely in its grasp. He clucks his tongue twice. "If your tears were any indication, you seem to be in a delicate situation, Reaper."

I hold his gaze. "You may remedy that delicacy by releasing me from this realm." *And letting me retrieve my sister.*

Because if thirty days go by and Kalmin has not been returned...

Eunbi will die. Because of me.

I cannot have more blood on my hands. Cannot have my little sister's blood on my hands.

Losing Eunbi would shatter me completely. She is all I have.

A brief moment passes as the Pied Piper sets aside his wineglass and laces his fingers. He props them underneath his chin, his expression concerningly contemplative. Finally, he straightens in his seat and narrows his eyes, as if staring at a puzzle he cannot quite complete. "I would like to offer you a bargain, Shin Lina."

A bargain. Every primal instinct in my body screams for me to run as far away from this Dokkaebi as possible. Yet it is impossible. I'm trapped here, and there is nowhere to go—except forward, toward the Emperor of the Dokkaebi. Steeling myself, I take another step closer to his throne. "Bargains involve promises. Agreements. Honesty. I have to wonder, Pied Piper, how much your word is worth."

"My word is worth whatever I decide it is worth." *Bastard.* I scowl, trembling with unrestrained hatred. "But your situation intrigues me," he continues. "I am eager to see how it unfolds."

My breath catches in my throat as I dare to hope. Perhaps there is a way out of this, after all. Perhaps I will escape with Kalmin unscathed, the threat to Eunbi's life null, perhaps—

"You and your crime lord—if you desire that he return with you—will be granted passage back to Sunpo…*if* you manage to assassinate the Emperor of Gyeulcheon."

What in the gods' names?

The wonderful hope warming my body gutters out, replaced by icy dread. I struggle to push words through my tight jaw. "*You're* the Emperor of Gyeulcheon."

"Yes, Reaper, I am well aware," the Pied Piper replies with a sharp, sly smile. "And I am also very bored. Such a game will keep me thoroughly entertained. There is nothing that we Dokkaebi love more than games of fortune. As for the rules…" The Piper tilts his head. "Well. I've always been fond of the number fourteen."

"Fourteen?" I rasp through a dry mouth, unable to understand the connection. My pulse thunders in my ears. I cannot think through my shock. I cannot do anything but sway where I stand.

"Fourteen," the Pied Piper confirms silkily. "It's my second favorite number, my first one being, simply, four. But four is far too small a number for my purposes."

Four. I shiver, suddenly aware of the clamminess coating my skin, the dampness under my arms, the way my heart pounds erratically as it sends wave after wave of nausea through my trembling body.

Four is an unlucky number. It brings bad fortune—at least, that's what the superstitions say, and the Eastern Continent's myths have so far proven to be true. I find it fitting that four would be the Pied Piper's favorite number.

"I could, of course, give you four days." The emperor slips a hand into the folds of his hanbok, as if looking for something. "But I am nothing if not magnanimous." A dark grin. "And so you have four*teen* days, Reaper, to kill me." He finds what he is looking for and tosses it toward me. I see only the glitter of a chain until I catch it in my hands, glass and metal cold on my skin.

It is a necklace, a small hourglass connected to the chain. The curving, eight-shaped glass is situated between two obsidian circles, the same material that makes up the elegant pillars on the hourglass's left and right. Inside, silver sand waits inside the top curve of glass, unmoving.

"Go on," says the Pied Piper. "Put it on. A fine piece of jewelry, is it not?"

My fingers tremble around the chain, and he laughs ever so softly.

"When the sand trickles out, little thief, your time is up. And if you have failed to kill me by the end of the fourteenth day... Well. I'll kill you," the Piper whispers softly. Lethally. "And I can assure you that it will not be pleasant. That tapestry was very important to me."

"Which is why it was sitting in a dust-covered box in Sunpo." The words spill out of my mouth before I can clamp my lips shut. My hands are still shaking violently around the necklace

I have not donned. This game he offers me—it is impossible to win. Fear and anger have quickened my tongue, and I regret the words as soon as they are spoken.

A cold shiver kisses my sweat-dampened back as the Piper straightens indignantly. Fury radiates from the emperor in powerful waves of unbearable heat that scorch my skin as I curse my foul mouth.

His silver gaze is unforgiving. "Perhaps my absence from your kingdom has helped you forget who I am, as so many of your kind have forgotten the names of the gone gods."

I hold my chin high, refusing to cower even as fear grips my heart. "*I* have not forgotten."

The Pied Piper considers me for a long moment, his scrutiny sharp. I stop breathing altogether as he tilts his head to one side, then another, before finally settling back in his throne with an air of disinterest that now feels…calculated. "Well then." His mouth is a cruel, crooked line. "Perhaps the fact that I have let your little kingdom live a full life apart from the power I hold over it has made you think that you can let your tongue run quick. But," the Pied Piper warns, his lips curving into a frigid smile, "it is so very dangerous to forget such things."

I will my knees not to buckle under the overwhelming strength of his glare. Will my eyes to resist flickering to his flute, Manpasikjeok, only a hairsbreadth away from his ringed fingers.

"You stole from me, Shin Lina. I have not forgotten, nor will I ever. I have some compassion, as you were only under orders, but we all have choices. Orders do not always require obedience. Demands do not always hold dominance over what is right."

His eyes narrow and he watches me struggle to hold his gaze, watches me struggle not to tremble. There is no amusement on his countenance now, only cold displeasure.

"This bargain is the best deal that you will receive. Take it or don't. If you kill me, my court will ensure your and your crime lord's safe return." He smiles thinly. "It grows so dreadfully boring here. I urge you to take this bargain. If not..." The Piper flashes his teeth, showing sharp white canines. "Well. The result will be the same as if you lose. Do you prefer a beheading? Or perhaps an arrow to the heart? Although in my opinion, a beheading seems rather quicker and much more entertaining. On my part, at least."

My stomach roils and I take a deep breath, my chest tight. With this offer before me, I suddenly miss the comfort of Asina's thirty days. For now that time means nothing, and I have been handed fourteen days in their place. Fourteen days to kill the Dokkaebi emperor and save my sister. Fourteen days of cat and mouse...but I will be the cat this time.

The room is silent, save for the torrents of thoughts pounding through my mind so loudly that I worry the Dokkaebi can hear them. I lift the hourglass, staring at the glittering sand as my mouth sets into a firm line.

I am a skilled fighter, quick and agile. A weapon honed by Yoonho himself, and deadlier than any of the Talons combined.

And yet...there is no way I can kill the Dokkaebi in front of me.

But I can try.

I can bide my time. Rebuild my strength. And strike.

Except if I end up dead, Eunbi will die, too.

I choke down a whimper and fight back a desperate, keening prayer. Shin Lina does *not* cry. Pain builds in my constricting throat as I will back tears. Weak. I look weak. There is a moment of silence that seems to drag on forever, as long as time itself...

But then I fasten the necklace around my neck.

The glass is cold on my skin, and I fight back a shiver. "Fine. I'll play your godsdamned game," I rasp as the Pied Piper's lips curve. I feel my face tighten into a puzzled frown as he extends a hand. The blood from my forehead is still on his fingers, spots of red on his silver jewelry.

I frown at it. *Am I supposed to—*

"Shake it," the Piper says, arching a brow. A taunt. A dare. A challenge.

I hesitate. But… *For Eunbi. For her chiming laugh and sparkling eyes.*

I make myself walk forward. Climb the dais. Force myself to grasp his hand. *For Eunbi.*

Despite its smooth, slender appearance, his hand is callused and cold. A shock of ice floods my veins, and I gasp, flinching away.

The Pied Piper merely laughs, soft and sly. "We have a deal."

CHAPTER EIGHT

When I was fifteen, I broke my arm.

It happened so fast that I registered only the unmistakable *snap* before it all went black.

Yoonho was working me into a drench of sweat as I punched, kicked, flipped, and twisted, determined to be honed into what Yoonho envisioned for me. A living weapon, and the Talons' greatest asset. It had been only a year since Yoonho had plucked me, a sticky-fingered urchin, from the street. Yet I was strong. Ferocious. I had already killed seven men—seedy, scowling men who believed that the Talons' Sunpo belonged to them. The very sort of men who believed everything and every*one* was theirs to take with force and unforgiving brutality. I took pleasure in seeing them cowering in their final moments, took pleasure in making the kills.

But when it all went dark, I felt fear. Sharp, stabbing fear. *Yeomra*, I thought. *Please do not take me yet.*

When I awoke, Yoonho's narrowed gaze peered down at me from where I lay on my bed. He had pulled up a chair, and by the look of the circles under his eyes, he'd been there for a while.

His graying hair was disheveled, and the wrinkles alongside his thin mouth and hooked nose seemed even more prominent.

I blinked blearily. "What happened?"

Yoonho was silent, yet his eyes spoke for him. I followed them to my right arm. To the heavy white bandages strapping it to my chest, immobilizing one of my body's most useful limbs.

Oh. *Oh.*

The training session, the burst of pain, the darkness... I blinked as realization struck me.

"You *broke* it," I fired, feeling tears prick at my eyes and threaten to spill out. "You broke it," I repeated quietly, furiously rubbing my eyes with the back of my left hand and fighting back those tears. "Why did you break it?"

Yoonho's face turned from haggard to steely. "You need to be lighter on your feet. Quicker. *Faster.* Had this been a real fight, you wouldn't have a broken arm. You would be dead. Do you understand, Lina?" He held my gaze, and a heavy silence settled between us, broken only as my anger reached a boiling point.

"How am I supposed to train?" I exploded. Everything I was working for, everything I'd achieved... "My arm is broken!"

"Who said anything about not training?"

"My arm," I repeated slowly, "is broken."

"And?" He sat back in his chair. "You have another arm."

"My *left* arm," I retorted, trembling with fury.

"Precisely. Your left arm could use more attention, regardless. Think of this as the perfect opportunity to strengthen dexterity on your nondominant side."

"It's not fair," I cut in, frustration making my voice small and tight. "You have both arms. Fighting you with one arm isn't fair."

"Life," Yoonho replied curtly, his patience finally slipping, "is not fair. Especially in this line of work. You want to survive? Then fight with what you have. And what you have is a perfectly good left arm. You'll have opponents bigger than you. Stronger than you. More powerful than you. Use every resource you can in order to win." He ran a hand down his face, which suddenly seemed haggard again. He looked old in that moment; a great deal older than his fifty years. And tired. So very tired. "You're on your way to becoming the Talons' greatest asset. Prove to me that you can be."

I clenched my jaw tight enough that it popped. But he was right. I knew he was. And, like any petulant fifteen-year-old, I hated him for it. "Fine," I spat out. "I will."

And I did.

Fighting the Pied Piper will be like fighting without an arm. And a leg.

And eyes, or ears.

I try to ignore the Dokkaebi's air of obvious satisfaction as he stands from his throne and gracefully makes his way down from the dais, his shoulder brushing past mine.

Heat blooms on the spot where our skin meets. "Your time starts tomorrow," he says with an air of dark satisfaction, eyes on the hourglass. "Consider this your day of rest."

I grit my teeth and imagine running him through with the dagger still strapped to my waist. But no—too risky. So I stay where I am as he once again parts his lips, which this time reveal words that are not meant for me.

"Your eavesdropping stops now," he calls, his voice tinged with dark laughter as he fixes his eyes on a point on the other side of the room, near the black doors.

There is a muffled feminine swear, followed by two low, masculine laughs—and then the heavy, dark doors slam open, accompanied by a burst of light.

My breath catches in my throat as more Dokkaebi appear, their footsteps echoing across the black marble floor. There are three, with pointed ears, and breathtaking in ways that humans can never be—one a beautiful female, tall and regal, with a waterfall of curly black hair. She carries herself with an air of haughty pride, emphasized by her narrowed eyes and upturned chin. A dress of glittering gold clings to her alabaster, freckled skin. The garment is one of the Northern style, skintight and utterly at odds with this continent's traditional hanbok.

She stands between two males, but her fingers are brushing those of a Dokkaebi who, despite his unlined face, harbors a shock of long white hair. His skin is a rich umber and his uptilted eyes—a deep emerald green—take me in with wary interest. He wears a black hanbok embellished with gray embroidery, a sash of silver secured around his waist, where a sheathed sword, along with various golden medallions, also hang. I wonder, warily, if he is some sort of general.

He scowls at me.

I scowl right back.

The final male, wearing a simple tunic and baggy pants, is clutching a staff of twisted black wood. He eyes me with a vague intrigue that unnerves me. His eyes are not a searing silver like the Pied Piper's—they are brown and rimmed with dark circles. Their depths seem to swim with infinite questions and answers, knowledge and thought, wisdom and wonder. His hair falls to his chin, the red-brown color of autumn foliage. Under my gaze, he tilts his head in what could be a greeting or a warning.

Probably the latter.

I don't return the gesture, but my fingers twitch to my dagger.

"It was hardly eavesdropping," the female Dokkaebi replies coolly. "Your voice is simply too loud to ignore."

The white-haired male to her right seems to swallow a laugh

with difficulty before composing his face back into stiff stoicism.

"I see we have a guest," the staff-bearing Dokkaebi murmurs before the Piper can reply. "I hope that you have not forgotten to introduce us."

The Piper casts a sparking look over his shoulder in my direction. "Shin Lina, meet Jeong Kang, Park Hana, and Kim Chan." He cuts a look to Kang, the one with the staff. "That satisfies you, I hope."

In the presence of these intimidating immortals, I suddenly become overly aware of the grime crusting my skin and the bruises dappling my face. I straighten and say nothing, gripping the hilt of my dagger so tightly that my knuckles ache.

"An honor," Hana says icily, lips twisting into a mocking smile. Her voice is slick with a distaste that sends me scowling.

"I truly wish that I could say the same," I reply sweetly before I can stop myself.

Chan tenses as Hana's eyes flash, but before she can reply, Kang turns to the Piper with a bone-weary expression. "Haneul Rui, you owe me a great explanation."

My eyes snap to the Pied Piper, who gives Kang a bland smile. *Haneul Rui*...of course the Piper has a name other than what Sunpo dubs him. Something roils uneasily in my stomach, the danger that I am in suddenly seeming much more real.

"Lina," the Piper—*Rui*—says, "and I have struck a little bargain."

"Dear gods." Kang's face pales and his eyes dart to the hourglass upon my neck. "Rui." I take pleasure in the fact that there is genuine concern in his voice, take pleasure in the idea that perhaps, somehow, I can pose a threat after all.

The emperor ignores him. "Hana, darling." Rui turns to the dark-haired female. "Show Shin Lina to the guest wing. She could use a bath."

My cheeks burn red as he and his companions chuckle.

Kang is the only one who remains silent, his brows furrowed in quiet contemplation. He meets my gaze for a moment, and it almost seems as if sympathy swirls in those dark depths.

I scoff. I don't want his pity. Don't *need* his pity.

"This way," Hana says with an elegant tilt of her head as she begins to make her way out of the throne room, her golden dress swishing across the glossy ground.

I don't move.

Instead, I turn my gaze to the Pied Piper.

His smile falters slightly as I hold his stare and let him see every bit of the Reaper that is still in me. Let him see every murderous and predatory gleam that shines in my eyes as if to say, *You've made a fool's bargain, Your Majesty.*

The Piper just curls his lips into a razor-sharp half-moon.

I cock my head and smile an awful smile for a split second before allowing my lips to flatten, allowing my eyes to bore into his.

Seconds pass before his jaw flexes—just slightly.

And with that, I taste triumph, sweet and spiced on my tongue.

Limping past him toward Hana, I make an extra point to shove my shoulder into his. He doesn't budge, but I do not miss his scowl.

As I follow Hana out of the room, Haneul Rui's glower is a sharp sword embedded in my back.

CHAPTER NINE

Whatever I expected Gyeulcheon to look like…it isn't this. It isn't that I'd thought that the Dokkaebi lived in dark, gaping caves slick with filmy puddles and scuttling with rats… It's simply that I hadn't anticipated *this*.

I try not to allow my face to slacken in awe as the doorway of the throne room opens to a sunlit grand plaza, with a glass ceiling displaying a brilliant blue sky.

Slowly it occurs to me that the sunlight isn't sunlight at all, but warm moonlight cast from the dozens of golden moons—all in various phases—hanging suspended between the clouds. There is no sun at all, only the sight of these moons that are a clear echo of the tapestry I so foolishly destroyed.

I swallow hard and tear my gaze away from the unnatural sky with difficulty.

The plaza itself houses a burbling fountain, crafted of emerald stone, in the center. Lilac liquid burbles out of the top and spills into a pool where koi dance in flashes of orange. My eyes shift to the small Dokkaebi children dipping hands into the fountain, their laughs merry as they echo through the plaza. A

Dokkaebi donning plain, servant-like attire hurries her way to them and hastily ushers them away.

I watch as the servant hustles her charges past a looming marbled statue that looks suspiciously like Haneul Rui, and into an adjoining hallway. To the right of the fountain is a sweeping staircase, and I watch a brown-robed Dokkaebi make his way down what must be fifty steps, carrying a pile of precariously balancing scrolls.

Above the stairs, a hallway is visible, lined with portraits of still lifes that I can just barely make out. One seems to be a painting of an emerald snake with glistening scales curled around a rotting cluster of browning grapes. The colors are vivid, yet edged with a layer of darkness that unnerves me. Even despite my trepidation, though, I cannot look away.

"The guest wing is this way." Hana nods toward the hall through which the Dokkaebi children have exited, her eyes narrow. "Are you done staring?"

I flatten my gaze at her tone. "I assume that this *guest wing* is more of a prison cell."

She gracefully arches a curved brow. "You'll find yourself mistaken."

"Because your emperor will give fine quarters to a girl who's to kill him," I scoff.

"Perhaps my emperor does not find you to be much of a threat." She smiles at my furious expression. "This way."

As I follow Hana across the plaza, noting how her skin glows with health, I try to ignore the envy that floods me. Try to ignore the fact that Hana has what I have lost. Has more than just skin and flesh that clings to her bones but color, fullness, and brightness in her face.

"Don't," Sang would say, sometimes catching me staring at the twins as they suited up in black lace and delicate ribbons for their mission. "Don't compare yourself, L."

But it is so hard not to long for what others have.

I roll my eyes as we pass the sculpture, which, I decide with absolute certainty, is in fact the Pied Piper. The marble rendition stands tall and proud, fingers elegantly curled around Manpasikjeok as his pursed lips graze the instrument's plate.

The statue seems to leer down at me with great amusement as I pass by. I feel a surge of satisfaction as I not-so-subtly send a vulgar gesture its way.

Hana's back stiffens, almost as if she's sensed my offense. For good measure, I send the gesture her way, too, before hastily tucking my hand behind my back.

I think that I hear her mutter an impressively uncouth curse.

The corridor we enter is composed of obsidian arches, and as I pass underneath, I take in an array of intricate designs that remind me of thorned vines carved into the dark stone of the overpasses. Flickering red candle flames illuminate the corridor and bathe Hana in a wash of eerie light.

She coolly glances over her shoulder. "This way," she says as she turns a corner.

The arches give way to two staircases, one leading up and the other leading down. Hana chooses the polished black steps leading downward. "From the looks of you, you'll enjoy your stay here. We have running water. And plenty of soap to go around."

I vividly imagine throwing Hana out of a very high window.

She leads me through another hallway, this one lined with dark marbled walls and golden doors. "Rui won't make this game of his easy for you. But I'm sure you already knew that."

I finger the hourglass and swallow hard. "Obviously."

Hana laughs quietly and I contain myself only barely, taking a shallow breath through my nose.

"Here." Hana halts in front of the last golden door. "This is you." She tilts her head, her long-lashed black eyes scanning me with a haughty sort of distaste. "I would wish you luck, but I would really rather have you fail. Do not expect to find any sympathy or blessings of good fortune from any Dokkaebi you may meet." Hana smiles thinly before turning to make her way back down the hallway. "You'll find the soap next to the bathtub. I suggest that you use it."

I seethe at her retreating back. "No key?" I call, but Hana says nothing as she disappears up the stairs. I turn toward the golden door and try the knob. Locked. Wearily, I run a hand through my hair and mutter a sour curse under my breath.

Of course there's no key.

"Very funny," I mutter.

A moment later, there's a hiss and a click that makes my hand fly to my dagger—but it is only the door, slowly inching its way open, unprompted.

Tightening my grip on my dagger, I step inside the room.

I blink. Then blink again as I slowly shut the door, keeping my eyes on the four-poster bed, the polished wooden floor, and the large cushions surrounding a low table adorned with a vase of white-petaled buckwheat flowers.

"Fine quarters for an assassin," I murmur under my breath.

My gaze flickers to the bathroom. And to the bath, which resembles a small pool. It is large and rectangular, carved from pale green onyx, and already filled to the brim with steaming water dappled by pink flower petals and crystals of blue salts. The air is warm, heavy with the scent of a sweet, biting citrus and cherry blossoms.

What kind of game is the Pied Piper playing?

The bed, the sofa, the chandelier, the *bath*…the luxury, the tranquility. I am going to murder him, and he's given me a room brimming with luxury as a reward?

Perhaps he doesn't find you to be too much of a threat at all.

I grimace hard enough that my still-beaten face barks in pain. He underestimates me. And I will use that to my advantage.

But first, a bath. And a godsdamned *long* one. I reek badly enough that I don't care if the bathtub is part of the Pied Piper's duplicitous game. I strip off my clothes and sink into the water, hissing slightly as the heat reaches through to my battered bones. The hot water feels divine on my left leg, soothing the injured muscles. But I did not take off the necklace, and the chain's metal is frigid upon my neck.

The water never seems to grow murky, despite the layers of grime coating my skin. It never grows cold, either. My skin soon shines raw from the fervent washing, and when I'm finally done, I rise from the tub, wrap myself in a towel, and walk over to my clothes, dirty and reeking of sweat. Stains crust the fabric in crude splatters. I look back at the wardrobe.

Fine, I think grimly. *Fine.*

I clench my jaw as I curl my fingers around the dagger still strapped to my grimy pants, choking back a gag. The aroma of citrus does little to block out the reek of sweat clouding my clothes. I hold my breath as I fish around in the pants' pockets until I locate the lighter and cigarette. An eager sort of itchiness begins to tingle in my fingertips.

I was interrupted before on the street, and gods, I need it *now*. I am in Gyeulcheon, surrounded by Dokkaebi, while my little sister's academy is surrounded by bloodthirsty Blackbloods waiting for thirty days to pass.

A smoke will calm my nerves.

I flick open the lighter and watch the small flame dance.

For a moment, I think I see Sang's face in the flame—haggard and weary as his eyes somberly meet mine.

If something happens to your health, I hear over the slight crackle of the flame, *I can't bear knowing that I handed you that first one.*

Flinching, I shut the lighter with a snap and send my old garments into the corner with a well-aimed kick. Later. I'll smoke later. Clenching my jaw, I yank open the doors of the wardrobe.

And my jaw drops.

CHAPTER TEN

Inside the closet, flowing and elegant evening gowns hang delicately on silver hangers. Tunics embroidered with golden thread rest next to cloaks made of thick gray wool. Patterned hanboks, made of shimmering silks and surely worth more than any item of clothing in the kingdom of Sunpo, catch my eye. I bite my tongue as I count twenty pairs of shoes, ranging from delicate slippers with dainty, low heels to heavy black boots that appear to be my size.

I admire one hanbok in particular. It hangs beside a plain nightdress, calling to me. The jeogori, the hanbok's upper garment, is a dark blue studded with golden embroidery, reminding me of the night's constellations. Its long sleeves are a delicate, sheer blue. The chima—the skirt—is black, and the material is flowing; I reach out to touch it. It reminds me of the hanboks I wore with the Talons, during those rare moments in between assassinations and thefts...the hanboks I wore for Sunpo festivities such as the Night of the Red Moon, standing with Sang underneath the sky's scarlet crescent, laughing ourselves hoarse. The hanboks I wore when I was happy.

But an inch away from the satin, my fingers freeze, hovering in midair.

The urge to try it on and feel the cool fabric brush my skin, to feel like the girl I once was, is overwhelming. But I do not forget who these clothes belong to.

"No," I mutter, combing my other hand through my hair in frustration and ripping my gaze, and hand, away from the gown. So Rui has chosen eveningwear and fashion as his weapon. Smart. But I will not be baited. I will not forget what I am here for.

I scour the closet for the plainest, dullest clothes I can find, settling for a simple gray tunic and baggy black trousers. I slip them on, trying my hardest not to marvel at the softness. I tuck the cigarette and lighter into the deep-set pockets, then knit my still-wet hair into a sloppy braid and cast a glance in the mirror next to the wardrobe.

I have almost forgotten what it is like to be clean. For once, my high cheekbones and pointed chin are visible—as is the dimple that indents my chin and the small black birthmark on my right cheek. I swallow hard. I almost look like the girl I was a year ago.

Almost.

A sharp rap on the door jolts me out of my haze.

Clenching my dagger as my heart rams against my rib cage, I inch my way to the door. A bead of sweat trickles down my back. "Who's there?"

A beat of silence. And then— "The Emperor sends you a meal." The voice is high and young, pretty and sweet.

It sounds harmless enough, but I know better. I myself have hidden behind shy smiles and soft-spoken words, only to reveal my true nature a moment later, lunging at my target with a gleaming sword.

Cautiously, I open the door, my dagger clenched behind my back.

A steaming bowl of rice drizzled with honey and sprinkled with crystals of brown sugar, a plate of glistening berries, and a platter of golden flaked fish greet me.

"For you," the bearer of the tray says, and I move my gaze toward her.

Ice rushes through my veins, and I lurch back in shock.

"You're human," I say slowly, taking in light brown eyes, rounded ears, plump cheeks, and an abundance of freckles. She is pretty, but it's a mortal sort of beauty, one that will fade. She cannot be more than twenty years old. There is a blank, dreamy sort of quality in her gaze, one that greatly unnerves me.

"The benevolent Emperor Rui sends you this." The girl presses the tray into my arms. I take it, still numbly staring at her eyes.

So the stories of the Pied Piper are true.

He truly does spirit away humans from the mortal realm of Iseung.

"Enjoy," says the girl in her high, young voice before quickly moving away.

I watch closely as she rounds a corner and vanishes from sight. My jaw tight, I finally firmly shut the door.

So that's what he does with the humans—the Piper turns them into blank-eyed servants in his palace. I don't know whether to be relieved or horrified. They're not dead as the legends allude, but they're not quite *alive*, either, existing only to do another's bidding. I know some semblance of the feeling myself.

I exhale shakily as I set the tray of food down on the sofa, slightly nauseated. There was no clarity in that human's gaze. There was only that fog, undoubtedly produced by the spell of the Pied Piper's flute, Manpasikjeok.

Has Kalmin met the same fate?

I find myself wishing for him to be enduring something far, far worse.

My stomach rumbles, but I ignore it, as I ignore the platter of food that could very well be poisoned.

Minutes tick by as I sit on the sofa, my hands knotted together as I try to ignore the cramping hunger twisting my stomach. Before I can stop it, my gaze flickers back to the golden fish.

No, I tell myself firmly. *No.*

But the aroma… I sigh. The Pied Piper seems to look forward to my assassination attempts—ones that I cannot commit if I'm dead. It is unlikely that he's taken the time to poison the meal; after all, our game of cat and mouse has only just begun.

I pluck a pink berry from the tray and examine it. After a few wary moments, I arrive at the conclusion that it looks and smells like a normal, mundane berry.

I hope that I'm right as I tear off the tip of the fruit with my teeth. When I don't die within moments, I take another bite and hold back a groan. It is delicious—too delicious. Before I know it, I'm tearing into the fish, hungrily spearing the crisp golden skin with my chopsticks.

As I eat, my mind struggles to compute that I am truly eating a real meal. The rice is sweet, and its sugar topping crunches beneath my teeth. The blackberries leave dark, syrupy stains on my lips. The fish's salty flakes melt on my tongue.

I'm eating. *Eating.*

My stomach cramps, but I ignore it, ripping into the food with an appetite akin to that of a starving animal. I pay no consequences for it until nearly halfway through the meal, when a sharp pain in my stomach sends me doubling over. A wave of sickness works its way up my throat, and I scramble to my feet, swaying unsteadily. Did the bastard poison me after all?

No. My body is just not used to so much food.

I stumble into the bathroom, clutching my stomach. A

couple of minutes later, I emerge with the taste of mint heavy on my tongue from the dental paste I used after retching my supper into the toilet. I'll eat again in the morning. Just a little, until my body can handle a normal amount of food.

I climb wearily into the bed and immediately frown. The mattress is impossibly cushioned under my battered body, the blankets wonderfully heavy and warm.

How dare this bed be so comfortable. I want to kill Haneul Rui even more for it. But my eyelids are heavy, and I struggle to keep them open.

I am in Gyeulcheon, where sleeping can do me more harm than good. I need to plot. Plan. I need to design the Pied Piper's death and Eunbi's rescue. I desperately hope that my sister remains blissfully unaware of the danger surrounding her — until I leave Gyeulcheon and can come for her, killing all those godsdamned Blackbloods in the process. I need to scheme until daybreak.

But I can do that with my eyes closed, can't I?

I slowly allow my lids to flutter shut.

My grip on the fraying thread of consciousness slips as a wave of sleep, heavy and dark, crashes over my head.

CHAPTER ELEVEN

"Lina," Chryse said, setting down her spoonful of porridge, "you look like shit."

"Hello to you, too." I stalked through the dining room, leaving a trail of mud behind me. Chara, Chryse, Sang, and Yoonho were all eating breakfast, gathered around the low table that groaned under the weight of still-steaming food.

I tugged out my pillow next to Sang and Chara and collapsed onto it. Sang sent me a brief glance filled with worry before reaching across the table for the platter of hard-boiled eggs and setting it beside me. I ignored him as I met Yoonho's gaze. At the head of the table, he drummed his fingers on the tabletop.

"The mission went well," I said, earning a satisfied nod in return. "Cho sends his greetings from the bottom of Habaek's River. He won't be bothering us, or the Doves, any longer." The Dove Coop was a brothel in the Boneburrow that paid tribute to us, one frequented by Cho often—much to the displeasure of the Coop's Doves. "And as for his assets…" I rolled my shoulders, still stiff from the fight. "I saw to it that they'll be transferred to your account this afternoon."

Yoonho inclined his head, the wrinkles around his eyes crinkling as he smiled. "You were gone long. Any interruptions?" Although his smile didn't falter, his tone carried an undercurrent of concern.

"Chara and Chryse did their work well. His guards were still hungover from last night." I sent the twins a knowing look. They giggled behind their hands and exchanged mischievous looks. "But Cho was stronger than I thought. He didn't go down easily." I fought the urge to massage my forehead, where I'd covered a fast-forming bruise with my hair.

Yoonho's brows lowered and he sent his spy a critical look. "Dig a little deeper next time."

Sang nodded stiffly. "Apologies."

"It's not Sang's fault," I quickly amended. "Besides, it all worked out in the end."

I felt my lips turning into a frown as Yoonho remained silent, sipping from his earthenware cup of byeonggyul-cha tea with a grim expression.

"You should eat, Lina," Sang said quietly, nudging me under the table with his knee. "You were out all night."

I ignored him again, still looking at Yoonho. "The pistol put him down eventually. And I'm fine. Not injured at all."

"Well." Yoonho took a bite of seasoned kelp. "If you had to resort to using bullets, Reaper, it is a sure sign that you went in unprepared. I was expecting a heart wound. Slower, more painful."

Grinding my teeth in irritation, I crossed my arms. It seemed I wouldn't be winning this fight, so I let it drop, turning to my next request. "I need more bullets. Cho was wearing some form of bulletproof material underneath his hanbok. The first two were useless."

"And the third?"

I shrugged. "He wasn't wearing the material on his forehead."

Chara made a face. "Lina, darling, we're eating. I can hardly digest with talk like this."

"I like to cover business over breakfast." Turning back to Yoonho, I cocked my head in interest. "Do they make those? Bulletproof face masks, I mean." I leaned forward, intrigued.

Next to me, Sang sighed impatiently and began loading my plate with a hard-boiled egg, a mound of fresh rice, spinach, and bulgogi. The beef was a rare treat. Wyusan, it seemed, had graced Sunpo with a morsel of their meat this week—probably taking pity on us for the fact that most of our protein came from the same salty fish swimming in the murky waters of the Yongwangguk Sea.

"Ask Sungho," Yoonho replied, naming the Talons' weapon dealer. "Get in his good graces and he just might make one for you."

"Sungho? It's impossible to get in that man's good graces. It's like he has something eternally shoved up his ass. Eat," Sang said, pushing my now-full plate toward me, along with a cup of citrus tea.

I obediently picked up my chopsticks, absentmindedly catching a bit of rice between the sticks.

Yoonho set down his cup and wiped his lips with a white cloth. "I'll be in my office should anyone need me. Lina, take the day off to rest. Chara, Chryse, you will be carrying out your assignment. Sang, locate Unima Hisao. I've heard a rumor that he plans to pull funding from us and direct it elsewhere. I want to know to who and where."

"Unima's cutting sponsorship?" I frowned, pausing with my chopsticks halfway to my mouth. Even the idea was ludicrous. Unima had been an ally for as long as I could remember. A wealthy nobleman and successful merchant hailing from the jewel-heavy kingdom of Oktari on the Southern Continent, Unima had many competitors within the world of trade.

He was also our biggest sponsor. He funded our properties, our taverns and gambling dens in the Boneburrow—the northern district of Sunpo, where the streets were lined with what Yoonho called "institutions of ill repute." I called them brothels and bars. We repaid him with protection and knocked out his competition in the precious-stone market. "That can't be true. It's likely a false lead."

Yoonho's face was grim. "Look into it, Sang. Tell me what you find, and we'll go from there." Yoonho sent us all a slight nod. "Good luck, and good day."

Once he left, Chara and Chryse stood up as well and sent us wicked smiles. "We'll see you two tomorrow," Chara said, tilting her head.

"Have fun." I grinned around a mouthful of rice.

"They will," Sang murmured softly as they retreated.

"What I'd give to have their job instead," I said ruefully. "Rolling around in lingerie with rich, powerful men sounds like the perfect Friday."

Sang huffed a laugh. "Does it, now?"

"Better than taking hit after hit from an asshole businessman just so I can set up a clear shot at his forehead." I scowled. "Bastard."

"About that… I'm so sorry, L. He must have been taking private training sessions. I completely missed it when I created his file." Sang cast his stare downward and ran a scarred hand through his perpetually messy hair. "I take complete responsibility. I…"

I furrowed my brows as I swallowed a bite of bulgogi. "It's fine, Sang. I got him, didn't I? He's dead now. I killed him."

"You did. But not without the marks to prove it." Heat bloomed on my skin as he brushed his fingers gently across my forehead, sweeping away the few strands of hair I'd arranged to fall over the bruise blooming upon my skin. I hadn't wanted to worry the twins—they always worried when I got hurt, no matter how small the injury.

But Sang knew my tells. He knew me.

My eyes met his, and for a moment, time seemed to still. I saw, rather than felt, myself moving forward a breath of an inch, my lips parting ever so slightly...

Sang moved away, his eyes widening.

Cheeks burning, I turned back to my food and stabbed at an egg. "It's just a bruise," I said stiffly. "It'll fade."

"Lina—"

"I'm tired. Thanks for the food." I glanced down at my half-eaten plate, at my now-cool cup of tea, anywhere but Sang.

"L..." he said. I cut a reluctant glance to Sang. His shoulders were slumped. "I'm sorry. It's just..." He paused, shaking his head. "I can't keep telling you, over and over, that it was a mistake. Please, just—"

"Just what?" I cut in. Sang was silent. I scoffed bitterly. "Right."

His eyes widened. "Lina, I—"

I forced myself to smile, to cock a brow, but I had a sinking feeling that Sang could see how fake it all was. "Don't get killed on your mission," was all I said before stalking out of the room, humiliation burning on my cheeks. As always, I'd misread the situation.

Fine. It wouldn't happen again.

I stormed down the hallway, but my steps faltered as my vision started to blur. The walls of the palace seemed to melt and congeal, trickling drip by drip into nothingness as the floor beneath me rolled and swayed, and then...

I was standing in a pool of blood.

It wasn't mine, I realized, slowly lifting my gaze from my feet.

No, it was *theirs.*

My breath caught in my throat as I took in the heap of bodies strewn across the floor of the corridor.

Two had blond hair. Usually sleek and glossy, it was now tangled and matted with dried blood.

Another lay limp and prone, a scarred hand I knew as well as my own outstretched toward a discarded sword.

Oh gods.

No. Not again.

It wasn't this day, not yet.

This day happened three weeks from when I was in the dining room. This day was in the future. No, not the future—the past. I was not here, not really—it was a memory. A year-old memory. A forever recurring nightmare...

Blood seeped into my shoes, soaking my socks in warm sogginess.

No. No. No.

I fought back a scream. The blood coating the floor slowly began to rise, inch by inch, until I was knee-deep in crimson. Waist-deep.

I needed to move, but I couldn't. My muscles were taut and frozen.

Chest-deep.

The blood was dropping in temperature. It was *cold.*

Chin-deep.

Cold, coppery blood filled my mouth, my nose. Everything was scarlet, a bloody, vicious scarlet, and I couldn't move, couldn't breathe, as I drowned in the ocean of blood, my lungs screaming for air—

. . .

I awaken tangled in layers of blankets, my head buried under a mountain of pillows. My racing heart steadies…and then resumes its relentless pounding as the past day's events come flooding back to me.

Gyeulcheon.

The Dokkaebi.

The bargain.

Fourteen days, beginning this morning, to kill the Pied Piper. If not, Eunbi dies. The hourglass has begun to spill shimmering sand through the thin, stemlike neck. It falls idly, like drifting snowflakes, to the glass below. My heart pounds against it, increasing in speed as I taste bile.

Shakily, I slide out of bed, my toes touching the soft rug. I pad to the bathroom, trembling as I splash icy water on my clammy face. The dream pokes and prods at me, but I will not think about it. I need to focus. To plan.

I am a trained assassin. Skilled and versed in every weapon and poison imaginable. This is just another assignment…only with higher stakes.

The only weapon I currently possess is the dull, battered dagger. But there has to be some form of an armory in this palace.

I suspect that the Dokkaebi here will leave me alone, gauging me to be a very miniscule threat. Neither Hana nor the two males seemed abundantly concerned for their emperor's safety. I can only hope that it means they won't target me. But why would they? I have a feeling that the Piper wouldn't take well to that. I'm his *entertainment,* after all.

I loosen a breath. Right. I can do this. This is my assignment. I will complete it, just as I have many others.

I'll start off by mapping the palace. Learning my surroundings inside and out is crucial. I'll look for weaponry as well. The dulled, flimsy dagger supplied to me by the Blackbloods will do little good in the long run. And I'll keep an eye out for Kalmin, too. He is now my ticket to Eunbi's safety, and therefore I need to ensure that the foul, cursed snake is still at least *somewhat* alive.

Somewhat being the key word. If I see him... I flex my fingers and imagine them wrapping around his pale throat.

I jump as a harsh knock sounds on my door.

Although it is most likely my breakfast, I grab my dagger before opening the door. Immediately, my lips curl into a hateful snarl. *"You."*

"Me." Haneul Rui smiles a razor-sharp smile as he braces a hand against the doorframe and leans over me, his head at least a foot above mine. "Good morning, Reaper. Aren't you going to let me in?"

I clench my jaw hard, gaze flickering toward the human girl standing behind him and carrying a tray of food. I send a glower demanding an answer toward the Piper.

He shrugs. "I thought we'd take breakfast together. Review our little bargain."

I tighten the grip on my dagger as my heart begins to race. He's so close to me... So close to his death. An opportunity to strike has presented itself quicker than I could ever have hoped. Grudgingly, I step aside, my dagger clenched behind my back.

He brushes past me into the room, his robes flowing behind him.

Today, he wears a hanbok of so deep a purple that it is almost black. The lines of his muscled chest are visible thanks to the robe's low cut, and I lick my lips as I imagine my dagger piercing the skin and spearing the heart underneath.

I watch the young girl place the food on the low table and quietly make her exit. As she leaves, I shut the door behind her and narrow my eyes at the Pied Piper. My fingers twist the door's lock upright with a soft *click*.

"The guest suite is rather lovely, don't you agree?" Rui's back is straight and proud as he observes the room, now thick with the smell of licorice and plum blossoms. "I see you've made good use of the bed." His back is turned to me. It is perfect.

"It's a fine bed," I say smoothly, calculating how far, exactly, I'll have to lunge to sink the blade into his lower back. Rui chuckles, beginning to turn slightly.

Now. I have to act now.

As quickly as a shadow flitting in the night, I lunge with my dagger poised in position to strike. But I hit nothing but empty air.

Rui laughs softly as I stumble. He moves so fast that I barely register it at all. A moment later, the emperor stands against the opposite wall, where he watches me with unconcealed amusement as I grit my teeth and hurl my dagger across the room, aiming to kill.

Rui looks bored as he plucks the dagger out of the air. "Really, Lina. Control your temper." He tosses it back to me, the beginning of an edged grin playing on his lips.

I seize my weapon and rush, a blur of movement as I dart toward Rui.

I will do it. I'll kill him. But a mere foot away from him, I freeze.

The Pied Piper holds his flute between his slender hands, having seemingly procured it from thin air. He raises Manpasikjeok to his lips, and a song, lilting and melodious, washes over me. Its sweet notes flutter along my skin like paper-thin butterflies, like soft snowflakes on a glistening sunlit morning.

Every breath I take is slow and deliciously deep, a sense of tranquility I've never felt before making my eyelids so wonderfully heavy.

Put the dagger down, the song whispers, and I do. My arm

drops limply to my side, and the dagger falls to the floor with a muted *thud*. *Come closer*, the song urges, and I do. *Good. Now look at me.*

Head foggy and vision blurred, I try to focus on the figure before me. I first make out the glittering silver earrings that sparkle tenfold before my blurred eyes, which soon move to the cheekbones that can cut glass. Heavy-lashed eyes filled with swirling silver storms...

Something shifts in the music.

I gasp, doubling over.

Everything is a roar of grating sounds. My breathing is too rough, too hoarse, too rasping. My vision swims, one moment sharp—too sharp—the next smudged and blurred.

My only relief from the grating in my ears is a quietly melodious laugh as the Piper tucks away his flute. "A valiant effort, but a failed one nonetheless." Rui kicks my dagger to the far corner of the room. "But now that you've gotten that out of your system, come eat. The food is growing cold."

I draw myself to my feet, breathing heavily as I swallow a curse of rage. Humiliation and fury heat my cheeks to a scalding scarlet.

So this is what it is like to be compelled by Manpasikjeok, the Flute to Calm Ten Thousand Waves. Bile rises in my throat and I swallow it down, struggling to control my rage. My hands shake.

First with Kalmin, and now with the Pied Piper.

Is it my fate to always be subject to another's will?

Rui sends me a glance as he lounges on one of the floor cushions in front of the table and pours himself a cup of steaming tea. "I've been told I'm quite the musician," he says with cold laughter in his voice.

"I've been told I'm quite the assassin," I retort viciously, still trembling.

"I was told that as well, but I have to admit that, so far, I'm disappointed." He shakes his head in a mockery of regret, his long blue-black hair fluttering slightly. "I was expecting something...more."

As was I, I want to hiss back, but I swallow the words whole as I acknowledge that I failed, for I attacked far too soon. I must learn more about this creature before I stand an irrefutable chance of slitting his throat. I should not be surprised that I have stumbled.

Rui gestures to the cushion across from him with long, tapered fingers.

He turns his penetrating gaze toward me as he raises his porcelain teacup to his lips. Tendrils of steam twirl around him like morning mist. "Dine with me," he says.

There is no choice for me but to obey, and he is perfectly aware of that. Rui's lips tilt upward in clear amusement as I snarl in aggravation.

I slowly drag my feet to the table and sit on the cushion opposite him. Despite myself, my stomach grumbles as I survey the spread of food.

"Pajeon?" Rui offers, gesturing to a stack of the savory pancakes with his chopsticks.

"No," I snap and instead snatch the bowl of hard-boiled eggs that Rui's chopsticks have just reached for. I take a too-ferocious bite of one. The grinding of my teeth is audible as I chew.

My resentment deepens.

These eggs are delicious.

This fact only upsets me more.

The Dokkaebi scoops a bit of danpatjuk into his bowl instead. "I've decided that there must be some sort of punishment for failed assassination attempts," he declares, raising a bite of the steaming red bean porridge to his lips, which are curled in amusement.

"Besides a beheading?" My fingers have begun to tremble. "What will it be? An arm? A leg?" I breathlessly wait for him to respond, eyes trained on his every movement.

Rui sets down his spoon and wipes his mouth on his napkin with precise, delicate dabs. "Those ideas sound terribly vulgar. Besides, I've ordered you to be untouched by my court. Our game is to remain between us."

He has ordered for me to be untouched by his court.

Relief floods my chest, closely followed by distrust. How can I know he's telling me the truth? The Piper's word is worth nothing.

I swallow my food warily. "Then what do you have in mind?"

Rui takes another sip of tea. "I was thinking of something more along the lines of kitchen duty, every day for the duration of your stay here."

I blink.

Kitchen…?

Oh.

I'm suddenly overwhelmed by a rush of relief. I'll be keeping both of my legs after all. "Kitchen duty," I repeat, careful to keep my tone dubious. "In the kitchen."

"Oh, it's fun," Rui says airily. "You'll quite enjoy it."

"I'm sure," I reply stiffly, glaring at his ever-growing grin.

"Your assassination attempt was almost impressive in terms of absolute recklessness and its sheer futility." Settling back in his seat and crossing his arms, the Dokkaebi waits for my response, as if he has just granted me a great compliment.

Unbelievable.

I clench my jaw as I reach for a cup of tea. That I tried to kill the Pied Piper just moments ago is topped in bizarreness only by the fact that I am now sitting and taking breakfast with him.

"I have to admit, this bargain of ours is the most fun I've had in quite a long time."

"I can't agree," I reply sweetly, clenching my fist around a dasik. The seed cookie crumbles through my fingers, and I dump the pieces onto the table. *If only I could crush his bones so easily*, I think as Rui watches me with raised brows before languidly rising to his feet.

"Get dressed and wash up. Kitchen duty is a full day's work. I'll wait outside." Rui tosses a wicked smile over his shoulder as he leaves, the door shutting firmly behind him.

I sneer at the door as I retrieve my dagger. He's undoubtedly playing a prank—delivering me to the dungeons when I expect the kitchens.

Exceedingly conscious that the Emperor of Gyeulcheon stands just behind my door, I take my sweet time washing up, savoring each minute that I keep him waiting. They pass by, one by one. Five. Ten. Fifteen.

Twenty.

I finally stride out into the hall, sending a shit-eating grin in the direction of the Piper, who looks entirely unfazed.

"Ah," he murmurs, arching a brow. "There you are."

"Here I am," I reply, tapping the hilt of my dagger, which is sheathed at my waist. It's an empty threat—I will not strike now, not when my failure is so fresh—but I still throw every ounce of hatred behind the words.

The emperor merely clucks his tongue in mock disapproval before starting down the hallway of the palace in a graceful, purposeful stride. I follow him, vividly imagining digging my dagger into the cavity of his chest.

As we make our way through the hall, my mind whirs. I'll be working in a kitchen. Perhaps I can poison his food with the churi-hyang plant, a poisonous flower that is deadly despite its delicate white appearance. Or stick a small blade inside one of those gods-damned dasik cookies. The opportunities will be endless—

"Your scheming is audible even from here," the Piper dryly announces as we pass under the stone arches into the plaza. "I suggest, little thief, that you research the art of subtlety."

I flash a crude gesture involving one very specific finger at his back, realizing only a moment later that the white-haired Dokkaebi, Kim Chan, is watching me with narrowed eyes from where he stands next to the jade fountain.

Furrowing his brows, he approaches Rui. "Your little pet has a nasty temper."

"I'm nobody's *pet*," I spit viciously.

Chan looks somewhat surprised that I can talk.

"Oh, I'm well aware. She tried to kill me just this morning," Rui says.

The other Dokkaebi's jaw tightens in rage. A vein bulges across his forehead. "Rui."

"Relax," Rui counters with a languid wave of his hand. "She obviously didn't succeed."

I hold Chan's gaze and smile, ever so slightly. *But I will.*

Kim Chan practically quivers with rage. My leer grows.

The Pied Piper seems to be oblivious to the silent battle waging between Chan and me. "I've decided to plant her on kitchen duty as punishment."

"Kitchen—" Chan whirls back to his emperor. "For trying to kill you?"

"On the contrary. For failing."

"What do you mean, *for failing*?"

Rui simply smiles.

"You—" Abruptly cutting himself off, Chan pinches the bridge of his nose with vast weariness. "Rui, really. This bargain of yours has all of us on edge."

I chuckle. Chan, it seems, has not made the mistake of underestimating me. But my laugh quickly fades at his next words.

"Not that we think she'll succeed," Chan adds with a sharp, pointed look in my direction, "but think of your image. A wily, fickle emperor who partakes in such bargains is not the best front for this realm. Especially now. If you would speak to Kang, if you would hear his words of wisdom…"

"Spare me your grief," Rui replies, flicking his eyes to the heavens and loosening a long-suffering sigh. "Don't you have a training quad to attend to, General?" He lowers his gaze, and a corner of his mouth quirks as Chan straightens.

My brows rise. I've been correct in assuming that Chan's uniform, his medals, indicate his position of power. As a general, it is given that he's a skilled fighter, and therefore a considerable threat. Although Rui claimed that he ordered his court to leave me be, I find that I do not quite trust him.

Chan's mouth presses itself into a firm white line. "Kang has asked to speak to you later."

"Tell him, then, that I am all ears," Rui responds in cool annoyance, examining the nails of his right hand before glancing at Chan with a raised brow. "He can find me in my quarters after I deposit our assassin into the kitchens with Asha."

"Asha?" Chan's eyes, green and bright with burning dislike, bore through me. "Ah. I see. Perhaps kitchen duty is a fitting punishment after all."

I send him a bored look. Whoever Asha is, she certainly cannot be worse than these two immortal assholes.

CHAPTER TWELVE

Plump, and at four-foot-five, Asha doesn't seem like much of a threat at first. I have faced ruthless Blackbloods and wrathful Dokkaebi, after all. I am not easily intimidated.

In fact, Asha reminds me almost pleasantly of my long-gone aunt—short and squat, with an array of frizzled hair and thinly plucked brows. Only when her beady eyes run over me do I begin to feel the slightest inkling of apprehension.

The kitchen is a stark contrast to the rest of the palace, resembling the inside of a humble cottage.

The walls are constructed of a dull brown wood, the tables and counters of crudely cut lumber. Fireplaces roar underneath heavy iron cauldrons that bubble with scarlet, savory-smelling kimchi jjigae. Cabinets gape wide open, displaying jars of herbs, spices, and colored salts.

A handful of Dokkaebi clad in white cotton hanboks sit on floor mats and bend over wooden vats filled with red paste that they work into cabbage leaves. At a flour-dusted table, a kitchen staffer huddles over a mound of pale dough. The kitchen smells of pickled vegetables and grilled meats, tinged with smoke from the fires.

Asha shoves me over to a wooden counter with heaps of fresh vegetables. "Cut," she snaps before bustling over to a handful of gaping Dokkaebi and barking orders.

My eyes meet theirs, and I enjoy the distaste that darkens their expressions. Before I turn back to the mound of vegetables, though, I pause. I caught a glimpse of a human boy stirring a black pot of steaming seaweed soup in an adjacent room of the kitchen. He seems content, unharmed, but I still feel an icy surge of alarm at the sight of yet another human in the Dokkaebi's realm.

It is an effort to tear away my gaze and focus on the task before me.

The knife Asha gave me is wonderfully sharp, and I enjoy rolling its weight around in my hands. It's considerably less dull than the dagger that hangs at my waist, and sinks into a violet, bulbous mushroom as if it is butter. I feel a sort of calm content overtake me as I chop and dice, cutting into inches-thick radishes and heads of cabbages. It's wonderful to have a knife in my hands again, wonderful to wield a sharp blade and overpower an adversary—even if my opponent is a pile of vegetables.

As I work, the hustle and bustle of the kitchen slowly becomes muted. Soon, the mountain of vegetables has dwindled considerably, replaced by heaps of chopped produce. I glance around the kitchen, breaking free of my trance.

Am I already done?

Perhaps in another life, I could have been a kitchen hand—although I prefer wielding my knives in much more exciting ways. I eye the kitchen knife. Will Asha notice if I take...

I stiffen as a hand swats at my neck and then plucks the knife out of my grasp. *Godsdamn it.*

"Up," orders Asha, pushing me aside as she examines

the vegetables. "Kitchen work is constant, girl. No time for daydreaming." She sweeps the vegetables into a wooden bowl and gestures to the heavily floured table laden with mounds of sticky bread dough. "Go. Make yourself useful. I trust you at least know how to knead dough. Soboro-ppang is easy enough to make."

I send a sour look in Asha's direction as I reluctantly make my way to the table where a Dokkaebi male glances up as I seat myself across from him. He is thin, with a hooked nose and dark eyes that widen curiously as I take a hearty handful of sticky dough and plop it onto a dusting of flour. I incline my head warily in response to his scrutiny. "What?"

He says nothing and quickly returns to his work.

I poke at the dough, amused at the indent that my finger leaves. I poke it again. Again—

"Hangyeol," Asha, still lurking behind me, says to the kitchen hand opposite me. "Make sure this one stays on task." She frowns ominously before scuttling away.

I snort, earning a frown from Hangyeol. "I'm Lina," I introduce myself, making an effort to be somewhat pleasant.

He says nothing, merely sprinkling flour over his dough and working it in with his hands.

I copy him.

I've never baked before, except once, when Chara was overcome with the sudden urge to become a world-class baker.

I volunteered to help her, resulting in various late-night baking sessions in between assassinations and seductions. We made cherry tarts, a staple of her Northern homeland…but they were so horrendous, even Sang, with his massive sweet tooth, spat his bite out into the wastebin with little hesitation. The only person who seemingly enjoyed them was Sungho, the weapons master, who ate anything that even remotely resembled food.

Suddenly, the kitchen, the clanging of the pots and pans,

the flour dusting my nails…it is too much. I swallow hard and clench the dough in my fist. I need to focus on something else. Old memories of time spent in a different kitchen are doing me no good.

Gyeulcheon. I'll focus on what I know about Gyeulcheon, and the Dokkaebi. I sift through all I've been told about the immortals as I continue to knead the dough.

The Dokkaebi were born eons ago from bloodied weapons used by the gods on a long-ago battleground as they fought against monsters in strife. It is said that the blood of the gods mingled with the blood of the monsters and dripped from their clashing silver blades onto the ground of the battlefield, where the first Dokkaebi were created.

The Dokkaebi are almost gods themselves, practically their children, made from their own flesh and blood. My morning encounter with the Pied Piper further proved their strength. My bargain also confirmed that Dokkaebi are indeed notoriously fickle—although they once were known to bring good fortune to the Three Kingdoms of Sunpo, Bonseyo, and Wyusan, they were just as often known to bring about plagues and poverty simply for the fun of it.

The *fun of it.*

Bastards.

It's therefore not a surprise that the immortal race eventually lost control of the other Three Kingdoms except Sunpo, and retreated to Gyeulcheon, a realm of their own creation. The exact reasons for their retreat still aren't known—perhaps forgotten through the centuries—but one can reasonably assume that the mortals grew weary of the Dokkaebi's capricious nature and drove them away.

And despite their absence from the kingdom for nearly five centuries, the Dokkaebi haven't forgotten about Sunpo. The Pied Piper still spirits humans away to Gyeulcheon. And judging by the boy I glimpsed stirring the soup and the girl who carries meals to my room, the stolen mortals work in Gyeulcheon as servants.

But there is only one kidnapped human I can focus on at the moment, and that human is Konrarnd Kalmin.

Intuition tells me that he is in this palace. But where? Despite myself, I feel a flood of satisfaction as I imagine Kalmin on hands and knees, scrubbing the floor of the Piper's bathroom until his hands shine raw and red from the harsh soap.

But the palace is large. Kalmin could be anywhere.

I tilt my head, furrowing my brows in thought.

Yes, I muse, *the palace certainly is grand… Grand enough for a heavily stocked weaponry, and certainly large enough to sneak around without getting caught…*

I glance back down at my dough. It looks kneaded enough, whatever that means. I reach for another lump and dust it with flour.

As I scrape bits of dough out from underneath my fingernails, I wonder what Asina is doing. Fear tightens my chest. If that bitch has strayed from our deal… If my sister has been harmed… I clench my jaw. My thoughts have drifted to Eunbi, to her relentlessly curly head of hair, gap-toothed grin, and her perpetually sticky fingers. The way she shrieks when she's tickled, the way she sucks her thumb in her sleep.

I can see how this is a punishment. I'm losing time—valuable time. With only fourteen days to assassinate the Dokkaebi emperor, every second counts. My fingers graze the hourglass at my neck, tracing the cold glass in which silvery sand slowly falls.

Taking a sharp breath, I warily glance around the kitchen. I will not, *can*not, spend more precious time attempting to bake bread instead of attempting a murder.

I eye the door from which I entered.

Rui said I had kitchen duty. But he didn't say for how long, and the sand in my hourglass is falling.

CHAPTER THIRTEEN

Smuggling myself out of the kitchen is even more difficult than breaking into the Temple of Ruin. Escaping Asha's watchful eye requires a rather unfortunate spilling of stew and an equally upsetting overturning of a vat of fermenting kimchi. But I make it out.

I'm unable to keep a triumphant grin from my face as I wander through halls of polished stone. Dokkaebi servants pause as I pass and I send them unbothered, disparaging looks. The palace, it seems, is more labyrinth than castle.

An hour later, I've discovered only the same halls that I already walked through, the same rooms, the same kitchen. Grimacing bitterly, I sit on the edge of the plaza's fountain and wipe a thin layer of sweat from the nape of my neck.

Behind me, the fountain burbles quietly as lilac spills onto small water lilies. It smells cloyingly sweet—like nectar. I absentmindedly dip a finger into the fountain, and to my surprise, my skin tingles where it meets the lavender. Before I can stop myself, I place my finger on my tongue. It's deliciously sweet, reminding me of honey.

"Nectar from the khana tree," a voice to my right says quietly. "A favorite here in Gyeulcheon."

I startle and yank my finger out of my mouth.

Kang, the Dokkaebi with the wise eyes and chin-length autumn hair, is leaning against his staff and smiling ever so slightly. "Hello, Lina." He looks at my hourglass with an indiscernible expression, but for only a brief moment.

"Hello." I scan him warily as I wipe my finger on my tunic.

"Rui told me you earned kitchen duty this morning." His voice is nothing more than a gentle murmur, but it is edged with a steeliness that I pick up on immediately. Caution straightens my spine.

"I did." I fight the urge to shift my weight from foot to foot under his stare that seems to ask, *Done so soon?* "But I was dismissed."

"Dismissed?" Kang arches a brow, clearly not believing me— but mercifully, he appears to deem the subject trivial. "You seem tired. I understand that Rui put you in a guest suite. Was it to your liking?"

"It was decent," I mumble. "It could use more wall decor. And the bed is slightly lumpy." A lie. The bed is the most comfortable thing I have ever slept on, but Kang doesn't need to know that.

"Ah. Well, my apologies, then." Kang laughs quietly, although light doesn't quite reach his sage eyes. They remain steely. Wary. "I assume that you've been exploring our palace."

I shrug again. We hold a brief but exceedingly awkward staring contest as Kang waits for me to reply, realizes that I'm refusing to, and sighs before tilting his head in reluctant acquiescence. "You must be looking for Konrarnd Kalmin. Your boss."

"Confirmation that he's alive could be exceedingly useful," I mutter, slowly tilting my head as I wait, wait for the offer.

"Understandably. Come, then. I'll bring you to him." Kang beckons with a slight tilt of his head, and I feel my stomach drop into my feet as I stand.

Kalmin. I am going to see Kalmin.

I swallow my bile. "Thank you." I hide my trembling hands behind my back.

"The palace grows as familiar as the back of one's hand over time," Kang says as we mount the plaza's U-shaped stairs. "Until then, it is a puzzling myriad of twists and turns." I glance at the portraits of fruit lining the hall, lingering on the snake coiled around rotten grapes. Noticing my gaze, Kang slightly inclines his head. "Rui has always had a fondness for art." Something in his tone shifts, dipping into a faintly troubled cadence, and I note how something solemn and sorrowful dims his eyes. "You'll notice that the palace brims with it. Do you have an affinity for artwork?"

Unexpectedly, the memory of my fingers shredding through the tapestry floods through me with a burst of guilt. I make myself smile rakishly. "Only art as fine as its beholder."

He chooses to ignore this. "The tapestry was a piece of art with great personal meaning to Rui," Kang responds placidly, unperturbed by my jest. "You should feel lucky that he chose such a bargain. He considered, ah, *other* forms of punishment."

I choose to ignore that little fact. "I would never have marked the Pied Piper as such an art enthusiast."

"The Pied Piper? Ah. I'd almost forgotten. Pied for his eyes, no? The silver within them, along with the occasional blue? And piper for Manpasikjeok, of course. An accurate nickname." He slows to a stop, gracefully halting before a staircase of stone. "Kalmin should be below. I'll accompany you."

"What's below?" I frown as I listen to the faint clanging of metal and the muted rise and fall of voices.

"You'll see," he replies vaguely before he begins his descent.

I don't move, glowering at his back.

Is this a trap? Kang seems mellow enough, but I can't put it past him to sabotage me—even if Rui has ordered for our game to remain between the two of us. But what choice do I have? If Kalmin truly is down there, I need to see him and make sure that the wormy bastard isn't dead, and this whole bargain a wicked prank.

I sigh. *Fine.*

Gritting my teeth, I follow Kang down the stairs, and am entirely unprepared for what awaits us below. I blink as I adjust to the flashing of sparks, the roar of fire, and the grating screeches of metal on metal as some Dokkaebi and some humans hunch over forges, their faces smudged with soot and oil.

I tilt my head, immensely pleased at this development. It seems I have found the weapon forge after all.

Scanning the workshop, I observe the rise and fall of hammers and the movements of the muscled arms that wield them. *Where is he?*

My mouth dries a moment later, and I feel Kang give me a sideways glance as my stomach tightens into knots and a cold sweat perspires on the nape of my neck.

Kalmin is bent over a pile of molten metal, grime coating his milky skin. His scarlet hair has been shaved to a cropped cut. I nearly choke in rage and hatred as I see the dark crane, the mark of the Blackbloods, inked on his bare forearm.

I shudder as I move my eyes to his, noting how his gaze never strays from the weapon he is creating. Even from feet away, I recognize the dreamy look of compulsion in his gaze. The same look that swims in the eyes of the girl who delivers my meals and the boy who stirs the seaweed soup in the kitchens.

Kalmin. The Blackblood. Reduced to this.

I feel a surge of smug satisfaction seeing *him* weak, seeing *him* at the mercy of another's whims. Before I know what I'm doing, I'm stalking past sparks of fire and bustling workers, only dimly aware of Kang's watchful gaze on my back.

I stop in front of Kalmin, who doesn't even so much as look up from his work. His hands are smeared with soot, fingers curled around a hammer that he brings down upon a pile of metal in a mechanical motion. My hands tremble.

He killed my friends.

My family.

And now he stands before me, nothing more than a husk. An empty shell.

Would he even fight back if I held the dull, old piece-of-shit dagger *he* gave me to his neck? The urge to hurt him as he's hurt me is overwhelming. But I cannot. Will not.

Slowly, my smugness crumbles into hollow defeat.

I need to get Kalmin back to Asina alive, in order for Eunbi to live.

And I want him to *feel* it when I kill him. Want him to scream in pain, to beg for mercy as I destroy him. Right now, I doubt that he would even register the feeling.

"Kalmin." The name tastes like dirt on my tongue. "You *fool*. Look at yourself. Look at what you got us into." I spit on his boots, then lean in to his ear, my eyes latching on that godsdamned tattoo. "You wanted the Reaper? Well, you have her. And once you're yourself, I'll show you exactly what it's like to die at my hands. I'll kill them first—starting with Asina. You can watch the entire time. Because then you'll know how it feels to stand in a pool of blood leaking from your family's bodies. And then I'll kill you." I pull away, breathing heavily. Kalmin says nothing. He is blissfully ignorant of my presence as I whisper, forcing the words past trembling lips, "Yoonho was ten times the man you ever were."

Nothing.

Not even a look in my direction.

I shake in fury. But I make myself turn away and take stiff steps toward Kang, whose brows are furrowed in contemplative concern. Over the din of the weaponry, I doubt he heard what I hissed to the vacant-eyed Blackblood, but there can be no mistaking the suspicion glimmering in his eyes.

"I see that he's alive," I say, stalking back to the stairs. "Thank you. This has been useful."

Useful, because I've located the weapons forge.

And I am in desperate need of some new daggers.

"The rumors are true."

In the parlor, I looked up from polishing my pistol.

Chara and Chryse halted in their application of their dark red lipstick. Yoonho set down his book in a swift movement, his eyes blazing.

Sang was dressed in all black, his hair slick from the rain outside and dripping rainwater onto the parlor's carpet. He'd been gone nearly two days. "Unima Hisao is pulling sponsorship."

Yoonho stiffened.

I set down my pistol in disbelief. *"What?"*

Yoonho looked grim as he shared a dark look with Sang.

"Unima is dropping sponsorship with the Talons," Sang repeated quietly. "And striking a deal with the Blackbloods."

Silence, stormy and dark, blanketed the room. The air grew heavy with crackling tension.

Yoonho laced his hands and stared coldly at the opposite wall. Somewhere down the hall, a clock ticked, the sound as abrupt and sharp as a gunshot. The twins jumped in their seats on the settee, their faces drawn and sober.

I was the first to speak. "The Blackbloods."

Yoonho's jaw tightened.

The Blackbloods, the Talons' rival gang, was run by Konrarnd Kalmin, who had nearly killed Yoonho in a failed sniping the previous spring. There were no borders in our gang war, nothing but undiluted fury and bloodlust. Sunpo belonged to the Talons, but Konrarnd Kalmin and his gang thought otherwise. It was hard to trace the feud back to any other point besides the Blackbloods' formation five years ago, when Kalmin had swaggered into the city from a Brigvallan ship docked at Fishtown, took one look at the derelict kingdom, and deemed it his.

I watched as my boss wearily rubbed the phantom injury haunting his left shoulder, where the bullet had buried itself deep. I would never forget those first few days after the attack, the hours of Yoonho drifting in and out of consciousness as his blood had steadily seeped through his gauze-wrapped shoulder.

"What did they offer him?" Chara asked quietly, tracing a line over her stockinged leg. Next to her, her sister anxiously bit her lip.

"Konrarnd Kalmin can be quite convincing, and Unima's appetite has always been insatiable," Sang replied quietly. "I imagine that some sort of mutually beneficial deal was struck. It wouldn't surprise me if the Blackbloods offered to give him a large share in one or two of the pleasure halls they own, on top of protection and competition elimination, in exchange for funding. I've heard whispers along my network that the Blackbloods are looking for a foothold into the Oktarian jewel trade, and it seems as if they've found it with Unima."

"It doesn't matter," Yoonho said, turning his head from the wall. His eyes were dark and troubled as they focused on me with acute clarity. "You know what to do, Reaper."

"Yes, yes." I waved my hand. Of course I knew. But… My eyes narrowed a moment later, and I leaned forward in my seat.

"Killing him will draw repercussions from the Blackbloods," I added carefully. "Significant repercussions."

"Let them come," Yoonho replied grimly.

"Unima is in Wyusan for the week, on business," Sang said somberly, naming the kingdom to the immediate north of Sunpo. "Presumably investing in their pelting business and selling his Oktarian jewels for far higher prices than they warrant."

"Is it too much to hope that he gets lost in the Wyusan Wilderness?" Chryse muttered. I considered this. Many were lost within the broad expanse of forest within the nearby kingdom, yet it was unlikely Unima entered the kingdom through the woodlands. A moment later, Sang confirmed my suspicions.

"He left today, taking the river route of Habaek's River," Sang continued. The river curved around the Yaepak Mountain Range that divided Sunpo from Wyusan and led all the way up to the very tip of the continent, where Bonseyo rested. "He's expected to return next Wednesday to his manor in the Coin Yard via the same route."

"Then we strike next week. We plan. Plot. And then you, Lina…" Yoonho leaned forward, and I watched as the thick vein on his forehead pulsed with fury. "You kill him."

CHAPTER FOURTEEN

So Kalmin is alive.

I sit on my sofa, chin propped on my fist and knees jittering beneath me. Kalmin is alive, so therefore, Eunbi is alive, too.

For now, at least.

And hopefully for a while longer.

Because I have a plan. Tonight, I will sneak into the weaponry and hoard as many weapons as I am able. Pistols, swords, daggers…anything that I am trained in enough to properly wield against the Piper. And then from there…

I huff in frustration. From there, I will have to formulate *another* plan.

Rubbing my temples wearily, my thoughts turn to my end goal. To kill the Pied Piper, he'll have to be caught off guard.

Very off guard.

I pause.

Dokkaebi sleep, don't they? But finding the emperor's bedroom without help will be impossible, and I doubt Kang would be willing to escort me as he escorted me to the armory. And I cannot simply *ask* the Piper to take me to his rooms.

Unless… I grimace.

Well. I suppose there is *one* way to make it into Rui's bedroom.

The thought sends a cold shiver down my spine. Oh gods. How am I supposed to seduce a Dokkaebi? *Can* one even seduce a Dokkaebi? What is he drawn to? Surely not a mortal, and certainly not the mortal who would love nothing better than to rip out his heart and hold it beating within her palm.

Tilting my head, I carefully consider how it could be done.

How I would run my one hand down his bare chest while twining the other in his long, silken hair. A soft growl would rumble in his slender throat as I slant my lips across his, the kiss hard and hot, so biting and bittersweet. I would press him downward onto the bed, straddling his waist as his head hits the pillows, softly laughing as his breathing hitches.

And when his eyes flutter closed, as he moans a sweet, soft sound… I would drag my blade across his bare skin in a lover's caress, letting my weapon paint itself with a rich, ruby red.

Completely immersed in my thoughts, I only notice that the air is moving, rippling, when the scent of licorice and plum blossoms slams into me with enough force that I jerk backward.

I choke as Haneul Rui gracefully appears, leaning against a bedpost with an air of boredom. "Hello, Reaper," he purrs.

I leap to my feet, drawing my dagger with lightning speed. "Couldn't you *knock*?" My voice is hoarse, my cheeks hot with rage and…something else. I pray that he overlooks the way my chest rises and falls unevenly to the beating of my thundering heart.

"I did. More than a dozen times, in fact." He waves at the weapon in distaste. "Relax. I'm not here to hurt you."

"I'm afraid that I can't express the same sentiment," I snap back.

A midnight laugh. "Already so eager for more kitchen duty?"

Rui mockingly clucks his tongue. "Which I heard you skipped, by the way. Asha expects you in the kitchen bright and early tomorrow morning."

My dagger is unwavering in my grip as I bite out a particularly vulgar curse.

"I have to admit, I'm impressed with the speed with which you overturned that vat of stew. Although I'm afraid Asha would disagree. She seemed a little less than happy while recounting your escapades." Rui's lips twitch impiously. "Please, Lina, put down the knife. We both know it won't do you much good anyway."

For a long moment, I refuse to move. But he's right—I remember my futile attempt at a headbutt and acknowledge that blunt instruments will do little against his strength, and this dull dagger is certainly no exception. I must play the long game.

Slowly setting down the dagger, I narrow my eyes. "What do you want."

"To take afternoon tea with you, of course." He flashes me a wolf's smile.

"First breakfast, and now tea?"

"Yes."

"No."

"Why not?"

"I hate tea," I lie, crossing my arms.

"I doubt that. I have a feeling that it's me you hate, rather than a steaming cup of oolong." His eyes flicker to my lips, which are curled in distaste. "Or would you prefer gyepi-cha?"

"Get out of my room."

"Technically," Rui says, arching a brow, "I own this room. And all the rooms in this palace."

Bastard. "Out," I hiss.

Rui simply winks. "Dinner, then. Tomorrow." The air begins to ripple once more, and Rui sends a final amused glance over his shoulder. "Wear something nice."

A rush of cold wind and he is gone, leaving me glaring at empty space.

Wear something nice.

A slow smile works its way across my lips as an idea, wicked and dangerous, crosses my mind.

Dinner will be perfect.

When the human girl brings me my food that night, I manage to eat more than half of the bowl of bibimbap before my stomach begins to ache.

I climb into bed and pull the soft blankets over myself, hugging my arms around my waist as I press my cheek into the pillow. I'll leave for the weaponry in a few hours, I decide, fighting back a yawn.

Until then, sleep sounds wonderful.

CHAPTER FIFTEEN

Eunbi frowned in my direction as she sat on the dirty floor of our chogajip, a grimy ragdoll in her chubby palm. "Lili," the four-year-old babbled, thin eyebrows furrowing together, "Eomma? Appa? Where are they?" Her concerned questioning interrupted my steady, silent stream of prayers.

Perhaps it was foolish to plead favors from the gods. Perhaps it was foolish to cry out for help from the deities who no longer paid attention to the mortal world, instead residing in their own world of Okhwang, hidden in the sky and beyond the reach of human hopes. But Eomma and Appa had always prayed to them, and so did I. "There is nothing wrong with hope," Appa would say, glancing up at the stars through the gaps in our thatched roof. "Perhaps they are listening, in the sky kingdom of Okhwang. Perhaps they will come back."

But Gameunjang, Lady Luck, had not answered me even once.

"Lili?" Eunbi asked again.

I looked up from where I was slumped against the wall with a sore back, sipping a cup of cold, watered-down barley tea.

At fourteen, my back shouldn't have been aching as much as it was—but with Mother and Father gone to visit our ailing haraboji in Bonseyo, I took up all the housework and the harvesting of our small farm of barley. "I told you, Eunbi," I said gently. "They're at sea—but they'll be back any day now."

Eunbi's nose crinkled. "Gone too long. I miss Appa. I want Eomma." A stray tear trickled down her cheek and into her mouth. "Write to them, Lili. Tell them to come back *now*."

"They could be here tomorrow." I scooched over to where she sat. "Or even tonight. But until then…" I wiped another trickling tear away from her face. "Until then, you're stuck with me. Am I really so awful, Eunbi?"

Her head whipped back to mine, her curls bouncing. "No!" She scrambled into my lap and threw her arms around my shoulders. "No, Lili. I didn't mean that."

"I know," I reassured her, rubbing her back. "We've had fun together, haven't we?" Just this morning, I had taken her out of the countryside and into Sunpo's Fingertrap, where we'd wandered around the marketplace, admiring the goods for sale. A stand of sugared pastries had caught both of our eyes, but we'd hadn't enough yeokun—and although it had been tempting, Appa had taught us never to steal. "I wager when Father and Mother come back, you'll miss the days when it was just the two of us."

Eunbi pulled away from my neck, and I was relieved to see a gummy smile. "Maybe I will," she admitted, and then burrowed her face in my neck again.

Despite the state in which we lived, with our baths reliant on rainwater, she had the sweet smell of a child—lavender and lilies. I leaned against the wall and cradled her in my arms as her breathing steadied and slowed. She was sucking her thumb, and when I glanced down at her small face, she was still smiling slightly, rosebud lips tilting upward.

My little sister dreamed vividly, had told me about her dreams of falling stars, swirling flocks of butterflies, and dancing tiger cubs. I hoped her dreams would always remain so, that she would never get nightmares about going hungry or falling ill like I did. That she'd always be so innocent, always dream of a butterfly's iridescent wings.

But...

The knot in my throat tightened to a point of pain and silently, I resumed my prayers to Gameunjang.

Because the truth was that our parents should have been back three days ago.

I lurch out of my bed with a sharp gasp, stuffing my knuckles into my mouth and biting down to hold back a scream. I taste blood. Pain shoots up my hand as my teeth pierce the skin.

That memory, that day...that was four years ago. Before we'd heard of the shipwreck that took our parents' lives, before we'd been turned out of our humble hut, before I'd begun to fight tooth and nail to survive, to protect my baby sister.

Before the Talons, before my mistake that cost us everything.

"Godsdamn it," I whisper as I pull my hand from my mouth, refusing to look at the bright red markings that my teeth have left behind. I shove that memory from my mind, shove Eunbi from my mind, and slide out of bed.

I need weapons. *Good* weapons.

And I'll be cursed to Jeoseung if I don't get my hands on some tonight.

I slip out of my room, into the quiet hall beyond, and retrace the steps to the weaponry. The palace is eerily silent, the corridors lit only by the flickering red flames.

A few Dokkaebi guards line the plaza, their faces drawn and solemn. I hold my breath as I count them from underneath the passage of arches. One, two, three…six, seven, eight.

I can slip by them to the stairs if I am silent enough.

Before I can think myself out of it, I move.

"It's like you're a river," Sang once said. *"Twisting and turning around bends so gracefully…like water."*

I was amused then, but as I make my way up the staircase undetected, I have to admit that perhaps Sang was onto something. My feet are light on the ground as I slink through the shadows. Holding my breath, I sneak by another scattering of guards before finally making it to the staircase to the weaponry. Only hushed silence greets me. Deeming the coast clear, I creep down the stairs.

And grimace.

It is pitch black.

I wait as my vision slowly grows adjusted to the velvet dark. When I can finally make out the faint outlines of worktables, I begin my theft.

I want a sword. Sharp knives. A pistol, if such technology is used in Gyeulcheon. And anything else I can get my hands on.

My steps are silent on the stone floor as I creep past iron chests holding unfinished weapons and fireless forges heavy with the smell of smoke. I furrow my brows at an incomplete sword, missing a hilt. I require weapons that have been finished, for I won't get far with only a half-made dagger. But… *There.*

Oh, thank the gods—however absent they may be.

I've reached the very back of the weaponry, where weapons of all shapes and sizes hang on the stone wall. They're newly forged and undoubtedly waiting to be distributed to the Dokkaebi.

It's too bad that I got here first.

My hand reaches out to touch a freshly sharpened blade. I

run my fingers over the glossy black hilt of a glinting jikdo and trace the sword's cold, straight metal. My brows lift as I catch sight of a perfectly welded dagger. The pommel is a shining gold, engraved with tiny red rubies similar to the gems that once constructed the tapestry that landed me in this godsdamned mess.

Just as I take the knife into my hands, the sound of footsteps approaching from the stairs jolts a terrible panic through me. I dive underneath a worktable as the low cadence of voices meets my ears.

"...heavily lacking," a voice is saying. I pause, recognizing it as Chan, the white-haired general. "They're a different breed altogether, barely able to hold a rutting *sword* without either impaling themselves or one of their friends. Impossible to train."

"They're young," a new voice, melodious and honeyed, replies quietly. Kang. "You cannot expect them to be excellent soldiers to start with."

"Excellent soldiers are what Gyeulcheon *needs* right now." The two stop at the foot of the stairs. "That metals were hijacked from the mines is cause for concern. Yet Rui has refused to take such threats seriously. The stolen material is known to be the best ore for weapon forging. You cannot tell me that this development is not concerning."

"The shipment was small," Kang responds reassuringly. "It was hardly a loss. I doubt that they even have enough supplies to stage a revolution. Or enough members. But your concerns are valid, my friend. I have been planning to speak to Rui—perhaps I will do so sooner than I'd planned."

Interesting.

How very, *very* interesting.

"Please do." Chan scoffs. "As small as they are, the thieves are impossible to track. My scouts have reported nothing." I tense as the footsteps resume and approach my hiding spot.

"They're elusive, curse them. They could be forging the stolen metals into weapons as we speak."

"I will make Rui aware of the threat's significance."

"I am willing to bet that he will care very little."

"He's not cared for anything in a very long time. We both know that." Kang's voice, soft and somber, pauses. "Rui and Hana expect us. Take your armament from the wall and let us leave."

I hold my breath as two pairs of feet appear near the table.

"That's odd," Chan murmurs after a moment. "Lee said he finished it this afternoon. And yet it's not here."

"Perhaps we could see it with a candle," Kang says wryly.

"It's a dagger." Chan clucks his tongue. "Damned trainee took mine by mistake. Tainted it with his grubby little hands. I had Lee craft me a new one—golden-hilted and crusted with rubies. It should be easy to see, even in such darkness."

The dagger grows cold in my hands. My heart rate quickens.

If Chan looks down, he'll see me.

And his dagger.

"We'll come back tomorrow and speak to Lee. But for now, we mustn't keep the two waiting. You know how limited Rui's patience is."

Chan mutters something unsavory under his breath, and I exhale in relief as he moves past my spot to the stairs. Kang begins to walk as well but pauses, his sandaled feet only inches away from me and the stolen knife.

I freeze, and time seems to tick by ever so slowly.

He's seen me.

But a moment later, Kang moves away, his footsteps receding up the stairs, following Chan. Relief limpens my limbs. They're gone.

I glance down at the dagger, aware that I should probably return it to its place on the wall. *But where is the fun in that?* I think, fighting back a snicker as I crawl from my hiding space.

How I make it back to my quarters lugging weapon after weapon undetected is nearly beyond me.

In the relative safety of my room, I plant my hands on my hips and observe the pile of weapons sprawled across my bed with immense satisfaction.

A short sword, a jikdo, a whip, throwing daggers, and, of course, the golden dagger. Giddy with my success, I tug my dull dagger out from the sheath at my waist and kick it to the farthest corner of my room.

I will not need it anymore.

I trace the handle of the jikdo lovingly. Oh, the things that I can do now.

I am the Reaper of Sunpo. And finally, after a year of working with that made-of-shit dagger, I have finely crafted armaments all to myself. It truly is a moment to rejoice.

Another reason to rejoice curls my lips into a grin.

From the conversation I've eavesdropped on, it appears that Gyeulcheon has a rebel movement. And what better allies than a rebellion? Tomorrow, I will find them.

My second full day in Gyeulcheon, it seems, will be a busy one.

Kitchen duty. Scouring the realm's streets for the rebellion. And dinner with Rui.

I wince as my cheeks flush, the mental image I'd conjured earlier rising back to the surface of my mind.

If all goes well during dinner—and, especially, *after*—perhaps the rebellion won't need to worry themselves about assassinating the Emperor of Gyeulcheon, as I shall do the job for them. But still, I have to find them. Because if what I have in mind for tomorrow night doesn't succeed, I will need all the help I can get.

Wearily, I climb back into bed and tenderly cradle the

whip as I pull my blanket up to my chin. Yet despite myself, excitement buzzes in my stomach. It seems that for the first time, I might be at least one step ahead in our game—and right now, I still have thirteen days left.

The excitement is hauntingly familiar, I think, as I close my eyes, holding the coiled whip close to my chest. I almost feel the way I felt as a Talon, the thrill of the hunt thrumming through my bloodstream.

I fall asleep with more hope than I've had in a long, long time.

CHAPTER SIXTEEN

Worn to the bone from a grueling morning spent toiling over a mound of onions, I yank open the kitchen door and tumble into crisp morning air.

It takes me a moment of gulping down the fresh air, my lungs burning from the acrid scent of onion, to finally take in my surroundings.

I am outside, in a tiny garden. Small plots of land hold lettuce, tomatoes, and vibrant produce I cannot quite place.

Trees dappled by afternoon moonlight provide shade to a bubbling creek. A stone wall patchy with moss encloses the garden. It is beautiful.

Marred only by the three human girls.

They are bent over a garden plot, their gloves crusted with dirt as they sink their fingers into thick soil and pull out bulging radishes. Their faces are tight and drawn with concentration, gleaming with sweat. And although I cannot see their eyes, I have a sinking suspicion that they are unfocused and dreamy.

"Hello," I say slowly, my breath catching in my throat as I approach them. They don't waver in their work. The smallest one of the three uproots a radish with a stiff, mechanical motion.

"Hello?" I repeat.

No response.

I grimace. Who were they, before the Piper brought them here? Do their families still grieve, mourning them as dead? Or do they know that they are here, trapped in Gyeulcheon, tending to a garden on dirty hands and knees?

I snap my fingers in front of the smallest one's eyes.

Not even a blink.

Heaving a sigh, I approach the wall. As disturbing as it is, I cannot waste my time on a lost cause. Grains of sand fall in my hourglass, a reminder of the time I have left to win—or to lose.

The garden wall will be easy enough to climb. Hopefully, it will deposit me outside the palace grounds, and preferably not atop a guard's head.

Digging my fingers into a crevice in the wall a few feet above my head, I heft my weight so that the toes of my boots wedge themselves between the gaps closest to the ground.

In only a few moments, I manage to reach the top. Standing on the stone, I peer down at a dirt road, lined with forest. Good— no guards to land atop.

"Lina," a too-familiar voice greets.

I whirl around.

My eyes land on Rui, standing below me with an expression of great amusement. His earrings sparkle in the moonlight, and his hanbok—today a shimmering silver with a sash of navy blue—matches his glittering eyes. The emperor's long, dark hair is pulled away from his face by a glossy black brooch that resembles two thorned branches, meeting each other halfway at the crown of his head.

A small part of me whispers that if he *wasn't* a dangerous Dokkaebi, I'd be more than ready to join him for dinner. I gnash my teeth and force that traitorous little thought away.

"You look...elevated today." Rui pauses, delicately sniffing the air. "Is that onion I smell?"

I wince. "No."

"Hmm." He doesn't look convinced, and wrinkles his nose. "I came to relieve you from kitchen duty, but it seems as if you've already taken matters into your own hands." Rui arches a brow. "Would you care to tell me why, exactly, you're climbing my wall?"

"No." I curl my hand around the hilt of my jikdo, although Rui doesn't seem to be attempting to stop me.

"Ah. Well, I wish you luck with whatever adventure you've decided to embark on. Perhaps I'll join you." A glint of mischief flashes across his face, and he half looks as if he's about to climb the wall as well.

I scowl. "Goodbye," I say, and jump over the wall before he can join me.

The sound of Rui's laughter, soft and low, follows me to the ground.

I roll my eyes as I begin to walk the dirt path, struggling not to limp as my left leg protests in pain. The jump hasn't been good for the perpetually wounded limb.

Taking a steadying breath, I focus on the road before me. Surely it will lead me into the city—assuming, of course, that Gyeulcheon *has* a surrounding city. But it has to, based on my eavesdropped conversation alone. Not everybody lives in the palace. Rebels especially.

The road is deliciously shaded, but I don't have time to savor the cool breeze that flutters along my skin and kisses the nape of my neck. After tonight, I will only have twelve more days left to kill the Pied Piper. If I am to find this rebel movement, I need to locate them as quickly as possible. Finding them on my second full day here is ideal, if ambitious.

So I walk as rapidly as I can manage with my aching leg, and soon the path slopes into a trail winding down a small hill, which overlooks a Gyeulcheon town. The town is expansive, yet quaint, surrounding a curving creek burbling with ebony water. Shops line a brown-cobblestoned street, where Dokkaebi roam, holding wicker baskets with fresh fruits, vegetables, small jars of preserves, and other goods. Puffs of smoke rise from the chimneys of small hanoks. I hear music—the sweet notes of a harp.

The scene is picturesque. Lovely.

I highly doubt that the town is home to rebels of any sort.

But I must try. The village seems to slowly extend into a city, and I can just barely make out a faint skyline in the distance. Perhaps if the town doesn't hold what I'm looking for, I will venture into that faraway city.

It is only when I stand on the smooth cobblestones that I realize I have very little to go on. What is the name of the rebel group? How am I to find them, when all I have is a vague knowledge that they possibly exist, in some form or another?

Dokkaebi steal double-takes as they pass me, clutching their baskets and protectively tugging toddling children closer to their sides. I send them what I hope is a nonthreatening smile as they furtively move by.

I grimace. I need to think. Need to find the rebellion. Frustrated, I kick at a loose stone with my boot. Godsdamn it.

Think, Lina. Think.

The answer finally, *finally* comes to me, and my eyes fly open as I scan the street for any sort of blacksmith's shop. Chan said that the "movement" stole a shipment of metals. He also mentioned that they are undoubtedly using their newfound material to forge weapons for their cause. To do so, they'll need a blacksmith and a forge.

So I shall find a forge.

Seeing only mundane shops and a few vegetable stands, I move deeper into the heart of the village. I pass glossy windows displaying everything from floral blankets to precariously tall piles of yellow-paged books.

I pause in front of a shop exhibiting a particularly magnificent window of sesame-sprinkled pork buns. The buns have been perfectly steamed into a lovely snow white that I know will be simultaneously chewy and soft, should my teeth sink into one. My mouth waters, and my fingers twitch.

No. I am here on a mission, not to steal food, no matter how mouthwatering that food is.

With great effort, I turn around. Perhaps I'll come back later.

"Chi Misook makes incredible pork buns," an unfamiliar voice says to my left.

I startle to see that a Dokkaebi stands next to me, also gazing at the still-steaming buns. My hand snaps to the jikdo at my hip, but he makes no move to attack. Instead, he merely smiles at my reflection in the glass panel. "I've told her to enter in the annual cooking competition, but still, she refuses. The entire town loves them. A crowd favorite." The Dokkaebi glances sidelong at me. "Have you tried them?"

"I'm not from here," I reply, carefully taking him in with a warily narrowed gaze.

He is tall, with tanned skin and amber eyes circled by wire spectacles. His brown hair is pulled into a small bun at the nape of his neck. His tunic is collared, and a worn-out satchel that looks as if it contains more than a few books is hitched over his left shoulder.

"My apologies," the Dokkaebi replies. "You must work at the palace. I'm Jiwoon. Wang Jiwoon."

I bristle. So he mistakes me for one of those washy-eyed humans. "I'm from Sunpo," I retort, "not the palace."

"Ah." Understanding flickers momentarily behind Jiwoon's glasses. "I believe I have heard of you."

"Have you?" I tighten my grip on the jikdo's hilt.

"You've caused Gyeulcheon quite a stir." Jiwoon smiles lopsidedly. "You're the gambling girl. If I heard correctly, you can purchase your freedom in exchange for killing our glorious emperor."

"Something like that."

"Intriguing." Jiwoon nods toward the window, toward the steamed buns. "Let me buy you one."

Wary, I frown. What sort of game is he playing?

"I'm afraid you can't depart Gyeulcheon without tasting one of Misook's pork buns," Jiwoon explains carefully, as if noting my suspicion. "And I'm interested in you. All of Gyeulcheon is. In exchange for a meal, perhaps I can unveil some previously mysterious story about you and the emperor's bargain. I have a paper due. My tutor has urged me to find an interesting topic, and everything about you and your situation is…"

"Interesting?" I guess wryly.

While I have no strong desire to sit down with Wang Jiwoon and share a meal, I have to admit that the scholar could be beneficial. He lives in Gyeulcheon, and most likely knows where to find a forge. Or better yet—he could have information on the rebels.

I may have to play the fool, hide behind flirtatious smiles and prompting silences, but I can do all that while sinking my teeth into a warm bite of food. I smile prettily. "You have a deal."

Jiwoon looks slightly surprised, yet delighted all the same. "Let me buy you your promised meal, then."

A pleased smile tugs at my lips as I watch the Dokkaebi duck into the shop.

CHAPTER SEVENTEEN

We sit on chairs perched outside of a small bookshop. I tip back in mine, the legs of the chair balancing precariously on the ground as I eat.

Jiwoon didn't lie. The pork bun he's bought me is nothing short of heavenly, hot and savory, with perfectly seasoned meat. Somehow it manages to be wonderfully tender yet chewy.

"This quill has written all my best papers," Jiwoon says as he pulls a black feathered quill out of his book satchel, along with a small pot of ink. "I guess I'll start off with the basics. Your name?"

"Lina." Jiwoon scribbles that down, then pauses, waiting for a surname. "Shin Lina." I take another bite of food.

"Well, Shin Lina." Jiwoon eyes me analytically. "Our emperor's been vague in the circumstances of your arrangement. All that Gyeulcheon knows comes from court whispers and gossips. There are rumors that you stole something from him."

"Yes," I say, swallowing a chunk of pork. "I stole a tapestry that he left in my kingdom, in a dusty old trunk in the middle of a dusty old room. You may feel free to quote me on that."

"So you're a thief?"

"When the opportunity arises." I lick my fingers.

Jiwoon pressed his quill into his paper. "Did you work alone?"

I sigh, weighing the benefits of divulging the details of my circumstances to the Dokkaebi. Perhaps I'll glean information about the rebels if I first allow him to glean information about me. "Not... Not exactly. My boss ordered the stealing and dismantling of the tapestry. Haneul took him first. Then me. If I kill the emperor, both he and I go free."

"A harsh punishment for a stolen piece of wall art." Jiwoon's ink flows across the paper. I eye his writing curiously but fail to make out more than a few jumbled words.

"The tapestry had many jewels on it," I explain. "I was to sell them to various Oktarian buyers in the city. The kingdom of Oktari is fond of precious stones and would pay large sums for Dokkaebi treasure. But..."

Something glitters in Jiwoon's eyes. "You were caught."

"Obviously," I reply sourly, unable to keep the bite from my voice.

"How many times have you been caught before?"

"Once."

Jiwoon pauses at the darkness in my tone, his pen faltering. "What happened?"

"It was a long time ago." *A year ago, to be exact.* A muscle jumps in my jaw. "I don't see what this has to do with my bargain with the emperor."

"Backstory," Jiwoon replies vaguely. "It makes the exposé that much better."

Backstory? What happened is not meant to be jammed into a composition. My irritation deepens. "It's none of your godsdamned business."

"My apologies." Dropping the delicate subject, Jiwoon

adjusts his spectacles. "I assume that the emperor is keeping you cooped up in ropes and chains?"

I pause before responding, my eyes still narrowed. "Hardly."

"How so?"

I describe the suite, enjoying Jiwoon's stunned expression. "He even sends servants to bring me breakfast."

"The human servants." Jiwoon's brows flick upward as he dips his quill back into the small pot of ink. "You'll forgive me for mistaking you for one of them. Sometimes they venture into this village to purchase goods. I should have known you were not of the same ilk—your eyes are too clear, your tongue too quick."

"They're under his compulsion." I shudder, remembering what it was like to be entranced by the sweetly sinister notes of his pipe.

"You've seen Manpasikjeok." Jiwoon's expression darkens. "He stole your consciousness."

"Don't look so miserable. I stole his favorite tapestry. We're even." I attempt to sound blasé, but Jiwoon's expression is devoid of any hint of humor, and I can't help but shudder at the memory of being compelled.

"Were you a well-known thief in your realm?"

I straighten. "I am the Reaper of Sunpo. I am more than just a thief; I am an assassin. The best. And the entire kingdom fears me."

An unreadable emotion flits across Jiwoon's face. Abruptly, he snaps his notebook shut and pockets his pen. "I've heard all I need," he explains, stuffing his notebook into the satchel. "Thank you."

My eyes widen. He cannot leave yet. Not when I failed to uncover any useful information from *him*— "Wait."

Jiwoon pauses.

I muster a smile. "I was wondering…" I trail off. How to

subtly phrase what I have to say? "If you knew of a certain…"
My smile begins to slip. *Shit.* "A certain rebel group's
whereabouts…"

Godsdamn it.

Expression inscrutable, Jiwoon adjusts the cuffs of his tunic
and hitches his satchel higher on his shoulder. "You don't find
the rebellion," Jiwoon replies quietly, turning away.

I open my mouth to protest. The scholar slides a backward
glance over his shoulder.

"The rebellion finds you."

And then he disappears, his stride steady.

Unable to wipe a frown of displeasure from my face, I spend
another hour scouring the streets for a forge. I ask a handful
of villagers, but they are unwilling to speak to a human—in
particular, the human plotting to kill their emperor. I stalk back
to the palace, muttering sour curses.

The rebellion finds you.

I have accomplished absolutely nothing.

I drop back into the kitchen's garden and nearly land on the
head of a servant girl. Seething, I stomp back into the palace.

It is almost time for dinner, and I've wasted the entire
day entertaining a scholar's eager queries. His exposition
will undoubtedly win him accolades, but I obtained no useful
information for myself. I shake my head, pushing away the
disappointment and replacing it with cold focus. I need to bathe
and make myself look as presentable as possible.

No, more than presentable.

I need to look *desirable.* Tempting. Sensual.

And right now, I'm a sweat-soaked, scrawny girl with a bird's
nest of hair. I certainly have my work cut out for me.

I lower myself into the bath and slather my skin with citrus-
scented oils before working a lavender-scented shampoo through
my tangled hair. One of the secrets to seduction imparted to me

by Chara and Chryse was to smell *good*.

Not like onions.

"Seduction," Chryse once said as I watched the twins slip their legs into sheer, lace-embellished thigh-highs, "is an art form." She cast a look at me over her shoulder. I was a stark contrast to the sleek-haired, red-lipped vixens with my bruised jaw and split lip, both courtesies of a rough training session with Yoonho the night before. "It takes calculation. Elegance. And grace."

"And a pretty mouth," her sister chimed in, running a brush through her river of golden hair. "Men especially have a fixation with lips."

"Run your tongue over your lips a few times. Bite them, play with them, smile…draw as much attention to your lips as you can. And," Chryse added coyly, running a perfectly manicured hand down her slope of cleavage, "your other assets."

In front of the vanity, Chara arched a brow. "Don't tell me you're learning all this for Sang. The boy fucks anything that moves. He visits the Boneburrow more than the two of us combined." Chryse snorted.

"I'm not," I snapped, even as I felt my cheeks burn with a flaming heat. "If I'd wanted to sleep with him, I would have by now." It wasn't that I didn't feel desire for Sang. I did. Gods, I did. I'd had my eye on the spymaster for more than a while—but if we did it… I wanted to do it *right*.

Chara didn't look convinced. "He would sleep with you. We see how he looks at you."

"And we see how you look at him," Chryse murmured softly, and for a moment, I thought I detected a hint of wistful longing. She blinked and hastily reached for a bottle of perfume. "Perfume is a must. Something sweet, alluring, tinged with a bit of darkness. Roses and sage. Honey and dianthus."

"Spray it on the sweet spots." Chara rose from her chair to

retrieve a staggeringly high pair of black heels in the Northern fashion. "Your neck, your throat. Behind your knees, your inner thighs."

"Your walk is important, too," added Chryse, eyeing Chara's heels. "Sway your hips, but not too much. You have to let them want more."

"Touch them," Chara said. "Run a hand down their arm, lean over their shoulder, whisper in their ear. Tease them."

"Your voice should be a murmur. Sultry and mysterious. Hand me that mirror, darling?"

I handed Chryse the small, golden handheld mirror. She eyed her reflection through slit eyes, tilting her head in a way that reminded me of a cat. "We're seducing another gentlemen's club tonight. We'll come back with your information."

Chara heaved a sigh. "These gentlemen's clubs reek. I miss the women."

"The women play our game. The men don't know that there is a game at all." Chryse set down the mirror and stood, following Chara to the door. "Tease them until drool dribbles down their chin. That's when you win."

That's when you win.

Now I climb out of the bath and wonder what the twins would say if they knew what I am doing. A familiar ache pangs in my chest. I swallow hard and run my hands through my knotted wet hair until it falls in damp strands down my back.

I eye the wardrobe. *Dress nice*, Rui told me.

Oh, I will. I allow myself a soft chuckle as I open the doors.

Tonight, I just may murder the Pied Piper.

Tonight, I just may earn my freedom.

I rummage through the gowns, the skirts, the tunics, the pants, the endless array of soft fabrics until my gaze steadies on a shimmering black slip dress. It is thin, teasingly low-cut, with dark satin that looks as if it will cling to all the right places.

Remembering the Northern heels Chara chose, I grab a similar pair, black and strappy, and more than five inches off the ground.

The dress is cool and silky against my skin, and I silently thank Yoonho for the weapons lessons I endured in heels. I glance in the mirror and frown in frustration.

The dress would be perfect, if I were more than just skin and bones.

With my face lacking fullness, my nose seems pointier than ever. My collarbone juts out awkwardly, and my arms have only the barest hint of muscle. Kalmin has wrecked my body, my most prized weapon.

But this is what I have now. I'll make it work. The miniature hourglass hangs just above my slight swell of cleavage. Barely any sand dusts the bottom half, but the silver grains are still trickling through, reminding me of all I have to lose, and that time is ticking past.

I purse my lips, gaze landing on a small drawer in the wardrobe's door. The contents are just what I'd hoped for.

I sweep powder across my face, covering my faded bruises. Next comes blush, swept over my sallow cheeks to create an illusion of health. Kohl and shadows are next, followed by lipstick. It glides across my lips, smooth as butter, leaving behind a beautiful, glistening red. I take a deep breath, analytically observing my reflection once again.

I can still see the hollowness in my gaze, the too-sharp cheekbones, the hint of shadows under my eyes. I look decent, not seductive.

Throat tight with disappointment, I shove the lipstick back in the drawer and glance at the stolen weapons on my bed. Contemplatively, I run my fingers over the golden hilt of Chan's dagger.

How ironic would it be to kill the Piper with his friend's

own weapon?

I sweep my hair into a dark coil, using the dagger to keep the strands in place. Hopefully, Rui will dismiss it as just an embellishment. Hopefully, he will see me as...captivating.

My hands begin to shake.

Tonight, I will seduce the Pied Piper.

CHAPTER EIGHTEEN

A brisk knock raps at the door, and I glance in the mirror one final time. I tuck a stray strand of hair behind an ear. Secure the dagger, hidden under dark locks.

Another knock.

I yank open the door, and my forehead nearly collides with Rui's hand, which is paused mid-knock. I attempt a demure smile through gritted smile. "Emperor."

He is dressed in a fine hanbok of black silk and golden embroidery, his lids lined in the barest hint of kohl. Rings rest on his tanned, still-curled fingers, and teardrop-like earrings twinkle and shimmer on his ears. Rui smiles, revealing sharp white canine teeth. "Lina." I bite back a shiver as his gaze runs over my body, lingering momentarily on the slope of my neck, the bareness of my legs. "You look ravishing."

Heat floods my cheeks as I wait for the punch line…but none comes. The emperor's tone is steady.

Honest.

Hurriedly, I will the pink flush across my face to fade. "Thank you," I murmur, tilting my head slightly to the side, not missing how his gaze snags on my neck a second time.

Perhaps this plan will work after all.

Perhaps I do look...pretty.

Rui's smirk grows as he extends his arm. "I've arranged for us to take dinner in the palace observatory. I think you will enjoy it, given your apparent enthusiasm for the exploration of my kingdom this morning."

I eye his arm warily before realizing that he means for me to link my own with his. Hesitantly, I do. Can I retrieve the dagger from my hair now, with my other arm? Can I plunge it into his back? I can't, I realize, as Rui escorts me down the hall.

Although he has a gentle, yet firm, grip on my arm, I have no doubt that the moment I make a false move, it will tighten into an iron grasp.

"Did you enjoy the village?" As we cross the plaza, his voice is tinged with an interest that surprises me. "That is, I assume you went there—the trail behind the kitchen gardens is the only direct path there. You'd be surprised how often Asha runs into town for so-called ingredient runs."

"So-called?"

"I have it on good authority that her ingredient runs are an excuse to gawk at the dresses in Madame Haa's," Rui replies as we take the stairs. He is brimming with amusement now, his eyes bright and sparkling. "I had Chan follow her once."

So Asha does have a soft spot. For dresses, at least.

I can barely keep track of my mental map of the palace as we turn through dozens of hallways and mount two more flights of stairs. I chew my bottom lip in worry. If I have to find my own way back...

"You're being suspiciously agreeable," Rui notes as we arrive at an ornate silver door. "Should I be worried?"

"Not in the least," I respond sweetly.

He laughs under his breath before opening the door with a

slight push of his palm. I bite back a grimace. Opening a door like that would require me to use far more strength. He is strong. Very, very strong. But is he stronger than this dagger?

For this is his general's dagger, forged of Dokkaebi gold, honed and heavy in my hair. And this time, I am determined to hide behind an element of surprise. Last time, I was too hasty, too *obvious*.

This time will be different.

"Our dinner." He gestures with a great flourish at what lies beyond the door.

My eyes widen.

The observatory is a rounded dome, its walls illuminated by a candelabra on the low dining table in the center of the room.

A panel of glistening glass in the ceiling pours starlight into the room. Plates of food, still steaming, sit on the table. Colorful cushions, plump and velvet, await us on the glossy black floor that reflects the shimmer of the stars. I allow myself to feel a surge of triumph as Rui shuts the door.

We are completely and totally alone.

Yet I know that Haneul Rui is dangerously clever. Know that this secluded dinner is somehow his move in our game, with a hidden motivation that I cannot quite decipher. But I highly doubt he knows that my own strategy is to take him down with sugared smiles and flashes of skin.

"This way," Rui murmurs, placing a hand on my lower back. Even through the fabric, his fingers are cool, the frostbitten metal of his rings biting on my skin. I am overly conscious of the sheer closeness of his body to mine as he guides me to the table.

Attempting to steady my fast-beating heart, I jerk away and walk the next few strides myself before settling down on a cushion. My cheeks burn as I avoid the Piper's gaze.

A small smile toying on his lips, Rui takes the one across from me. He gracefully folds himself onto the pillow, crossing his legs and adjusting his flowing black robe. "I hope you're hungry, Shin Lina," he murmurs as he picks up his chopsticks and twirls them idly between his fingers.

My stomach grumbles in response as I take in bowls of soup swimming with chunks of tofu and green ringlets of scallion. Glazed meats are artfully arranged on wide platters next to glass noodles mixed with vegetables atop a porcelain plate. Tendrils of steam curl up from shiny white rice and fat mandu, filling the room with a savory aroma.

"It won't serve itself," Rui says, reaching for a platter of meat. "However useful self-serving plates would be, I fear it's even beyond my own capabilities to procure such an invention. Duck?"

"Fine." I watch as he loads heaps of food onto my plate before turning to his own. I cautiously pick a piece between my chopsticks and raise it to my lips. The duck is tender, almost sweet, and the glaze sticks to my lips even as I swallow and reach for more. This is the sort of food I wished for in Sunpo, the kingdom where children eat the same salted fish every day and pretend it's pork or beef or chicken.

Rui takes a bite of rice. "I'm pleased to see that you put the wardrobe to good use."

I smile over my glass of wine. *Draw as much attention to your lips as you can.* "This dress was irresistible."

"So I see," he murmurs. My breath hitches momentarily in my throat. As if he can hear it, Rui gazes up at me underneath his lashes as a wicked laugh flickers in his eyes. "Is the sky to your liking?" He gestures to the expanse of night that looms above us.

I lift my eyes to the pearlescent silver moons, the shimmering stars, and the small, lightning-quick flashes that can only be comets speeding through the eternal expanse. "If it isn't?"

The emperor shrugs languidly. "Then I will change it for you."

"Change…the sky?"

Rui waves a hand upward. The sky ripples and shifts, until the white stars and moons glow varying hues of gold and the blue-black depths of the sky change to a sunset orange. The shining light encases the emperor in an aura of gold. "Perhaps this is preferable." His eyes glint. He looks almost…shyly hopeful, as if he is itching for my approval.

For the sky has gone from dark to vibrant in a matter of moments.

Quickly, I compose myself. "I liked it better before."

Rui twirls a hand again, and I watch orange melt back into velvet darkness.

"You can change the sky."

"And you can state the obvious."

I furrow my brows in annoyance, and he shrugs laconically.

"Gyeulcheon is a realm of my own creation. Whatever I wish for it to be, it will be. It bends to my will." *Gods.* "At the very least, it is an impressive party trick."

My party trick is my ability to juggle three knives. I take another moment to compose myself, conscious of Rui's gaze. He's trying to distract me from my goal. I must stay focused.

I tilt my head and eye him with demure intent as I sip my wine. It tastes strangely familiar, rich and almost nutty, and I have a feeling that the twins would be proud as I run my tongue over my red lips.

His gaze darkens, lingering on my mouth, and I mentally applaud myself. "It is from your realm," he informs me as he reaches for the platter of plump dumplings. "The best vineyard on the Northern Continent. The Lunshel Vineyard. I believe they call this particular wine *Sallinna.*"

The name rolls from his tongue smoothly.

Sallinna.

I struggle to keep my composure.

That's why the wine tastes so familiar. Yoonho had it imported for the twins' nineteenth birthday party as an homage to their Northern heritage. There was a mistake in the shipment, an overstock, and the Talons sipped from bottles of the wine for months after the party. Does Rui somehow know what memories the wine brings forth? No. He cannot. Can he?

"You look distracted, Reaper." His voice comes from far away. It almost sounds concerned.

I tear my gaze from the opposite wall, where I've been staring blankly, mind running through images of that birthday party. Of the Talons, grinning from ear to ear as Chara and Chryse, stunning in matching dresses of emerald, twirled and danced to the rhythm of the band. "No," I say quickly. "Not at all."

Rui laughs that rich, velvety laugh. "Plotting my demise?"

I can't hold back a smug scoff. "Who says that I haven't already?"

"Speaking of." He arches a brow. "I've meant to ask you, little thief: Armaments from my weaponry have mysteriously disappeared. Would you happen to know where they've gone?" Wry cunning dances across his face. "Although my blacksmiths are talented, I do doubt their ability to create weapons that simply wander off on their own."

"I've no idea," I reply mildly, acutely aware of the stolen dagger that holds up my hair. "But your friend Kang did indeed bring me into the weaponry as part of a little palace tour." I watch him carefully, but the emperor looks only vaguely entertained.

"I assume, then, you saw that your friend is alive and well."

"Kalmin is not a friend," I snap hotly, momentarily forgetting myself. "He's anything but. Yet I know him, and I know that he's never worked in a forge a day in his life. You compelled him. Compelled *all* the humans in this palace. The girls in the garden, the boy in the kitchen. And I know there are more."

"And your qualms about this are what, exactly?" Rui coolly arches a brow. "I thought you would be relieved that I haven't killed them."

I seethe. "Do your kind have an aversion to manual labor? Is that why you turn to humans instead?"

"Perhaps," Rui replies calmly. "Mandu?"

I say nothing but still, he plops one onto my plate. I don't touch it.

He fixes his attention on me as he lingers, leaning forward. "Do tell me the full story behind you and our scarlet-haired blacksmith. You work for him, yet you despise him. You entered Gyeulcheon with more bruises than I could count, with tearstained cheeks and a bloodied face. Such a story piques my curiosity." Rui settles back in his cushion, his fingers toying with a chopstick. His gaze refuses to part from mine.

A dare. To see what I will say.

Fine, then.

"He killed my friends." I will my expression to remain a mask of icy calm.

Rui sets down his chopsticks. "Ah." There is no pity on his face, but for a moment, I think I may see a light in his eyes momentarily dim. "I assume you won't be going into detail."

"No." I take a shallow breath. Godsdamn it. How has this conversation steered into such precarious waters? It was meant only to be a distraction, a veneer for me to hide behind before I stab him. But it has gone on long enough—I should be seducing him. Not sharing a snippet of my sob story. I must get this back on track.

"Fair enough," Rui says, and he dips his head in acknowledgment as I take a cautious bite of mandu to mask my disconcertion. It's filled with savory shrimp and the dough is steamed, chewy. As I eat, Rui eyes me appraisingly.

"What?" I demand in annoyance around a mouthful, yet again forgetting my determination to be coy, seductive.

"I am just realizing," Rui says, "that I put you to work in the kitchens." He twirls his chopsticks between his fingers, looking faintly amused.

"And?"

"And the kitchen is an opportune place for poisoners." The emperor takes a bite of duck and chews contemplatively. "Hmm," he muses. "I taste duck, obviously. Ginger. Sesame. No hint of poison, unfortunately. How boring."

"You haven't tried the japchae," I say sweetly and gesture to the bowl of clear noodles. Rui raises a brow, helps himself to a serving, and takes a bite.

"I'm not dead," the Dokkaebi emperor informs me. "Why is that?"

"I might be an assassin," I mutter, "but even I doubt my ability to poison food under Asha's eye."

To my surprise, Rui laughs. Although quiet, the sound is rich and velvety. "That's well enough. Poison is a coward's tool. Easy, with no skill required. Besides, I wouldn't put it past Asha to kill you herself should you try anything of the sort." At my expression, his smile grows. "Are you not fond of Asha?"

"Asha," I retort, "hits me with spoons."

His eyes glint wickedly. "Yes, she does have a tendency to do that. She's hit me, as well. As a child I'd often sneak into her kitchens and steal sweets. One time, she threatened to boil me along with the stew."

I snort through my nose before I can stop myself. "Perhaps I'll borrow her idea." But then I blink, mulling more carefully over his words. Asha looks no more than a squat thirty or so, but she's an immortal—and looks are deceiving. If she was in the kitchens when Rui was a child… "How old is Asha?" I ask. And then—before I can stop myself—"How old are *you*?"

"I'm twenty," Rui says, and I can't help but raise my brows dubiously.

"Only twenty?" That can't be true. He's been alive for much longer, I'm sure of it. The tales of Sunpo's Pied Piper stem back centuries.

"In a way." He takes another bite of food. "Dokkaebi age much slower than mortals, you know. In Dokkaebi years, I'm twenty. In human years…" Rui shrugs, unconcerned. "I don't quite feel like doing the arithmetic at the moment."

It's my turn to eye him appraisingly. "When is your birthday?"

"The winter solstice." The emperor's smile is a curved blade. "Would you care to bring me a gift?"

"It's only spring." My responding look is falsely saccharine. "You'll be long dead by then. But perhaps I'll give a eulogy in your honor. The starting words, I think, would be *'this bastard.'* The ending words would be *'got exactly what he deserved.'*" I violently stab my chopsticks into the mandu to punctuate my point.

Rui's lips twitch, and then almost as if he tried to prevent it, he is laughing once more. I stare at him, at his eyes sparkling with amusement, his sharp canines glinting as he throws his head back in now-unconcealed mirth—and I can't help but laugh as well before I guiltily clamp my lips shut. *Just part of the game,* I tell myself and eye him speculatively.

The emperor seems to be genuinely enjoying my company, as bizarre as that is. And…we are secluded in a small room. Perhaps I won't need to find his bedroom after all. I could…do it here. Kill him in the observatory. Plant the dagger through his chiseled flesh.

As his laughter quiets, I fix my gaze on my nearly empty glass. "Pass the wine," I request, unsure of how else to proceed through the night without the buzz of alcohol warming my bloodstream. To my surprise, Rui stands with his hand wrapped around the carafe. I hold my breath as the emperor gracefully makes his way toward me and pauses, hovering over my shoulder.

"Here," he says, still sounding vaguely entertained, and pours the dark liquid into my glass.

I place a slender hand on his own, my skin warm against his cool. "That's enough," I murmur.

He pauses. The trickling of the wine slowing to a stop.

I look up at him from underneath my eyelashes. "Thank you."

His gaze is so impossibly silver. He makes no effort to move, his expression dancing with a bright, cold wickedness. I have a feeling that my own reflect the same iciness as he moves closer, lessening the space between us until there is less than half an inch separating us.

I tilt my head. A question.

He smiles. An answer.

I stand in an elegant, graceful movement and raise my hand to his face, tracing the angular curves of his jaw, his cheekbones. His eyes flutter shut for a moment, only a moment… My mouth flattens into a hard, straight line.

And then my hair tumbles down my back as my free hand closes around the cool hilt of the stolen dagger. *Steady my hand, Yeomra.* I imagine the god standing behind me, hand on mine, mouth grim.

The game is over. Now.

I grab his shoulder with my free hand as I dig the blade into his chest, gritting my teeth as I *twist*, twist the dagger *hard* as Rui gasps. His back arches and blood streams onto my hand, hot and…*golden.*

Rui stumbles backward, his face deathly pale as his hand grasps that golden, ruby hilt of the dagger. His mouth is slack in agony. Golden blood trickles past his ashen lips.

I stand grimly at the table, my heart racing as Rui looks at me in shock. Disbelief. His fingers are still wrapped around his friend's dagger.

And then—he falls.

The emperor lies on his back, a hand on the hilt, the other outstretched, his eyes shut as his gasps slow and…stop.

I don't dare to move, my chest rising and falling in rapid breaths as I dig my fingernails into my palm, adrenaline pulsing a hot buzz through my body. Because… Because…

I killed the Pied Piper.

Shakily, I exhale as my chest tightens with emotion.

Joy? Relief? Triumph? The emotions are splendidly mixed, warming my blood and bringing color to my cheeks. I imagine the God of Death standing behind me, smiling in approval.

It is done. It is over. I have *won*.

I can go back to Sunpo. Return Kalmin. Eunbi is safe.

Yet I don't move. My eyes are fixed on Rui's body, limp and prone, on the floor. I feel no remorse, no regret. Just a relentlessly burning triumph.

Of course I did it.

I am the Reaper. Why did I ever even doubt myself? I've killed, maimed, and fought more men than I can count. I was Yoonho's pride and joy. A Talon.

Slowly, I take a few cautious steps toward the fallen emperor and prod him with a toe. No movement, no motion, no whisper of life.

His hanbok is soaked in his inhuman blood. On the table, his platter of food sits patiently waiting for a diner who will never return.

The Pied Piper is dead.

A cruel grin twists my lips as I lean down to his ear, my breath grazing his cold, still skin. "I win," I murmur, unclasping the hourglass necklace and letting it fall to the folds of his hanbok, where it shimmers underneath the moonlight.

I'll find Kalmin now. Drag him to Kang, or Hana, or Chan,

or *whoever* will take us back to Sunpo. I'll dump the bastard at Asina's feet and demand to see my sister.

My back is straight and proud as I stalk toward the door.

But I never make it.

Instead, I hit the wall hard, stars dancing in front of my eyes as my vision ebbs into momentary darkness before swimming back to reveal a pair of glittering silver eyes and red lips pulled back into a dangerous grin.

Shock rips through my chest like a bullet, leaving a gaping wound.

"Not quite," the Pied Piper replies with a double-edged smirk as he leans over me, dangling that godsdamned necklace before my eyes.

And I see that the sand still trickles, steadily falling in silver flakes.

"I'm afraid, little thief, that our game happens to be far from finished."

No. *No.*

Panic tightens my throat.

I killed him.

I dug a dagger into his chest as far as it would go.

He was dead. He is *supposed to be dead.*

Yeomra has betrayed me.

I cannot help the ragged breaths slipping through my lips. The Piper's arms trap me against the wall, caging me eye level with his chest, where the dagger still gleams, embedded in his blood-crusted flesh.

"I've always been a fan of theatrics," Rui says as I begin to shake. "A lover of theater, some may say. I've been known to participate in a few shows here and there. My court tells me that I'm quite the actor."

"The dagger," I rasp. "The dagger. I killed you. You're bleeding." Bleeding *gold.* It never occurred to me that a

Dokkaebi's blood didn't run red. I gape at the ichor-like blood.

"Ah. The dagger." His lips pull up in derision as he flicks his gaze toward his chest, where the hilt gleams almost tauntingly. "Funnily enough, Chan approached me just this morning, complaining that his newly crafted dagger had gone missing. I suppose I found it."

I swallow hard as he lifts his gaze from his impaled chest.

Dokkaebi fire, blue and unforgiving, dances within the depths of his silver eyes.

I fight back my trembling as the temperature drops around us, my skin shivering against the bite of ice now palpable in the air. As goose bumps creep down my body, I can only hope that Rui does not release his flame. That it dances only in the silver of his eyes.

"You have much to learn about Dokkaebi, if you truly believe that a blow to the heart delivered with the force of a small human girl is enough to murder their emperor." Rui plucks the dagger out of his chest. I watch with wide eyes as his ruined flesh slowly patches together until the bloodstained tear in his robes surrounds nothing but smooth, tan skin. "Unluckily for you, I heal rather quickly. But you have good aim; I'll give you that. And I must confess, I didn't see your attack coming. Although I realize now that I should have been far warier from the second you opened your door wearing that dress. I see now that seduction was your second weapon of choice this evening."

I say nothing.

He won this round. And I…I lost.

Losing, it seems, is all I have been able to do recently.

"Perhaps I feel even a bit jilted that our friendly meal was all an act," Rui adds, a peculiar dryness to his tone.

"I can agree to that," I hiss, and Rui chuckles.

"Another failed assassination attempt under your belt means another punishment. One that suits the crime." He sighs, running a hand through his hair, the other planted on the wall next to my right cheek. "The options are, indeed, bountiful."

My blood runs cold.

"But I have one in particular in mind." Rui's breath tickles my neck.

"And what's that?" I grit out through clenched teeth, jaw aching. I am holding back tears—tears of anger, tears of frustration.

I've gotten nowhere tonight.

"Tomorrow evening, there's a ball," Rui murmurs, his voice velvet soft. He tucks a strand of my loose hair behind my ear, and I fight back a shiver at his cold touch. "And my court is *dying* to become acquainted with you, Shin Lina." He chuckles softly. "I believe you've already seen the evening gowns in your wardrobe. They happen to be hung right near this lovely dress you now wear." His fingers trace the satin fabric clinging to my waist in a featherlight touch, and crackling flames heat my blood as he clucks his tongue. "You do know, little thief, that this is a nightdress. Don't you?"

As a matter of fact, I hadn't known that—but that is irrelevant now. My cheeks burn in fury as I snarl up at him. *This* is to be my consequence, then. To stand in Dokkaebi finery in the midst of a crowded ballroom, enduring dirty looks. "Fine. A ball."

"A ball," Rui confirms. A wicked glimmer shines across his face. "Tomorrow will be quite a busy day for you. I believe Asha mentioned something about your next shift's length."

"Let me guess," I mutter darkly. "It will be ten times as long."

"Preparation for the ball takes all day," Rui replies, tilting his head and arching a brow. "I would expect you to be aiding Asha in her work through the late evening."

I grimace.

"Until then," Rui murmurs, his breath tickling my neck as he refastens the necklace around it, "I suggest that you keep yourself out of trouble."

CHAPTER NINETEEN

Sparkling light falls from the grand, glittering chandelier like snowflakes, illuminating the glasses of champagne balancing precariously on silver trays carried by dazed-looking servants.

There is laughing and chatter as the Gyeulcheon court spins and twirls, whirling gracefully around their partners. Swirling stairs lead to a balcony on which the Piper lounges atop his obsidian throne, one leg swung over the other while his fingers tap to the rhythm of the music as he observes the merriment of his court.

He is dressed as finely as I have ever seen him, his deep obsidian robes high collared and elegant midnight silk spreading across the floor. A silver headpiece sits on his forehead. It seems to be crafted of thorns, twining around one another as they twist upward. In his lap rests Manpasikjeok.

I have not been able to look away from him since the moment I arrived.

And with the way his eyes roam, the way his brows touch… I have a dreadful feeling that Rui is searching for me. Not that he will find me anytime soon.

It isn't that I'm hiding or at all daunted by the ocean of Dokkaebi. I'm simply concealing myself behind a scarlet curtain, my back pressed against the cool glass of the window.

I have stayed here for nearly an hour now, watching. I tell myself that I am plotting, that there is really no shame in standing behind a curtain, since I am planning the Piper's downfall. But really, there is nothing I can do with murderous intent at the ball. The hanbok I wear, with the jeogori reminiscent of a night sky that I spotted during my first day in Gyeulcheon, is nearly impossible to move in.

I paired the hanbok with one of the small throwing daggers stolen from the armory. It is strapped to the back of my right thigh with a strip of black fabric underneath the black chima. But it is useless to wield—Rui will see me scaling that curved staircase before I can even draw it. And besides…after last night, I doubt that this small dagger will do any good.

Underneath the hanbok's fabric, my hourglass necklace is cold on my skin as I seethe that there will be no killing tonight. I can practically *feel* that godsdamned sand falling, *feel* my time running out. My third full day in Gyeulcheon, spent lurking behind the curtains at a ball and decidedly *not* murdering the emperor.

My eyes land on Hana, who is smiling as she leans on the arm of Chan. He gazes down at her with a fond expression that sends a bizarre sort of pang through my chest. Both are dressed in hanboks the same shining shade of silver—perhaps a tribute to their emperor.

The couple talks to Kang, who wears a white silk hanbok and carries a golden scepter in place of his staff. A server— Hangyeol, I realize, from the kitchens—approaches the trio while balancing a tray of wineglasses. Hana plucks a glass from the array and clinks it against Kang's, then Chan's. Chan says something with a wry smile that has Kang laughing and Hana rolling her eyes good-naturedly.

They remind me of the Talons. Of the twins and Sang and me, drinking on rooftops, proposing outrageous toasts that had us howling with laughter for hours on end.

I tear away my gaze.

A part of me still marvels that the Dokkaebi are *real*. For so long, they seemed like characters of a long-forgotten story. The Pied Piper was almost an urban legend in Sunpo, a kidnapper in the dead of night who disappeared without a trace. But he is real—so very real.

And he is looking for me.

I feel the change in the music before I hear it. Feel the shift in the air, as if an invisible fog, thick and heady, has blanketed the room. *No* is my last coherent thought before I feel my head go light, my eyes un-focus, my ears prick up as the melody, high and lilting, twirls into the air like a gracefully unfurling ribbon.

Lina, the song purrs, running invisible hands down my neck, my chest, the small of my back. *You've been hiding. Please come out to play. I am ever so bored.*

In a fluid, barely lucid moment, I step around the curtain. I blink dreamily as a Dokkaebi couple twirls by, their faces slackening at the sight of me.

Why have I been huddling behind the drapery at such a lovely ball? There is music, and food, and— Oh! I spot Rui, lounging on his throne, his lips parted above that beautiful flute. This is his ball, thrown in honor of his need to be entertained… surely it would be polite to greet him.

I am only dimly aware of the hushed murmurs that arise from the crowd of Dokkaebi as I make my way across the ballroom floor, swaying slightly as I mount the steps.

The song is so beautiful. High, sweet notes cloud my mind, but it doesn't matter, *nothing* matters except reaching the throne and greeting the handsome, regal emperor with my best smile and telling him how wonderful this ball is... How absolutely delightful...

I nearly stumble over my gown as I reach the top of the staircase, overcome with eagerness to sink to my knees before Rui and bow in respect.

His eyes are twinkling—*like stars*, I think, caught in admiration. He is playing Manpasikjeok with nimble fingers and glossy lips. I sway before him and wobble as I sink to my knees. My gown spreads around me, an ocean of silk in which I am an island. I bow my head, and my hair tumbles past my cheeks in a waterfall of dark waves.

"Your Majesty," I murmur, delightfully content as his eyes rest on me, drinking me in. The effect of his gaze is draining and relieving all at once, in a way that reminds me of the ashes of a halji tree. And the music... I sigh in bliss as I savor the song of the flute.

Until it comes to a stop, the beautiful melody crashing into nothingness.

I gasp at the abrupt absence as my ears ache and ring in protest, leaving me winded, weak, at the feet of the Piper.

The Pied Piper. And that godsdamned flute.

I shake in fury. Enchanted. Again. I was a fool not to expect this, but after the dinner, after making him *laugh*—I thought perhaps Rui would rely instead on his wit to lure me out, the same way he used it to engage me in conversation over our meal. He didn't use Manpasikjeok then, so I didn't expect him to use it now. My skin crawls and my fingers tremble.

Naive, I seethe. It's never that easy, not in this godsdamned game, and I should *know that.*

Always controlled. Always at another's whims. Whether it be at the behest of the Blackbloods or at the will of the Dokkaebi emperor, I am never anything but a pawn to be moved around the chessboard by another's hands. I am nothing but a plaything.

"You insufferable *ass*," I hiss in fury. My fingernails dig into the palms of my hands as if the pain could jerk me out of this seemingly endless nightmare. "You *bastard*." I have killed men for less—so much less. I jerk to my feet, back burning from the scrutiny of the guests down below. "I will make your death a very, very slow one," I spit viciously. "And I will enjoy every moment of it, you *gaesaekki*!" A hushed gasp from the crowd below meets my ears as the vulgar expletive leaves my lips in a shout, but I don't give a shit. I have had *enough* of being others' puppet.

Somewhere, I think I hear Chan choke in outrage.

As Rui's expression stills at the name, I realize with mortification that my vision has become blurred with hot tears. Angrily, I smear them away, even as my mind runs with memories. Kalmin, ordering me to kill a young wife when her husband refused to pay tribute. Demanding that I stand guard outside the gang's giwajip for twelve hours straight in the freezing rain. Commanding me to steal a seemingly innocuous tapestry from the Temple of Ruin.

Rui, ordering me to his throne. Forcing me out of my hiding space. Stealing my will, my mind, my *choice*.

Any amusement on his face has vanished as my chest heaves furiously and he tucks away Manpasikjeok. The ballroom is so still, so silent. He regards me for a long moment, and then I watch as a muscle in his jaw jumps. As he lithely stands and cuts a look toward his people.

His voice, when he speaks, is light. Only I can see how stiff his fingers are as he spreads his hands. "Carry on with your dallying," he tells his court, and then turns to the musicians. "A waltz," he snaps. The musicians quickly close their gaping mouths and procure a waltz, which the court ignores. Their stares are still fastened to me as I seethe. My nails cut into the palms of my hands as Rui turns back to me.

Although his eyes are dark, he smiles almost *cheerfully* at me. "Let us enjoy this ball. Dance with me."

"Or what? You'll compel me?" I gesture angrily to the folds of his robes, where I know Manpasikjeok rests. "It seems, *Your Majesty*, that my will isn't my own in this matter."

"You called me a son of a bitch in front of my entire court," he hisses back from the corner of his mouth, barely audible. "You've not only insulted me, but my mother, the former empress. I've ordered for our game to remain between us, but these guests are drunk on wine and dancing. I wouldn't put it past them to attempt something unsavory to avenge my, and my mother's, honor. If you dance with me, we show them your good faith, and you remain unscathed."

"Except for when you *behead me*."

He takes a small breath through his nose. "If you would like to take your chances, you may. But your safety relies on my order, and their obedience—which you have challenged. I cannot do more, for it is royal law that I do not use Manpasikjeok on my court—or on any of my kind, for that matter, unless they have committed a serious offense. But even then, I do not enjoy it, and rarely resort to it."

"But you *do* enjoy using it on defenseless humans," I fire back as I look down at the sea of dancers below. Dozens of angry scowls and blazing eyes are still on me. Mouth suddenly dry, I wet my lips nervously.

Perhaps I shouldn't have called Rui a gaesaekki, I realize somewhat belatedly as I note that many of the angry Dokkaebi seem to be military—and have jikdos sheathed at their waists. Others have no weapons, but I stand no chance against an angry mob, for I am armed only with my tiny dagger.

"You're anything but defenseless," he says in an undertone. "But don't underestimate the loyalty these guests feel for me."

Rui offers his hand to me slowly, as if approaching a wild animal.

Reluctantly, I take it, despising myself for the corner I've backed myself into.

His skin is icy, yet a flicker of heat blooms as our palms meet. I squeeze his hand as hard as I can, wishing I could crush his bones into powder.

Rui gives no sign of discomfort and slants his gaze toward me, and I wonder if he is aware of the effect his godsdamned *hand* has on me. "Shall we?" he asks, and I think that his voice might be hesitant.

"Fine," I manage to snap, tightening my grasp even further on his hand. Rui leads me down the stairs and twirls me to the center of the ballroom floor, a hand on my waist, the other intertwined with my own. I wonder if he can feel how I shake with fury. I sense his muscles tighten and realize that it's likely he can.

Some of the ballroom's tension seems to disperse as Rui spins me. Yet my cheeks still burn under dozens of glares, and I can tell that they will not be done gawking anytime soon.

Fine. Let them look.

Let them know the face that will kill their king.

As we dance, I lean closer to Rui so that my whisper reaches his delicately pointed ears. "If you *ever*," I snarl, voice quavering with emotion, "use your godsdamned flute on me like that again, I won't stop at just killing you. I'll take Manpasikjeok from your dead body and I'll crush it underfoot. I'll set your throne on fire and then burn your entire realm to the ground. Do you understand me?" Heat sears my eyes, and with some horror I realize that furious tears have once again caught on my lashes. *"Do you?"*

Rui hesitates, and then—barely audible—says, "Forgive me."

My mind swirls to a halt and I think that perhaps I've misheard him. But then he says it again and I realize that he's...

apologizing to me.

"Forgive me," he says again to my complete and utter shock. "It will be added to the rules of our game. I will not wield Manpasikjeok against you again…unless, of course, you're attempting to murder me. I see now that it is unfair. Wrong. Cheating at our game."

Rui is…apologizing.

The shock of it is so strong that I nearly stumble.

Of all the things I expected Gyeulcheon's emperor to do, asking my forgiveness was not one of them. After a year of remorseless abuse, I've forgotten what it's like to be offered an apology. Forgotten that there can be power in two small words, that guilt and contrition *do* exist. That I deserve to see them.

There is power in being apologized to, I realize. *I do not need to forgive him.*

So I don't.

But I remember his remorse and tuck it away into my heart, where I can pull it out and scrutinize it later.

"Thank you," I say stiltedly. "For the apology."

And I mean it. It has not fixed what he has done, nor has it quelled my hatred of him—but he has sworn not to do so again. I will hold him to his promise, and myself to mine.

The emperor bows his head, and we dance in silence for a while underneath the acute attention of his court.

"The hanbok looks lovely on you," he murmurs after a while. "Do you find it to your liking?" Rui is close enough that I can feel the hum of his power, thrumming from him in freezing, sparking pulses. I grit my teeth.

"I despise this dress." In response, Rui twirls me under his arm. My skirts spread into the air, a whirl of shadow.

"Really," he says, looking down at me. "Because I find that I enjoy it even more than that little black nightgown you wore last night." A wry smile. He has returned to being infuriating, then.

A large part of me is relieved. My hatred banked when he apologized, the flames of it stuttering. We are back on solid ground now, and for that I am grateful. I return to imagining the many, many ways I could kill him if he were human. "And I find that I enjoy you more with a dagger in your chest."

Rui chuckles and brings me closer to his body as another couple waltzes by and sends dirty glances my way.

"You look well recovered from the loss of your dignity last night." Rui's hand is gentle on the small of my back as we dance.

"At least I know now that you bleed," I retort mock-sweetly.

"Is that resentment I hear?" Rui tugs me closer to his chest in time to the swell of the music, and it's an effort not to let my breath hitch as the space between us lessens. "Your hatred pierces my heart as much as your dagger, Reaper." His eyes glitter. "If your dagger had struck my heart at all."

"It will," I promise him as we circle each other, our hands pressed together.

"You'll find that I guard my heart very closely."

"It's easy to bypass the rib cage. All I need is another chance. I assure you, Pied Piper, that I will hold your heart in my hands before the days of our bargain come to a close."

The waltz quickens into a lively pace. I can barely think straight as we sweep across the ballroom floor. It is a struggle to maintain my balance when our speed increases.

Rui laughs under his breath. "Destroy me, then," the emperor says, holding my gaze as we swirl through the sea of colors. "Pierce my heart with one thousand daggers. Let the kingdom shine golden with my blood. You'll find that I will enjoy it."

I gape at him, perplexed at the rough cadence of his words.

For the first time since I stepped foot in Gyeulcheon, Rui looks away first.

The dance has become a quickstep. Rui moves quickly,

gracefully, with the agile fluidity that only a Dokkaebi can possess. "So kill me, Shin Lina." His words are low and steady underneath the orchestra's melody. "If you can."

"What do you think I was trying to do last night?"

"I think you were trying to do many things." He pulls me closer to his chest. I can smell him—plum blossoms and licorice. "And that little dress you wore tells me that murder wasn't the only thing on your mind."

My cheeks burn scarlet. "Last night you gave me a false victory," I grind out.

Rui laughs under his breath. "All in good fun. And you had your own fun as well. You laughed, Lina—I saw. You must admit that at least part of our dinner was enjoyable."

I shove aside the memory of how the emperor's eyes fluttered closed as I traced the smooth, statuesque lines and curves of his face. "Up until you spitefully deceived me, I was quite enjoying myself."

"I suspected as much. Tell me, Lina. What exactly was your plan?"

"To murder you," I reply flatly.

Rui smiles slightly as our pace quickens further. For all my years of training, of working my muscles and limbs until I became agile and fast, I am beginning to lose my breath as the music becomes a rapid flurry.

The notes pound through the air like raindrops in a storm. Pain shoots up my scarred leg but I ignore it as best I can, for I will be damned if I stumble before Rui's court. My hair whips through the air, and I realize that we are the only two on the dance floor. The rest of his court hovers around the ballroom, murmuring. I twirl and pivot as Rui leads, his eyes gleaming with excitement. *Let them watch*, his gaze seems to say. *Give them a show, little thief.*

The air seems to crackle between us, heavy and thick with

lightning-hot tension.

And then he is spinning me, the ballroom becoming a blur before my eyes.

The song reaches its crescendo, sweet and piercing, as I collide with his chest. I am breathless and glisten with a thin sheen of sweat as the musicians finish their song.

Gyeulcheon's court holds their breath as Rui, still holding me in his arms, bends to whisper in my ear.

"I meant your *other* plan," the emperor purrs, his voice low and husky. His lips graze my jaw as he pulls away. I briefly close my eyes and shiver at the featherlight touch.

His laugh tickles my skin as he releases me from his grip and turns to his court with a magnanimous smile. "Go and make merry, for this is a revel, and we dance until sunrise."

I watch as his people return his smile, some throwing their heads back and laughing in joy as they swarm to the dance floor.

Rui turns back to me. His sparkling smile is gone, something more serious in its place. "Would you save me the last dance, Reaper?"

I blink as he returns to his balcony, his gaze finding mine once more as he reclines on his throne. Something stirs in the pit of my stomach. I yank away my gaze and pivot on my heel. I will return to my curtain now. The whispers have become murmurs, which are slowly becoming blunt mutters. I hear my name, repeated with sour distaste throughout the ballroom.

I push past a gaggle of finely dressed females and nearly crash into Kang, who stands with Hana and Chan. The couple gives me identical dirty looks. *A match made in the heavens*, I think bitterly.

"Lina," Kang greets, his voice holding none of his companion's animosity.

"Kang." I force what I hope is a polite smile and flick my gaze toward Chan. If the general knows that his missing dagger embedded itself in his emperor's chest, he gives no indication.

"It's a lovely hanbok. The colors suit you."

"I enjoy your…" I pause, searching for the word. Cane? No. "Scepter."

Although Hana scoffs, leading Chan away to the floor, Kang seems pleasantly amused. "Your dance with the king was a sight to behold. You're a graceful dancer. Would you grant me the pleasure of a waltz?"

"Ah," a voice wryly comments from behind me. "I see you beat me to it. I was hoping to dance with you. Perhaps you'll find me after the waltz?"

In a moment of surprise, I take in the newcomer's amber eyes and wire glasses. Recognition thrums in my chest. Wang Jiwoon, in a hanbok of simple black. The scholar from the village. I open my mouth, but Jiwoon shakes his head ever so slightly. His face is dark with what almost looks like a warning.

"Find me after this song," I say slowly, my brows furrowed. Jiwoon dips his head in a nod and melts back into the crowd. I watch him go with unbridled scrutiny.

"Do you know him?" Kang's tone is mild, but as always, the undercurrent of wariness persists.

Lie, a voice murmurs in my mind. "Not at all," I reply smoothly, allowing Kang to take my hand and waist.

"I see that you've captured eyes in more ways than one, then," he says dryly. "And how have you found these past few days?"

Something in his voice makes me jerk. "I assume that Rui spoke to you of last night."

Kang winces at my frigid tone. "He did. But I must say, he seemed quite entertained. It has been many, many years since I have seen him so lively."

"Wonderful," I mutter. Only Rui would be entertained by a knife protruding from his chest.

A bitter taste floods my mouth. I cannot imagine what it is

like, to live a life so peaceful, in such splendor, that one chooses to manufacture danger. Cannot imagine the privilege of being *bored*, for I have been fighting for my life for years—as an impoverished child, as an orphan on the streets of Sunpo, as a Talon, as a Blackblood, as the Pied Piper's captive. I have never been bored. I've never been given the chance.

"Ever since your arrival, he has grown more and more cheerful. The distraction of your game has been good for him."

"And I suppose he was dreadfully morose before?" I scoff, casting a hateful glance to the throne. Rui sips from a glass of wine and questioningly raises his gaze to mine. Quickly, I look away.

"Quite, in fact," Kang replies quietly. "He lost somebody dear to him."

This piques my interest. "Who?"

"It is not my place to say." Kang dips into a bow as the waltz comes to an end. "I wish you a good evening."

"Kang." I catch his wrist as he turns to leave. "You have been…kind to me. Showing me to Kalmin, complimenting my attire, asking for a dance. Why?"

Sadness flashes across his countenance before it is quickly replaced by a small smile. "I am kind to most. Despite your circumstances, you are no exception." He pauses, his eyes landing on something—someone—behind me. "Your next dance awaits you." With a slight nod, he departs.

"Lina." Jiwoon extends a hand, gracefully loping into my vision. "A dance?"

"Jiwoon," I say warily, taking his hand. I begin to step in time to the music, letting him lead. He is a fine dancer, but I can't help but compare his ability to that of Rui's and note that he is no match for the emperor. "I didn't know you were a member of the emperor's court."

"I'm not."

I arch a brow. "Oh?"

Jiwoon nods. "I hold no place in this court." His tone is bitter.

I'm not quite sure what to make of Jiwoon's presence, then. "I assumed that only members of the court are admitted."

"Do you recall my parting words to you that day in the village?"

I feel a twinge of foreboding as I think back to that day outside of the bookshop.

You don't find the rebellion.

My eyes widen.

The rebellion finds you.

Jiwoon glances down at me, his lips a tight line of confirmation. "Hangyeol told me you would be attending this ball tonight. He let me in."

I slacken in shock.

Jiwoon is part of the rebellion.

His grip tightens on me as I put together the rest of his words. "Hangyeol?" The kitchen hand? I blink once. Twice. "He's with you?"

"One of the very few who are. He's also the one who notified me that you would be coming into the village that day. Thanks to his word, I was able to find you."

I shake my head in disbelief. "Why didn't you just tell me what you were a part of?"

"If we were to alliance ourselves with a young human, we needed to be sure that it was the right move."

"The questions weren't for a composition."

"Hardly." Neither of us dares to speak in anything but a whisper. "They were necessary for your file, though."

I frown. "Clever. But you are either very brave or very naive to come dance with me right under the emperor's nose."

"A mixture of both, no doubt." Jiwoon's gaze shifts. "And he is watching us right now."

My head snaps in the throne's direction.

Rui is indeed watching, his eyes dark with an emotion I cannot put my finger on. He doesn't pull away as I stare him down. Instead, a crooked smile curves his lips.

"I will enjoy killing him," I breathe to Jiwoon. "But I have tried, and my efforts have been futile. If you truly are a part of the rebellion, I need your help."

"And us yours. Misook's bakery. Tomorrow at midnight." The dance ends, and my eyebrows furrow in confusion. Aren't waltzes typically much longer? I glance at Rui, who shrugs far too innocently. "Be there."

"I will."

Jiwoon nods—and then he is gone, as quickly as he appeared. My heart pounds wildly.

A chance.

I have a chance. A real, solid chance at winning this godsdamned game.

I throw a wicked grin Rui's way. Let him make of that what he wishes. I am on a wonderful high as I make my way toward a server carrying champagne. The small orchestra starts a song of sweet sorrow and longing lust as I reach for a glass.

I feel, rather than see, Rui rise from his throne. *Would you save me the last dance?* he asked.

But now, I am one step ahead in our game. I can afford a little recklessness.

Tossing Rui a wicked look, I drain my champagne and slip through the doors just as the emperor parts his lips to call for me.

CHAPTER TWENTY

The next day passes as slowly as molasses.

I suffer through Asha's squeaky reprimands with an impressive amount of self-control. Hangyeol expresses no change in demeanor toward me, despite what I've learned—that the discreet kitchen boy has been a rebel all along. The two of us sit quietly at the flour-dusted table, filling sweet rice dough with a thick red bean paste and listening to the rest of the kitchen murmur about last night's ball.

More than a few glances are tossed my way as Dokkaebi mutter something about a waltz with the king. I return these looks with a flat one of my own.

When I am finally released, I take dinner in my room, devouring a steaming bowl of rich pork bone soup that scalds my lips. I can eat now without feeling my stomach roil. And is it just me, or are my cheeks becoming just slightly fuller? I pause, feeling the new softness of my face with my fingertips. I certainly look at least a smidgen healthier.

Impatiently, I wait for midnight. *Misook's bakery*, Jiwoon said. Jiwoon, the rebel who will help me put the Pied Piper six feet under.

I take the route through the kitchen garden, scaling the wall easily, relying on my years of working in light-deprived rooms as I pass through the dark woods.

It's easy to retrace my steps to the baker, and when I get there, I touch the glass door. A slight rotation of my wrist tells me it's locked. Carefully, I knock once with a hand as the other drifts to the whip at my waist. Could this be a trap? A cruel twist in the game orchestrated by Rui? I cannot put it past him.

There. I see a figure in the shop, tensing as they approach the door. What if it is Rui, laughing at how foolish I am, how gullible?

But it isn't. It's Hangyeol who opens the door.

"Lina," he says quietly. "You made it." I incline my head in a nod. It's odd, seeing him out of the kitchens with hands clean of flour. "This way."

As I step into the bakery, he locks the door with a brisk click.

I shoot him a wary look, but Hangyeol shakes his head as if to say, *Relax.* He leads me around the counter and its encasing of pastries into a small back room. "They're waiting for you," Hangyeol says, gesturing to a ladder, half concealed by bags of rice. It leads down, through a hole in the floor, into darkness. I narrow my eyes in suspicion. "It's not a trap," Hangyeol promises quietly.

"That is exactly what a person orchestrating a trap would say," I hiss.

Hangyeol looks exasperated. "Go down the ladder, please. I'll follow you."

I send him a look of warning as I grip the rungs of the ladder. They are cold and rusted under my fingers. I descend quickly, nimbly jumping to the cold, hard ground, then squint through the darkness as Hangyeol joins me.

There is the sound of a match striking and then a burst of light.

"Lina," Jiwoon says, sitting at a round table, a flame flickering between his fingers. "Welcome."

He sits with a female, who takes me in with a steady inspection. Her brown hair falls to her chin in choppy strands, and she wears an array of colorful necklaces, all varying in size and material. Some are beads, polished and black, others chains of gold, green, and violet. Black shadow dusts her eyes, matching her ratty black tunic. "Chi Misook," she says. "I own this bakery."

I raise a brow. "Is it just the three of you?" Disappointment, and skepticism, have me frowning. I was expecting dozens of rebels, and this…this is not what I hoped to find.

"Yes." Jiwoon lights a trio of candles in the middle of the table. "But you'll find that we're more than enough." Something in his voice—perhaps its cold determination—momentarily lessens my concerns, and I observe the room analytically.

The floor is a hard cement, holding the table and chairs. The walls are covered in papers, some maps, some seemingly ripped out of books, all marked up with red ink. Trunks of gleaming weapons, crafted of polished silver, sit in various corners of the room. I catch sight of a shining silver ax and can't help but nod in appreciation.

Jiwoon follows my gaze to the weapons. "We stole a shipment of metals from a Gyeulcheon mine not too long ago," he says, pride tingeing his voice. "A difficult heist, but we pulled it off. We've been using it to forge our own weapons."

"So I heard," I confirm, finally allowing myself to relax. "You got under the general's skin. Quite impressive."

"Take a seat." Misook waves to an empty chair, her fingers fluttering in a way that reminds me of the ruffling feathers of a bird. "We have much to discuss."

I do, for they wear expressions that stir something deep

within me. Hope.

"It's important that nobody followed you." Jiwoon glances to the ladder, as if half expecting Rui to drop to the floor.

"Nobody did." I shake my head. "They leave me unsupervised in my quarters. I passed no soul on my way."

Misook looks impressed. "They leave you alone? No guards, no overseers?"

I dip my head in a nod. "It's part of the Pied Piper's game."

"Jiwoon told us that you stole a tapestry from him, and now you pay the price." Misook twirls a strand of hair around a ringed finger. "If you don't kill him, I assume he kills you?"

"He's still trying to decide between a beheading or shooting an arrow into my heart," I reply, pinching the hourglass between my thumb and forefinger, drawing the Revolutionaries' attention toward the falling sand. "Today is my fourth day in Gyeulcheon." Four. Rui's favorite number, and an unlucky one, at that. I suppose I should be glad that thus far, my luck seems to be fully intact, for I've found the Revolution. "I have ten days left to kill the Pied Piper. If I fail, my life is forfeited."

"And all for a tapestry," Misook muses.

"This tapestry." Hangyeol scans me in puzzlement. "What do you know of it?"

"Only that it was left unattended in Sunpo, yet apparently was close to Rui's heart. If he has one." I scowl.

"Only one thing has ever been held that close to his heart." Shadows dance across Jiwoon's face. "And she died a near century ago."

"She?" I feel a flicker of triumph, knowing that Rui has suffered, has lost as I have—but it soon gutters out, replaced by an uncomfortable feeling in the pit of my stomach. It's a feeling that I can't quite place, and I do my best to ignore it as Hangyeol shrugs.

"He was in love. Or so they say. His long hair, it is a symbol of mourning. When Dokkaebi grieve for lost partners, we grow our hair long. But for him to have *loved*…" He shares a doubtful look with Misook.

"He's incapable of such a thing." Misook is now toying with a heavily beaded necklace. She rarely seems to keep still. "He's a monster. A tyrant."

"Agreed," I say in barely concealed delight, finding that I quite enjoy these people.

"Lina." Jiwoon leans forward. "Your arrival here, and your unprecedented access to Haneul Rui, has let us dare hope. We have been set on bringing a new reign to Gyeulcheon for so long, yet have never been given an opportunity, an in. But you, if you join our ranks, you give us that in, that opportunity. But you must promise that you will stay loyal and true to the cause."

"I promise." I straighten in my seat and meet his eyes. "But you must promise to stay true to me, as well." I am no stranger to the inner workings of groups, of the deceit and duplicity that stem from collaborations. "And I want collateral."

"Collateral," Jiwoon repeats. "That can be arranged."

I am no stranger to being betrayed. "If you cross me," I say quietly, "your names will be turned in to the emperor." It is a gamble—the names they've given me, other than Hangyeol's, could very well be false. But by the way Misook flinches, Hangyeol chokes, and Jiwoon blinks in surprise… I smile grimly. "My collateral."

There's a long silence. Wary looks are exchanged before Jiwoon nods. "Agreed. And as for collateral on our side…betray us, and we kill you." His stare is steady, even. So is mine as I incline my head in a nod. That's simple, and standard enough. During my time as a gang member, I've had many dealings along the lines of this.

"Fine."

"Then we'll begin." Jiwoon gestures to Misook, who nods.

Hangyeol straightens in his chair.

"Jiwoon founded this group twenty years ago. We call ourselves the Revolution—for obvious reasons." Misook's gaze crackles with intensity. "Haneul Rui is unfit for the throne. The bastard lost control of our empire centuries ago. Our land."

"You mean my realm," I say slowly. "Iseung."

Misook nods darkly. "Once, the Dokkaebi ruled your Three Kingdoms. Now we are a forgotten myth, tucked into a corner of that mortal realm of yours."

"You can't say that you mean to reclaim Iseung."

Silence.

When I speak, my voice is low in warning. "Humans have done well on our own. We have built our own empires, our own cities. We would not bow down as easily as you think. If that is the goal of your group, then I will have no part in it." Anger thrums in my chest.

"Misook misspoke." Jiwoon hastily shakes his head. "We do not wish to reclaim your realm as our own. We wish only to reclaim what our lives were like when your realm was ours.

"When we ruled over the human realm, resources were plenty. Infinite resources. Infinite land. My family lived comfortably from dominating the fishing industry. Hangyeol and his brother created their own businesses as both jewelers and miners. Misook…"

"Trade," she says. "I was a trader. Furs, pelts, jewels, silks. I made a good living, enough to support myself and my family."

"When Haneul Rui lost control over your world, we were crammed into this one, an artificial realm made as an escape route. Five hundred years ago, we were forced to leave our hard-earned empire for a tiny world named Gyeulcheon, sealed in with no way to escape."

Hangyeol nods. "Only the emperor and members of his inner court, can utilize teleportation to travel to Sunpo, our last remaining territory. They're called Gaksi Dokkaebi…the strongest of us, the most powerful, the hardest to kill."

I think of our dinner, how Rui cared not that he had a blade protruding from his chest. Gaksi Dokkaebi are indeed difficult to kill.

"But Sunpo provides nothing for us. No food, no resources. It crawls with crime, with dirt. Many of us have even forgotten that we still hold power over Sunpo." Misook sighs.

"We lost our riches with your realm." Jiwoon stares at the flickering flame of the candle, his fists curled. "Lost our lifestyles, our identities."

"I have a bakery now," Misook says quietly. "It barely makes enough money to pay rent."

"I work in the kitchens. As a spy, yes, but for pay as well. I earn close to nothing." Hangyeol shifts uncomfortably in his seat.

"And I work double shifts at an apothecary," Jiwoon concludes. "We went from riches to rags in the blink of an eye."

"Haneul enforces a tax too high for any of us to pay. He traps us within the walls of this damned realm. He demands our respect, and yet gives us none." A muscle in Misook's jaw jumps. "We have families. Children. Siblings, young brothers and sisters who are hungry and hurting."

An image of Eunbi flashes across my mind's eye, and a surge of sympathy twists my heart at the pain in Misook's eyes.

"How can we support them? How can we provide for them when our meager earnings go to the tax?" Misook shakes her head. "It is impossible."

"Killing Haneul Rui will lead to a crisis that can spawn a revolution, the means to a greater good. Haneul has no heir. His general or adviser may step to the throne, but they have no experience in ruling. There are many more of us who lost our livelihoods when we were forced to retreat into Gyeulcheon but are too scared to act. Killing the emperor will put the kingdom in a place of turbulence, and that is when revolutions begin to grow." Jiwoon's gaze is dark behind his glasses. "We will weed out his court. I see a realm ruled by the people, a realm grounded by the moral of fairness for all. We could live how we once did, in prosperity."

"You're our hope," Misook says. "You're Sunpo's Reaper. You live unsupervised in the palace. The king is literally inviting you to murder him—and nobody's standing in your way."

"When we first heard of you, we thought it was too good to be true. But Hangyeol observed you for a few days. Saw how you came and went as you pleased. Then I, hopeful, met with you in the village. And you were looking for us."

"If we play this right," Hangyeol says quietly, "we will all get what we want. Us, a new empire. You, a return home."

I nod slowly. "A win for us all."

"Exactly."

Jiwoon's eyes are dark. "We will make this worth your time, Lina. My family, we are descended from the blood of Hwanung, God of Laws. He is, in many ways, our father. When his blood spilled onto that ancient battlefield, my lineage began. I believe that even absent, Hwanung watches over us still, steering me toward justice. He is the patron of the Revolution. And he will watch over you as well."

I feel a burst of pleasure at the thought of Hwanung fighting alongside us against the Gyeulcheon emperor. My heart begins to beat excitedly in my chest as I lean forward in my seat.

"You need me and I need you. I have tried and failed to kill Haneul Rui twice. He's strong. Fast." I scowl. "I'm a trained assassin, a warrior. I've killed and maimed and stolen nearly my whole life. I've failed only once before this. But Rui is proving impossible to kill."

"We know," Hangyeol says simply. "And we have a solution."

"A solution?" I repeat hungrily.

The trio exchanges glances before Jiwoon stands and pulls a piece of parchment from the wall. Wordlessly, he slides it over to me. The edges are frayed, like it has been torn from a book. I hold it to the candlelight.

It's a watercolor of a berry bush, painted in smooth, elegant strokes. The berries are gleaming and plump, as big as the tip of my thumb, and colored a shining blue-gray.

Wongun berries, the dark ink above the illustration reads.

"These berries are a mutation," Jiwoon explains. "A side effect from artificially creating a realm. They line the Black River that our village's creek leads to. Word has it that Haneul tried to stop them from growing, but the bushes are relentless and cannot be controlled by even him. So he's kept them a secret. The emperor decreed that the Black River is dangerous—but we know it's not because of its rushing waters. He doesn't want us finding these berries."

"What's so special about them?" I trace the watercolor with a fingernail. "They look very plain."

"Alone, nothing," Jiwoon admits. "But within the apothecary, I have learned that when you mix one ingredient with another, the result can be incredibly useful."

"The wongun berries contain a protein that, when mixed with a few other ingredients, increases power within the body," Misook says.

"What kind of ingredients?" I ask warily, still processing their words.

"The kind of ingredients that you can find in an apothecary," Misook explains slyly. "But the point is, for a human, consuming such a mixture will heighten your strength to that of a Dokkaebi."

"And if a Dokkaebi were to take it?" I question. The Revolution exchange indeterminable looks as I frown. "What would happen then?"

"Their strength would be heightened to that of a Gaksi

Dokkaebi," Misook says after a few moments. "Their powers would grow significantly. The enhancer doesn't do anything to Gaksi Dokkaebi," she adds before I can ask. "It works only on lesser beings, like us—humans and plain Dokkaebi."

"If that's the case," I reply slowly, "why can't one of you take it instead? Why do you need *me*?"

"Because even if one of us consumes it, we lack your proximity and bargain with Haneul—and that is the greatest weapon of all, Lina. The emperor is inviting *you* to kill him, not us." Jiwoon's eyes are dark. "Even without the enhancer, you stand a better chance of succeeding where we will surely fail. If *you* consume it, you'll stand an *irrefutable* chance of killing the emperor." Jiwoon's voice hums with determination. "You'll kill him. And we'll all get what we need."

My heart is pounding. An enhancer, to increase my strength. To level the playing field. I know that I'll take it, despite any risks, despite any possible side effects. I *need* to take it. "I have to kill him," I whisper. "We need to get those berries as soon as possible."

"We will. Tomorrow night. We'll meet here." Jiwoon pauses and stretches out an ink-smudged hand. "Welcome to the Revolution, Shin Lina."

CHAPTER TWENTY-ONE

I had killed Unima Hisao about a dozen times.

If Unima Hisao were a mannequin, that was.

Wearily, I set down my bow and frowned at the arrow-embedded dummy some length away. The plan was barely formulated—I still had no clue whether the kill would be a long or short distance away, as Sang was still mapping the layout of Unima's mansion and the twins were still drawing out information regarding the rotation of its guards.

So for now, I was practicing both long-range and short-range kills. Today had been long range. I brooded over Unima's betrayal as I yanked my arrows from the dummy's chest and stuffed them back into the quiver.

"The poor mannequin," Yoonho's voice, low and gravelly, said behind me. "Your aim is something to be admired."

I turned around and straightened. "Unima will get what he's earned. Pulling sponsorship, redirecting it to the Blackbloods? The man must have a death wish. Lucky for him," I muttered, hitching the quiver over my shoulder, "I plan on granting it."

"Unima will pay. As will Konrarnd Kalmin." Yoonho rubbed

his left shoulder with a grimace. "The Blackbloods are a pathetic excuse for a gang. I want them out of this kingdom. Gone."

"As do I." I leaned against a wooden wall, folding my arms. "But you have to admit that what they lack in sophistication, they make up for in force." We'd been fighting them for years.

"They do," Yoonho agreed. "But all fights must end eventually, and killing Unima will send them into a frenzy. We must be more than ready for retaliation." He paused and I frowned. Were the circles under his eyes darker than usual? The wrinkles on his face deeper? "This could be our final fight. Kill Unima, Lina," Yoonho said, turning away. "Then we will strike."

The note arrives the following morning, slipped underneath the crack in my bedroom door.

I pause where I am sitting at the low table, chewing on a bite of honey-drenched rice and massaging the crick in my neck — courtesy of my restless sleep the night before.

Even in the world of drowsiness and dreams, I do not escape my past. It haunts me relentlessly, slithering with the cold grace of a deadly serpent, following my every movement.

Words of inky black, thin and slanted, have been etched across a slip of thick, cream-colored parchment.

Little thief, the unfamiliar hand reads, *in retribution for that last dance you so wickedly deprived me of, you will find me waiting for you on the opposite side of the garden wall that you are so very fond of climbing. I do not suggest being late, for I'm waiting most impatiently, and there is nothing I hate more than boredom.*

His Royal Majesty,
Emperor Haneul Rui

My jaw works as I reread the note before crumpling it into

a ball, the still-wet ink running down my fingers like blood.

A morning spent with Haneul Rui does not sound altogether appealing, despite the fact that I now harbor the upper hand in our game—that I now have the Revolution behind me.

I hesitate as my throat tightens. Is it possible that Rui knows of this development? I am overcome with the desire to hide underneath my bed instead, armed to the teeth as I avoid what is surely a punishment of pain.

Yet it is clear that I have no choice but to follow the emperor's demands.

I recall how his lips parted during that final song to call for me… And how I darted away, delighting in taunting him.

There is a price to pay for everything, and I suppose that Rui has already arranged the particular price for my deceiving him.

I reluctantly knot my hair back into a tight braid and secure my jikdo to the belt cinching the waist of my cotton pants. There's no telling what the Piper has planned for today, but it's safe to assume that being armed won't hurt.

After yanking on a pair of heavy black boots and rolling up the sleeves of my lightweight tunic, I shove the crumpled note into my pocket and stalk through the palace.

Hangyeol and Asha send me wary looks as I storm through the kitchens, but there's no time for either to question me before I'm ducking out the kitchen doors into the garden and stomping toward the wall. The human girls look vacantly after me as I haul myself over the wall, my fingers gripping the rough edges of stone.

As I swing one leg over the other and drop down onto the blanket of grass and moss below, my leg barking only slightly in protest, my eyes meet Rui's.

"Hello, runaway," he purrs.

The emperor is leaning against a nearby oak tree, his face half concealed in darkness by both the shadows of the looming forest and the wide bamboo rim of the gat he wears atop his loose hair. The cylindrical hat is crafted of a sheer, dark material with a beaded string looping underneath the chin and accompanied by ribbons of black cloth as well.

To my surprise, he is wearing a relatively simple hanbok—one that lacks the intricate patterns, the flowing fabric, and trailing silk ribbons. The jeogori top is simple gray cotton, as are the baji bottoms. Both are plain, light, and easy to move in. A moment later, I see why.

Nickering a few feet away, two white stallions nibble at a patch of grass, their tails swishing as they eat. One is saddled and harnessed, the other bare.

"What is this?" I demand cautiously. I try not to look at his hair, at the long straight locks rippling in the wind. Who did he love? Who did he lose?

"Those are horses. I assume that you have them on Iseung as well." Rui smiles at my frown as he pushes himself from the trunk of the tree. His silver eyes glimmer as he follows my gaze. "I thought I would show you the finer parts of my kingdom," Rui says as he turns back to me. "I assume that you can ride?"

I can't help raising my brows. "You're giving me a tour?"

He smiles, slyly magnanimous. "And why should I not? Your little trips along this trail have showed me your curiosity." Rui strides over to the saddled stallion and leads it by its reins to where I stand. It's large, sleek, and powerful, with dark eyes narrowing down at me as if it can sense my secrets. "This is Byeol," he says as he pats the horse's well-groomed flank. "He's a mellow steed, and easy enough to ride." Rui cuts a gaze to me over his shoulder as he makes his way toward the other horse. "If, of course, you already know how."

I bite the inside of my cheek at his wry tone. I'm a decent rider—growing up, a fellow farmer gave me horseback riding lessons on his mare. But I do not trust Byeol, a creature of Rui's realm.

Especially as the horse whickers in my ear and foul-temperedly stomps his foot.

Mellow, my ass.

Rui has already mounted his stallion, and waits for me by the edge of the shadowed forest, near the beginning of the trail.

My cheeks heat as he watches me struggle to clamber onto Byeol. The stallion is clearly not fond of me—he bucks and snorts, sending me toppling to the ground, biting back a cry as sharp pain shoots along my left leg.

I drag myself upright, glaring at the horse as he turns back to his grass. His tail whips me in the face, and I'm left pulling a frown at his rear. "Foul thing."

Rui clucks his tongue, and his mare trots closer to me. "I suppose that you can always walk."

Not with my left leg hurting so. I grimace, unwilling to allow him to watch me limp behind him. "I would rather ride." I approach Byeol's flank again, determined to succeed in mounting him this time.

But the stallion rears back as I come closer, a high-pitched whinny tearing through the air—and then he is gone, galloping around the wall, his hooves clopping on the ground and sending clods of dirt flying in his wake. Furious, I gape in disbelief at the patch of grass where Byeol stood just moments before.

Rui chuckles. "How incredibly unfortunate." He arches a brow down at me as I glare upward. "I suppose that you'll have to ride with me." The emperor extends a hand down, the invitation clear. Ride with Haneul Rui or walk. "Duri won't mind."

"*I* will," I mutter, even as I grab his hand.

A ride on horseback, even with Rui, is much preferable to walking. I crush his fingers in an iron-tight grip as I swing myself up, settling so I sit just before him. My back rests against his chest, and I can't help but suspect that the bastard has somehow *planned* this.

I grind my teeth as my cheeks heat. Memories of our dance come flooding back to me. His hand on my back, the fragrance of plum as he tugged me closer, the way he led me with the grace of a swan.

I lean as far away from Rui as I can. He chuckles in my ear as he gently twines his hands through Duri's white mane and clucks his tongue. The beads of his juyeong tickle my neck as the horse begins to trot into the forest, hooves clopping against the trail.

"You don't need reins?" I ask suspiciously. "Or a saddle?"

His voice is a soft rumble from just above my head. "Duri is fond of me. There's no need to harness and saddle her. She will listen to me and obey my commands."

The smell of the forest, sweet and thick with late-spring foliage, quickly overtakes us, along with a blanket of cool shadow. Duri nickers slightly as a squirrel darts across the winding trail with acorns bulging in its fat cheeks. I watch it go.

"Do all creatures of your realm do that? Obey you, I mean?"

Rui snorts slightly. "How easy life would be if that were true," he dryly replies, and I can't help but suspect that perhaps he is thinking of the rebel movement. "The realm may obey me, but the creatures are their own. Duri is unique in this way."

As if in confirmation, Duri snorts.

Birds sing in the high treetops, chirping and chortling as their wings flutter through the foliage. I crane my neck, studying the way the morning moonlight pours through the leaves above, dappling the forest with butter-yellow patches that glisten and gleam. As we ride, I cannot help but wonder which god or goddess Rui's family line is descended from. I open my mouth to ask but abruptly close it. To question him may signify that I have been speaking to other Dokkaebi. He must not suspect my involvement with the Revolution.

The back of my head bumps against Rui's shoulder, and I abruptly look down, reminded of the way his arms are enwrapped around me as he holds the strands of Duri's mane. I can feel his steady heartbeat through my back. Unconsciously, I have leaned back into him. I bite the inside of my cheek, hating how my own heart has begun to hammer.

"I am aware that you've already seen the nearest village," Rui murmurs, steering Duri off the trail. She picks her way through the tall grass and winding trees, carrying us deeper into the heart of the forest.

"I have," I say noncommittally, my hand drifting toward my jikdo. I do not like how far we are venturing into the woods. Unease prickles my spine, and I mark each passing tree, determined to be able to find my way back to the trail, should the need arise. "Where are we going, exactly?"

I feel Rui shrug, the motion smooth and graceful. "Gyeulcheon is a realm of wonders. I was thinking of showing you the hill lands or the forest glades. There are other villages that we can venture into as well, although if you'd like to observe the caves, we may do that, too. It is your choice."

The thought of entering a dark, grimy cave with only Rui for company does not quite pique my interest.

As if sensing the direction of my thoughts, Rui laughs softly. His breath caresses the side of my face. "I am not attempting to assassinate you in some hidden place, Lina. I keep to the rules of our game. Your fourteen days are not yet up, and I still haven't decided between a beheading or an arrow to the heart. Perhaps the latter would be fitting, after your attempt during our dinner...but it's still a debate."

I swallow, my mouth suddenly dry. "I'll see the hill lands," I answer as coldly as I can, even while my heart lurches uneasily in my chest. As Rui clucks his tongue to Duri, who nickers in response, I frown. "Your punishments are never what I expect them to be," I find myself muttering. "Kitchen duty, a ball, a grand tour…"

"Would you prefer a dungeon of torture? It could be arranged."

"In place of spending a morning with you?" I twist and flash him a sweet smile. "Oh, most certainly."

He smirks back. "You know," he says as I turn back around, "I was quite looking forward to our last dance."

"A shame that I had to leave."

"A shame. Although there was no shortage of others who were willing to take your place," he adds.

"Oh?" I reply, struggling to keep my voice nonchalant. This is ridiculous. I should not care who he dances with. I *do* not care who he dances with. The idea that I would is ludicrous. "Are you seeking to be congratulated?" I demand when a few moments of silence pass.

His shoulders shake as he laughs, midnight soft. "Perhaps I am."

"Well then." I twist my lips, even though he cannot see them. "You'll be disappointed."

"There's no need to be jealous," he murmurs, and I swallow hard as he leans closer to me, his lips grazing my ear. "I didn't dance with any of them."

A strange emotion, cool and soothing, washes over me. I narrow my eyes in displeasure, even as I question: "Why?"

"Well," he replies, brushing aside an overhead branch as we ride, "I find that the possibility that my dance partner may stab me to death at any moment adds a certain thrill that simply cannot be replicated by those who are *not* determined to stab me to death."

Not entirely sure what to make of that statement, I settle on rolling my eyes and watching as the trees and undergrowth of the forest begin to grow sparser. It is hard to tell how long we have been riding. Perhaps it has been an hour, maybe two. Either way, as Duri exits the forest, I blink back surprise as rolling slopes emerge into view. As I take in the sight, Duri lingers on the edge of the woods, nibbling on a bit of grass.

The hill lands are vast and impressive, a shade of deep emerald that I have never before known. The mounds of earth stretch as far as the eye can see, rippling waves in an ocean of greenery, and embroidered with forests of vibrant flowers and snaking lines of trees.

I see a glimmer of aquamarine in the distance—a lake that reflects the cerulean sky above. Birds fly in *V* formations through the clouds, their voices high and sweet as they cry out in rapture.

"The hill lands," Rui says softly behind me. "Are they to your liking?"

They're beautiful, I want to say. *They are utterly unlike anything I have ever seen.*

But I remind myself who has brought me here. Who created them. And I say nothing.

When I don't reply, Rui slides from Duri.

It is only when he's on the ground that I realize how accustomed I've grown to his touch. Disliking the notion, I ignore Rui's extended hand and jump down to the ground, gritting my teeth against the impact. Yet it is still jarring against my leg.

"*Gods*," I curse before I can stop myself, unable to refrain from bending over and bracing my hands against the aching thigh and rubbing it in an effort to relieve the pain.

Rui watches me with an inscrutable expression. His visage is devoid of any amusement, but there is a flash of concern, which is soon replaced by intrigue.

I grit my teeth. I don't want him to inquire how it happened—how my leg was ruined—because it is a story that I do not give out willingly to those I cannot, or do not, trust. But his question diverges from what I expect.

"You take the names of the gods." He's frowning slightly, as if I'm a puzzle he cannot quite figure out. "You told me, in the throne room, that you had not forgotten. I see now that it is true."

I straighten, my hands falling to my sides. I shift my weight onto my right leg. "Some of us still hope." *As futile as it may be.*

His eyes glitter. "Hope for their return from Okhwang?"

My lips twist downward. "There is nothing wrong with hope," I bite back. That is what Eomma and Appa used to say as we gazed up at the night sky to the hidden world of the gods, our bellies aching with hunger and muscles sore from working the farm. *There is nothing wrong with hope.*

They may be gone now, but my belief—my hope—is not.

Rui cocks his head. "I did not mean to offend. I simply did not expect you to be religious."

"Why? Because I'm an assassin? There is a god of death, no?" I straighten indignantly. "Emperor Yeomra of the underworld, Jeoseung. And there is a god of trickery. Seokga. And the creator god, Mireuk, did he not also birth suffering? Pain? These three will be my patrons, if they are to return."

"But even Jeoseung is abandoned now," Rui replies, his eyes still on me in clear curiosity. "Emperor Yeomra has abandoned it for Okhwang, where the gods and goddesses pay no heed to mortal strife. They feast and drink and make merry, unconcerned with the problems of your realm of Iseung. They are not coming back, Shin Lina. Even the Dokkaebi have not heard from the gods and goddesses for centuries upon centuries. There has been no whisper from Jacheongbi, even when the soils yield no crops. No sign of Samshin-Halmeoni, even as mortal women die in childbirth. And where is Hwanung when laws are broken and promises betrayed? They are gone, little thief. And I very much doubt that they plan on returning."

"That doesn't mean that they will not come back," I insist, my throat tight. How dare he dismiss my hope? "My prayers could one day be answered."

Rui's gaze grows somber as a warm wind dances through the hills, fluttering his hair and brushing a hand against my hot cheek. "And what do you pray for?"

I open my mouth, tasting the words on my tongue.

For Eunbi's safety. For Kalmin's death.

For a life away from the Blackbloods.

For forgiveness.

"I pray to Yeomra that next time, you'll stay dead when I kill you."

CHAPTER TWENTY-TWO

Rui's eyes glimmer. "Well then," he says. "I hope that for my sake, the gods remain absent."

Snorting lightly under my breath, I turn back to the hill lands.

It's strange that such beauty can exist within a realm belonging to one so notorious. Duri and I watch as Rui begins to stride down the forested slope, tossing a wicked smile over his shoulder.

"Where are you going?" I demand, guarded.

"I said I'd show you the hill lands, Shin Lina," he replies. "So follow me, and allow me to show you."

I grimace as I trail after him, my limbs aching as we climb over sets of rolling hills. I keep one hand on my jikdo as I walk, boots sinking into soft mounds of flowers. As they are crushed underfoot, their fragrance reaches my nose—saccharine and sweet, like raw honey and crushed sugar.

My breathing is a rattle in my chest by the time Rui finally takes pause atop a towering hill. I'm some ways below him, and struggling hard to conceal my limp. He stands on the hill with his back to me, straight and proud, his hair rippling in the air. When I finally stand at his side, unable to level my ragged breathing, I look daggers at him.

That this outing is a punishment makes much more sense now.

But he doesn't turn to me. At least, not at first.

Instead, he leans down to the ground, long fingers grazing the pale pink petals of a flower clump. I watch as he plucks one at its stem and then, finally turning, extends it to me.

My mind eddies out as Rui arches a brow at me. "For you."

I blink. The Dokkaebi emperor has offered me a flower. I wonder what he's plotting. "No," I say, and abruptly clear my throat. My voice is hoarse.

Rui's smile is sharp, as if my reply is exactly what he expected. Shrugging, he turns back around and gathers more flowers in his hands—some of pastel colorings, others rich and vibrant—and takes a seat on the hilltop, seemingly content to weave their slender stalks together and gaze out at the sea of sloping verdure. Still standing, I can't help but feel the slightest bit awkward—and when minutes go by without a word from Rui, I begin to pick the flowers myself.

I do it angrily at first, ripping the stems from the ground with harsh fingers. Although the hill lands are beautiful, I'm still at a loss as to Rui's motives for bringing me here. Lurking under the guise of a pleasant outing, what are they truly? At the end of this game, one of us will die by the other's hand.

He must be plotting something. If I were him, I would be.

But the flowers are as delicate as they are beautiful, and soon, I find myself picking them with care, selecting a rainbow of colors for my quickly growing bouquet. Baby blues, sweet lavenders, subtle creams. A butterfly flits past, pink wings shimmering in the golden day's moonlight. Slowly, my frustration eases and, although wariness remains, my chest is no longer tight.

Cautiously, I sit next to Rui, glancing out at the scenery beyond our hill before focusing my attention on what the emperor is doing.

He's woven a crown of flowers, I see — a crown of pinks and reds, stems laced tightly together. His fingers move nimbly as he continues to weave. "My mother taught me," he says. "When I was young."

Unbidden, an image of Rui as a small child rises in my mind — with rosy cheeks and mussed hair, sitting in his mother's lap and watching as she weaves a crown of daisies and other blossoms. I wonder what she was like. Beloved, if his court's reaction to my calling him a gaesaekki is any indication.

Rui plucks a blue flower from the ground and begins to add it into the circlet. "The pollen always made her sneeze," he continues with a fond smile. "But she would weave regardless, sneezing the entire time. Her hands were always sticky with pollen afterward."

I fiddle with a flower stem, remembering my eomma. A strong but quiet woman, her hands were callused and her nails bitten.

It has been long enough that I feel only a dull ache at the memory of her and Appa, so at odds with the raw scraping pain that followed the shipwreck.

Even then, I hadn't let myself feel it for very long. There was Eunbi to take care of. So I shoved that pain aside, and when I met the Talons it became a bruise — hurting only if I pressed down on it too hard.

"One time," Rui continues, "I stepped on a wasp's nest. The infernal things chased me all the way into the mortal village. I imagine it was quite the sight — a young prince running away from wasps, chased by the continent's empress and yelling his head off."

I can't help but smile at the vision. "Did you get stung?"

"You sound hopeful." The emperor chuckles softly. "You'll be pleased to hear that I did, and screamed the entire time. The stings burned rather badly despite my ability to heal, and there was a pond nearby—so I jumped into the water. My mother jumped in after me, royal robes and all. We spent the afternoon splashing each other, much to the bemusement of the human townsfolk. She was spirited, my eomma."

Something in my chest cracks a little bit. All the times he has spoken of his eomma, it has been in the past tense. It is a pain I understand. A part of me wants to reach for him, to ask what happened, but I hastily stomp out the urge. *I don't care*, I tell myself. *I don't care.*

After a moment, Rui points to the glimmer of blue I spotted earlier. "Over there," he says, "is a pond that is popular for swimming among the children here." I follow his gaze to the glimmer of blue I spotted earlier. "I based it on the one my mother and I played in. It's beautiful, is it not?"

It is. Light catches on the lazuline waters, glistening and glittering. It's a large body of water, encircled by the hills. Even from far away, I can make out white blurs that can only be swans, gracefully floating on the sparkling surface. His eomma's memory, eternally enshrined.

"And if you look farther north," Rui continues, "you'll see the barest hint of white-capped peaks. Gyeulcheon's mountain range. It is always wintertime on the mountains, no matter what the true season of the realm."

There are indeed faint shadows of craggy mountains, half obscured by a few low clouds. I glance sideways at Rui. "By your own design, I assume."

"I do have a fondness for the winter season." He turns to me now, and there is again that strange, shy hope that I have spotted once before—as if he wishes for me to find what he has created beautiful. It shines through his perpetually sly, wicked face as clearly as the sun that does not shine here in Gyeulcheon.

That look is so utterly different than what I expected from the Pied Piper, the Dokkaebi emperor. Swallowing hard against an emotion that tastes strangely like guilt—bitter and acrid, edged with a terrible dryness—I look back to the mountaintops. "How large is Gyeulcheon?" I force myself to ask, shoving aside that foolish sense of shame.

"It is as large and as small as I wish for it to be." Rui shrugs. "Pocket realms work differently than normal realms. There is no set size, not when they are outside the regular planes of existence. Perhaps Gyeulcheon is no bigger than a leaf, or your pinky finger. Or perhaps it is as large as your Eastern Continent. There is no such thing as relative size, not in Gyeulcheon."

"And you created it," I say, unable to keep a hoarse cadence of horrified wonder out of my tone. "You created it all."

"I did." He inclines his head. "No doubt you are wondering why."

I cut a look at him from the corner of my eye. "Everybody knows the story."

A muscle in Rui's jaw flexes. "I very much doubt that," he quietly replies.

"Oh?" Straightening with the desire to prove him wrong, I lift a brow. "The Dokkaebi lost control over Sunpo, Bonseyo, and Wyusan. With nowhere else to go, you created this realm with your power, and your kind retreated here." *Without any chance to escape*, I add silently, remembering my conversation with the Revolution.

"Ah." His lips curl upward ever so slightly. "So I see that everybody knows only what they think they know. You mortals amuse me. Filling in the gaps of your history with stories of your own. You intermingle fiction with fact."

"Is that not what happened?" I narrow my eyes suspiciously. "Tell me your fact, then. Or your fiction."

"No, I don't think I will." The Pied Piper shrugs idly. "It's a very long story that is known by very few, and one that will undoubtedly put a damper on an otherwise pleasant conversation. Although I must admit, I am curious. I'd assumed that another assassination attempt was guaranteed today. Perhaps I was wrong. How incredibly disappointing."

With my hand that is not holding the flowers, I unsheathe my jikdo. The sword's sharp metal blade gleams as I level it at him, the blade caressing his neck. "Perhaps I am just biding my time."

Rolling his eyes, Rui brushes the blade away. I allow him, for what I have said is true. I *am* waiting for the perfect moment: for the enhancer to be consumed. "You will have to do better than that, Reaper."

"Oh, I will." I tilt my lips into a cruel smile as I tilt my sword this way and that, letting it gleam in the sunlight before deftly sheathing it. Rui watches the blade in clear entertainment as it disappears. "You may rest assured that your blood will coat my hands soon enough."

"How delightful. I do look forward to it," he purrs. "It is most anticipated."

"Good."

"Good." A wicked glimmer shines in his lustrous eyes. "I wish you the very best of luck."

"I don't believe I need luck anymore," I reply coolly, standing, my fist tight around my bouquet.

Rui simply looks amused. "As you say, little thief." He rises smoothly and—to my shock—places the crown of flowers upon my head. It's too big, and it slips down to my brows, bringing with it the honeyed scent of sweet, fresh nectar. Rui steps back, admiring his handiwork as I attempt to decide whether I should be angry or bewildered. I settle on both.

Yet I am feeling another emotion alongside those two—

something warm, and light, and altogether forbidden.

My face suddenly feels hot, too hot. Quickly, I remove the crown from my head. There's no denying that it's beautiful, intricately patterned, and despite myself I hesitate to crush it underfoot. The memory of Rui's fingers carefully looping the stems together lingers in my mind, refusing to fade.

Sensing my uncertainty, Rui takes the crown and begins to untangle the stems from one another. "For Duri, then."

For a confusing, awful moment, I want to snatch the circlet back before he can deconstruct it completely. I want to wear it, to claim it as mine. But I don't, and when we return to Rui's stallion, he weaves the flowers into her flowing white mane. Duri nickers happily, nuzzling the emperor and stomping her feet, clearly delighted by her new accessories.

Rui mounts her gracefully and extends his hand to me. "We should return," he says as a warm wind sweeps through the forest's edge. My fingers are too loose around my bouquet and the gust sweeps the flowers away, carrying them to the hill lands beyond.

"Welcome back." Jiwoon inclines his head as I nimbly descend the ladder that night, followed, once again, by Hangyeol.

"We won't be here long." Jiwoon is dressed in all black, as are Misook and Hangyeol. A night of stealth is clearly ahead.

"To the berries, then," I say slowly. The berries, the key component of the enhancer. The berries, which will help me win this godsdamned bargain.

"The Black River." Misook nods.

"You have a weapon?" Hangyeol asks.

I nod, tapping the jikdo sheathed at my waist. "Stolen from the Gyeulcheon armory itself," I reply to the delight of Misook, who crows with laughter.

Even Jiwoon cracks a smile, but it falters as he meets my gaze. "I trust that you can swim."

It's a long walk from the village to the Black River, a walk that brings me through yet another shadowed forest humming with the eerie song of a night bird.

As I fight my limp, I wish for Duri. Rui's stallion is steady and sweet, and with her, I'm willing to wager the trip could take half the time. I'd even settle for Byeol. But I have neither.

By the time the Revolution and I finally reach the rocky riverbank, my limp is prominent.

I take a moment to massage the aching muscles as I take in the Black River. It roars as its frothing obsidian waters crash and churn over slick black rocks.

"The berries," I say, scouring the shore for berry bushes and seeing none. "Where are they?" Annoyance tightens my jaw as I turn toward the Revolution behind me. A finger taps the hilt of my jikdo in impatience as a muscle pulses across my temple. If they have lied to me, they will find that my wrath is not something that can be easily escaped.

"Look." Light from Jiwoon's lantern dances across the barren bank, flickering as a cool gust of wind sweeps through the night. His expression is somber as he directs his light across the rushing waters, illuminating an array of foliage, among which are berry bushes.

They are a dark, leafy green, and I can just make out the plump blue-gray berries glistening under the lantern's orange glow.

"They're on the other side," Hangyeol says, looking at me. "There's only one way to get to them."

I grimace as the river's water froths and swirls. "You're

Dokkaebi. What of your teleportation?"

"I'll remind you that teleportation is a power now reserved only for Gaksi Dokkaebi. Once, all Dokkaebi could materialize wherever we pleased. Now, we are confined within Gyeulcheon. Rui knows that if this land allowed us to teleport, we would leave. Return to the world that he lost control over, despite Haneul's belief that Iseung is no longer meant for Dokkaebi." Misook shakes her head. "We've tried to swim across to the berries before. The water is mind-numbing."

"Misook almost drowned." Jiwoon glances at Hangyeol. "Hangyeol went under for several minutes. I made it halfway before blacking out."

"You've tried before and failed? This particular bit of information seems to have been withheld from me." Disappointment, sharp and cold, bites at my chest. If these three immortals failed to make their way to the berries, how do they expect me to?

It is yet another dead end, another false start. My jaw tightens as I turn away, seething. I will find a way. Without these berries, without the enhancer they can create. Without the Revolution.

"Lina." Jiwoon grabs my arm. I stiffen but halt, yanking myself out of his grip. "Wait. You must at least try." Nervously, he pushes up his glasses. "Please."

"The three of you failed. I can't see how I would not."

"Because you've had years of training. You've tested your bodily limits hundreds of times," he replies solemnly.

"Besides," Misook says, quirking a grin that doesn't reach her eyes, "I can't swim. Which explains the near-drowning part."

"You can swim, Lina, and you're strong. You must at least try." Jiwoon closes his eyes. "Please." I see desperation on his face, the same sentiment mirrored on his companions. Loosening a deep breath, I eye the dark waters. I am a strong swimmer. Yoonho saw to that. Once, I had no choice but to leap off a pirate's ship in Sunpo's harbor. I swam the six miles back to shore, slicing through warm, murky water until my feet touched the silky sand of the harbor's bottom.

Fine.

I will try, but if I fail and somehow manage to escape a watery death, I'll ensure that these Dokkaebi regret sending me to the river.

"How many berries do we need." A demand. Not a question.

"As many as you can retrieve. You have pockets?"

"Some." I ignore the hope flaring on the Revolutionaries' faces as I kick off my heavy boots and shrug off my thick cloak so I am clad in just a tunic and pants. My hourglass necklace gleams in the darkness. The top half is almost half empty. Gritting my teeth, I reach for my sword, still strapped at my hip, but Jiwoon shakes his head.

"Keep it."

Warily, I oblige. Perhaps I'll need it to cut through the thorns of the berry bush. Before me, the water swirls with fragments of dark ice. "How deep does it get?"

"Deep enough. Twenty—maybe thirty—feet."

"If I drown, rest assured, I will haunt you as a Gwisin for eternity."

Jiwoon, at least, has the grace to look worried. I send the trio a final dark look before beginning to wade into the Black River.

"Oh, and Lina?" Misook calls. I turn around to meet her eyes, which have darkened with worry. "The fish have teeth."

Delightful. How absolutely delightful.

CHAPTER TWENTY-THREE

The water numbs my legs as I wade in to my knees and brace myself against the rushing current. I'm conscious of the rebels' unwavering attention as I shiver, the river swallowing my thighs. My waist. The current strengthens, and I grasp onto a slippery rock for support.

The berry bushes are at least fifty yards away. I take a deep breath.

I can do it. I can. I just have to take the plunge.

"Habaek," I whisper to the river god, "do not let me drown."

I can do this.

"Keep the light on me," I shout over the crash and rush of the river.

For Eunbi, for myself, I *will* do this.

Gulping a breath of air heavy with the salty, egg-like smell of the river, I plunge into the pounding water. I'll swim underneath the current, under the crashing waves.

My muscles strain against the cold water. It's all blurry, all dark, beneath the water. I will my strength not to give out as I kick, swimming in strong, swift motions. My lungs burn like fire, and I push myself back to the surface, gasping as my head breaks through.

Almost halfway there. I am almost halfway there.

Liquid burns my nose, and I choke on the flavor of brackish water. Grains of silt crunch between my teeth as I grit them, submerging myself once again and pushing farther through the river.

No fish so far—although my body is so numb that I doubt I would actually feel their bite. I can barely even feel the pain in my left leg.

Riverweed tickles my stomach and winds itself loosely around my limbs. My knee scrapes against something rough, maybe a rock. The warmth of the pain is almost welcome. But the water has grown slightly shallower, and—

I am there.

I choke on a breath as I shoot through the water, the cold night air flooding my lungs.

The shore. I made it.

Dimly, I register the cheers of the rebels but don't bother turning.

Shaking violently, tunic crusting my skin with tiny icicles, I crawl toward the bushes on hands and knees across the riverbank's rocks.

The berries are hard and smooth in my hand, refusing to break from the bush. They resemble the watercolor perfectly. With a trembling hand, I saw through the branches with my jikdo. One, two, three...ten, eleven, twelve. Twelve berries, bulging in my pockets.

I button them closed and take a moment to gather my strength before turning to the water again. The swim back will undoubtedly be just as tiring.

But I'll do it.

Taking a deep breath, I dive back into the churning waves. I am so godsdamned tired as I push my way through the cold. I have just begun to surface for air when something catches my eye.

It's long and lean, almost like an eel, but not quite. Bulbous red eyes latch on to me as it slinks in a circle around my body, the small black hairs coating its body waving in the water. Pointed yellow teeth protrude from its gaping mouth as it leers.

The fish have teeth.

But this is no fish. This is a—a *snake*.

And underwater, as terror lances through me like a red-hot knife, I scream. Bubbles surround me as I frantically kick upward, away from the water serpent. My limbs are suddenly too slow and so uncoordinated as it shoots toward me. I am pathetically clumsy in the water, but I manage to twist out of its way. Panic is engulfing me, my chest is aching, for I'm still screaming. I can't stop, no matter how hard I try.

I have—

Weak as it is to admit, I have always feared snakes, and this, this *thing*—oh gods oh gods oh *gods*.

With a high-pitched whining, the creature twists and redirects itself toward me once again. I flinch and kick upward just after a burst of pain slashes its way across my cheek. I manage a shallow gulp of night air before the cursed thing wraps around my legs in a tight hold and yanks me back under the surface. I scream again in undiluted terror, and I have just enough time to spot Jiwoon, his face tightening in panic, before water fills my nose, my ears, as I am dragged down, down, down.

Serpent, my mind is thinking nonsensically. *Serpent. Serpent. Around my legs.*

For a moment, I am back in my chogajip, young and screaming in the night as snakes sneak through the hut's flimsy walls and coil around my ankles, sinuous bodies tightening.

I shove away the memory and choke on water as I draw my jikdo and desperately stab the creature. I am slow and clumsy under the water, but there is still a high-pitched shriek of agony and rage that sends me reeling. We hit the bottom—hard—and only then does the creature let go.

All I can see is a blur of red as it shoots toward my throat. My lungs burning with lack of oxygen, I bring my sword forward. Although the water makes my movements ungainly, I manage to rip through the creature's skin. Blood fills the water, and there is that unbearable shriek again, but louder this time.

Almost as if there are more of them. My limbs turn to jelly.

I need to return to shore. *Now*.

The creature writhes, bleeding on the riverbed. I swim past it as the screams grow louder. And louder.

I will my body to move faster as I bend my knees and shoot upward, nearly blacking out from both the lack of air and the abrupt motion.

My head breaks through the frothing surface, and I suck in a breath as I begin swimming toward the shore. Water still fills my lungs, but I am fueled by adrenaline.

I pump my legs, my arms, calling on years of water training with Yoonho. I am a fast swimmer, even in the cold.

Kick. Kick.

I turn my head from side to side, gulping down air whenever I can.

Faster. Faster.

With no small amount of horror, I sense the creatures following me, the water shifting with their motion, the river quickening. I hear their screeches, muted and muffled beneath the current. *Faster, Lina. Faster.*

Grunting, I push myself past my limit, slicing through the icy water like a knife. I choke on the flavor of fish and riverweed as I keep going, feeling those godsdamned creatures come closer and closer. Is that a scale scraping against my leg?

*Godsdamnit, godsdamnit, gods*damnit—

I scream, redoubling my efforts. My chest burns as I swim. I am nearly there, nearly to the shore. I can make it. I *will* make it.

Just as something long and hairy brushes against my skin, I escape from the water and throw myself onto the rocks, as far away from the river as I can manage.

I hit the ground hard, teeth rattling as I curl my knees to my chest to regain some semblance of warmth. A low keening is escaping my lips, hoarse with terror. My throat is scraped raw, and every note hurts, but I cannot cease the noise.

"Lina," I hear through my gasps and chokes. "Lina."

Then somebody presses on my chest, and I gag as water rushes out of me, spilling onto the rocky shore. The sharp rocks dig into my back as I violently shiver. My vision is blurred and my body suddenly feels limp and heavy. Water streams from my hair, my clothes, my skin. I'm trying so godsdamned hard not to cry, but my adrenaline is fading, leaving me cold and scared and wet.

"Misook," Jiwoon shouts. "Her cloak. Get me her cloak."

I am bundled and wrapped, Jiwoon shouting orders to his two comrades. Hangyeol stuffs my feet back into my boots, and Misook holds my bedraggled hair back as I retch out the brackish water. Jiwoon tears a piece of fabric from his shirt and holds it to my skin. Red blooms onto the white cloth. Blood, warm and wet, trickles down my cheek from where the creature slashed it.

"Lina," Jiwoon says urgently, kneeling over me. "Shit," he mutters, and gently curls his arms around my shoulders as I shake. I close my eyes, hating myself for needing the comfort, the reassurance. But I do. Oh gods, I do. "You're okay," Jiwoon says softly into my ear. "You're okay."

"What were those things?" Hangyeol asks slowly. "The screams in the water…"

"The river serpents," I hear Jiwoon reply over my head. "Damn Haneul for putting them here. I didn't expect them to emerge tonight."

"Of course they emerged," Misook mutters. "Their sole purpose is to prevent the berries from being reached. Lina got farther than any of us ever did."

"At a cost." Hangyeol sounds horrified and guilty all at once. "Oh, Lina."

Misook mutters a curse in agreement.

"Does she have them?" Hangyeol asks hesitantly.

Trembling, I lift my head. "My pockets," I rasp. My vision is beginning to clear, and I shift away from Jiwoon. His arms fall, releasing me, and I tug my cloak closer around me. Although my body is warming, I still shake violently. That water must be colder than ice.

Silence falls.

"You did it," Jiwoon whispers as I unbutton my pocket and allow the trio to gape at the blue-gray berries peeking through the waterlogged folds of fabric. "You got the wongun berries."

"Of course I did." I sneer past chattering teeth, doing my best to push aside my remaining terror. "Next time, you give me *all* the fucking details. This is not how a team works. This was not fair, and yet you say that Hwanung is your patron god." With great difficulty, I clamber to my feet, withdraw the berries from my pockets, and shove them into Jiwoon's hands. "I'm going back to the palace. Tomorrow night, whatever it is I must do, I expect a proper briefing. If not, I'll take the berries and I'll work alone."

Although I lack Jiwoon's apothecary, and his training to create a potion, I spit out the words with enough conviction that the Revolutionaries exchange wary glances. I send them one last dirty look over my shoulder as I stalk away, my body shaking. The perennially wounded leg is no longer numb, and I walk with a bitter limp, hissing through my teeth each time I'm forced to set down my left foot.

The fish have teeth, indeed.

CHAPTER TWENTY-FOUR

The tone of today's letter is colder than its predecessor.
Reaper.
Skip kitchen duty today. Meet me at the plaza instead.
-His Royal Majesty,
Emperor Haneul Rui

I examine the paper, which has once again been slipped under my door. The writing is familiar by now.

Does Rui know that I have collected the berries for the Revolution?

I worry my lip as I slip into a clean tunic and pants and tie my hair back into a simple braid. The slash across my cheek from the river serpent shines bright and red.

My dreams of the past night were filled with red-eyed creatures leering at me from murky underwater depths, their teeth bared as they circled me. Filled with snakelike bodies weaving through river rocks, coiling around my ankles. I woke drenched in a cold sweat, gasping for air as if I were still in the Black River and wheezing through a tight chest and sore throat.

As I make my way to the plaza, I try my best not to sniffle.

My throat is knotted and sore, my nose horribly hot and stuffy. The cold is undoubtedly the aftermath from my late-night dip into the Black River. I despise being sick.

I sneeze into my elbow just as I arrive at the plaza. With blurry eyes, I locate Rui.

He stands beside the fountain, his hands tucked into the folds of his midnight blue hanbok. Warm moonlight streams through the windows, bathing the emperor in an almost heavenly glow.

He lifts his head as I approach and arches a brow. "Good morning, little thief."

"Yesterday, and now today." My voice is raspy and horrendously congested. "What do you want this time?"

Rui raises his brows. "Have you fallen ill?"

"No. I'm quite well, thank you." I straighten as a cough pinches my throat. I hold it back, more than certain that a vein on my forehead bulges with the effort.

"You're sick." His eyes move to the wound on my cheek and darken. "And injured. Where did you get that?"

I open my mouth to tell a quick lie, but instead the cough, deep and rattling, bursts through my lips. Rui frowns as he watches me furiously wipe my mouth on the sleeve of my shirt. It's impossible to discern whether the frown was one of disgust or concern. Probably both.

"I was going to offer you a walk in the gardens," he says, "but now I see that will have to wait."

That is why he summoned me? I shake my head. This bastard. I start to stalk away, but Rui smoothly blocks my path.

"Surely you're not too eager to rid yourself of my presence."

"I would like nothing more. Hence my various attempts at murder." But it is hard to sound threatening with a stuffed nose.

Rui sighs as I sneeze. "Come with me, Lina." Gently, he takes my arm and leads me out of the plaza. The desire to lurch from his grip is not as prominent as it once was. The thought is not comforting.

I half close my eyes and imagine breaking all the bones in his hand until they are nothing but splinters. *Ah. That's better.*

"You're scheming," Rui notes as we stride down a small corridor half hidden behind one of the palace's many stone archways.

My eyes fly open. "No."

"You always look as content as a cat while plotting my untimely demise," the Piper murmurs as we approach a small wooden door engraved with swirling symbols at which I narrow my eyes. I am fluent in various languages, but these are otherworldly and unfamiliar.

Noticing my stare, Rui gives me a sidelong glance. "The Elder Language of the Dokkaebi. My father spoke it, and his father before him. It's a near dead language now, but a few have not forgotten it."

"Like who?" I ask warily, wondering who the door belongs to.

In answer, Rui raises his fist and knocks briskly on the rune-embellished entryway.

A moment later, the smells of various herbs and spices waft into the hall as the door opens and reveals Kang.

I suppose I shouldn't be surprised—Kang's gaze is perennially full with an ancient, unnerving wisdom.

"Rui," Kang says quietly, inclining his head in a respectful nod. "Lina. This is a surprise." He steps to the side and extends his arm in welcome, the gray-trimmed sleeve of his robe rustling. "Come in."

I fight back a sneeze as I follow Rui into the adviser's room, the strong scent of herbs torturously tickling my nose.

Through watery vision, I take in the great walls of stone, towering bookshelves, and jars upon jars of strangely colored herbs on wooden shelves. There is a thick, ancient-looking rug on the floor and a desk with dozens of heavy scrolls and teetering inkpots. In the corner there is a small cot, neatly made.

"My apothecary and study," Kang says in way of explanation. "I hope that you'll forgive the mess."

"Ah," I say, and squint at a jar containing a luminescent jellyfish in a pale pink liquid. I reach out to poke at the glass container, but my hand is swatted away by another's. Rui's.

How dare he—

"Kang," the emperor says, leaning against the disorderly desk and pinching a quill between two ringed fingers, "Lina seems to have fallen ill."

Kang's face is etched in concern as he glances toward me.

"I'm not sick," I hiss.

"Oh, she is, just too proud to admit it. She also seems to have miraculously procured an injury on her cheek." I clench my jaw as Rui waves the feather in my direction. "Do treat her, Kang. Our game will surely slow to a standstill if she's in such a condition. I can hardly imagine her being capable of sneaking up on me while sneezing."

Fury reddens my cheeks. "I don't need your help. Nor do I want it." The bastard seems to want me in perfect health should I lose the game. Beheading a sickly assassin is hardly fun, apparently.

The two Dokkaebi ignore me.

"Of course," Kang replies, dipping his head to his king before turning his gaze toward me. He places a cool hand on my throat, prodding at my neck with gentle fingertips. I seethe, meeting Rui's eyes. He gives me a too-saccharine smile, twirling the quill between his fingers.

"Your throat is sore?" Kang's brows are slightly furrowed. "And you're congested as well?"

I mutter something unintelligible in confirmation. He nods before shifting away, rummaging through his herb-filled jars. Rui tilts his head as he joins my side, his gaze probing. I refuse to turn toward him, my chest clenching as I feel him zero in on my cheek.

"I don't suppose you'll tell me where you contracted a cold and a cut."

"Hardly," I retort smugly. The smugness quickly vanishes as a vision of the river serpent rises in my mind's eye. Goose bumps erupt along my skin. It's safe to say that I will not be going for a swim again for a very, very long time.

"I expected no less." I can *feel* Rui's eyes narrow at my back. "Although I am dreadfully curious."

"Poor you," I croon sweetly, turning to face him.

"Was it a member of my court?" Suddenly, his gaze sears with Dokkaebi fire. "I ordered for you to remain untouched."

"Until I lose our game and you get to murder me yourself?" Crossing my arms, I send him an eye roll. "Have you decided yet between chopping off my head or an arrow to the heart? Or perhaps you've come up with something more creative than either of those two?"

The cobalt fire in Rui's eyes flares. A muscle in his jaw pulses, and his lips part, forming words—

"Lina." Kang has returned and now holds out a wooden mug with some sort of steaming liquid. "A tonic. For your illness."

Slowly, I take it, peering down at the amber liquid. "What's in it?" I think of the jellyfish and my brows draw together in suspicion.

"A few remedial herbs," Kang replies, clearly noting my hesitancy. "Nothing too strong, but it should clear you of your sickness."

Cautiously, I sniff it. Through my clogged nose, I'm just able to smell something tangy and sweet.

"Drink it," Rui says firmly, his mouth tight and eyes lingering on my cut cheek.

I pause and frown at him. He seems a bit too eager.

"There's no toxin, if that's what you're wondering," Kang gently assures me. "It's a recipe from the old days. The ingredients are fairly simple and will cause you no harm."

"Poison is a weak man's weapon, as I've said," Rui murmurs. "A coward's tool. Trust me, Reaper, if I wished to kill you, it would not be by something as simple as poison."

Kang sends him a nearly unfathomable look. But if I had to guess, it is a look of utter exasperation. The emperor just shrugs in return.

"How comforting," I snap, but raise the mug to my lips all the same. It is hot, sweet, and soothes my throat as I drink. Rui carefully watches me until I've drained the concoction to dregs. Only then does he appear satisfied.

I wipe my mouth. To my surprise, my throat no longer aches. Gone is my stuffy nose, my watering eyes. "Thank you, Kang," I say hesitantly.

Kang bows his head. "Would you mind if I examine your cut now?"

"It's shallow," I say quickly. If Kang somehow recognizes it for what it is… "It'll heal within the week."

Rui cocks his head. I can practically see the gears turning. "How did you say you got this wound again?"

"I didn't." I stiffen as Kang gently places a delicate finger to the wound. It stings underneath his touch, and I grimace— but Kang is already moving away, collecting herbs from the jars, murmuring something about "sealing."

"You ought to be more careful." Rui's voice is quiet. Low. My muscles tighten as he takes a few steps closer and pauses a mere inch away from me. "Whatever it is you're doing, I can assure you that if you're too rash, you'll end up with far deeper cuts. Your plays in our game have been admirable thus far. But I would warn you to examine the chessboard before you make another move."

I ignore the sudden twist in my stomach. *He doesn't know. He cannot.* "It was an accident," I grind out. "It happened in the kitchens."

"I don't believe you," he whispers. A cruel smile lacking any amusement tugs at his lips. "I've specifically instructed Asha to keep a close eye on you. I would have been informed of your injury by now."

"Why do you even care?"

His smile disappears, replaced by lips pressing into a firm line of displeasure. "Because it's more than a scrape." I swallow hard as he reaches out his hand, his fingers brushing against the cut. I flinch at the sting, and his hand falls back to his side. "You're hurt."

"I've taken worse."

His eyes are sad. "I know."

I flinch away, my chest tightening as I remember the state I was in when he captured me on the street—bruised and bloodied and broken. *Why do you care?* I want to ask again. *Why?*

Rui is silent as Kang returns carrying a small clay mortar with a thick paste. He steps aside and allows Kang to gently dab the cool substance to my wound. The skin itches violently, and I move to jerk away, but Kang stops me with a shake of his head.

"The skin is knitting over," he warns me. "Let it seal—don't scratch."

Grudgingly, I oblige. Kang continues to gently apply the paste, and as he works, I take in the Pied Piper. The sadness I thought I saw is gone, replaced by that constantly cold glitter of amusement. I quickly look away, disliking how something in my chest stirs under his regard.

Does he suspect where I've been? Jiwoon mentioned that Rui placed the river serpents in the river, no doubt understanding the risk that the berries pose to him. It wouldn't be difficult for the emperor to realize that I got both my cut and my cold from swimming across that dirty, frigid current.

I risk another glance toward him, but his face is now entirely impassive and blank as he nods his thanks to Kang, who bows in return. Then he jerks his head to me. "With me, Lina."

I mutter a thank-you in Kang's direction before following Rui out the door.

His stride is purposeful, his back straight and his shoulders stiff. My left leg aches as I quicken my pace to keep up. Even if he notices my limp, Rui says nothing as we make our way back to the plaza. I note that his jaw is tight as he finally turns to me.

"Reaper," he says, pausing next to the fountain burbling with the lavender nectar. I feel a cold trickle of apprehension slide down the nape of my neck as he gives me a long, searching look.

"Dokkaebi," I retort, crossing my arms.

His attention is fixed to the spot where the cut used to be. I tense, preparing to be exposed, but he merely shakes his head. "Tread carefully," is all he murmurs before the air ripples and he disappears, leaving only the lingering scent of plum blossoms and licorice behind.

I seethe at the spot where he was just a moment before.

"He's always been one to come and go," a smooth voice notes from behind me. Hana. "But I'm sure your kingdom knows that as well as any." She is clad in a flowing hanbok of petal pink, and I warily notice that a rose-gold sword is strapped to her back.

"Hana," I greet flatly. "I haven't seen you since the ball."

"I could say the same. I have to admit, I'm clueless as to what you do, holed up in your room all day." She smiles thinly. "Plot? Scheme? Perhaps dwell on the fact that you're the laughingstock of this entire court?"

"If you're so convinced that I'll lose the bargain, why do you insist on bothering me?" I grin as I brush past Hana with a little more force than necessary. "If I had to guess, I'd say you were concerned for your king's well-being." I toy with my hourglass necklace and enjoy the way she stiffens. "In eight days, he could be dead."

"Hardly," I hear Hana scoff, but I am already stalking away, tossing Rui's statue a crude gesture as I pass it by.

CHAPTER TWENTY-FIVE

With nothing to do with the rest of my day, I take to once again exploring the palace.

My alliance with the Revolution makes the prospect of a potential assassination even more probable, and I must know this palace as well as the back of my hand if I am to pull it off.

I wander through the corridors, chomping on a handful of deliciously tart kumquats that I snatched from the kitchen and piecing together a mental map of the palace as I walk. The kitchen, throne room, plaza, and armory are some of the few rooms I'm able to locate by myself. Slowly, after around an hour of careful exploration, an art gallery is added to the list.

I hover in the space, drinking in the paintings, the colorful pieces. I pause as something catches my eye — a tapestry, similar to the one I stole.

It's smaller, depicting a cloudy sky. Tiny jewels are raindrops as they fall from white clouds. It seems to have been created by the same artist as the garden tapestry.

My eyes slowly move from the tapestry to a collection of paintings that hang on the black walls of the gallery. Some are painted in glossy oils, bright colors blending together to form images of a dark sea, a glowing sunset, and various other landscapes. Others display portraits of Dokkaebi. I tilt my head as I gaze at a canvas glossy with strokes of color forming hard, chiseled cheekbones and short locks of black hair tumbling into argon eyes crinkled with laughter.

A gasp of shock lodges between my lips.

It is Rui, and yet it is not.

This Rui lacks the long, silken black hair—instead it falls just to his cheekbones in black waves. I reach out a finger to trace the lips curved into a full smile and the eyes wrinkled with fondness. *This was before he went into mourning.* Whoever his lover was, she was alive when this painting was created. It is clear from both the look on his face and the length of his hair.

Never before have I seen Rui's expression devoid of the underlying dark amusement that seems to constantly haunt the curvatures of his visage. There is nothing but pure, unadulterated joy on this Rui's face. It is as if a completely different Haneul Rui gazes at me through a gloss of paint. My lips purse as I scan the canvas for a signature or a date.

There. A date from a little under one hundred years ago. And there, in small looping letters below. *S.A.*

I examine the artist's autograph curiously before a slight unease settles through me and I move on, turning my back to the gallery. A vision of the emperor's happiness captured through paint nags at the back of my mind as I walk, and my stomach clenches in envy. When was the last time I wore an expression of such carefree happiness? With a tightening throat, I search for the answer, sifting through memories of pain and anger and grief until Eunbi's small face comes into focus, grinning wildly as a chubby hand stretches out toward me, holding a steamed mandu in its small palm.

When I was with the Talons, I would visit Eunbi at her

mountain school as often as I could manage. She would hurtle down the academy's glossy wooden halls and throw herself into my arms, squealing in delight.

During my last visit there, we snuck into the kitchens and stole as many dumplings as we could manage, huddling away in a broom closet to sink our teeth into the savory treats. We laughed ourselves hoarse, feeling a breathless pride at escaping the shrewd eyes of the academy's Sisters—stern-faced matrons with strong disapproval for theft of any sort. If Eunbi remembered that our father taught us not to steal, she didn't show it as she gobbled down the food with a smug triumph. Any rules Appa made had been abandoned in favor of survival the moment news of the shipwreck reached my ears. I became, in many ways, Eunbi's father and mother. My rules triumphed over theirs, and I said stealing was perfectly fine as long as we weren't caught.

"Here," Eunbi said through a big mouthful of kimchi, scallions, and pork. "You can have my last one, Lili." She pressed the mandu into my hand, ignoring my gentle protests—it was Eunbi's favorite food. But my little sister shook her head stubbornly, dark curls bouncing. "It's a present," she insisted. "Take it! Take it, take it, *take it*!"

It was a silly thing, just a dumpling, but her generosity filled me with a love and happiness so potent, I pulled her into my arms and smothered her with hugs as she squirmed and giggled in delight. That was the last time I saw her. I still remember how crumbs dusted the sides of her mouth, how her tiny yellow hanbok was slightly crinkled and stained with something that looked suspiciously like red bean paste.

Four months later, I was working for the Blackbloods.

Now, my eyes prick with tears and I shove the memory aside. I can almost taste the mandu, but it fades, leaving me empty and hollow.

I miss my sister.

Shaking my head, I attempt to clear the sadness that has blanketed my mind and return to puzzling over the portrait.

S.A. Who is S.A.?

Is she the one Rui lost? The one Jiwoon spoke of? The reason Rui wears his hair long in mourning?

A small pinching in my chest reminds me almost of jealousy, and the question hounds me until I find myself entering a quiet, empty wing isolated from the rest of the palace. So lost in my thoughts, I wandered around the palace in a daze, and my feet brought me here of their own free will, it seems.

The dimly lit corridor is empty, save for the simple black door at the end of the hall.

I survey that door in a mixture of intrigue and confusion.

What lies beyond it? Why is this wing so isolated, so abandoned?

I quietly approach the door and place a hand on the black paint. With the slightest movement, I push — and to my surprise, the door cracks open.

My heart pounds as I slip inside, breathing in the smell of soap and fresh sheets.

It is a small room, plain and simple, with a neatly made bed and wooden walls, barren save for a silver-framed mirror. There is a wardrobe tucked in one corner and a desk stacked with a few papers and books in the other. Other than those simple features, the bedroom is empty. I let the door close behind me with a click.

Who lives here?

My fingers trail over the smooth mahogany as I scan the loose sheets of parchment.

On one, *meeting with court- discuss budget distribution.*

On another, *import metals for weaponry. Iron and steel preferred.*

Some phrases are crossed off, others circled. I shift through the papers and my back stiffens as I catch my name. *Shin Lina.*

Taking the paper in my hands, I scan the small black writing. *Show my assassin the observatory. The moons are to be bright.*

The hairs on the back of my neck rise as I reread the note through the thin, precise line that has been neatly crossed over the words. I recognize Rui's narrow handwriting from the notes that he's delivered to my quarters.

So this is *his* bedroom.

I set down the paper and glance about the room with new eyes. It is surprisingly plain for Haneul Rui, who embellishes himself with sparkling jewelry and fine silk hanboks every day and every night. I run a hand over the bed's duvet and frown slightly. Now I understand why the door was unlocked.

There is nothing to steal in here. And judging by the too-silent corridor outside, this wing is rarely disturbed. It is almost as if Rui is hiding from his court, from Gyeulcheon.

Interesting.

I turn back to the papers, hoping to find something useful that I can bring to the Revolution. But the lists are simple, indicating nothing of plans to increase taxes, acknowledgment of the rebels, or, honestly, anything even remotely interesting. My gaze flicks to the stack of three books. Cautiously, I heft one into my hands and turn a yellowed page.

It is not enough
to hold your hand in my own, my love
I desire your heart instead,
pulsing in my hand
beating against the cage of my fingers
Totally and completely
mine.

I lift an eyebrow in wry amusement.

I didn't mark Haneul Rui as the dark, romantically brooding

poetry type. The initials from the portrait swim in my mind's eye as I trace the page with a finger, running it over the black ink. Perhaps he read this poem to the portrait's artist. As I consider it, my jaw clenches and an unpleasant surge of envy heats my bloodstream.

Quickly, I repress it. It's of no concern to me whether he read it to her or not. I reach for the next book.

My fingertips have just barely grazed the front cover as a hand grips my arm and I stumble back, hitting something hard and firm.

"What are you doing?" hisses Rui's voice in my ear, low and cold.

I whirl around in a heartbeat, shaking off Rui's grip as I hit his chest hard. Rui stares down at me, his eyes a dark storm. There is no hint of amusement on his face. Only cold, hard wrath.

Suddenly aware of the danger I am in, I make to dart out of his arm's reach, but with immortal grace, the emperor of Gyeulcheon sends me flying through the air. I land on the bed, cushioned yet winded.

In a flash, Rui is there, towering over me. Baring my teeth, I curl my fingers around the hilt of the jikdo at my side and level it at his throat before he can come any closer.

"You went exploring, I see." Rui's face is a mask of ice, mere inches away from my own. He eyes the sword with little more than a vague, disdainful interest. The temperature in the room has dropped considerably. Blue flames blaze in his gaze.

I tighten my grip.

"What was it I told you this morning?" Rui reaches out a slender finger and traces the blade. Golden blood blooms on his finger, but he doesn't seem to mind. His eyes are intent and searing as he cocks his head. *"Tread carefully?"*

My jaw clenches.

"Really, Lina." Rui's hand falls back to his side. "I'm

disappointed in you."

His voice is cold. Venomous.

My heart is in my throat as I slowly edge off the bed, careful to keep the jikdo erect and ready to slash, even though I know that it will do little good in the end. Gracefully, Rui steps closer to where I now stand. "Put down the sword, Lina," he murmurs. "We both know that any effort to kill me will most likely be amusingly futile."

"Bastard," I spit.

"Old habits seem to die hard. This is not the first time I caught you lurking in places where you are not welcome, little thief." He clucks his tongue. Blue fire is burning in his gaze, and the air has become frigid, so much so that goose bumps run up and down the lengths of my arms. "You never seem to learn," he whispers, and takes a step closer.

My body tenses. I try in vain to ignore my own uneven heartbeat as Rui holds my gaze in a burning sort of silence.

But my mind once again drifts back to the ball, to the heat of our dance and the way a small fire warmed my stomach as my skin touched his in front of the entire court of Gyeulcheon. That same fire crackles within me now, slowly flushing my cheeks.

No.

I hate Haneul Rui.

That will never change.

"My, Lina," he notes coldly. "Your cheeks are the color of roses. It's quite entertaining."

Embarrassment and fury crush any semblance of desire underfoot, and I ferociously jab the jikdo toward his chest. Rui sidesteps easily, looking bored. But he's breathing hard, his chest rising and falling unevenly. Mine is, too. I feel as if I can barely breathe around my hatred, my rage.

We glare at each other over the sword.

"Nobody enters my bedroom." I didn't think it was possible

for Rui's eyes to narrow any further, but they do. "You seem to have considered yourself the exception."

"The door was unlocked, you fool."

"Even if it was," Rui replies harshly, "were you never taught the common courtesy of keeping to what is yours? If you recall, I do not take kindly to *trespassers.*" His voice trembles on that final word, only slightly—but it's enough for my eyes to widen as he shoots a look toward the table, where the poetry books lie.

In all the days I've spent in Gyeulcheon so far, today being the sixth, I have never heard the emperor's voice anything other than steady. But there is a quake in it now, a tremor.

And as his attention returns from the books to me, I realize why.

Those books are personal to him, perhaps for the very reason I theorized over. They mean something, something that is not for me to see.

Suddenly I feel a surge of remorse, along with something else. Something warmer. I have seen something I was not meant to see, but it is not only the books. It is the way the Dokkaebi emperor's voice shook.

It was—at least for a brief moment—a flash of humanity.

"Ah, but I forgot." He laughs, low and cruel, and the moment is over. His voice is once again steadily cool. "You're a thief."

"Don't speak to me of courtesy," I retort, but it is only half-hearted. I'm still wondering at the chink in his armor. At his brief second of pain. I suddenly have the ridiculous urge to apologize.

"Why not?" His voice is a whisper now, soft and husky and low. "Have I not been gracious? Have I not been kind?"

"You have been the *exact opposite* of those words," I hiss, snapping back to attention and wishing his room had a window that I could push him out of. I'll sooner do that than tell him I'm sorry.

Rui chuckles a low laugh that has my toes curling in my boots. "I suppose you have an arsenal of words that you believe would suit me better," he purrs. "Don't you?"

"Evil," I fire back. "Foul. Conniving. Cruel."

"Impossibly handsome."

"Impossibly *vile.*"

He stiffens at that. "Don't come in here again," he bites out shortly. "Or you'll find yourself groveling for mercy."

"I will *never* grovel to you."

"You seem to be feeling better." His words are cold and probing. "I regret bringing you to Kang. I find that I prefer you ill."

I straighten and touch my fading cut as his attention flicks to it. "You still want to know where I was, how I got this cut, don't you?"

His silence is my satisfaction. And perhaps it is that smugness that makes me do what I do next. Or perhaps it is a desire to rattle him, to shock him enough that I win a point in this godsdamned game of ours.

Either way, I take a step closer to the emperor. My body thrums with a mixture of rage, humiliation, and something far, far more threatening.

Rui says nothing, almost unbearably icy. No matter. I will melt him soon enough.

Smug satisfaction surges through my bloodstream as he lets me approach, lets me run a hand up his chest and tilt the jikdo so it rests only an inch from his swanlike neck. My fingers explore the dark silk of his robes as I lift myself onto my tiptoes, angling my head so that my lips brush his neck before hovering near his alert ear.

"Do you want to know?" I whisper, my own voice quiet but throaty, tinged with fiery promises and edged suggestions.

A muscle in Rui's jaw jumps. "Don't toy with me."

I smile slightly. "I'm not." I let my hand play with the collar of his hanbok for a moment longer before I draw back, widening my eyes ever so innocently.

A flicker of something burning flashes across Rui's face. His jaw clenches, as if he is willing himself to remain still. I watch this with an incredible amount of amusement. "Shin Lina," Rui says quietly. The flames in his eyes bank.

I wait, but no other words come. Rui is simply watching me, his gaze heavy with what looks like a warning but feels like a challenge. My face burns and my smile drops as my skin tingles in response. Suddenly, I am fearful, and not of Rui…but of myself.

I…I want him.

Perhaps that flash of humanity has softened me. Weakened me. But whatever the case, I want him.

Want to feel his skin against mine, icy cold against my burning hot. Want to brush my lips against the column of his throat, coaxing sounds of lust, of desire, through his mouth. Want to—

I flinch from my own thoughts. My free hand drifts to my hourglass, then jumps away as if scalded.

Rui watches me carefully. "Is something the matter, little thief?" he asks hoarsely.

Yoonho drilled it into me to retreat only when necessary, and standing here, my skin burning with traitorous want, retreat is the only option.

Because if I stay…

I hold Rui's heavy look a moment longer before I turn and, with the speed of a viper, dart from the room. His gaze is heavy on my back as I slam the door to his bedroom with enough force that the entire corridor shudders.

CHAPTER TWENTY-SIX

I am in a black mood as I stomp through the forest that night on my way to meet the Revolutionaries, crushing sticks and fallen leaves underfoot and muttering curses.

Curse Haneul Rui. Curse him for eternity.

Hangyeol's brows raise at my dark expression as he opens the door to Misook's bakery. "Is all well? I noted your absence in the kitchen today."

"Everything is perfectly fine," I snap.

Hangyeol wisely chooses to remain quiet as we descend the ladder into the hidden room.

Jiwoon is hunched over a ratty book, his lips pursed in concentration as he scours the tattered yellowed pages by the glow of candlelight. Ink smudges his fingers, and his hair is messy, as if he has been raking his hands through it.

Perched at the table in an oddly birdlike pose, Misook twirls a beaded bracelet around a finger as she sifts through a pile of heavily marked papers. Neither of them notices me until I sit down, pointedly clearing my throat.

"Lina," Jiwoon says abruptly, startled. "You're here." His

gaze moves to the fading cut on my cheek, and guilt flashes across his face. "It's healing, I see."

I give him a tight nod, not willing to spend precious time recalling the previous night's adventure. "What is this?" I take in the book, the pile of parchment.

"Our next step." Jiwoon adjusts his glasses and slides the book over to me.

I cock a brow at the thick pages. *Wongun berries*, it reads. *Preferably seven. Nine petals of saengbulkkot, the flowers of life, finely ground. Three petals of honsalikkot, the flowers of soul revival and rebirth. Kecan seeds. Black sand from the Black Sea. One dried sparrow's tongue.* And finally—*scale of an Imugi (to be finely powdered).*

I slowly raise my head. "Ingredients."

Jiwoon nods. "By themselves, the wongun berries won't achieve what we need them to. By creating this concoction, they will grant you the strength you need to kill Haneul."

"And you have the ingredients?" I grimace. Tongue, *scales*... It's already apparent that the taste will be horrid.

Misook sets down her bracelet. "Not quite." She gestures to the book. "Jiwoon was able to obtain the flowers, the seeds, and the tongue from the apothecary. The sand can be found at the Black Sea. And thanks to you, we have more than enough berries. The only thing we don't have is—"

"The scale of an Imugi," I guess. Misook nods in confirmation. "What is an Imugi, exactly?" The word is not familiar.

"One of the many monsters that used to prowl your lands," Jiwoon replies, his countenance somber.

"I've never heard of an Imugi before."

"You wouldn't have," Misook says. "Its kind vanished five hundred years ago, retreating to Jeoseung. And they weren't creatures your kind would like to recall."

"An Imugi," Jiwoon continues, "was a serpent. A giant, clever serpent with a maw large enough to swallow a human whole. With the power to summon rain and storms."

I feel my palms begin to sweat, my neck become hot and itchy. My heart is pounding in my chest. After last night's encounter with the river serpents, this is simply too much.

The twins used to tease me relentlessly for my fear of snakes. The Reaper of Sunpo, terrified of a mere serpent? They laughed themselves hoarse when they first found out—when we were shopping in the Fingertrap and from a wicker basket a snake rose, brown scales shining in the sun. The Wyusanian snake charmer laughed, too, as I shrieked, stumbling back into the twins, tripping over my own feet and landing on my rear with a crash.

Sang was the only one not to laugh, helping me up with a look of concern. Later, I confided in him the origin of my fear. Growing up, my family's chogajip was not well built. Rats would slip through the cracks and burrow into our meager bags of rice. Sometimes, snakes would come, too.

They would slither over me as I slept on the floor, twining around my ankles, causing me to wake with a scream. As I kicked at the sinuous bodies tightening around my legs, my father would have to pull them off with grunts of exertion, and more often than not, the snakes would drag their fangs down my calves to prevent their removal from my flesh.

Appa would envelop me in a hug in an attempt to soothe my shaking body. When Jiwoon did the same to me on the riverbank, I could not stop myself from leaning into his touch. From needing the familiar comfort.

But even with Appa's comfort, I often came away from the encounters with long, jagged snake bites that left me feverish and ill for days. Eunbi, teary-eyed and distressed to see me ill, would sit by me for hours and sponge my forehead with the clumsy hands of a child. For nights after, she would try to stay awake and on guard for serpents. Yet my little sister was only a baby, and always fell asleep with a determined frown on her face, as if she were pummeling the snakes in her dreams.

"I've never…been able to let go of that fear," I confided to Sang, shamefaced. "I don't… I don't know why."

For a moment he was silent, but then: "You are the Reaper," Sang replied with a small smile as he gently pushed a strand of hair behind my ear. "The Reaper can never be scared. The next time you see a snake, Lina, you give it a piece of your mind. The serpent versus the assassin. I place good money on you, L. You're the one with a collection of very pointy swords. Promise me you'll fight tooth and nail."

"I promise." I laughed, but couldn't help thinking that with the death of my father, there was nobody to haul the serpents off me.

My fear is silly, perhaps, but it is also real enough that my experience at the river—facing down those fanged serpents—was more than just scary. It was horrifying, harrowing. As I remember it, I dig my nails into the palms of my hands while Jiwoon continues his description of the Imugi.

"They were vicious," he says, and I swallow nervously. "Even the gods could not control them. Entire villages were wiped out overnight. Your kind tried everything to appease them—some even worshipped them in hopes of avoiding their wrath—but nothing stopped their bloodlust until they retreated to the underworld realm of Jeoseung, where all go after death. But they went of their own accord, for reasons we still cannot quite determine."

"I never knew that." I shake my head to clear it, even as my heart pounds unevenly in my chest. "They're gone, but we need their scales." I wearily rub my temples. *Shit.*

"Which is the problem," Misook agrees. "Without the scale of an Imugi, the enhancer will be incomplete. As will our mission."

My fear is beginning to recede, replaced by irritation. I loosen an exasperated sigh. "This was not mentioned to me until now. I thought I asked for transparency."

Jiwoon raises a brow. "We told you the enhancer required ingredients other than the berries in our very first meeting."

"You *said*," I grit out, "that they were ingredients able to be found in *apothecaries*, not in *Jeoseung*."

"Well—I suppose it's possible that another village's apothecary somehow still carries it," Jiwoon says defensively. "For a heavy price, of course."

"Wait." I pause, an idea forming in my mind. "Jeong Kang, Rui's adviser. He has heaps of herbs and items in his study. I was there just today. Kang treated my cold."

"You had a cold?" Jiwoon frowns.

"As surprising as it may be, one can get a cold from swimming in freezing, murky waters. Especially when said freezing, murky waters likely contain river serpent shit and brim with all sorts of potential for illness." The Revolutionaries grimace as I briskly move on. "It could be possible for him to have the scale. His room is crammed with all sorts of bizarre ingredients."

Eagerness shines bright on Misook's face. "So we look there first."

Hangyeol frowns. "I've never seen this room."

"Which is why I'll be doing the breaking and entering. I remember the path. He's one of Rui's closest confidants; I doubt he's holed up in his room all day."

"Brilliant." Jiwoon offers me a hesitant smile. "Search tomorrow. Bring us the scale and we can start brewing the concoction."

"I need to have a description. I don't plan on doubling back because I stole the wrong item."

"The scales are a deep, sparkling teal," Misook replies. "You'll know them when you see them, trust me."

• • •

The scales are a deep, sparkling teal.

I shelve those words in my mind, planning to scour Kang's small apothecary tomorrow, as soon as the adviser leaves his rooms. But for now...I climb into bed.

It is nearly morning already, and I have only three hours before reporting to the kitchens. Yet I cannot sleep, cannot even so much as close my eyes. Worry after worry, scheme after scheme, chase their way around my head.

I tremble as I feel a familiar craving burn my tongue and throat.

My hand twitches toward the pocket of my pants, where I've tucked away that final cigarette and my lighter. I've waited long enough.

I need it, the crushed halji leaves to burn my lungs and unfurl smoke in my mouth. I fumble in the dark until my fingers close around the object.

"Reaper."

I jolt, gaze snapping to my door as there is a soft knock. The voice is Rui's.

My lights are off—surely Rui can see that. I will feign sleep. I have no interest in speaking to him.

"I know you're awake," Rui continues dryly, slightly muffled through the door as he cuts my plot short. "I saw you tiptoeing through the corridors not ten minutes ago."

Godsdamn it.

I was sure I snuck back to my rooms unobserved. A chord of worry thrums within my chest. Does he know where I've been? Grimacing, I pinch the bridge of my nose. My mouth is on fire with the need for my cigarette, for the sweet, sweet inhale of dust.

"Leave. I'm in bed." I give a dirty look to the doorway as I part my lips, wrapping them around the cigarette. It is slightly bent from the months of disuse, but it will more than satisfy my craving. My vision blurs and my fingers itch with anticipation as I light the flame.

Through the doorway, Rui says suspiciously, "What, exactly, are you doing in there?"

I pointedly ignore him. My attention is focused solely on the flame as I raise it closer and closer to the cigarette that waits patiently between my lips.

The door has fallen suspiciously silent, the Piper's knocking having ceased.

A ripple of air, a gust of icy wind, and then the emperor is standing at the foot of my bed. "Where did you get that?"

I choke in surprise. "Out," I order sharply, regaining my composure a moment later. "I don't recall extending an invitation to my bed. I'm occupied." As I hiss the words at him, the flame wavers, only a mere hairsbreadth away from my cigarette.

"I can see that." Rui curls a hand around a bedpost, his knuckles shining white as the wood creaks under his grip. He is almost the picture of a furious god, I think, taking in his bloodless lips, blue flaming eyes, and furrowed brows. "You smoke, then."

Is that disappointment buried underneath the otherwise cold words? I feel a funny sort of tug in my heart. He almost sounds like Sang.

Almost.

I snap the lighter shut, the flame disappearing with a metallic click as I smile contemptuously. "I asked you to leave. I have business to attend to." I wave the cigarette in his direction and watch through slit eyes as his lips curl into a snarl.

I have a throwing dagger underneath my pillow. I should reach for it.

But I don't.

"Have you forgotten the fragility of your human lungs?" Rui very well near growls. "I won't have you destroying yourself. Give it to me."

I match his glare, tunneling as much fire and flame as I can through my narrowed eyes. "This is my last one." Even I can hear the desperation in my voice. "It won't hurt me."

"I've seen that kind before," comes the cold reply. "It's crafted of halji leaves. Have you any idea what those do to your body?"

Irritation tightens my throat, and I begin to slide my hand underneath my pillow.

"They decimate it," Rui says quietly, moving with slow grace until he stands before where I sit. "Completely destroy your muscle mass. Obliterate your lungs until they are nothing but two blackened shrivels." His tone hardens. "Give it to me. Now."

I am still for a moment longer.

Rui waits.

And I strike.

It may not kill him, but it can damn well drive my point home. I withdraw the throwing dagger and with a grim grunt, I raise my arm, the tip of the dagger gleaming as it moves toward Rui's chest. But Rui is quick, nimbly moving aside as the weapon clatters to the floor.

"Give it to me, Lina," he says with quiet coldness as he makes his way to my bed.

"No," I snarl, voice quavering. "You've taken everything from me. My freedom, perhaps my life. Let me at least have this." This last piece of the Talons. This last piece of who I was before everything fell away at my feet, leaving me so impossibly alone.

He halts at that and closes his eyes briefly before saying, "You will take your *own* life by putting halji into your body. Tell me, Shin Lina." Rui moves closer once more. "What do you think it will fix? Your exhaustion? Your confusion? Your fears?"

"You don't know how badly I need this," I whisper. "You

couldn't understand."

"So tell me." The small space between us crackles with tension and something else that is much deeper, much darker. "Why?"

I tremble under his blue-burning gaze with a shameful mixture of hatred and desire. I feel my lips parting as words, bitter with treachery, form on my tongue. "Sang…gave me my first."

The words hang in the air like wisps of smoke curling from a cigarette.

Rui's anger seems to flicker. It is almost as if he is relieved—relieved that I am speaking to him. "Sang?"

"My friend." I cannot clamp my lips shut. "He was my friend."

"Was." The emperor's jaw loosens. An odd dullness fades his expression. "He died, then."

"They all did."

Rui blinks. "I see," he says softly.

"Sang, Chara, Yoonho, Chryse…even Sungho, the weapons master. All of the Talons dead. Except me. But I might as well be. I'm bound to the gang who killed my own, doing their dirty work to prevent them from killing my sister. Eunbi." My voice cracks on the name. "I'm one of them anyway. I helped kill my friends." My throat is tight, and hot tears prick my eyes.

Furiously, I press my lips shut in disbelief that I've allowed those words to spill from my mouth. *Godsdamn it.*

I dig my nails into my palm. Why did I tell him?

The emperor is quiet. "You're in pain."

"And it's not like you're helping matters. In fact, you've made them much worse by stealing away Konrarnd Kalmin." I snap the lighter back open. "I'll smoke if I so wish."

"No," Rui says, his voice freezing back to ice, "you won't."

With a bitter, twisted sneer and tears still precariously clinging to my lashes, I curve my lips around the cigarette.

And I light it.

CHAPTER TWENTY-SEVEN

I forgot how good it is.

As I inhale, I'm sent reeling—that burning ash searing my throat as hot smoke folds itself around my tongue, tasting of something spicy yet bitter. Tasting of days long over, never to come again. Tasting of home.

My eyes flutter shut, and I blow the smoke out into a wavering gray ring. A delicious type of fog clouds my head, and my tears dry on my lashes.

Until the cigarette is snatched from my lips by two ringed fingers.

My eyes fly open as I blink away the fog to send one of my most raging growls toward Rui, who pinches out the butt of the cigarette in a cold, precise gesture. Anger sends hot shards of flame through my chest, and before I can think, I lunge at him with as much force as I can summon.

"Give it back," I hiss as Rui sidesteps my attack. My cigarette still dangles between his fingers. I am on the verge of tears again.

"Make me," is the cool response.

Fine.

I will.

The two of us edge around each other in a small circle. My snarl is as hot as fire, Rui's as cold as ice. I make the first move. A feint to the right, a dart toward the left.

My fist curls as it nears Rui's jaw but hits air as he gracefully moves away. Desperation makes my movements choppier than usual—gone is the grace of the Reaper. I need that cigarette back.

I need the taste of rooftop smokes with Sang, of laughing around the rolls until our lungs hurt, of hours spent gazing up at the stars. I need it. I need it—I need him.

I need them.

I *need them*, but they're not here, and all I have left is the cigarette, the tiny, flimsy cigarette.

But even that's about to be taken from me. No matter how much I lunge and claw and scratch, the cigarette still remains pinched between Rui's fingers.

Dimly, I note how his eyes have widened with something like distress and alarm, but I do not care. He has my cigarette. The cigarette I saved for months, resisting temptation upon temptation until I needed it, and damn it, I need it now. I finally had that taste of the halji leaves, and my body screams for more.

"Lina," Rui says sharply. "Lina—"

"Give it to me. Please." My voice breaks on the word, and I know how pathetic I sound, but what else is there to say? I fight my way toward the Piper once again, but this time, he doesn't move back.

"You're ill," he notes quietly. His face is white with…fear? Worry? Truthfully, I don't give a damn what it is.

"I'm no such thing."

"You are. I've seen it before, in people within your kingdom on my visits. You're addicted. Tell me, Lina, how many cigarettes did you used to burn through per day? How many inhales of smoke did you breathe? How many—"

"Stop." I squeeze my eyes shut. *You're a living, breathing*

smokestack… Lina, I… If I had known, I wouldn't have offered…
"Shut up," I snarl viciously to Sang's voice. Forcing my eyes open, I meet Rui's. "Give it to me."

Rui shakes his head. "No."

I shatter completely as Rui closes his fist around the cigarette, crushing it until there is nothing left but a pulp of ash and dust. The debris trickles out of his fist, floating to the floor. His face was impassive, but not anymore. There's another flash of concern. Wariness. "I won't have you destroy yourself."

I shake as I stare at the nothingness that my smoke has become.

"You are here to play a game. And you *will* play until it is finished. I won't allow you to destroy yourself until we are done."

The cigarette. Gone.

Sang. Gone.

Chara. Yoonho. Chryse. All gone.

All my fault.

"Lina. Look at me."

No.

"Lina."

Slowly, I turn my brimming hatred onto the Emperor of the Dokkaebi.

Whatever desire for him I felt earlier seeps away, crumbling into rubbish akin to what is left of my last cigarette.

"Leave me," I demand hoarsely. *"Please."*

And so he does.

"You kill him tomorrow."

"Gladly."

Yoonho and I sat in front of the warm fire, watching the

orange flames dance. He swirled his wine within its crystal chalice.

"You go at night, when there's a rotating of the guards. Scale the building, find his room. Kill him." Yoonho took a sip of his wine. "Feel free to make it a slow death, my Reaper."

I raised my own chalice to my lips "The Blackbloods will be angered. Has Sungho finished the weapons?"

"Nearly."

"Good." Yoonho musingly ran his thumb across his chalice. "By the way, Lina… There is something I've been meaning to speak with you about."

I straightened, uneasy at his tone. "What is it?"

"I'm getting older. And I'm injured." Yoonho shifted uncomfortably. "Konrarnd is young and strong. Should anything happen to me, the Talons will need a new leader—somebody who knows the ins and outs of this kingdom as well as the back of their hand, and somebody who isn't afraid to lie, cheat, steal, and murder."

A new leader. I shook my head as a grimace twisted my lips. "Nothing will happen to you."

Yoonho gave me a long look that sent something cold slithering down my back. "The Talons will need a new leader," he repeated. "And I want that leader to be you."

There was no sound save for the crackling of the fire.

"Me," I repeated hoarsely, but what I really want to say is, *No.* The thought of Yoonho dying is like a shard of glass in my heart. The thought of anybody else leading the Talons—the thought of that person being *me*—is terrifying. I'm not Yoonho, sly and natural-born leader. I'm only Lina, assassin and older sister. I do not have his years of experience, of expertise. The room spins. "Why?"

"I can think of no one better. You're the strongest of all of them. I've trained you since the day I saw you stealing in the market—even then, I knew your potential." Yoonho smiled faintly. "Do you remember that day, Lina? Dirt was smeared all over your face; you were dragging your sister behind you as you ran. She couldn't have been more than four, toddling to keep up."

"Eunbi." I could still feel my sister's small hand clenched in my own as we'd darted through the streets, the stolen buns still warm in my other hand. Our hearts had still been ragged with the grief that the shipwreck had imparted upon us. Sometimes we thought they'd stop beating.

"The Talons are my legacy. I know that you would protect them like you protected her. And that is why I want you to be my successor." He sighed, wearily massaging his temple. "Of course, it's preferable that I survive this war. But in the case that I don't…"

He wanted me to lead.

I should have felt honored. But all I felt was apprehension. Not once had Yoonho ever spoken of dying. To us, he was immortal. I took in the man before me; he suddenly looked eerily old, and so very tired.

"Maybe it would be best if we postpone tomorrow's assassination," I said. Because then, the gang war would be postponed, and with it, the possibility of Yoonho's death.

"No. It must be tomorrow. Promise me, Lina." Yoonho turned his head toward me. His features were etched with horrendous desperation. "Promise me that you will lead."

My lips parted in alarm, and my heart cracked a bit at the sight of him. "I promise," I replied hoarsely, my tongue heavy and leaden in my paper-dry mouth. "I promise."

Relief flooded his face as he let his head rest on his chair. His eyes fluttered closed. "Thank you," Yoonho whispered.

Leaving the study, I went to find Sang, who was right where I suspected he would be—on the roof, lighting the cigarette that dangled between his lips.

"Lina," he said, turning his gentle hazel eyes toward me.

"I need to talk to you," I mumbled, watching the kingdom below us. I saw the lights of taverns and nightclubs, heard distant laughter and bawdy shouts.

His hand, warm and callused, took my own. "Look at me, L." I turned my gaze toward him. Worry widened his eyes. "What is it?"

"Yoonho."

Sang frowned ever so slightly. "What happened?"

"It's what will happen that worries me." I fumbled for my own cigarette. Sang watched with obvious regret as my fingers drew the roll from my pocket. "Can I have a light?"

"Lina."

"Sang." I began to tremble. "Please. I need a smoke."

Silently, he passed me the flame. With a click, then a hiss, I lit the roll and placed it between my lips. My nerves soothed at once, and I handed the lighter back to Sang. "Yoonho spoke to me about tomorrow's assassination."

"Ah." Sang nodded. "He's been anticipating it for days. He'll be on edge tonight."

"More than on edge." I blew a puff of smoke off the rooftop, watching it waver unsteadily in the air. "He told me that he wants me as his successor."

"His successor." Sang's tone was unreadable, carefully measured. "And what did you say?"

"I said yes." I tapped ash from the butt of my cigarette. "Sang, you should have seen him. I tried to convince him to postpone the assassination, but he would hear none of it. Something's coming, Sang. Something big."

Sang exhaled slowly, forming a ring of smoke. "What do you plan to do?"

"I still have orders to kill Unima. I must follow them, and I will. But this is the beginning of a war. The Blackbloods will strike back hard."

"They can't kill Yoonho." But even Sang sounded unsure.

I shook my head. "Their boss nearly ended him last spring with a single shot. Yoonho said that this could be our final fight." I remembered his words to me in the training room with a heavy heart.

"Shit," Sang murmured softly, tipping his head back as smoke blew from his lips. "I'll protect Yoonho with every last breath in my body," he promised, his voice low and quivering. "But I cannot promise that nothing will happen to him."

"If only I could tell the future," I murmured and felt a bitter twist of anxiety. "Godsdamn Unima."

"Unima or not, this would have happened eventually. Our proxy wars and rivalries were always bound to become something bigger. We'll deal with the aftermath as best we can. The Talons are strong. And we have you, Lina." He smiled, his teeth white under the moonlight. "And I know you would never let anything happen to this gang. Not over your dead body."

CHAPTER TWENTY-EIGHT

As I get dressed the next morning, the events of the previous night slowly come trickling back into my mind.

My last cigarette.

Haneul Rui.

I bare my teeth in a scowl.

Damn him.

Godsdamn him.

I press a shaking hand to my mouth, trying to steady my breathing as it quickens and hitches. Last night—I needed the halji, needed it so badly. But Rui cruelly, callously, destroyed my cigarette. Cold fury sets in.

I will steal the Imugi scale for the Revolution. After that, I will take the wongun enhancer and kill him. And I will be sure to savor every godsdamned moment of it.

My hourglass is halfway drained. Seven more days to kill the Pied Piper.

I open the door just as the human servant raises her hand to knock. I grab a persimmon from the breakfast tray before stalking down the hallway, seething as I chew.

"Shin Lina. You're up early." Kim Chan leans against a pillar with an expression of immense mistrust. The general's green eyes search me, landing at the whip and jikdo that I have secured to my waist.

A flicker of surprise darkens his face, and I smirk as I watch him put two and two together. His missing dagger, the stolen weapons at my waist. Chan tightens his lips, and my pleasure only grows. At my rising amusement, the general straightens, tearing his gaze away. "To kitchen duty, then?" Each word sounds as if it has to be forced past his lips.

I don't reply, stalking past as I send him the most vulgar gesture I know.

I'll kill him, too. Cocky bastard. But that will have to wait. For now, I'm focusing my time and energy on finding the scale of the Imugi, even though the idea of touching snakeskin makes me feel slightly ill.

With a surge of annoyance, I realize Chan is following me. I place my hand on the hilt of the whip as I grudgingly stalk down to the kitchens, seeing no other way to get him off my tail.

Does he know where I plan to go?

Asha pays me no heed as I sit down in front of Hangyeol. Chan still hovers near the entrance, watching her. Hangyeol gives me a questioning look that only I can see as I finish my persimmon and toss the core over my shoulder, not caring who I hit.

"He must be bored," I mutter through my teeth as Hangyeol passes me a ball of dough to knead. I watch in resentful dismay as a passing kitchen girl turns bright red after catching a glimpse of the white-haired general. The girl rushes to whisper to her friend, who freezes in the middle of stirring a vat of stew to ogle Chan.

An idea slowly forms in my mind as I watch this odd exchange.

I will get Chan off my tail. Of that I am certain.

I tap Asha's shoulder as she hobbles past. "Asha," I say sweetly, "I see that we have a visitor."

"Why are your eyes anywhere but your work?" Asha snaps back, but her ire dies as I silently point a finger toward Chan. Her eyes find Chan's and, to my immense pleasure, Chan stiffens in dread. "Eyes on your dough," Asha mutters, but I know I am not imagining the roses blooming on her wide cheeks. To my delight, she begins to waddle over to the general—but not before shooting a dirty look my way. I grimace as Hangyeol sends me a sympathetic one in return.

"Clever," he says, loud enough for only me to hear.

"I know."

"General," I hear Asha say excitedly. "You come to the kitchens."

"Asha." Chan responds stiffly as she practically glows with admiration. I gape. Is Asha batting her lashes? I stifle a laugh.

"Perhaps to visit me?" Asha pauses. "But certainly not. Are you hungry? Is Hana?" she adds, her voice dripping with contempt on the name.

It's impossible not to snicker into my dough. Beneath the table, Hangyeol kicks me. I send him a glare, but my smarting knee does little to dissuade my feeling of triumph.

Sending Asha over to Chan will surely drive him away—he already looks miffed. Asha is blabbering on in her nasally voice and showing no signs of stopping anytime soon. Satisfaction blooms in my chest as a clearly exasperated Chan mutters an excuse to Asha before slowly retreating, casting a withering look over his shoulder in my direction.

I cock a brow.

Asha deflates as Chan leaves, and I watch as she immediately barks reprimands at a young kitchen hand who apparently chopped the carrots all wrong.

"What was that about?" Hangyeol asks cautiously, eyeing the spot where Chan stood only moments before.

"He followed me," I mutter. "I was planning on visiting Kang's apothecary, but lo and behold, the esteemed general appeared."

Hangyeol tenses. "He's watching you. Did Haneul send him?"

"How should I know? It's probable, but Chan could have acted on his own. It's no secret that Rui's inner court despises me. He and Hana especially." I recall their looks of disgust as I spoke to Kang at the ball. The couple is truly perfect for each other, the bond between them strengthened by their mutual hatred of me.

"Perhaps it would be best to bide your time before searching for the Imugi scale," Hangyeol suggests under his breath. "Wait until you're not being watched."

"I'll find that cursed scale right under their noses if I have to," I snap irritably, and then glance around to ensure nobody heard me. All the other kitchen staffers are bent over their work, and the clanging of pots and pans assures me that my words have gone unnoticed.

"We cannot risk being caught," Hangyeol hisses back, barely audible. "You must wait. Chan could be watching for you just outside these walls. Nothing can go wrong—you must know that as well as anybody."

"Oh, I do," I mutter. "Believe me."

Hangyeol sends me a final look of warning before turning to dip his hand in a bag of flour and coat a sticky lump of dough in the fine powder.

My mood curdles, becoming increasingly sour. So Chan is watching me now. That makes my situation much more complicated. I pound the dough with my fists, sweating in the cramped kitchens until Asha dismisses me.

Returning Hangyeol's last warning glare with a grimace, I leave the kitchens.

To my relief, Chan is nowhere in sight—but Hana is. She pauses from examining her glossy red nails, catching sight of me.

I mutter a stream of vile curses.

Hana flicks her brows upward as I stalk down the corridor. "You have dough in your hair."

"Are you watching me, too?" I snap.

She shrugs, turning back to her nails. "Hardly of my own free will. Don't be flattered. I can assure you I have much better and more interesting things to do than babysit a human girl."

My cheeks burn with fury. So Rui is behind this after all. "I'm not to be supervised. That's not part of the game."

"Speak to Rui, then." Hana holds her manicure out to the light streaming from the candles lining the stone hallway. She purses her lips, seemingly unsatisfied, and drops her hand back down to her waist.

I fight back envy. Her scarlet dress accentuates her hips perfectly, and I suddenly feel horrifyingly scrawny in comparison. I push the feeling away.

"I've been given strict orders to keep you under my watch," Hana says. "He mentioned something about withdrawal symptoms?" A cruel grin twists her lips.

I can barely breathe past the fury, the rage. "Where the hell is he?"

"Who?" Hana asks silkily, clearly feigning ignorance. She twirls a strand of raven hair with a slender finger, enjoying my frustration.

"Your emperor," I hiss. "Where is he."

"I haven't a clue."

I growl low in my throat as I shove past Hana with as much force as I can summon.

"But you might check the throne room," Hana calls as I

storm away, vividly imagining all the ways I want to kill Haneul Rui.

Dokkaebi servants gape at me in surprise and horror as I shove past them and stomp through the halls, aiming toward a certain enemy of mine, who is undoubtedly lounging on his throne and laughing to himself.

"Withdrawal symptoms?" I hiss as I stride into the throne room, where Rui lounges on his throne, murmuring to Kang, who stands beside him. At my entrance, Rui gives a slight nod to Kang. The adviser makes his retreat at once, sending me a quizzical look as he leaves.

I stand before the dais, near shaking with anger. I place my hands on my hips, dangerously close to the weapons at my waist. "I was to be unsupervised. This isn't part of the game."

"Consider it an intervention," Rui replies, infuriatingly patient.

"I don't need," I say very slowly, "any of your *interventions*."

"I disagree." There is a cold glint in his steady gaze. "Have you any idea what you looked like last night? I've seen people like you—"

"People like me?" I abruptly interrupt, earning a look of utter exasperation in reply.

"Smokers," Rui elaborates calmly. "Addicts."

"I'm no addict." I snarl. "I held on to that cigarette for months without touching it. Could an addict have done that?"

"If you're not addicted, then you're balancing on the brink of it. I know what those halji leaves do to your kind. The smoke is addictive, certainly, and the effects of withdrawal are not to be taken lightly. I've seen it firsthand." Rui tilts his head. "I refuse to believe that you have not."

Seething, I avoid his gaze. It is true—I'd seen a man once, his eyes widened as he stumbled through the streets of Sunpo with twitching limbs and a shockingly slack mouth. Watching him trip over his own feet and foam at his limpened mouth was one of Sang's many attempts to coax me off halji. It failed, of course. By then, I'd already been dependent enough on the smokes to not want to give it up. And so had Sang. "Why do you care," I hiss, "when you're more likely to kill me than halji anyway? A godsdamned smoke won't *behead* me."

Rui rises from his throne in a smooth, languid motion. "I cannot say that I particularly wish to have a rabid human girl trotting about my kingdom. That's why I sent my confidants to observe you. You cannot blame me."

I give him a long look, gritting my teeth so hard that my jaw aches. "I will enjoy killing you, I think."

"Oh, of course you will," Rui replies breezily. "You've assured me of such multiple times. And I'm sure you'll take your time. But now, my inner court and I have a meeting." He sweeps by me, his arm just barely grazing mine. A spark erupts between our skin, and I jerk away with a vicious hiss. "I'm sure you're able to keep yourself busy. Try not to cause too much chaos. I have enough on my hands already with our game," Rui adds pointedly before disappearing through the grand doors of the throne room. They shut with a bang, and I glower heatedly at his throne, imagining setting it aflame with an immense amount of satisfaction.

Yet a moment later, my jaw relaxes, and my eyes widen. I am alone. He and his court have a meeting, which means...

I rush to Kang's apothecary, its door clearly discernible thanks to the symbols engraved into the wood.

My heart thumps rapidly in my chest as I try the golden knob. It holds fast, locked from within. I glance around at the empty corridor before drawing my small throwing dagger and jimmying it into the lock, sticking my tongue between my teeth in utmost concentration until it unlocks.

The room is quiet and deserted, with Kang nowhere to be

seen. I smile to myself as I slowly shut the door, eyes roaming across the shelves groaning under the weight of glass jars filled with unidentifiable substances.

Deep, sparkling teal. Deep, sparkling teal. The words run through my head like a mantra as my fingers skim across rows of containers.

One jar holds some sort of pale, crushed herb, another something that looks suspiciously like a wrinkled finger suspended in murky yellow liquid. I grimace as I shift through jars small and large, sharply scouring their contents. But there is nothing on this shelf, and so I move on to the next.

It is the same. Containers of herbs, the occasional dried insect, and other substances better left unidentified. My lips begin to tighten in frustration. What if Kang doesn't have what I need? He could be back any moment now, and as courteous as he has been, I doubt that he will take kindly to my burglary stunt.

Shells, dried honeycomb, wasp nests.

I huff a sigh of frustration as I finish scouring the second shelf. I glance at Kang's desk, eyes widening. *It has drawers.*

I hurry over, acutely aware that time is passing quickly. I yank open one drawer to nothing but a handful of mothballs and a stack of tattered books. The second one reveals capped bottles of a brackish gray liquid. I try the third door.

It is stuck.

Interesting.

If it won't open, that certainly means something of great value rests within. I work the drawer with my dagger, prying the stuck board until it gives way. I scan the drawer's contents eagerly as it slides open with a low, hoarse creak.

Jars. Dozens of them.

I fight back revulsion. Is that a bird's head? And that jar of thick, golden liquid can be nothing but Dokkaebi blood. I see now why Kang kept the drawer inaccessible.

I hold my breath as I catch sight of one large jar in particular. Within is a single scale, long and oval, nearly the size of my head. It shines and sparkles with a beautiful shade of blue-green that reminds me of the ocean, bright lazuline waters smudging with the vibrance of swaying seaweed. My heart jumps in my chest and my palms begin to sweat as I pick up the jar, thankful for the thick barrier of glass between my skin and the scale.

"Imugi," I breathe shallowly.

I make to shut the drawer and slip out of the room before Kang returns. But something else catches my eye—something that makes the ravenous burning in my mouth resume, an intense pang of longing crashing down upon me like an ocean wave.

Halji leaves.

I would know them anywhere. They are sickly thin and ash-colored with jagged black veins running across their blades. There have to be at least a dozen of them within that container. Before I can change my mind, I have snatched that jar, too, and tucked it under my arm with an unsteady heartbeat.

What luck I have, I think as I slip out of the apothecary and make my way back to my quarters, throat scratching with craving. The scale—*and* halji leaves. I'll win this game now. I know I will.

I shut the door of my room with a broad grin. I shall take the scale to the Revolution tonight. But for now…

My gaze turns toward the sickly gray leaves.

For now, I am occupied.

I roll up my sleeves and get to work.

Sang once taught me how to roll my own cigarettes with nothing but a scrap of parchment. I need only to rip out a page from one of the horrendously boring books on the low table near the sofa to create my cigarettes.

Maybe Rui is right, I think as I wearily inspect the homemade roll pinched between my fingers. *Maybe I am on the brink of addiction.* But I cannot stop—godsdamn it, I cannot stop. I need the bitter inhale to feel alive.

I breathe in the smoke and finally feel as if I've found some semblance of peace. If I close my eyes, I can nearly sense Sang sitting next to me, lighting his own roll under the pale moonlight. I can almost feel the cool wind brush against my face as Sunpo sleeps, exhausted after a day of mischief, and hear the low hum of Sang's voice as he murmurs something about his latest mission.

Tears burn my eyes. Godsdamn it.

He's gone, a small voice whispers in my head, cruel and malicious, yet honest all the same. It is the Thought, seeping shadows as it snakes through my mind, caressing it with a taloned finger. *And whose fault is that?*

"Mine," I whisper, hands trembling. I exhale smoke. "It's mine."

CHAPTER TWENTY-NINE

"Y**ou got it.**" Jiwoon shakes his head in disbelief as he holds the jar in his hands, examining the shimmering snake scale. "The scale of an Imugi. I can hardly believe it."

"Let me see." Misook grabs it with eager hands, pressing her face to the glass. "It truly is an Imugi scale," she confirms a moment later, her lips stretching into a wide smile. "Let's hope that nobody realizes it's gone."

"It's unlikely that Kang will notice," I reply, remembering the sheer number of items hidden within the stuck drawer.

"But not impossible." Jiwoon straightens where he stands at the head of the table, his eyes beginning to blaze behind his glasses. "I should get started immediately."

"Jiwoon will be taking the ingredients to his apothecary," Misook explains. "He'll create the mixture while we formulate a plan."

"I should be done within the week, well before your fourteenth day." Jiwoon packs the jar into his satchel and hitches it over a shoulder with ease. He makes his way to the ladder but pauses a few inches before me. "Now's the time for you to lie low," he says quietly. "We cannot afford any suspicion on Haneul's end—not if we're to make this work. Understood?"

"Of course."

"Good." He turns to the two other Revolutionaries. "And that goes for you, too. Keep under the radar. Especially you, Hangyeol."

Hangyeol agrees with a small inclination of his head. Jiwoon claps me on the shoulder. "By the way," he says, "you did well. Thank you, Lina." I allow a small smile to grace my lips before he scales the ladder and disappears.

Misook turns to me with an expression of pure merriment and mischief. "This calls for a drink."

Who would have known that the rebels have such exceptional taste in wine? I savor the dull ache in my head as I awake sprawled across my bed in a tangle of sheets and limbs. My eyes are wonderfully bleary, my mind beautifully numb as I gaze at the ceiling.

Last night, the Revolutionaries and I spent hours drinking wine straight from the bottles until our heads swam and every little thing seemed to us hilarious beyond belief. I smile as I remember the hysterics the three of us fell into as we played a game of tujeon. I hadn't enjoyed the card game since...since the Talons.

The game is one of gambling, and I distinctly remember snorting in mirth as I drew two tens—the highest score—resulting in Misook having to run to the bakery above and return with four pork buns, all of which I practically inhaled through my giggles. The three of us were drunk on triumph, but Hangyeol was the drunkest of all, singing a bawdy tune at the top of his lungs until Misook— suddenly practical—asked in a hiss if he meant to bring Rui's soldiers down upon us. But Misook was even drunker than Hangyeol and nearly fell out of her chair as she spoke. Hangyeol and I were snickering through our fingers, doing our best to smother the noise, which somehow made the situation all the funnier.

Jiwoon will be in the village now, creating the enhancer in the apothecary where he works. It will be done within the week, he said. If Gameunjang deigns to lend me luck, I will win this game within the *week*. Today is my eighth full day in Gyeulcheon. I'm nowhere near Asina's thirty-day mark, and although Rui's deadline is approaching faster, with only six days left, the progress I've made is enough for me to breathe a bit easier—at least for a while.

Smiling as I sit up, my undone hair spilling down my back, I reach for a cigarette I rolled the night before. Everything is working out perfectly. The plan is finally—*finally* in motion.

Haneul Rui will die by my hand.

I exhale a puff of smoke and imagine Asina's face as I stalk through the door of that cursed complex, dragging a dazed Kalmin behind me, two weeks before her pathetic deadline. I imagine the gasps of those Blackbloods as I throw him at their feet. I imagine the rush of relief that will surely come as Asina calls off the men in the mountaintops, leaving Eunbi safe and secure in her school. I will enjoy every moment of it.

But what will become of me then? I feel an uncomfortable pinch of foreboding. It will be back to the filthy bedroom and stale rice for dinner. Back to the Blackbloods to resume my role as their executioner. My throat tightens.

But Eunbi will be safe. And that is enough.

Until when? a small voice questions in my mind. It is Eunbi's voice, high and girlish. *Until you say the wrong thing? Until you make the mistake of crossing Kalmin? I will never be safe, and neither will you, sister.*

I choke on an inhale of smoke. Hacking, I thump my chest, every breath searing. *Shit.*

I extinguish the handmade roll and stumble to the sink, where I cup icy water in my hands. Trembling with pain and unsteady on my feet as halji smoke scorches my throat, I gulp down the water until the quivers and pain cease. I splash a few more handfuls of water onto my face and slip out of my pajamas, examining my body before I slip into a tunic and loose pants.

Thanks to the meals during the past week, I almost look like the girl I was before that fateful night at Unima's. My torso has regained some fullness. My ribs are no longer as visible, and my skin has a tinge of a healthy flush.

Yet I know, even without looking in the washroom's mirror, that my eyes are still as dark and haunted as ever. They grow only more somber as Eunbi's voice rings in my ears. *I will never be safe, and neither will you, sister.*

I close my eyes and brace my hands on the sink as I remember the day I said goodbye to Eunbi.

We stood within the palace of the Talons, fat raindrops splattering on the windows as a Sister from the school waited patiently by the large doors. Yoonho watched from a balcony, with an older boy positioned beside him with a hazel gaze soft with concern, scarred hands gripping the balustrade as he watched as well.

"Where am I going?" four-year-old Eunbi asked, her lower lip trembling as she gazed up at me. Her hand clutched mine. "I want to stay."

My throat was almost unbearably tight. "You're going to school," I said very gently as I squeezed Eunbi's small hand, kneeling before her. "In the Yaepak Mountains. Where the sunsets are very pretty and the air very fresh." *And where your teachers still believe in the gods. Perhaps their belief holds them in favor with the deities—perhaps it will keep you safe.*

"No," Eunbi snapped stubbornly, her cheeks flushing a dark red. I sensed that a tantrum was on its way as she yanked her hand away with a huff of irritation. "I am staying with you, Lili. Tell her to go away." Eunbi sent a petulant frown toward the Sister.

"Eunbi, it's not safe for you here." I glanced at Yoonho. Some nights, my mind still struggled to comprehend that I was a member of the Talons now. A gang member at fourteen. But what choice did I have? They fed me, clothed me, paid me... At a cost, of course—a cost that I hoped small Eunbi would never need to pay. "Bad things can happen."

"I don't care." Eunbi's lower lip quivered violently. "Don't care, Lili." Her small voice cracked, and then she buried her head in my shoulder, wetting the cloth of the shirt with tears. I shoved down a sob of my own as I held Eunbi tight. I had to be strong. I would be. "I want to stay with you. You haven't let bad things happen to me. You'll protect me! You always have! Why can't I stay?" Her voice was high and plaintive, cracking with frustration and fear. Her small body shook with tears as I scooped her into my arms and pressed a kiss to her forehead.

"This *is* me protecting you," I managed through a tight throat. "Sunpo isn't safe, Eunbi. If anything happened to you—" The mere thought sent a wave of sickness through me, and I breathed in her scent of lavender and lilies, trying to force the bile down. In a kingdom of grime, it was a wonder she didn't yet smell like the many odors plaguing the streets. She was still innocent, a budding flower. "You must go, little sister. For me."

Eunbi wiped her eyes with her fists. "For you?" she hiccupped.

"For me," I whispered. "Be brave, Eunbi. I'll come and visit. I'll write to you every day." Eunbi's wails began once more as I took a few small steps toward the Sister, who gave no indication of any emotion besides tranquility. "Be brave," I whispered one last time. "Be strong."

Now, my eyes fly open, and a small noise escapes my lips.

Be brave. Be strong.

A moment later, I blink in confusion. The marble floor of the bathroom is cool under my skin, which is coated in a thin sheen of sweat. Wasn't I standing just moments before? Perhaps I fell.

Wearily, I wince, my head throbbing in pain. I drank too much. No longer is my clouded mind enjoyable. I am hot and flushed, a dull ache pounding through my body. My throat burns. A smoke—another smoke might make it better. I open my eyes with great difficulty. The rolls are too far away, in the other room. I mutter a curse as the pain in my head grows worse.

I don't know how long I stay there, sprawled on the bathroom floor, but what I do know is that when I finally open my eyes again, Haneul Rui is kneeling over me with an expression of icy concern.

"I was not aware that you take your naps on the floor."

I bite back a bark of surprise as he places a cold hand on my burning forehead. I jerk away from his touch, but not before concern replaces confusion on the emperor's face. "You're hotter than a campfire," he murmurs.

"Go away," I snap. He is misty around the edges, and his face is blurred. I drank more wine than I realized last night, that's all. Sweat trickles down my neck, my back, and I shift uncomfortably.

"Lina." His tone is sharp. "You smell of wine and smoke."

"Don't *sniff* me," I bite out in great disdain. My vision begins to focus, and I tense. I undoubtedly missed my kitchen shift, prompting Asha to complain, and therefore prompting Rui to track down his missing human.

"I don't need to." His eyes slowly scan the bathroom countertops and the drawers. "Your entire suite reeks of halji."

Alarm crashes down on me in a great wave of ice. I struggle to sit but give up as the room tilts and turns much too precariously for my liking. "You took my last cigarette. I don't have any more to smoke." I wave a hand toward him. "Now, shoo. Go away."

"As much as I may hope that's true, the stench of the leaves is nearly overwhelming." He stands in one languid movement, and before I can open my mouth to deliver a biting reply, he disappears into my bedroom.

Godsdamn it.

I draw myself to my feet, stumbling to the door just as Rui pinches the handmade roll I discarded on the floor earlier. He looks down at it with an unidentifiable expression. "Where did you get this?"

"Get out of my room."

Rui slowly turns toward me. "Where," he repeats quietly, brimming with coldness, "did you *get this*?" The room seems to be encased in ice. Cobalt fire blazes in his accusatory stare.

I shove down a surge of panic. The scale—he cannot know I've taken the Imugi scale, too. So I shrug and give him an innocent little smile. "I went into the village. I stole it."

"Did you not hear what I told you?" He lets the cigarette drop back to the floor. "Your lungs are crumbling as we speak."

"I don't particularly care," I croon back. "Now leave."

"You do not care." His voice has changed into an unfamiliar cadence. It is almost gentle. "You think you deserve pain." Rui furrows his brows. "Your friends. You hurt them. You punish yourself for their deaths."

I shake in the doorway. "Leave," I hiss.

"No." Rui shakes his head. "Not this time. Tell me, Lina. Tell me what happened. Perhaps then I can help you."

"*Help* me?" My voice is ragged and vicious. "Why would you want to help me? Have you forgotten your game? Have you forgotten that I stole and destroyed your precious tapestry?

Have you forgotten who I am?" I tug the hourglass in between my fingers and tug it forward. The sand of the top half is a little more than halfway gone, drained to the glass below. "Have you so easily forgotten?"

He looks at the necklace, and a muscle twitches in his jaw as I let it drop back to my chest, where it hits my skin with a dull thud that I feel more than I should. "No, Reaper, I have not. And yet I know what it is like to lose and punish oneself for the loss." There is a flash of that cold, familiar smirk, but it is faint and fleeting. "Perhaps you wondered why I chose such odds for our game. Why I let you roam through my palace as you wish." He pauses, tilting his head all too knowingly. "Why I allowed you to pillage the weaponry that night."

My lips part in slow realization.

He somehow knew, that night, that I was pilfering from the forge. Yet I walked away with a fine assortment of weapons, believing myself to have gone undetected.

And then he'd invited me to dinner. A dinner where I'd planted one of the stolen weapons in his torso.

My heart twists peculiarly in my chest.

Rui's dance with death stems from far more than just boredom and his hunger for entertainment.

"We seem to be two sides of the same coin, Shin Lina," Rui murmurs, making his way toward the door. "As surprising as that may be."

"Wait." I hesitate, suddenly overcome with a desire to *know* him. Know his loss, his pain. "Who was she? The one you lost."

Rui pauses with his hand on the doorknob. When he looks back at me over his shoulder, there is a flash of sadness across that beautiful, immortal face. "Achara," he replies quietly. "Her name was Shuo Achara."

I taste words on my tongue, feel questions on my lips, but remain silent.

"She made the tapestry," Rui says quietly.

The tapestry.

A small noise escapes from my mouth, but he is gone, the door shutting closed behind him, as if prompted by a phantom wind.

*A*chara. *Shuo Achara.*
S.A.

The name rings as clear as a bell in my mind as I gingerly slide out of the bed I've been lying in all day as I've fought my hangover.

It is more than obvious that Achara meant something to Haneul Rui. I recall the way his eyes dulled in pain as he spoke the name, the way his jaw tightened almost imperceptibly. She is the one Jiwoon spoke of, the reason the emperor wears his hair long.

Now his rage at the destruction of that tapestry makes sense.

I swallow as I realize how lucky I have been for my life to be spared—for the time being, that is.

She must have been an artist. The artwork lining the walls of the palace, the Piper's affinity for paintings...it is all the handiwork of Achara.

Achara painted that portrait of Rui, her looping signature signed *S.A.* in the glossy oils. I remember the fondness crinkling Portrait Rui's eyes, the happiness curving his lips as he gazed through the canvas at the artist.

At Achara.

How did she die? In sickness? An accident? Perhaps something more nefarious?

My mind swarms with questions as I make my way to the

bakery, boots crunching on fallen leaves. My brows are still furrowed as I sit at the Revolution's table and prop my chin on my palm.

"Lina," Misook says, abruptly jerking me out of my thoughts. Her mouth is curved into a sharp grin as she twirls a golden ring around her pinkie finger. The metal twinkles merrily under the light of the table's candle. "You seem preoccupied with your thoughts. Reminiscing about your tujeon victory?"

"You weren't in the kitchens today." Hangyeol looks at me charily. "Did something happen?"

Shuo Achara, I almost say. *Do you know who she was? Do you know what happened to her?* But strangely, the words stick to my tongue and clog my throat. "Nothing," I murmur quickly. I will not ask. Not yet. Something, some hushed voice within me, whispers to wait. "I simply had difficulty handling the liquor from last night." I add a wry smile as Misook snorts. "And my stomach still hurts from how quickly I ate those four pork buns."

"They were gone within moments. I didn't even see you chew." Misook snickers. "It was truly impressive. And also concerning. Concerningly impressive."

I grin at her.

"If I were you," she continues, "I would begin to ready myself for Jiwoon's concoction. It'll be far stronger than the wine and the buns."

"And then, once you've taken the wongun enhancer, you'll need to find Haneul alone." Hangyeol drums his fingers on the table.

"That's easy enough." I offer a sly smile. "I know the location of his bedroom."

Misook's eyes widen. She casts a glance toward Hangyeol, who stiffens. "Do you?" she asks.

My smile falters as Hangyeol scans me with what looks like a flicker of distrust. "You know where Haneul sleeps?" His gaze is dark and his mouth a tight white line. Next to him, Misook is tilting her head in contemplation.

"How would you know that?" she asks, the laughter having faded entirely from her face.

Unease prickles at my spine, and I straighten in my seat, jutting my chin. "I told you before," I snap with as much venom as I can summon. "Rui allows me to roam his halls alone. Of course I found his bedroom."

But there is a drop in my stomach. Do they somehow know the wanting that I felt as Rui towered over me in his bedroom, pressing his body to mine? Do they suspect that the flush now spreading across my cheeks is not from anger but rather from shame? Ridiculous. My cheeks cool. I have no reason to feel shame.

The only desire I feel for Haneul Rui is the desire to kill him.

"You should be thanking me instead of wondering if I slept with the enemy. I found the only room in which he is alone, in which he lets down his guard." I hold Hangyeol's stare until he cedes, his glower flickering toward the table. "I've given you my life as collateral. Learn to trust me," I demand quietly. "Otherwise, this team will never work."

"She's right," Misook murmurs, her face relaxing.

As Hangyeol mumbles his apology, I cannot help but exhale in relief. My irritation fades as Misook pulls out the stack of tujeon cards, and we begin another game.

CHAPTER THIRTY

I have just left the kitchens when an icy hand closes around mine and yanks me into a shadowed corner of the palace corridor.

Rui smiles down at me, lips tilted upward in a wolf's smile that fills me with dread. "Reaper."

"Dokkaebi," I reply warily. I have not seen him for two nights now. The memory of our last encounter—the handmade halji roll, his confession—flashes through my mind's eye.

The words have haunted me ever since, echoing in my ears on repeat. *Her name was Achara. Achara, Achara, Achara.*

Haneul Rui dances with death as much as I do.

He taunts it, he teases it, he seduces it because it has stolen something from him. It holds what he has lost, and he wants it back. Wants *her* back.

Gazing at him now, I wonder how I missed it before. The lines of grief etched atop his chiseled face are deep and haggard, veiled only slightly by the perpetually sly smile he wears like a mask. His eyes contain a deep, unfathomable sadness that I know is reflected in my own. It is a look that only those who have lost wear.

But that look of grief flickers, replaced by something bright and burning, as I narrow my gaze at him. "Is there something in particular you want?" I lean against the palace wall and toy with the hilt of my jikdo, glaring up at him. I have not forgotten his cruelty. How he steals mortals from my realm, from Sunpo. How he is so eternally cold, razor-sharp entertainment constantly dancing across his marble-hewn visage.

How he crushed my last cigarette in his fist, the ash running down his hand and staining his skin dusty gray.

"Yes, actually," Rui replies, tilting his head ever so slowly as his gaze drifts to my lips. "I thought that perhaps we would put aside our differences for the day."

"I am trying to kill you. More so now than ever."

"All in good fun." He waves a hand dismissively. "I thought, little thief, that perhaps I would take you on another tour and show you my favorite place in all of Gyeulcheon."

"No."

"Yes." His eyes glimmer. "Or, of course, you can report to Asha again. I'm sure that she misses you dearly." I grimace and Rui chuckles. "You'll accompany me, then."

"I'm taking pity on you," I snap. "Forced to take company with the assassin. Has your precious court abandoned you?"

Rui shakes his head. "I wasn't forced." There is something… *gentle* in his gaze, gentle in a way that stirs warmth within my chest. But then it is gone, replaced by a hunger that darkens his eyes into a storm-tossed gray.

I hastily focus my gaze on a point over his shoulder. "Where are you taking me? Somewhere quiet and isolated, I hope?" With a sharp grin, I tap the hilt of the jikdo.

"As predictable as ever, I see." Rui sighs. "Come now. As I said, our differences will be put aside for today."

"And where is the fun in that?"

"Did you not find my showing you the hill lands enjoyable in the slightest?" He rolls his eyes, a gesture that seems so human. So *normal*. I blink away my surprise. "I believe that you will find that you'll enjoy the scenery much more if you're not distracted by attempting to murder me. Come with me, Lina."

"If only to avoid kitchen duty," I mutter.

With a small smile that is nothing short of triumphant, Rui leads me through the corridor.

I feel myself sneaking small glances at the Piper, taking in the golden sheen of his skin, the silken shine of his dark hair, the elegance to his every step, and the sharpness of his jaw.

It is almost unfair how handsome he is, I think sourly. It's an unfortunate distraction.

"Do you like what you see?" Rui murmurs as we turn the corner into the plaza. He casts me a wry look of amusement, hot and probing. I feel it run up my lips to the too-pointed arch of my nose, the gaunt curves of my neck. I flush in discomfort and insecurity, fighting the urge to comb a few strands of hair over my face and hide behind the dark locks.

Instead, I force myself to turn back to the Piper, my eyes bright with challenge.

His lips twitch. "Because I do."

"You what," I demand.

"I do," he purrs, "like what I see."

The burble of the fountain is soft, and the light of the plaza glows. Early-afternoon moonshine dapples Rui in a blanket of shimmering gold.

He looks nothing less than ethereal as he tilts his head, his smile growing. My heart stumbles a beat. I feel terribly human, and though I am loath to admit it, even more self-conscious as I stand next to the beautiful immortal.

"Stop looking at me," I say hoarsely, curling my hands into fists. But that traitorous blush is still lingering on my cheeks, and by the way Rui's eyes dance, he sees it, too. He takes a half step toward me, and I summon a vicious scowl. He cocks his head.

"You'll have to come a bit closer," he murmurs. "I think it's time for us to leave."

I hesitate, remembering my arrival to Gyeulcheon, the way I fell through darkness and shadows, held tight in the Piper's embrace. "Can't we use a palanquin?" I think of the portable carrying-box with a sedan chair inside with some longing.

"No." A half-moon smile. "Come here, Lina."

Grimacing, I step forward. I close my eyes as he wraps me in his embrace, his hands gentle yet firm on my back. My face against the slope of his shoulder, I mouth a silent curse, my heart thundering in—

Anticipation for the drop.

That is all it is.

"Hold tight," Rui whispers, his breath hot on my skin as the floor drops into nothingness and the walls melt away, replaced by swirling shadows.

Cold wind whips through my hair as we fall into oblivion and dancing darkness, jolting from side to side. I tighten my grip on Rui, fighting back a scream as his shoulders shake with *laughter.*

And then there is an eddy of shadows, a burst of light, and my feet touch solid ground. I pant as my vision swims. Godsdamn Haneul and his fancy tricks.

"I would say that was a smooth trip." His voice is a low rumble in my ears. His hands rest on my back and his chin atop my head. Only then do I realize that I am still clinging to Rui, my face buried in his shoulder, my eyes seeing nothing but the black silk of his robes.

It is tempting to remain there, encircled by his arms, pressed against his chest. There is a feeling of comfort that I never thought I would find in being held by him.

I haven't, until now, truly realized how much I missed the touch of another. A touch that makes my heart stumble a little.

And Rui… Rui is holding me. Delicately, like I'm made of brittle, breaking glass… But firmly, like he knows every battle I have won, every fight I have fought. Every droplet of blood I have spilled and delighted in.

No. No—this is wrong.

I jerk out of his grip and shoot him a look of pure contempt before turning my gaze to where, exactly, Rui has taken me.

Dark water peacefully laps at a shore of gray rock. Moonlight dances atop small crests of gentle waves, which sparkle under its soft shine. My lips part in surprise. We stand on a beach surrounded by fields of tall grass swaying in the cool wind.

"It's beautiful, isn't it?" Rui is watching me closely, and I am almost unnerved by the intensity in his scrutiny. "The waves, the water."

"It is," I reluctantly agree.

He does not take his gaze from me. "These are the shores of the Black Sea. The water of a river flows into it—the Black River."

Oh gods.

I will my face to remain expressionless as I watch the sea ebb and flow.

Does he know that I swam across the river and stole the berries? I had that incriminating cold, and he saw the river serpent's cut firsthand. I fight back a grimace and don a mask of cool calm as I watch the ocean. "How pretty," I say flatly.

"You'll find the sea to be warm year-round. The river, on the other hand…" A wicked glint flashes in his gaze. *Shit.* "You'll find the water of the river to be beyond freezing."

"How terribly fascinating," I reply, acutely aware that if needed, my sword can be in my hand in a matter of moments. But Rui is perfectly still as he watches me. Only his hair moves, the ends fluttering in a soft breeze.

It is quiet enough on the beach for him to hear my every breath and detect an unevenness that would signify what I'm hiding. The beach is yet another move in our game. But now it's my move, and I will counter Rui's.

In and out. My breathing is steady and honest.

"Crossing the river is near impossible," Rui continues softly. "Very few can withstand the temperature. Some have drowned playing in the currents. Many who survive fall ill."

Godsdamn it.

I take a moment to compose myself under his shrewd regard, suppressing a flare of alarm. "Then I suppose I should be grateful you brought me to the Black Sea, rather than the Black River." Innocence flickers on my face, and I doubt that Rui will fall for it, but it is worth a try. "You said that this is your favorite spot in Gyeulcheon. Is this all you wanted to show me?" I examine my nails with an air of haughty superiority, as I saw Hana do the other day. But unlike hers, my nails are ragged and bitten. "I'm bored. The hill lands were far more exciting."

Amusement shines on Rui's face. "Look at how the sea meets the shore. How the sky meets the sea."

I do. "It's beautiful," I mutter reluctantly.

"Yes," Rui agrees quietly. "It is." There is a soft cadence in his voice that prompts me to glance at the emperor—who, to my surprise, is looking at me in a way he has not looked at me before.

His visage… There is that cruel, cold glee there, yes. A lingering hint of dark entertainment, a hint of that sharp sarcasm that I have come to associate with Haneul Rui. But blanketing it is an admiration.

And hunger.

It is a lustful, sinful hunger in his gaze, mirroring the same desire that hums in my own chest. His stare does not flicker as he drinks me in.

No. *No.*

Before my mind can catch up to my body, my jikdo is in my hands, the blade pointed unwaveringly at Rui's throat.

A soft laugh curls through the air. "Lina," he purrs. "I thought that perhaps we were having a moment."

"We weren't," I hiss. Naive of me to be distracted by his beauty. He is the Pied Piper, and my enemy in this game. I tighten my grip on the sword. "We were *not*," I insist again, as if I can convince myself through repetition.

Rui's smile broadens as he complacently raises his hands. "Put down the sword, little thief. You're unnerving me." Yet his tone suggests that I am doing anything but. I tilt it forward, the tip nearly slicing open Rui's silken hanbok. His eyes widen in momentary surprise, soon replaced with wry caution. "Truly, Reaper. Must you punctuate your every point with violence?"

"Yes."

"I doubt that it is necessary."

"It is until you cease your pathetic attempts at seduction." The words rip from my lips like bullets. "It's a desperate move in your little game."

Rui's lips part in incredulity.

My chest heaves as I breathe unevenly through my anger.

And then, after a moment of silence, Rui throws his head back.

And *laughs.*

Rage reddens my gaze as his laugh, husky and wicked, fills the beach. But the bastard continues to laugh, doubling over so my sword now points to the midnight hairs atop his head. "It is not *funny!*" I snarl, and before I can fully comprehend what I'm doing, I deliver him a hearty kick in the shin.

It makes no difference. Rui's shoulders shake as he continues to laugh. There is nothing for me to do but wait as he slowly straightens, undiluted mirth dancing in his eyes. "What," I demand icily, "was so amusing about that?"

He is grinning. "That you think I am attempting to seduce you." A wave of fury and humiliation rocks through my body. But then Rui cocks his head. "As only a part of our game, that is."

I freeze, confusion clenching my jaw.

And there it is again—that desire brimming in his gaze. "Come here, little thief," he says softly, sparking a myriad of responses within my body—and none of them is hatred.

None.

Oh gods.

My body pushed into motion by shock and bewilderment, I move forward.

But not to embrace him.

The tip of my blade has just grazed the top of Rui's torso when he nimbly moves to the side and avoids my strike. With a flash of his argon eyes, he grabs my shoulders and pulls me against the hardness of his chest.

The shore rocks beneath my feet before I can wrest myself away, and then there is that ocean of shadows and darkness and—

I hit the water hard, my jikdo vanishing from my grip as I sink into the depths. My hair swirls in the darkness, and my clothes become heavy as I push myself up. My head breaks the water as a venomous curse spills from my lips.

He dropped me in the godsdamned water.

Panting, I tread as gentle waves lift me up and down.

The middle of the Black Sea.

I am in the *middle* of the Black Sea.

CHAPTER THIRTY-ONE

The shore is only a thin strip of hope on the horizon, miles away from where I now swim. Curse Rui to Jeoseung forever. I will kill him with or without Jiwoon's creation. The fury fueling my body is enhancing enough.

I clench my jaw as my gaze lands on Rui, only paces away, calmly treading the water with a relaxation that enrages me. He grins as he catches sight of me.

"*You*," I snarl.

"Me," he confirms calmly.

I am as fast as a minnow as I dart over to him.

"You're a strong swimmer, I see," Rui notes. "You may be due for a new nickname. The Fish, perhaps, instead of the Reaper."

A huge crest of saltwater crashes over his head as I swipe my arm. He blinks, shaking the rivulets of water from his hair.

"Gods*damn* you," I nearly shriek.

Rui looks as if he is about to laugh again. "You don't enjoy the ocean, Lina?" He pauses. "Perhaps you enjoy rivers more." His lips quirk infuriatingly upward.

"Perhaps I will drown you," I pant, tasting salt and brine. Oh, if only my sword hadn't sunk to the bottom of the sea. A gentle wave lifts the two of us up. My legs kick as I stay afloat. The left burns in pain and exertion, but I shove down my agitated curses and silently fume at the Piper.

"You'll find that to be rather difficult." A cocky beam.

"Try me."

He only smiles.

I open my mouth to snarl a sharp retort, but words fail me as something brushes lightly against my leg. Memories of the river serpent with its long, yellowed teeth and beady black eyes rush my mind in a flood of distress. Rui watches me carefully as I jerk my head from side to side, scanning the waters for the hungry grin of the creature. *Yongwang save me*, I silently pray to the sea god.

"What is it?"

"Nothing," I mutter warily. There it is again—that phantom brush. I flinch and kick violently, but my foot connects only with water. Mouth tight, I send Rui a vulgar gesture. My heart is racing, and I struggle to keep my composure through my rising fear.

"If you're worried about sharks, you'll find them quite peaceful here. Unless it's another type of creature you're worried about." Rui tips his head back, moonshine illuminating his face, long dark hair fanning out on the equally dark water. "Perhaps one that gave you the nasty scratch on your left cheek."

Shit.

It is definite, then. He knows where I have been. Horror tightens my chest momentarily as my clothes, heavy with the ocean, threaten to drag me down. I quickly work my arms and legs as I fight to stay afloat.

Think, Lina. Think.

He knows I swam the Black River. Fine. Admittedly, it wouldn't take a genius to put that together. But does he know I took the berries? That's also probable. But if he does—does he even know what is to be done with them?

My resolve strengthens. Although it's more than likely that he knows why I crossed the river, I doubt that Rui knows with whom I work. I am still one step ahead.

And I will continue to play the fool. He'll get no answers, no glimmer of satisfaction, from me. "I don't know what you're talking about."

Rui snorts.

I admit I could have perhaps tried harder to add more conviction to my tone—but what is swimming underneath me? I try not to imagine various horrors moving beneath my legs, their mouths open wide as they rush upward, ready to tear into my flesh.

Shit. In my panic, I choke on seawater. It stings my throat and burns my nose. Concern flashes across Rui's face as he lifts his head from the water. I splutter in protest as Rui swims toward me, and I send another forceful wave of water over his head with my arm. But the effort causes my already sore limbs to falter, and then I am sinking down, down, down into the deep depths of the black, sightless sea.

Strong arms wrap around my waist as Rui hauls me upward, back into the moonlit air. Seething, I spit out a mouthful of salty water as Rui holds me tight with one arm and treads the water with the other. Rivulets of sparkling seawater trickle down his face. "And here I thought you were a strong swimmer," he mutters in my ear.

"I am," I rasp, voice hoarse from the salt.

I slowly become aware of the way his arms encircle my waist and the feeling of my body pressed so close to his. My face is mere inches away from him, and his breaths are warm against my damp cheek.

"Your near-death experience may say otherwise." His eyes

flicker to the still-fading scratch upon my cheek. "You're in deep waters, Shin Lina. You must be more careful."

My stomach drops at the double meaning, but before I can stammer an attempt at a quick-witted retort, his arm presses me even closer. The water begins to tremble, the air begins to move, and then—shadows, darkness, and weightlessness all over again.

I stumble as we land.

The water reaches only my waist now, and sand is soft underneath my boots. To my immense relief, the shore is well within reach. Rui releases me from his grip, but I make no move to swim to land and instead let the waters lap at my waist.

"It's almost as if you dropped us in the middle of the ocean to prove a point."

"Did you not enjoy the swim?" The sea reaches only his lower hips. His robes are wet from the swim, and the material clings to his chest as tightly as a second skin. I can clearly see the contours of strong, defined muscle under the black fabric.

I clench and unclench my fists as my eyes refuse to depart from him.

What is wrong with me?

Rui's eyes rest upon my face, questioning and taunting. I take a moment to glance at myself—my shirt clings as tightly as Rui's robes do, every inch of my body visible underneath the tunic. His gaze dips down for only a moment, but it is enough for that dark yearning to ignite within my stomach again.

My breath hitches as he moves closer, now only a breath away.

"Whatever it is you are doing with those berries," he murmurs in a husky whisper, a slender finger tracing where that cursed cut used to be on my cheek with featherlight softness before dropping silently back to his side, "I must warn you to be careful."

Heat trails over my skin at his touch. "It is you who should be careful."

"Perhaps. But I have played and won many games, Shin Lina. I know many tricks. The berries come with a price." His gaze flickers to my lips. "Be cautious. There are other ways to win."

"Oh?" I demand. "What are these other ways, then?"

A glimpse of that wicked smile. "As if I would tell you." He tilts his head in a feline gesture. "Your cheeks are aflame."

"It's hot," I reply curtly, unable to repress the shivers that roll down my back as he cups my jaw in his hand. He smiles ever so slightly.

"You don't mind. Me touching you, I mean." His voice is soft, wondering.

I am silent. The color flushing my skin seems to speak for me.

"At least you haven't yet tried to kill me today. So I suppose that must mean something." Rui pauses, his gaze dropping once more to my lips. "Does it?"

"Does it what?" Something inside me has begun to stir, as if awakening from a deep slumber. I feel my lips curl into a wicked smile as I hold his stare.

Foolish, a voice within me chides. *Foolish to toy with him, foolish to feel such heat under his gaze.* But what do I care? My smile grows.

"Mean something," he says—and I could swear that his voice softens, if only for a moment.

I have seduced him, and he, I. But what a fool he is. I can use this newfound seduction as a weapon of my own and win this cursed game.

So I smile that cruel little smile, and feel my breath hitch as Rui's eyes darken with desire. "No," I murmur. "It means nothing."

The air seems to thicken as we hold each other's gaze. Quicksilver sears within his eyes.

"Does it, little thief?"

I swallow hard, my smile faltering as I hide my trembling

hands behind my back. *No. No, it means something—it means something. Even though I do not want it to, even though it cannot... It means something.*

He must see the answer in my eyes, for he sucks in a sharp breath.

And then he is crushing me against his body, tilting back my chin as his lips hungrily meet mine.

Heat sends trembles through me as I kiss him and run my hands down the hard muscle of his chest, curling my fingers in the damp strands of his hair. I gasp as he nibbles on the softness of my bottom lip, his hands gripping my waist.

I feel him smile against my mouth as he lifts me from the water and I wrap my legs around his slim waist. His lips move to my neck, trailing fire across my already burning skin.

"I wanted this from the moment I saw you on the rooftop." Rui's voice is husky and filled with gravel as he tightens his hold on me. His eyes are hungry, sparkling with feverish desire.

I part my lips in surprise, but then his mouth is on me again and I forget all words. His teeth nip my neck and send a small burst of pain through my skin, but then he kisses the hurt away as he moves through the water onto the beach and gently lowers me to my feet on the soft black sand.

My breathing is ragged as my fingers scramble with the sash of silk that encircles his dark robes, untying the knot as my lips once again meet Rui's. I tug the fabric away from his body, revealing taut muscles and tanned skin shining with sweat and seawater. Now clad in only his black satin pants, Rui pulls away from me slightly, his long hair falling over his face and hiding us in a curtain. "Are you sure?" His voice is husky and desperate—but worried. Hesitant. His cheeks are flushed pink as he holds my arms gently.

And despite everything, there is no echo of that hesitancy within me as I draw him closer to me and stand on my tiptoes to press my lips again to his, running my hands up his chest. His breathing is ragged. A soft sound escapes him. "Lina," he murmurs against my mouth, and my name is like a prayer on his lips.

"Rui," I reply breathlessly, grinning up at him.

Slight surprise flashes across his countenance, and I realize that this is the first time I have ever called him by his true name out loud.

My cheeks flush, and I look away, my heart tightening at what this could mean…

A glint in the emperor's eyes warns me that he has not missed the significance of that name, *his* name.

Not the "Pied Piper," not "Dokkaebi," but Rui.

Rui.

I roll the name around in my mouth. *Roo-ee.* The syllables taste like sweet sparkling stars against a velvet black sky. Like crushed sugar that crunches between my teeth. Like winter's first snowfall and an icy wind carrying the rich scent of crackling fires and warm spiced wine.

"Do you know, little thief," Rui whispers, gently guiding my head back to him, "I think that you're in danger of mixing business with pleasure."

"Rest assured," I reply, smiling sharply up at him to mask the way my heart has begun to stutter, "if my sword had not sunk into the ocean, it would be you it would sink into instead."

"So bloodthirsty," he murmurs, pressing a kiss on the underside of my jaw. My eyes flutter shut as he plants another onto the column of my throat. "Don't you ever grow bored of daydreaming about killing me?"

"No," I reply as my skin burns in the wake of his lips. He laughs against me, and I shiver.

A small noise catches in my throat as Rui brushes a wet strand of my hair behind my ear. His gaze glitters. "I want you,

Lina," he says quietly. "But I need to know that you want me, too. That you're not doing this for…another reason. That this is what you truly desire."

I make to kiss him again in response, but he draws away. His chest rises and falls unevenly, his every breath ragged.

"You must say it," he says quietly but firmly. "Please. Tell me that you want me, little thief, and I am yours."

"I do," I whisper. Gods, I do. I know I should not, but… "I want you."

And with those three damning words, he is unleashed, his eyes shining as brightly as the moons above. His lips are hot against mine, and his hands cup my face as he deepens the kiss. I am sure that he can hear my heart ramming against my rib cage, sure that he can hear every hitch in my breath. Tears prick my eyes as I wrap my arms around his shoulders. For the first time in a year, my head does not roar with guilt and shame and mourning. For the first time in a year, I am able to lose myself with wild abandon.

For the first time in a year, my heart is beating fast with something other than fear or anger—and I feel like maybe, someday, I'll be okay.

A tear slips down my cheek, but it's not one of sadness. It's one of relief. There is an end to this suffering, after all—a balm upon the gaping wound of my heart.

Rui's breath hitches slightly, and a slender finger wipes away the tear. He pulls back, eyes wide. I shake my head gently, trying to explain as I pull him to me again. Yet even without words, it seems that Rui understands.

His lips are gentler this time, softer, his initial hunger sated. He strokes my jaw lightly as he smiles against me and quietly breaks our union.

The Dokkaebi emperor holds me against him, and I wrap my hands around his waist, content to remain like this for some time.

With my head leaning against his chest, I can hear his heart beating, fast and uneven.

So he does have a heart.

I close my eyes. We remain like this for what may be a minute, or an hour, before I hear Rui start the formation of a sentence, some jest. I narrow my eyes and just like that, the spell is broken. I step away, smoothing my hair and crossing my arms as my cheeks burn pink.

"Don't," I warn, breathing heavily and unwilling to hear whatever clever joke he has undoubtedly thought of.

Rui chuckles, dragging a hand through his hair somewhat ruefully as he reaches down to the sand below us for his waterlogged hanbok. Suddenly self-conscious, I turn and look away as he puts it back on.

Oh gods. What have I done?

What have we *done?*

"Lina," Rui says warily, and I turn. He stands on the beach, dressed once more, his tangled hair rippling with a stray wind. His brows are drawn in concern even as he gives me a wry, half-moon smile. "Are—"

"This," I say shortly, "is not happening again." I shove the panic from my mind as I stalk toward him. "Although I suppose that I should thank you for the distraction." Because that is all it should be. All it was.

All it can be.

If he is hurt by my jab, the emperor does not show it. He simply cocks his head. "You're welcome."

"You—" But suddenly I cut off, my eyes snapping to a point behind his shoulder, in the tall grass that surrounds the beach.

There, in the weeds behind the shore on which we stand... is that not a glimpse of a figure?

I scan the land, but there is nothing except rock and greenery. The grass sways and rustles in a phantom wind.

"What is it?" Rui twists, his eyes narrowed.

"I...I thought I saw something."

"I see nothing."

Apprehension creeps through me, dousing me in cold water. "We should go back." I do not look at Rui. I cannot. *I imagined it*, I tell myself, but still, I'm not so sure. *It was nothing but a shadow.* Yet my nerves are not so easily dissuaded. I have felt in my heart something forbidden, something dangerous, for my enemy.

"Lina—"

"We should go back," I repeat firmly, still refusing to look at him. My fingers graze the hourglass, steadily trickling sand. "Now."

"As you say." If Rui is disappointed, no hint of it shows. His voice is once again that familiar, coldly mischievous tone. His hands tighten around my midriff as the air ripples and shadows overtake us.

As we vanish, a lone seabird cries out, its song echoing across the ocean's rippling waves.

The moment my feet touch the floor of the plaza, I tear myself from Rui's grip. As his eyes dim in clear concern, I stagger away. He reaches for me, his face wary. "Lina—"

But I am already sprinting back to my quarters, ignoring the baffled Dokkaebi who gawk as their emperor arrives with the assassin, both dripping puddles of seawater onto the floor, faces damningly flushed.

"Lina." I hear him call again, but I don't slow until I burst into my rooms.

Shit.

My legs shake as I lean against the door, closing my eyes

and recalling what just occurred. I can still feel his lips on mine, pressed against my neck. Can still feel his hands around my waist, hear his ragged heartbeat.

I glance in the mirror. My entire face is flushed, my eyes bright as they take in the swollen lips and messy hair.

"I wanted this from the moment I saw you on the rooftop."

I run a shaking hand through my hair. I…*seduced* him.

I—I *kissed* him. I let him *hold me*.

Oh gods.

But… Good. That is good. Hasn't that been one of my goals from the start? When required, I can once again seduce him to my bed, strength enhancer humming in my bloodstream, and finish the job when he is most vulnerable. Good. It is good. I can win.

I *will* win.

I imagine sliding a knife between his rib cage, expecting to feel smug satisfaction…but none comes. Just a feeling of complete and utter reluctance.

What is wrong with me?

Gritting my teeth, I strip from the water-heavy clothes and tug on a plush white robe.

I need to finish the job. For Eunbi.

Smoke. I need a smoke. I hurry to where I've stashed the halji underneath my pillows, my fingers closing around a roll.

"I cannot say that I particularly wish to have a rabid human girl trotting about my kingdom."

Slowly, I set down the cigarette. I need to take care of myself. Need to appear as beguiling as possible. Rui has made his position on my smoking clear.

I'm to meet with the Revolution tonight. And I will. But… *I won't mention the beach to them*, I resolve as I climb into bed. Hangyeol's suspicion as I'd announced my knowledge of where Rui sleeps had been warning enough. They need to trust me. So

I will keep the day's events to myself. Nobody needs to know that I...that we...

Nobody will know.

I close my eyes, needing to rest for the night to come. But sleep seems impossible, for images of Rui with his wicked grin relentlessly dance across my mind.

CHAPTER THIRTY-TWO

As I step into the bakery, I feel a surge of guilt.
I quickly stow it away. There's no need to feel such
emotion. I've seduced the most powerful Dokkaebi alive, and
I plan to use it to destroy him. If anything, I should feel pride.

I compose my expression as I make my way down into the
secret room.

"Lina." Misook raises her gaze from the stack of papers she
is hunched over. "You're late." Next to her, Hangyeol silently
flips through an old, weathered book.

"I had a long day." I cut a glance at Hangyeol. Did he hear
how I arrived in the plaza, drenched in seawater and clinging to
Rui, my lips damningly swollen? I will explain, if so, that I plan
to wield my seduction of the emperor as a weapon and have
therefore broken no bonds of trust. But Hangyeol's face gives
nothing away as he focuses on the black text of the storybook.
"I took a nap and overslept."

"Ah." Misook smiles, but the light doesn't quite reach her
eyes. "It happens to the best of us, I suppose."

"Is something wrong?" Do they know? And if they do—does

it matter? Rui's seduction has brought us one step ahead, after all. There would be no need for them to collect their collateral.

But Misook shakes her head, her short hair whipping through the air. Some good humor returns to her eyes as her smile becomes apologetic. "We received word that Jiwoon will be finished with his concoction tomorrow. Much earlier than we anticipated. Everything suddenly seems so much more in reach than ever before…" Misook beams, shaking her head in disbelief. "We've waited for this for centuries, Lina. It's truly so hard to believe it's really happening, that we'll finally heal this place, this people. I've been in shock all day."

I blink at her words. *Tomorrow.*

Tomorrow, I could win.

Tomorrow, my strength could match that of Rui's.

Tomorrow, I can kill him.

My eyes widen. Something catches in my throat and I dig my nails into the palm of my hand, breathing becoming shallow.

Across from me, Hangyeol looks up from his book and frowns.

Shit. I twist my faltering lips into a grin.

"Tomorrow," I repeat. It is only years of training under Yoonho that allows me to summon that eagerness into my voice.

"Tomorrow we win," Hangyeol confirms. His eyes are solemn and tinged with something that causes me to pause. But then it is gone, and Hangyeol turns back to his book.

"You remember the plan, of course." Misook twirls one of her bracelets thoughtfully.

"Slip into his bedroom in the dark hours and finish the job." I cut a reassuring smirk at Misook that feels like plaster on my face. "It's simple enough."

But is it?

A rising surge of hesitation tightens my stomach.

It is.

It has to be.

"Return tomorrow night." Misook's smile is as bright as the moonlight that dazzled the beach of the Black Sea yesterday. "We'll be ready."

Morning moonlight has just begun to slip into my rooms, but I barely even notice.

I am staring at the wall, my lips pressed together in a tight white line. Dark circles ring my eyes, and there is a sallowness to my skin.

Sunpo, although suddenly in reach, seems so very far away.

Tomorrow, I will be back in that wretched kingdom, eating the scraps of food that the Blackbloods toss away. I will be carrying out their dirty business, my skin dappled with cuts and bruises from their abuse.

Tomorrow, Asina will welcome Kalmin's return, and the next day, I will be dispatched to get my hands filthy again at Kalmin's command.

But Eunbi will be safe.

That is what matters.

But for how long?

I told myself, over and over, that once I returned to Sunpo, I would spirit her away from that mountain school and the two of us would escape Sunpo forever. But...

That plan suddenly seems so farfetched, so improbable.

A sudden burning heats my eyes.

How will I kill him? I swallow hard. A knife to the throat? A sword to the stomach? I know many ways to kill—some quick, some slow. Quick. It should be quick. Before I lose my nerve.

But maybe I already lost it.

My hands quiver. The truth comes to me in an inevitable

wave of guilt.

I do not want to kill Haneul Rui.

Perhaps it is because of the way I feel when he looks at me—angry, yes, and bitter, but *alive*, for once. I close my eyes as I remember how he lifted me from the water, my lips tasting the salt of the sea on his. As I remember how it felt to live again, in his arms.

But the Revolution will kill me if I betray them.

And *Rui* will kill me if I lose his game.

I shake my head, pressing my palms to my eyes. I'm foolish to falter in my determination. I kill him, or he kills me. That is his bargain. Am I truly so naive to think that perhaps his decision has changed? That the kiss meant as much to him as it does to me? To hope he will neither behead nor shoot me?

More likely the kiss was just a lapse of judgment on his part. An ache of pain spreads through my chest. *Alone*, I think. *I'm still alone. There is nobody for me here.*

But there is Eunbi, in the Yaepak Mountains.

Eunbi. Her name is a crash of icy water upon my head, sharp and chilling to the bone. I still have Eunbi, with her trills of laughter and bright, vivid dreams. Eunbi, with her love of food— and strong hatred of vegetables. I still have her, and so there is no choice for me here. There never has been.

It is kill or be killed.

I will kill the Pied Piper and return to Sunpo.

For Eunbi.

For my little sister.

The hourglass, cold on my skin, is a reminder of my place in this palace. An assassin. A bargain. A game. Nothing more.

A gentle knock on my door has me hurriedly smearing my tears away with the heels of my hands and swallowing the salty tang of sadness with a swollen throat.

It must be my breakfast, delivered by a washy-eyed human, but I still curl my fingers around my golden dagger in precaution.

I crack open the door, but it is not a mortal face that greets me. It is Rui.

"You were crying." Rui leans against the opposite wall, idly lounging across my door, an eyebrow arched even as I point Chan's golden dagger unwaveringly in his direction. "Was yesterday truly that awful?" A half-moon smile, even as his eyes darken with worry. "I suppose it must have been, for you to run away so quickly."

Haggardly, I glare at him. I did not sleep all night, tossing and turning in my bed, haunted by searingly silver eyes glimmering with both malice and mourning. The dagger feels icy cold in my hand. "What do you want."

"Do you *really* need to ask?" he purrs, tilting his head in feline interest. "The pleasure of your company, of course."

I am too exhausted to do anything but seethe at the Piper, who waits for a sharp retort. When none comes, his brows draw together ever so slightly. "Lina," he says quietly. "Lina, I wish to speak with you about something."

Throat tight, I look away.

I will not hear his words, for tonight, I must kill him.

Tonight, I must return to Sunpo and resume my position as Kalmin's faithful lapdog. My vision swims with tears that I angrily force down, but not before Rui notices.

In a single stride, he is next to me, his hand curving delicately under my cheek as he gently turns my face toward him. At my expression, the emperor flinches.

Flinches.

"If I overstepped…" he whispers, and his voice is softer than I've ever heard. "I am sorry. For the beach, for all of it."

I jerk away. Looking at him hurts somewhere deep within my chest.

"Lina."

Fury rises inside me, great and swift, as I snap my head toward him. I hate that I love the way my name sounds on his lips. Hot tears of anger spill down my cheeks before I can stop them. I taste salt as blood roars in my ears. Rui's face grows taut as he watches me tremble, a helpless look in his eyes. He gently reaches to wipe away a tear that races down my cheek, but I tighten my grip on the dagger and lift it in warning. He steps back. "Please. Please let me help you."

"No," I snarl as I wipe away the wetness on my cheeks. I cannot look at him, cannot look at the distress in his eyes, the worry. He pretends to care—and that makes it all the worse. "If you don't leave me," I say, somewhat more composed, "then I will put this dagger to good use. Even if it cannot kill you, I am more than certain that you would hate to lose a hand."

Rui opens his mouth but shuts it as a battle between submission and defiance wages war on his face. Finally, he dips his head in a slight nod. "If you need anything—"

"Go." I force hate to brim in my eyes. Because I do hate him— hate him filling me with something other than the dark, persistent pain that has tortured me for a year now. I hold firm even as I shake with a storm of emotions, each a lashing of lightning across my heart. A deep, biting sadness. A sharp clawing of anger. And a dull ache of regret, one that weighs me to the ground, sucking the air from my lungs. *Kill or be killed.* I am not so foolish as to hope that he has changed his mind.

If I fail, my fate is a beheading or an arrow to the heart.

I will not allow myself to forget that, no matter the games Rui chooses to play. No matter how he excels at manipulation, at deceit. I will kill him, or he will kill me, and there is nothing more to it than that. There cannot be.

Rui swallows hard. "As you wish," he says quietly.

A ripple of air. Rui gives me one final, searching look of worry before disappearing into that dark, endless corridor.

It is only after he's left that I allow myself to crumple to my knees, my shoulders heaving with deep, rasping sobs.

CHAPTER THIRTY-THREE

I t is time.

My fingers quake as I fasten a dark cloak around my shoulders. I have tugged its hood over my face, and its inky shadows mask how my eyes are rimmed red from furious weeping, how my skin is pallid, beaded with cold sweat. Beneath the cloak, and attached to my hip, the weight of the golden dagger seems heavier. It is a damning reminder of what is to come.

Tonight, Haneul Rui dies by my hand.

A quick death is all that I can hope to give him. Quick and clean.

The moons of Gyeulcheon seem dimmer, the stars lackluster, as I slip into the small vegetable garden behind the kitchens.

My heart slams irregularly against the hourglass as my boots tread across the soft ground toward the wall. I clamber over it with trembling limbs. As I hit the grass below, my eyes snap to the oak tree against which Rui leaned, his silver eyes glittering underneath the rim of his gat as he gestured to the horses with an indolent hand.

I half expect him to be standing there, his smile thin, his gaze narrowed. But he is not here.

Not now.

I'm completely and utterly alone.

This is how it was always meant to be, I tell myself as I enter the forest and sidestep a puddle of murky rainwater. Somewhere, a bullfrog croaks, low and keen and hoarse. *This is how it always is.*

I am the Reaper of Sunpo. Grim, violent, and a harbinger of death. This is who I am.

My steps falter, and I recede from my haze of thoughts.

Something… Something is amiss. Yet I cannot quite place what is different. As my spine stiffens, I glance around the dark wood, taking in the gnarled trees and their tangled branches, the shadowy overgrowth, and the impenetrable darkness beyond. It is quiet here, so very quiet.

My eyes narrow.

The crickets have stopped their infernal screeching.

The silence is suffocating.

I am no fool. I unsheathe my dagger in one fluid motion, the metal singing as the blade scrapes against its sheathe. I scan the forest around me as I turn in a circle—waiting, watching, for what is coming.

Perhaps it is Rui, I think, still turning in a circle. *He has come to stop me. He has come for me.* I cannot tell if the emotion that rushes through me is hope or dread.

But there is no hint of plum blossoms, nor of licorice. Just wet earth and pungent mud.

My eyes snap toward a spot just outside my peripheral vision, where a shadow in the thicket darts just beyond reach.

"Who's there?" I demand, low and sharp, whirling around as another shadow rushes through the forest to my left, nothing but a phantom in the night. I hold my dagger tightly, sinking into the space in my mind reserved for evenings like this. Where I am nobody and nothing but swift, bloody death.

Nothing but a faint rustling in the woodland answers me.

I press my lips together in a tight line, displeased. "I suggest," I say quietly, "that whoever is in these woods with me makes themselves known. Perhaps then I will show mercy." A lie. Whoever is toying with me will pay dearly.

There is a shard of silence so sharp that my skin stings.

And then—the forest erupts.

I barely have time to bite out a curse as figures burst from the darkness, moonlight flashing on the long, straight blades they wield.

Dokkaebi.

I recognize none of them—they are all unfamiliar, two females, two males, all corded with muscle underneath the dark hanboks they wear. Guards from the palace? Those who want me dead before harm comes to their emperor? Subjects enraged by how I called Rui a gaesaekki at the ball?

Whoever they are, they have me trapped.

My knuckles shine white as I glower at one of the females, a Dokkaebi with stringy black hair and dull brown eyes. Her blade is level with my throat. The other three stand behind me, their blades at my back.

"Put down your dagger," she says, and her voice crackles with hoarseness.

Slowly, I obey.

The Dokkaebi's smile grows, and she kicks my weapon into a nearby puddle. I watch her carefully, my expression devoid of fear. Of rage. I push the shock and confusion from my mind and replace it with cold lethality.

"So," she says, cocking her head. "You're the traitor."

The traitor.

I struggle to remain expressionless as I remember the shadowed figure standing in the tall grass at the beach.

Traitor. Traitor.

The word rings in my head, a sharp bell of warning and recognition.

Somebody saw. Somebody *knows*. And that somebody…

Traitor. Traitor.

A member of the Revolution.

They know.

And my life is the collateral.

These are the consequences for the kiss on the beach. And I know, standing here, that any explanation I try to offer—any excuse—will only be met with the same end result. A blade through the heart.

They can try to kill me. But I won't let them succeed.

So instead, I bide time as best I can, running strategies of defense and offense through my mind as quickly as possible. "Jiwoon sent you," I say, for it is clear that these Dokkaebi have been dispatched here by another Revolutionary. And that somebody…Jiwoon, the figure on the beach. Jiwoon, the leader of the Revolution. Which means… "Who are you?" I demand, although I already know the answer. Time—I need more time. I make note of the female Dokkaebi's stance. She is alert yet indolent. I am outnumbered, and she is quite aware of it. I'm willing to bet that the three behind me rest in similar poses.

They underestimate me.

That I can use against them.

A male Dokkaebi behind me laughs. The sound is wet. Awful. "You didn't think that there were only three Revolutionaries, did you?" The point of a blade prods into my back, and I grit my teeth. "Foolish girl."

I am.

Stealing a shipment of metals… That obviously requires more than just three Dokkaebi.

But I trusted them when they said it was only the three of

them. And that godsdamned trust could be my undoing.

"Jiwoon's network is expansive," the second female purrs at my back. "You've met his right-hand man and right-hand woman. But there are dozens more of us, scattered throughout all of Gyeulcheon."

"Why didn't he tell me?" The words are nearly mechanical as my mind continues to sift through my priority, the various methods of escape and attack. Perhaps Gameunjang has thrown me a bone after all, for it seems as if this quartet of Revolutionaries loves to hear themselves talk.

"Your kind is never to be trusted." The second male's voice is hard and brittle. "Humans," he spits in disdain. Some splatters on the hem of my cloak. "So weak-minded, so shallow. Festering on the realm that is rightfully ours—Iseung. When we kill you, girl, and once we kill *him*, rest assured that the Dokkaebi will take their rightful place on the thrones of the Three Kingdoms once more."

"As rulers," the second female says. "Emperors and empresses. You will shower us in riches, worship us on your knees." The hunger is clear in her tone, in the way her words half catch on her tongue, clumsy with eagerness.

With a cold jolt, I taste sickness. Jiwoon promised that control over Iseung was not on his agenda—

But it does not matter what he has promised.

He has betrayed me. They have betrayed me.

A part of me itches to spit that the seduction of Haneul Rui is part of my winning strategy. Surely, I can attempt to talk reason into them. But my tongue remains leaden, refusing to taste the burnt sugar of a lie.

I have kissed him.

And I have liked it.

"It was only a matter of time before you betrayed us," the first female says, narrowing her eyes. "Jiwoon was wary of your treason from the start, for mortals are so shallow. They are easily corrupted. Fooled. But no matter," she continues, exchanging a look with the male Dokkaebi who stands just behind my right shoulder. "You'll be in Jeoseung soon, regardless."

I've had enough. "Maybe," I retort, muscles tensing as cold determination floods me. This is not how it will end for me. "But you'll go first."

Before they can strike, I drop to the ground and grit my teeth as the blade against my back tears down my skin. The cut is mercifully small and shallow, and little pain shoots through me as I roll in the mud and grime.

My hand closes around the golden dagger within the cold puddle as the Dokkaebi above me bring their jikdos down to where I lie. Silver flashes, but then I'm on my feet—dodging two blades, parrying one, and sending the first female Dokkaebi staggering backward with a well-placed kick to her abdomen. She stumbles into the forest, loses her balance on a loose stone, and lands out of sight within the shrubbery.

Stay down.

I snap around as two more blades aim for me and block the blows with lightning-fast speed. The food and rest I've received here has allowed me to transform back into the Talon's Reaper—strong and swift and utterly unforgiving. I barely pay attention to the dull throbbing in my left leg from the exertion, concentrating only on the battle before me.

I grit my teeth as I chance a few steps closer to one of the male Dokkaebi, and feint left before sinking my dagger into the right side of his chest. I feel a surge of relief. He is not as strong as Rui, not by far. He is an ordinary Dokkaebi—not a Gaksi Dokkaebi, the powerful members of Rui's inner court.

Golden blood, hot and thick, coats my hand as I yank my blade away, ducking as the other male roars in outrage. As his comrade falls, his eyes dull, and he rushes toward me. The veins crisscrossing his forehead bulge in fury, and spittle hangs in lines from the top of his mouth as he screams in a mixture of horror, agony, and outrage.

His grief has made him sloppy. He doesn't even see the gap in his defenses until my blade is singing through the air.

I smile at him as I slash his throat.

His hands rise to the golden wound, and with a soft gurgle, he collapses next to the other.

There is no sign of the Dokkaebi with the stringy hair, whom I sent reeling into the forest. My smile grows, cold and terrible, as I fixate my attention on the remaining Dokkaebi. She is taller than me, long and willowy, with a pinched face.

"If you were wise," I say glacially, "you would run."

Her eyes are fixed on the two dead immortals. "You killed them," she whispers, as if she can hardly believe it. *"You."*

"Me," I confirm, approaching her. My dagger drips their blood.

They are weak—so incredibly weak compared to Gaksi Dokkaebi. I see now why the Revolutionaries were so desperate for the strength enhancer. These mere Dokkaebi cannot hope to defeat Rui, a Gaksi, in their base form.

I imagine Yeomra watching me from the woods, the god of death smiling in pleasure as I twirl my dagger.

The Dokkaebi raises her gaze to mine and lunges, still ashen-faced. I allow it.

I allow her a few desperate parries. I duck, dodge, and sidestep them.

And then I disarm her.

Her eyes are horrified for the split second before they dim into nothingness.

I yank my blade out of her chest and she falls like a rag doll to the ground. Breathing heavily, I glance down at the bodies below. Their blood mingles with one another's, running in rivulets through the mud.

Curse Jiwoon. Curse him to Jeoseung for all of eternity.

A shiver crawls down my spine at the knowledge that he was *watching*. Watching as Rui and I found pleasure and solace in each other. Standing there, observing, unseen and unnoticed.

I will kill him for it.

And for *this*.

Sending assassins to the assassin. The irony is almost too much to bear.

CHAPTER THIRTY-FOUR

Panting hard, I wipe sweat from my brow as I survey my surroundings, the forest now quiet. My back has begun to sting from its cut, despite its small size. It feels almost like a burn—a burn that is growing more and more scalding. The fabric of my shirt must have rubbed against it, must have irritated it. I roll my shoulders in discomfort and do my best to ignore the growing pain.

With still no sign of the one remaining Dokkaebi, I step over the sprawling bodies and roll my shoulders. The path I should take now is not so clear.

Perhaps I will storm into Jiwoon's hidden room underneath the bakery and slaughter him. Or perhaps I will return to the palace as if nothing happened and do my best to create this enhancer by myself, plunging once again into the Black River for those godsdamned berries. But…if Jiwoon truly wishes to overtake Iseung… I cannot allow that. Cannot allow Dokkaebi to rule my realm once more.

From my time with the Blackbloods, I know enough about the nature of followers to understand that if I murder the leader, their devotees will scatter.

Doing my best to ignore the burning on my back, I turn toward the trail leading into the village.

And pause.

She is blocking my path.

The Dokkaebi with the limp hair now ridden with leaves and twigs stands perhaps twelve feet away, her jikdo leveled at me. I am flooded with a rush of irritation rather than fear.

"You," I drawl, clenching my dagger. "I thought you'd run off." I step on one of her companion's limp fingers as I stalk toward her. "You should have stayed away."

"Maybe." Her eyes glint in a way that sends a cold shiver down my spine.

I twist my lips into a grim smile. "You—"

I am cut off as a hand wraps around my throat from behind, pulling me backward. I press against a body, one that is hard and thick. I grunt in surprise, straining to lurch forward—but another hand wraps around my waist.

The female Dokkaebi steps forward and plucks the dagger from my hand as I struggle for air. My windpipe is being crushed; I can scarcely breathe, black dots swarming my vision.

A familiar voice mutters in my ear, "You really should have known better, Lina."

Jiwoon.

I choke on my hatred, scrabbling to drag my nails down any part of him I can reach, but the bastard holds true.

"Imagine my surprise," he continues, "when I came to collect the black sand for the enhancer and spotted the two of you in that embrace." He squeezes harder in his fury, and I gag. "But of course, I had my doubts about you from the start. Trusting a human, and an assassin at that. I was willing to take a chance, but I should have known that your bargain was too good to be true. The emperor clearly had ulterior motives. As did you."

I need air.

Oh gods oh gods oh gods I need air.

"Aecha," he says calmly to the Dokkaebi, "you may do the honor. In their names, of course." His eyes slide to the dead Dokkaebi in cold distaste.

"I'd be happy to," I hear Aecha say. She walks toward me, unsmiling. "For Gyunghui. For Beomsoo. For Namjoon. For the Revolution."

No. No no no no *no*—

Jiwoon's hand wrapped against my throat prevents me from screaming as Aecha's blade rips into my skin, digging into my abdomen.

Dagger scrapes bone and I wheeze, hot tears spilling from my eyes. Only then does Jiwoon release me, and I drop to my knees, blood leaking from my mouth.

Through my tears, I can see Jiwoon and Aecha as they crouch over me. Their eyes gleam with sordid pleasure.

"You filthy traitor," Jiwoon says almost pleasantly. "You filthy, filthy traitor." He clucks his tongue.

My hands weakly grip the hilt of the jikdo embedded in my flesh as I remain kneeling. It sits deep, the blade protruding through my back. Tears of the purest agony stream down my cheeks.

It is a burning, searing, blistering pain that racks my entire body. I shake with violent tremors. Everything, my bones, my muscles, the innermost corner of my very being... It all screams in agony.

Please, I think weakly. *Seokga... Mireuk... Yeomra...*

Hwanung, do you call this justice?

"This blade," Jiwoon says—and it sounds as if he's speaking underwater—"and all the others, were dipped in Imugi venom." His smile grows as more tears—tears of defeat—spill down my cheeks. "Yes, that's right. Imugi truly are the most useful creatures. Their poison is quite, quite potent. Some say it feels like being flayed alive. So, Lina, even if you do not die now, you'll pass within the hour. Food for the grubs and beasts." Jiwoon rises, and the stars and moons above are reflected in his spectacles. "Worry not. I will finish what you started. Thank you for retrieving the berries for me. I'll ensure that Iseung knows of your contribution when we reclaim it as ours once again." Jiwoon laughs, and it's a half-hysterical sound, bubbling and high. "Are you *crying*?"

The tears flow freely now at this final betrayal. "You said," I rasp, barely audible as I remember my first meeting with the Revolution, "you...said you would leave the mortal realm... alone." Each word scorches my throat and tastes like bile. "That all you wanted...was to improve Gyeulcheon. To make this world...fair."

"Did I?" Jiwoon grins, and the curve of it, the bared white teeth, are terrible. "I lied. Haneul"—the name is a disgusted snarl—"was a *fool* to forfeit all but Sunpo, a *fool* to trap us in this pocket realm. We were meant to rule. The Three Kingdoms are ours, not yours. Not the mortals'. They are our heritage. Did you think I'd forgotten?" He throws his head back and laughs bitterly. "I have not. I will not. Our rightful place is on those three thrones."

Aecha doesn't laugh, still staring at her fallen friends.

My mouth trembles violently as I take in Jiwoon's words, the truth he has given me as I die on the ground. *What have I done?*

Jiwoon will take the wongun enhancer, and Iseung, as soon as he's able.

He will be a cruel king. A tyrant. I see it in his eyes, the disgust as he speaks of mortals. The hunger as he speaks of the Three Kingdoms. Jiwoon will be Iseung's undoing, and it is my fault.

I think of Eunbi, huddled away at her mountain school. I have failed her.

I am dying, I can feel it. Killed not only by a blade but by venom—by a snake. My fear, come to fruition.

I am barely hanging on to the threads of life, and already, they are fraying. My blood is boiling, blistering from the poison. Past the splotches of black, I see triple. I sob weakly, wishing fervently for the gods to help me.

"Tears fit for a playhouse." Jiwoon's face is grim as he lifts the golden dagger from where it lies next to me. "And although they may be crocodile tears," he says, and I sob through my teeth as its blade approaches the skin just underneath my right eye, "I'd like to immortalize this occurrence. Shin Lina, defeated. Shin Lina, crying."

So lost am I in the thrall of the poison that I scarcely feel physical pain as Jiwoon presses the blade lightly into my skin, then slowly drags it down to just near the corner of my lip in a long, shallow cut. All I feel is a complete and unending terror.

"There. An eternal tear." He snorts in mirth and tosses the dagger to the side again before rising. "Farewell, Shin Lina. And my thanks, again. Come, Aecha. Time is of the essence, and there is nothing of great import to keep us here." As he rises, he looks down at me one last time. "Only food for the flies and the vultures."

I stare at the sky as they disappear. This is the end. I can feel it.

Life, gone so soon.

Is this how I will die? Staring at the moons of a foreign realm, supine on the cold ground? *Dalnim...* But the goddess does not answer me. These moons are not hers, they are Rui's, and she is so very far away. She won't come now. Nobody will. I am alone.

Alone, on the cold ground, unable to move. Unable to fight.

I always expected to go down in the heat of battle, streaming sweat and bleeding scarlet.

But there is so much that I still want to do.

Still need to do.

A dozen wasp stings puncture my stomach. A wildfire burns my skin. A low keening, as grating and desperate as a wounded animal, fills my ears.

Only when the whimpers grow in volume do I realize that the moans are escaping from my own lips. I turn to the side, sick. It splatters against the mud, trickles down my chin.

Pathetic, I think through the agony. *Absolutely pathetic.*

I stare at the sword embedded in my abdomen, wrapping a hand around the blood-slick hilt. There is no possibility that I would survive withdrawing it, none at all.

I look up at the moons above as the knowledge sends a wave of horror through me. The crescents dull further, as if they, too, feel my raw grief.

There is no possibility that I will survive—

I scream through my teeth as the pain grows.

Imugi venom. The cut on my back—that's why it burned so. And now I have a whole fucking *sword* coated in the poison jutting out of my back.

Seokga… Yeomra… Mireuk… Anybody… Please.

The night is so silent.

My vision descends into complete darkness before reemerging a few moments later, blurred and hazy. My fingers claw at the dirt.

This. This is how it ends.

And maybe this is how it *should* end. After everything—

"*Lina.*"

My eyes snap open. That voice—I would know it anywhere.

CHAPTER THIRTY-FIVE

"S ang?" I rasp. Blood bubbles in the corner of my mouth. Have I died and gone to join him? And if I have, why does that relentless pain still slam into my body and rake it with tremors?

I search for him in the dark woods.

A bluish glow at the corner of my eye has my head turning. A small noise tears from my lips, because…

It is Sang, but it is not. It is as if I'm looking at him through a river's reflection.

His edges are blurred blue, his face watery and shifting as he kneels beside me, slightly pellucid under the moonlight with those kind, gentle eyes and chestnut hair.

"Sang," I croak again, reaching for him. But my hand passes through him, feeling nothing but a waft of cool air. My arm falls back to my side.

I am hallucinating. Hallucinations are, no doubt, one of the many effects of the poison. But still, I attempt to squint past the mist clouding my vision. *Sang, my Sang.* Could he be a Gwisin? My lover's ghost, walking upon Iseung once more?

"It's not your time yet, Lina." Sang brushes a phantom hand against my cheek. I feel nothing, but I gaze at him, trembling. *"You must fight."*

I cannot speak, not when my strength is sapping so quickly. *I have a sword in my belly*, I think, for somehow, I know that he can hear me.

"The palace," Sang says gently, even as panic flashes in his eyes. *"They can help you there. You just need to make it."*

Do you not see the sword in my body? I cannot stand.

His face, ghostly and yet as open and understanding as it always was, slackens in grief. *"Yes—you can. You are stronger than you can ever possibly imagine. You are Shin Lina. The Reaper. You've killed men with your bare hands. You've haunted Sunpo in the darkness. You've collected that kingdom's souls with your blade, and you've spilled oceans of blood."*

I shake my head weakly. *The woods are dark*, I think almost nonsensically. *And I am scared.*

"You are the Reaper," he says again, almost with a hint of humor. *"The Reaper can never be scared."*

I swallow hard, thinking back to that day I confessed to him my fear. I promised him I would fight, tooth and nail.

"And besides," he adds. *"Think of Eunbi."*

Eunbi.

My baby sister.

My family.

Eunbi.

As blood spills from the corner of my mouth, I nod in grim determination.

For Eunbi, I will stand.

For Eunbi, I will try to survive this.

I do not want to descend into Jeoseung. Not yet.

For I am Shin Lina. The Reaper of Sunpo. The last remaining Talon. Orphan. Assassin. Thief.

Warrior.

I will not go to my death kneeling on the cold, wet ground in defeat.

Sang bows his head. *"You will not die alone in the forest, L. Follow me."* With a small incline of his head, Sang begins to drift along the trail, lighting the woods in a flickering blue light.

And I rise.

I roar, sobbing, as I force myself to one foot and then the other, a hand gripping the hilt of the jikdo embedded within my body.

I cannot walk. I cannot move. I nearly collapse again, but I force myself to stay upright. For Eunbi.

I plead for my limbs to move, and they do, albeit painstakingly slowly and with no small amount of sickening torture. And although each step brings me closer to the palace, they also bring me closer to death.

I groan, stumbling. Sang does not slow. I desperately fight to keep up as he guides me, sick and trembling, through the forest. Tears stream down my face and sweat slickens my skin. I lurch over protruding tree roots, and low-hanging branches scratch at my arms, my face. I can barely breathe, every inhale a wet, rattling wheeze that tastes of blood. There seems to be no end to the forest, no way out of the dark woodlands. Yet the trees slowly recede, standing instead at my back as I gasp for air and take in the garden wall.

I made it. I—

"You were always a good climber." Sang hovers before me, coating me in that blue light. *"Just remember, Lina. You're the Reaper. I'll be waiting for you on the other side."*

My eyes widen, but then Sang vanishes through the cobblestoned barrier. He meant only the opposite side of the garden wall.

Despair rises in me, but I force myself to grab one of the

wall's stones with one shaking hand and place a foot on another. Up. Up. *I am the Reaper.*

I am whimpering in pain, blacking out as my feet finally touch the garden's ground. I come to seconds later before I fall, delirious with torment. Sweat dribbles down my skin, sticky and hot, the beads tinged with blood.

Sang, I think, barely holding on to consciousness. *Sang— where are you?* I want to hold him, to touch him. Perhaps if I let the darkness take me...

"Not yet." His voice is sharp and cold in my ear. I force myself to open my eyes, force myself to follow him through the kitchen, down a myriad of corridors...

Sang. My Sang. There is so much I want to say to him, so much I want to ask, but...

My mouth. It is filled with enough blood that I choke on it, tasting strong copper. It overflows from the corner of my mouth and streams down my chin, warm and sticky.

I freeze, swaying in my spot as I meet Sang's somber gaze.

This is the end. I can feel it—the exhaustion and pain overcoming me.

Sang's eyes widen. *"No."*

Blood hits the marble floor. There is a small puddle below me now, crimson and thick. A crest of sadness rises in me as the barest hint of morning moonshine tinges the plaza in a bath of gold. I lasted through the night, yet the morning has come to take me.

"Sang," I whisper. It is the end. I know it, and so does he. The phantom is silent. The world is so very, very quiet in these early hours.

But then—

A figure dressed in silken black stands frozen at the top of the U-shaped stairs.

Rui.

His face is taut with fear as he meets my gaze, taking in the blood spilling from my mouth onto the stone floor. The cut on my face. The jikdo still embedded in my abdomen.

"LINA."

My name wrenches from his lips in a singular, horrible gasp before the air around him moves, rippling with a violent urgency as he steps into the corridor of darkness behind him...

And then he is before me as I fall, catching me in his arms and cradling me against his chest as I writhe in pain, choking on my own blood.

"*Kang!*" His voice is thunderous, booming through the palace with enough force that the entire structure seems to shake under his command. "Lina. *Lina.* Stay here, little thief; you must stay here—"

A thousand fires scorch my body, and I am screaming as the venom holds me in its grasp. Screaming as I die. Screaming as Sang watches with an expression of insurmountable grief, only an arm's length away from my bloodied fingertips that stretch toward him in utter futility.

"Who did this?" Rui is bent over my body, shielding it from the world, anything and everything that could harm me. His voice is a furious growl. *"Who did this to you?"*

But my vision is already going.

The last thing I see before it all goes utterly dark is Kang as he appears out of undulating air, his face as pale as death.

CHAPTER THIRTY-SIX

I tread the water of unconsciousness for just enough time to realize I am lying atop something soft, something warm, something wet.

A cot. The sheets are soaked with my blood.

The hilt of the jikdo swims in my gaze, fuzzy before my failing eyes and crusted with dried blood. Blurred figures stand over me, their voices blending together in a mix of panic and horror and anger and rage and confusion and fear... I sink down and down and down and down, the terrible waters of oblivion swallowing me whole.

And now I am not on the bed but above it, staring down at...myself.

It is *me*, it is my dark hair spread across the white pillow and my left hand dangling from the edge of the bed. And that is Rui, disheveled and pale as he dips a small cloth into a bucket of ice water and places it on my forehead with a tenderness I didn't know he possessed.

His black robes are crusted with blood. *My* blood.

We are in Kang's apothecary.

The stone walls are lit by the orange glow from the fireplace, and the collection of glass vials lining the walls shines under the light. The adviser himself is speaking to Rui, his mouth firm with determination. Chan, white-haired and solemn, stands beside him, his eyes on his king. Hana is next to him. But Rui's gaze never once leaves my face. My body is so still over there.

As still as a corpse.

I regard this scene with interest. My emotions are…detached, somehow. I feel only the faintest prickling of intrigue. This scene, it is like a playhouse drama unfolding before my eyes. I would like to see what happens next.

"Rui," Kang is saying, low and urgent, "there is no choice. This is the only option for her." He holds something in his hands. I can't quite tell what it is, not from my strange vantage point, but it's small and glitters slightly. A vial, perhaps. But what is in it?

Rui lifts his head from my still face. Anguish racks it, contorts his handsome features into a mask of desperation and agony. "It could kill her," he snarls. "It could *kill* her. You do not know that it will work. No human has ever—"

"She is dying anyway." Chan speaks impassively, even as a muscle in his jaw works. "She has a damn *sword* stuck in her body, Rui. I've never seen anybody survive this long, never mind a mortal. I give her another few minutes at the most. Probably less. Look. She's barely breathing."

"Rui, listen," Kang says again, voice tight with urgency. "If she ingests this concoction before we pull out the sword, there's a possibility that she will heal. But we must act quickly. Time is of the essence, and already we have lost so much of it."

"But if not," Hana adds, "she will die." There is no malice in her tone. Just plain, hard fact. "You must choose, and you must choose now."

"It should be her choice," Rui whispers, still gazing at my

pale face. "It should be her decision."

"Rui." Kang sounds impatient now. "She's slipping to Jeoseung more and more with each passing second. Either you lose her now, or you lose her later. It may not work, but you will loathe yourself forevermore if you do not at least *try*."

I tilt my head in interest, trying to see what is in the vial Kang holds. Medicine, perhaps. It must be.

"I beg you to consider the facts," Kang continues, and it's clear that he is losing patience. "The girl swam across the Black River to collect the wongun berries. You knew that, for is that not why you commissioned me to create a batch of enhancers of our own, should Lina's fall into the wrong hands? Should our soldiers need to heighten their powers as well, as a last resort?" He searches Rui's face as he attempts to reason with him. "Chances are, Rui, that she was planning on taking the potion anyway. That she found out how to create it. Allow me to give it to her now, my friend—I think she would want that."

The enhancer.

I hover in the air, blinking in surprise. They have a set of their own, created as a backup plan of sorts.

And they are going to give it to me.

I tilt my head again. This is quite interesting.

Rui's silver eyes are dim as he takes in the jikdo. As if he cannot bear to look at it a moment more, he ducks his head, his long hair hiding his face. His hands find one of mine, cupping it, embracing it as though it is a baby bird fallen from its nest. "Do what you must," he whispers.

The trio exchanges looks. Hana shakes her head almost imperceptibly at Chan, who places a comforting hand on Rui's shoulder.

And then Kang approaches me, pulling the sleeve of his robe back to reveal the vial—no bigger than the length of my pinkie finger, and containing a singular droplet of dark, shimmering emerald liquid.

I watch as he uncorks it, still unable to feel anything but a faint curiosity.

Gently, he lifts my head and presses the rim of the vial between my lips. He tilts my head back and pours the drop down my throat...

And I fall—fall back into my body, tumbling through the air, crashing down into flesh and blood and muscle and tendon and bone and pain... But the feelings begin to fade. Slowly, at first, and then quickly...

Until I am not there at all.

Until I am in darkness, complete and utter darkness.

All alone in the unending night, the pain finally fades. I let myself breathe, my heartbeat slowing from its thunder.

But the darkness, the silent nothingness, seems to shift. All around me, things feel as if they're moving, shadows of unidentifiable objects grating as they slip into place, positioning themselves as if they're a set for a play about to begin. I tremble as the gloom swirls, shifts, whispers...

A flare of white, like stage lights coming to life.

The show has begun.

CHAPTER THIRTY-SEVEN

The day had finally arrived.

Standing in Unima Hisao's Coin Yard manor, I felt a deadly sort of calm flowing through my veins. I straightened and cast a glance about the dark hall that I'd entered only moments before through the rain-splattered window. I was on the fourth floor.

According to the blueprint of the manor that Chara and Chryse had obtained, Unima's bedroom should be just down the hall. I kept my eyes on the shadows lining the corridor, slowly drawing the pistol from my belt. One click, then two, and it was ready. I was light on my feet as I made my way down the hall, keeping to the shadows as thunder rumbled outside.

Foolish, foolish man.

He had signed away his own life when he'd withdrawn his alliance from the Talons and had instead given it to those godsdamned Blackbloods. I reached the end of the hallway and pressed myself against the wall, peering to my left.

No guards.

In fact, it seemed that Unima Hisao had only Blackblood guards on the outside of his very considerable manor.

Flipping my braid over my shoulder and then tightening my grip on the pistol, I made my way to the door of Hisao's bedroom. It was painted a shining black, the doorknob a glistening gold. I pressed an ear to the door, listening.

Not a peep.

My fingers slowly wrapped around the doorknob. A slight twist of my wrist told me all I needed to know. The door was not locked.

Something almost like pity made me sigh. To think that he'd aided in his own undoing. A bullet to the heart shouldn't surprise him at all, really.

I checked my pistol. Unlocked. Ready to fire.

The moment one of my bullets ripped through the air, the war would begin. Blood would be shed. Lives would be lost. My mouth tightened in displeasure, and my stomach twisted with an uncomfortable apprehension. Some of those lives would be Talon lives. Others Blackbloods.

But Unima betrayed us. That cannot go undealt with.

I took a small breath and burst through the door.

The room was dark.

I could just barely see the outline of a bed. The figure lying underneath the down quilt could only be the dozing Hisao. Slowly, I raised the pistol.

Make him suffer.

And just when my finger curled around the trigger…

"Shin Lina," a voice crooned in the darkness. Husky and feminine, it sent a startled jolt through me. A thousand thoughts raced in my mind, but years of training kept my heartbeat steady and fingers unwavering around the cold steel of the pistol's trigger.

My eyes narrowed as the figure on the bed slowly peeled back the blankets to reveal a lithe feminine body clothed in a stealth suit similar to my own. There was a flash of white in the darkness as the woman smiled.

"Who are you?" I kept my pistol trained on the woman's forehead. "Where is Unima?"

"Unima is far gone from this place." A whisper of movement. A flare of flame as the candle resting on the bedside table was lit. The stranger was bald, her light eyes fishlike and cold as she tugged up the sleeve of her suit to reveal a forearm inked with the image of a graceful crane captured mid-landing.

The brand of our enemies.

Horror scraped its nails down my spine as I realized who the stranger was.

Asina. Konrarnd Kalmin's right-hand woman.

A Blackblood.

I'd seen her once before, only briefly, in the chaos after Yoonho had been shot. Asina had sent me that same flat smile as the Talon's leader had fallen to the ground. And that she was here and Unima was not...

Played. We had been played.

Shit. Anger tightened my jaw.

Asina's smile broadened. "You know who I am."

I sent her a sharp grin. "A mildly annoying pest. Easy to swat away and even easier to crush under my boot."

Asina slowly tilted her head. "Is that so? The Blackbloods are stronger than ever. As for the Talons..." She eyed me with obvious mirth, despite the pistol that pointed at her head. "Well. They fell for the trap we set."

"What *trap*? Kalmin replaced Unima with his little crony in the hopes of killing Sunpo's Reaper?" I laughed, the sound brittle and harsh. "No matter. I'll kill you, and then I'll kill your fool of a leader, too. And wherever Unima is, whatever rock he's hiding under, I'll find him." I scoffed. "You Blackbloods. Always so desperate to get ahead in the game."

"You're more foolish than I ever realized," Asina said softly as her lips curled in bitter satisfaction. "You think this was all for *you*? No, girl. This was for something much bigger."

I stiffened, dread sinking claws in my heart. *"What."*

Asina laughed. "Tell me, Shin Lina. Are your friends in that palace all alone, devoid of their precious Reaper's protection? And tell me this. How many more Blackbloods are there than Talons? It's *our* kingdom, girl, and it always has been."

No.

No.

In that moment, a dreadful understanding fell upon me.

The treachery of Unima Hisao had been orchestrated by the Blackbloods.

One step ahead, they'd hidden the merchant away as they'd awaited the Reaper's inevitable visit. A visit that would separate me from the others, separate my skills as a fighter from my gang.

And while I was gone...

An animalistic growl escaped my lips as fury turned my blood to flame. Fear like I'd never felt squeezed my chest tight enough that I choked on my own breath, stomach plummeting into an endless abyss of terror.

Sang.

Chara.

Yoonho.

Chryse.

They were all back in the palace, accompanied by the dozens of novices, the fledglings. And I was here, in a dark room, facing a smug Blackblood with a shit-eating grin.

I struggled to breathe. I'd walked right into their trap.

My family.

I would not lose my family.

I whirled toward the door. Godsdamn Asina. I'd deal with the bitch later. But for now—

Stuck.

The door. It was stuck.

I heaved my weight against the wood to no avail. Somebody had shoved something horribly heavy up to it. I pushed, straining against the weight. Warm sweat dribbled down my back, my neck.

It was useless. True fear, dark and trembling, settled in the pit of my stomach. Slowly, I turned back around.

Asina smirked, now standing in front of the room's large window. The only way out. She held a dagger in one hand, the golden metal gleaming in the candlelight. "Something wrong?"

I didn't hesitate.

The sound of the gunshot shook the giwajip, ripping through the air in a flash of violent silver.

But Asina was quick on her feet, nimbly stepping out of the bullet's path.

Another shot. Another. One by one, they rattled the room. And one by one, Asina dodged them as they instead shattered the window.

Shards of glass exploded into the air in a storm of white, coating my hair in a sharp powder. The acrid scent of the outside kingdom filled the room, icy gusts of damp night air whipping my cheeks raw. Asina guarded the open window, grim-faced as she was drenched by the relentless downpour of rain.

The pistol clicked. Empty.

I kicked it aside. Asina tilted her head as she watched me draw a jikdo from the sheath at my waist. With a feral snarl, I attacked, launching myself at the Blackblood with the swiftness of a viper. Blade met blade, the clashes drowned out only by the thunderous roars of the storm raging outside.

Blood wet the tip of my sword as it sliced down Asina's right thigh. I bared my teeth in triumph as Asina's parries became increasingly desperate, my blade singing through the air in a blur of steel.

I would not stop until I stood over her dead body. Until I could make it to the palace.

"You're too late," Asina spat as I stalked forward, ruthless with fury and ready to land the final offense. "Precious time has already been lost."

I didn't allow myself to feel the panic building up in the pit of my stomach. Instead, I kept my breathing as steady as my body allowed and focused solely on my next move.

"Give Emperor Yeomra my regards," I spat, naming the long-gone god of Jeoseung, and with a swift roundhouse, sent the woman toppling out of the window and into the screaming storm.

I did not waste any time checking whether the Blackblood would survive the fall.

I had to get back.

Every breath burned.

Roof tiles, slick from the rain, groaned under my feet as I hurried through the night. My lungs screamed in protest, but I pushed myself harder, faster. Rain lashed at my skin with each leap from building to building, nothing but a shadow in the night.

A trap. It had been a fucking trap. And I had fallen for it like a godsdamn fool.

One mile. Two.

Three.

Four.

My breaths came in short gasps. *Faster, Lina. Faster.*

There—I was almost there. My legs smarted as I threw myself to the ground, then scampered up the large wooden gate that guarded the palace.

"Please," I panted, "please. Seokga, Yeomra, Mireuk… anybody…"

No gods answered me.

Please. Please.

When I reached the top of the gate, horror tightened my throat. I struggled for breath. Through the scarlet archway and between the emerald columns, the door was ajar, a thin strip of light filtering into the dark, storm-tossed night.

The front entrance was to always be kept locked and bolted, especially at night. The fact that it was open now… I ignored the pain that shot up my legs as I jumped to the ground.

The night was silent. So very silent. Even the storm seemed muted as it drenched me in gushes of icy water. My legs turned to lead, and I found that I could not move to take another step toward the palace.

"Please," I whispered.

There was a single cigarette in my stealth suit, packed in a pocket along with its lighter, which I'd planned to enjoy after Unima's death. The urge to press the smoke between my lips and inhale bitter ash to calm my nerves almost overwhelmed me. My legs wobbled. I couldn't. I had to see what awaited me inside.

Every step up the front stairs stole air from my lungs. With a shaking hand, I pushed open the door.

Red.

Everything was red.

The wooden floor was stained with it—a red that trickled toward my boots in a stream of warm, wet crimson. A cold sweat ran down my back as my heart clenched and unclenched. The air was thick with a sickeningly sweet metallic scent that I knew all too well.

The smell of blood.

I was dripping rainwater onto the floor, watching as it mixed with the crimson, diluting it to a sickly pink.

"Yoonho?" The name, overripe with panic, wrenched from my lips. "Yoonho?"

Nothing but silence met my ears.

"Chara? Chryse?" My voice was shrill now, ringing through the night with a piercing desperation. "S-Sang?"

My vision blurred on the rivers of blood trickling across the floor.

I had to look.

Trembling, I wrenched my gaze from the red-stained tiles.

My eyes met a battlefield.

The carnage sprawled across the palace in heaps of limp, disfigured bodies seeping scarlet as they lay flat and unseeing on the bloodstained floor. Weapons rusted with crimson lay scattered on the ground. Others were embedded into still flesh with grim finality.

Some faces I didn't recognize. Blackbloods, given to death, their bodies still and splattered red. But the others…

I bent over and was violently sick.

That was Yoonho, slumped against a wooden column with a bullet hole dark on his forehead. And that was Chara, sprawled across the embroidered carpet, her blond hair limp and matted with blood as it hid her face while a sword rested in her back. Chryse was not far from her sister, her green eyes dull and unseeing, her pale hand curled loosely around the hilt of the dagger embedded in her chest.

And Sang…

The spy's face was still, but contorted with pain as he stared blankly at the looming ceiling. His body was horribly pale and bloodless, patched with bullets. His lips were blue. A scarred hand was stretched futilely toward a sword.

"No," I panted. "No, no, no, *NO!*"

The scream that exploded from my lips shattered the silence into a million pieces. My knees hit the ground, dampening with blood as I sobbed, racked with a sharp anguish.

They were dead.

My friends.

My family.

The Talons.

They lay broken and lifeless on the floor. Dead.

The scream broke off into hoarse, ragged breaths as the floor swam beneath me, darkness ebbing at the sides of my vision. Hot tears slid down my face, where they mixed with rainwater and grime. It was silent in the palace. So very, very silent.

The only noise that met my ears was the faint drip-dripping of blood as it spilled from Chara's body to the floor, each drop erupting onto the carpet in a burst of crimson.

The Mouse Trap.

My fault. This is my fault.

I killed them.

A hand touched my shoulder. Cold and clammy, it tucked a strand of hair behind my ear and lingered on the nape of my neck. I whirled around with a guttural noise, lacking all semblance of humanity.

Konrarnd Kalmin straightened under my gaze, a cold smile curling his lips. His hair was as red as the blood spilling on the floor, without a strand out of place. He wore a fine emerald suit that matched his snakelike eyes, which flicked over to me with no small hint of triumph. "Lina dear," he crooned. "You seemed in need of comfort."

I moved so fast that the Blackblood didn't even have time to blink.

Screaming in pain and grief and rage, I slammed him against the wall, breathing in the overpowering smell of cologne as I wrapped my hands around his throat.

I was white with fury as I *squeezed*, watching as Kalmin's face grew ruddy and horribly veined. He spluttered and clawed at my wrists. Through red-tinged vision, I watched as Kalmin's eyes moved to a point just past my shoulder. I barely had time to react before I was roughly hauled off him, leaving the crime lord gasping for breath as he leaned against the wall for support.

I hit the ground hard. Asina snarled down at me, flanked by two hulking Blackbloods, the tip of her blade pointed unwaveringly at my chest. Blood was leaking from the corner of her mouth, and the stiff fingers around her sword's hilt lacked any nails. She was carrying her weight on her right leg, but she was alive. The bitch had somehow survived the fall. I blinked numbly as Kalmin, slowly returning to a normal color, waved Asina aside. His second obliged, albeit reluctantly.

"You'll excuse the mess." Kalmin glanced around the palace in thinly veiled disdain. "Your friends did put up quite a fight."

I said nothing, retreating into myself and crawling desperately back to a hidden crevice of my mind where nobody could touch or see what I had done.

"No words from the infamous Reaper?" Kalmin looked almost disappointed. "I had expected a bigger reaction. Although perhaps you tired yourself out." He rubbed his neck, which was still red with marks left by my fingers. "I assume you've realized how perfectly everything came into play for us. Not even your precious Yoonho saw tonight coming."

Asina chuckled and glanced to where Yoonho lay dead and stiff.

"You Talons were always so lofty," Kalmin muttered disdainfully. "Waltzing around Sunpo as if you owned it. Well," he added softly. "No more." His lips split into a horrible grin. "Sunpo belongs to the Blackbloods now. And you with it."

I tensed, just barely.

Kalmin chuckled. "A weapon can switch its wielder, can it not? A sword passed from father to son as an inheritance? Well, Shin Lina. You are my inheritance." Kalmin gave a slight nod to

Asina, who drew something from within her stealth suit.

I found words, as rasping and as hoarse as they were. "I will *never* work for you."

"I beg to differ, Lina dear," Kalmin purred, watching his second approach me. "You have a younger sister, don't you? Up in the Yaepak Mountains? Quite lucky that she wasn't here tonight. Don't you agree?"

Eunbi. My mind eddied out, focusing only on my baby sister. A crushing terror enveloped me, and for a moment I could not see, could not *breathe* around my love and fear for her. If she had been here tonight, if I hadn't sent her off to the mountain school—oh gods. I doubled over, fighting down vomit.

Kalmin nodded to one of the Blackblood grunts, and a moment later I hit the ground hard, my teeth rattling in my jaw as Asina limped to stand over me with a cruel, cold smile and wet her lips in clear anticipation.

"This is for throwing me out of the window," she spat before she slammed her dagger into my left thigh, blade biting bone and bringing blood. A scream ripped through the palace as she dug it in deeper and *twisted*. An agony of scorching flames and cruel cuts overtook me.

But perhaps I deserved it.

As I screamed, hoarse and desperate, Kalmin chuckled.

Through tear-blurred vision, I looked at the Talons lying feet away, cold and dead.

The pain in my leg was nothing compared to the pain in my heart.

"That's enough." Kalmin's voice, cold and bored, reached my ears. "Sedate her. I grow tired of her protests. We'll drag her back with us prone."

No. *No.*

But when Asina slammed that rough cloth heavy with the bittersweet scent of sedative over my nose and mouth, when I choked for air, fighting to throw the Blackblood off me...I felt something within me shatter completely, shatter irreversibly.

The war had ended before it had even begun.

The serpentlike green of Kalmin's eyes was the last thing I saw before my world crumbled like ash in the wind and disappeared.

CHAPTER THIRTY-EIGHT

I am no longer in Sunpo.

No longer in the palace of the Talons.

No longer in Gyeulcheon.

Instead, I am in another world altogether.

Dark purple flowers brush against my calves in a phantom wind that carries with it the smell of sweet cherry blossoms. Sparkling light, a shade of pale blue, streams down from an endless sky of lilac, upon which a periwinkle moon hangs among diamond-shaped stars.

I blink slowly, glancing down at myself. I'm clad in only a thin white dress—a nightgown, fitting for the sudden heavy fatigue I feel. My hair hangs loose down my back, and in my right hand, I hold a tall white candle with a flickering yellow flame. The wax has begun to dribble down the stick, slowly bubbling pale white.

This world is beautiful and carries with it the slow feeling of a deep slumber. Yet I do not quite think this is a dream, not at all.

A name, a place, inches hesitantly into my mind.

But it simply isn't possible. *That* place is a realm of shadow and darkness, so at odds with the glittering moonlight falling upon my upturned face. *That* place is one of dark mist and blood. The fields of purple flowers, the smell of blossoms, the dreamlike feeling of peace… Surely this is not Jeoseung.

I look around, my movements slow, idle. The field of flowers is bordered by a stretch of woodlands where hundred-foot trees as white as bone stretch thin branches up to the sky. If I listen carefully, there is the sound of a river. It's so faint that I've almost missed the quiet churning entirely.

Sighing a little, I move slowly toward the noise, fueled by a languorous intrigue. The hem of my dress trails first through the field of flowers, then the sweet-smelling grass of the forest. I gaze up at the trees, marveling at their luminance, their skeletal bark. Hot wax from the candle dribbles down onto my hand, but the pain is warm, soothing.

I cannot tell how long I walk. It may be a minute, an hour, or a year. I follow the noise of the river, forging a path through the woodlands and breathing in the scent of cherry blossoms. When the faint noise heightens to a crescendo of roaring waves, and as mists of cold water spray my face, I finally halt and tighten my hold on the candle. It softens under my grip. My fingers dig into the warm wax, denting the column with their marks. Some of the sleepy fog departs from my mind as I see that I now stand on a cliff of lavender stone.

White mist wraps its tendrils around me as I peer down at the river below, taking in the rose-colored waters. Schools of iridescent fish leap from the shimmering depths, their scales reflecting the stars above. The air is now tinged with the faintest scent of salt, and something else, something that smells of copper.

My feet edge closer to the end of the cliff. Beyond the river and its bordering forest of white trees, there are mountains— huge stone mountains, some jade, some onyx, others quartz. Another cliff is directly across from the one I stand upon, the rock a shimmering white crystal. "Beautiful," I murmur, stretching out a hand toward the mountaintops.

"Lina," a voice says gently behind me.

Slowly, I turn, and the white mist parts to reveal Sang.

His brown eyes are deeper and darker than they were in the woods, and gone is the bluish tint to his borders. There is warmth in his gaze, color in his cheeks. He looks alive, solid and firm, save for a smudged blurriness coating his edges. I blink groggily as shock and happiness deliver swift blows to my heart.

"Sang," I whisper. Tentatively, I reach out a hand and touch his face. His skin is smooth and whole underneath my fingertips. "How... How can this be?" My hand falls back to my side.

"I think you know," Sang replies gently.

Again that name, that place, creeps sluggishly into my mind.

This time, I allow it.

Jeoseung.

The underworld. The realm of Yeomra, God of Death.

"I'm dead," I say slowly. "I've died." The words don't frighten me as much as they should. This world is far too peaceful for me to feel such an emotion.

But Sang shakes his head. "Not quite." He offers me a small smile, but it's strained. As if he's fighting hard against some invisible tether of sorts. "Not yet, Lina. You still stand on the side of the more-or-less living. Look," he murmurs, and gestures to a jade bridge a dozen or so feet from us. It is curved and glossy as it connects the cliff on which we stand to the one across from us. "Only when you cross the Hwangcheon Bridge over the Seocheongang River do you truly die."

I ponder this, but my mind is still moving slowly, as if attempting to wake from a deep sleep. "I see."

Sang sharply turns to me, his hazel eyes wide and urgent, a strand of curly chestnut hair flopping into his eyes as he grabs my free hand with one of his scarred ones. "Lina, I don't have much time left on this side, and neither do you. When your candle disappears, so does your choice. You have to decide, L. You have to decide where you want to be."

I blink, disconcerted, and glance toward the candle that I hold. Fat rivulets of candlewax drip down it and onto my hand, hardening in a cake of waxy white around my wrist and fingers. Already, the candle is half of what it was when I first emerged into this side of Jeoseung.

"What do you mean?" I ask, frowning a little. "What do you mean, that I have to choose?" My voice is plaintive. I am exhausted, and this conversation is confusing to my weary mind. I consider taking a nap in the field of flowers, but Sang's hand tightens on my own.

His expression is so raw, so tender. "If you want to live or die," he whispers, his thumb tracing circles on my hand. "If you want to cross the bridge of your free will, then you must do so before the flame winks out. And if you want to return to life, you must decide that soon. I know it's hard, Lina. You're slipping away, even now. It's making you tired. But you need to focus." Sang scans my eyes and then gently tugs me toward him and brings his lips to my forehead, kissing me there ever so softly.

His touch affects me as it always did, sending a jolt of warm adrenaline through my body, and I shake my head—free of the sleepy trance imparted on me by Jeoseung's tranquility and my own mortality. My thoughts are once again clear and sharp. "Sang?" I whisper after a long moment. "Was it really you in the woods? Were you really…a Gwisin?"

Sang smiles, and there's a hint of bitter humor in it. "Jeoseung lacks its god," he says, looking toward the Seocheongang River and the sprawling palace beyond. "Emperor Yeomra has abandoned it in favor of Okhwang. Chaos reigns, and the rules are easier to bend. But I do not think I will be able to do it again, L. It cost much. I heard you," he adds quietly. "Screaming in the forest. And so I came. I thought I could save you. You were never supposed to come to me, not here."

But it was my time. "I should have been at the palace," I whisper. "That night. It should have been me, too." *I should have died with you.*

Sang's hand clenches tightly around mine. "Lina—"

I look toward the Hwangcheon Bridge. "Are the others on the other side? Chara and Chryse? Yoonho?" Butterflies of hope begin to swarm in my chest and flap in my stomach as I imagine running into the twins' arms, breathing in the scent of their vanilla soap and spiced perfumes. "Are they across that bridge?" And perhaps my eomma, my appa—they could be there, too. "The Talons?"

"They are."

"I want to tell them how sorry I am," I whisper, and turn back to him as I fight tears. "I want to tell *you* how sorry I am." My throat clenches painfully. *I'm sorry.* How pathetic that those two tiny words will never reverse that night.

"It's not your fault. Lina." A look of pure horror flashes across Sang's face. "What happened was a tragedy. A miscalculation. It was a lot of things, but it was never your fault."

Tears fall silently on my cheeks. "But I left, ran right into a trap. Just like they wanted me to. If I had been there…" I choke. "Oh gods. Sang…"

"If you had been there, you may very well have been killed, too." Sang's face is firm. Unyielding. "You lived, Lina, and for that I am grateful." A soft pause. "And so are the others. You're the last of us, Lina. The last of the Talons. And we never blamed you. *Never.*" He meets my eyes. "The others understand. *I* understand."

My face crumples, hot with a rising grief that not even Jeoseung's tranquil peace can suppress. I think I catch a tearful glimmer in his eyes, too. "They're waiting for you," he says quietly. "It's your choice, Lina, which way you go now." Sang steps away, and his expression is gentle—soft and encouraging, but sad, too, as he watches me turn my gaze back to the bridge. The jade arch shines in the sparkling moonlight. I imagine myself walking its length, holding Sang's scarred hand in mine. I imagine feeling this peace forever, living in a world that smells of honey, where there is no danger of death or pain. I could be reunited with them again, my Talons. A small smile curves my lips.

"It's so different than I thought it'd be here. It's…beautiful. It's quiet. Peaceful. So different than Sunpo." The sky is so clear, and its moon rivals even Gyeulcheon's in beauty. I stare up at the stars.

"It is," he admits softly. "There is beauty in death."

"I could finally…" My voice wobbles. "I could finally rest." It is overwhelming, how much I want that. "I'm tired, Sang. I'm so tired."

"I know, L. I know."

I look at the candle in my hand, the wax melting steadily. I look at the bridge. *Eunbi*, I think, and hesitate. *My Eunbi.* She is not here in this world. She still suffers in the world above.

"It's your choice, Lina." Sang cups a side of my face in his hand, stroking my cheek with a thumb. "But," he says, "promise me that if you do choose to go back, you will let yourself live. Truly live. Promise me…"

He swallows hard, and I know that he is thinking of those nights spent smoking halji on the rooftops of Sunpo.

"If you choose to return, promise me that you will stop before it takes you. That you'll find a happiness in something other than the ashes of a cigarette. I wish I had… I wish I had learned this before it became too late. But for you, it isn't. Not if you so choose." Sang takes a rattling breath. "If you choose to return, I hope for you to find peace within your lifetime. Not the peace of death," he clarifies a bit sadly, "but the peace of the living."

Peace. My heart pounds at the word. I'm not sure I've ever felt it before, in the world of the breathing. To have such a thing would be a luxury. I would treasure it above all else.

Sang's eyes meet mine. "Find love. True love. That being, the one with the silver eyes… I don't pretend to know who, or what, he is. But what he felt for you in the plaza…"

My breath catches in my throat. "Love?" I ask hoarsely, and my mind drifts to Rui—the way he shouted my name with such fear, such grief—how he cradled me in his arms, silver eyes radiant with fury.

"Who did this? Who did this to you?"

I think of our kiss on the beach, the happiness I felt in his arms, and I wonder if it was the peace of the living Sang has mentioned. If it exists after all.

If I can find it, with Rui.

If he would call off our game.

Sang nods, a small dip of his head, and steps away from me. His hand falls from my face, and he avoids my gaze. "I recognized it, for I felt it, too. I *feel* it, too. It was never a mistake, Lina," he whispers in a thread of a voice.

Silken sheets. A bottle of champagne.

I blink rapidly, but even as I try to focus on Sang, my mind's eye is still picturing Rui. Rui, leaning against the tree outside the garden wall with a smile. Rui, apologizing. Twirling me around the ballroom to the beautiful, lilting music. Offering me a flower, weaving me a crown. Holding me in his arms as I bleed out.

Kill or be killed.

But what if neither of us wants to land the final blow? What if the connection we have transcends the rules of our game?

"You said… You said that it was a mistake," I finally manage to say to Sang, shaking my head. "You told me, over and over."

"I lied to you. And for that…" Tears run down his face, and he looks toward the forest of pale trees. "For that, I am infinitely sorry."

A sob works its way up my throat. "Why? Why would you lie to me?" *You, who I trusted more than anyone. You, who I loved. We could have done so much together.*

"Because…" Sang's hazel eyes dull as he turns back. "Because I was scared. Because with you, it was more than just another tumble. More than… I didn't know what would come next, and I feared that you would make me want a life outside of shadows and spies. And because I thought… I thought you deserved better than me, Lina."

"Better?" Tears flow freely down my cheeks now. "No. There was nobody else—there *is* nobody else." Burnt sugar on my tongue. I want to spit the taste out.

"You do not need to lie, L." Sang smiles gently, even as his eyes gleam with unshed tears. "I know that there is. And if you go, whatever it is that you have with him…chase it. You deserve love." He takes a shuddering breath. "Out of all of us, you deserve it the most."

"Sang," I sob, clenching my shrinking candle tight. I can barely breathe through my hiccups, my tears. "Sang." This is goodbye. I know it, in my bones. I cannot stay here. There is too much waiting for me above.

He steps closer to me and wipes a tear away with his thumb. I sob harder as he presses another kiss to my forehead, then enfolds me in his embrace.

Even in death, he smells of soap, sweat, ginger tea, and the smoky scent of halji. My fingers cling to his back and I bury my face in the crook of his neck, wetting his skin with salty tears.

"We'll see each other again, L," he murmurs into the crown of my head. His voice is tight, straining. He will have to leave soon. But I do not want him to go. "Whatever you decide, we'll see each other again. I promise."

"Tell the others," I choke out. "Tell the others—" *That I'm so sorry. That I miss them, I think about them every single day. Tell them I love them, my family, my friends.*

And I can see from those words that Sang knows I have decided.

There was no choice in the end, not really.

Too much is left unfinished in the world of the living.

"I know. I will." Sang gently leaves my grip. His absence stings like one thousand swords set to my skin. The image of him is rippling, flickering in and out of existence with every passing second. He smiles, one last time, crooked and small and shy.

My heart breaks into ten thousand shards at the sight of it.

I reach for him, even as he begins to vanish. "If you remember one thing from this conversation, Lina, remember…"

"Remember what?" I whisper.

"Death does not die," he says, meeting my eyes for the final time, "and neither will you, Shin Lina. Remember that."

And then he is gone, nothing but smoke left in his wake.

CHAPTER THIRTY-NINE

I bow my head over the candle as tears roll down my cheeks. *It's time*, I think, and my body moves of its own accord toward the field of flowers—as if it innately knows the way back to life. The flowers tickle my skin as I walk, but a heavy blanket of dark fog has rolled in, and they're no longer visible.

A feeling of foreboding unravels in my stomach, and I stop walking, eyeing the black fog warily as it conceals the lilac sky. Thunder rumbles, deep and low in the suddenly humid air. Jeoseung's cherry blossom air now smells like acrid lightning. The hairs on my arms rise, and tension prickles down my spine as I realize, with horror, that the mist around me is shifting...as if something is moving through it, circling where I stand. There's a faint rustling, and the smell of crushed flowers is suddenly sickly sweet in my nostrils.

Tendrils of the fog rise into the air, curling and coiling. I catch a glimpse of a large form slithering through the darkness for a moment, only a moment, before it is gone.

Cold rain begins to fall in rapid sheets, and I cover the flame of my candle as best I can, blinking rainwater from my eyes. I swallow hard and brace myself into a fighting stance. My legs are crouched, and my mind is unnerved. I feel ill, so very ill, as a flash of shimmering blue-green bursts through the fog for a split second. Inhumanly fast, but it is long enough for me to make out a large, glittering scale, the size of my head. Maybe larger.

My blood runs cold. My hands are shaking violently.

"An Imugi was a giant, clever serpent with a maw large enough to swallow a human whole," I hear Jiwoon say. *"With the power to summon rain and storms."*

A crack of lightning splits the dark sky, and I flinch. *Imugi. Snake.*

"Even the gods could not control them. Nothing stopped their bloodlust until they retreated to their underworld realm of Jeoseung for reasons we cannot quite determine."

Fueled by fright, I suddenly have the instinctual urge to cry out as I used to in my chogajip, lurching upward in fear as snakes slithered atop my legs. But I bite down on my terror and force myself to think. Imugi. The same serpent whose scale is in the enhancer, whose venom is in my body. A large monster, powerful beyond belief. They reside here, in Jeoseung. I am in their domain.

I squeeze the candle, denting the hot wax. My eyes have begun to water, and I feel shame along with horror. I must be brave, not a sobbing child. Every inch of me is shaking violently, and I struggle to control my bladder, which has threatened to loosen from panic.

"The next time you see a snake, Lina, you give it a piece of your mind. The serpent versus the assassin. I place good money on you, L. You're the one with a collection of very pointy swords."

Clinging to Sang's words, I take a deep breath and focus. If I strain my ears through the booms of thunder, I can hear that faint susurration as whatever circles me winds its way through the flowers. Mist swirls upward as the creature of Jeoseung circles me. I can feel it now, the invisible serpent eyes pinned on me through the pounding rain.

But it is not a hungry stare.

It feels…inquisitive.

I do not know how I know such things. I do not want to know.

I swallow hard against my dry mouth. The candle is little longer than my pinkie finger, barely sheltered from the storm by my hand. I need to leave. Now.

Wetting my lips, I slowly grow aware of another feeling creeping over my fear, soothing its jagged corners. Impossibly, my heart rate has steadied. My eyes are suddenly blurred only by the rain, with no trace of frightened tears. A feeling of peace has settled upon me, but it's not the peace I felt earlier, the sleepy sort that's warm and quiet. It's a cold, quiet sort of stillness. A dragonfly in amber.

And there's longing, too. Longing, swirling in my blood. For part of me wants to…wants to see it, this creature, this snake.

Yes, I want to see it, just once, before I go.

I wonder what it would feel like to run a hand over those twinkling teal scales, what it would feel like to be pinned under the gaze of the serpent.

Ignoring the sputtering flame of my fast-melting candle, I make to step forward, tracking the sound of the monster, my heartbeat slamming against my chest in eager, almost hungry, anticipation. My thoughts creep across my mind in a sluggish pace, blanketed by a fog of morbid yearning.

But my foot freezes in midair as I attempt to take a step to where I know the serpent will come around, cutting a trail through the eternal mist.

My candle is nothing but a puddle of wax in my hand. There is no time, none at all.

Closing my eyes, I whisper my choice, just as the flame of

my candle winks out, trailing a thin wisp of smoke. And a wave of shadow looms toward me, blinding and ice cold as it envelops me into its embrace of nothingness.

And just as I disappear into that nothingness, I think that I hear words, spoken on a forked tongue.

"Child of Venom," I think the Imugi might say, but then it is gone, and I have forgotten it ever spoke at all.

For I am no longer there, no longer in Jeoseung. I am once again floating, floating through an infinite darkness. I am alone in an infinite, eternal sea of shadows.

I am floating, detached from the physical, and yet...

There it is.

A tether of some sort, weighing me down from floating further into that darkness and what awaits within.

And there is a...a feeling of light seeping into my body, despite no light existing within this void.

The peculiar sensation grows deeper.

Stronger.

And then it is overwhelming, relentless, that strange feeling of invisible light pounding into me, bursting through my body.

The darkness surrounding me, the pain encompassing me, I flicker and falter as that beautifully mysterious light encircles me in its warm embrace, that tether coaxing me down, down, down...

The darkness disappears.

Bright white light takes its place.

That white light is familiar somehow.

As if I have encountered it before, many, many years ago. There is something maternal about it, something so strangely comforting as it glows with the brightness of a supernova, pulsing with power. With *life*.

The light brightens. And brightens. It is awful and beautiful at once, pain mixing with pleasure as it streams into me.

Life. But not as I have known it.

There's something foreign about the life that flows into me, something strange and unfamiliar. And even with the beautiful brightness, I can sense something cold and cruel, something as ancient as the stars, underneath that warm glow. It blazes inside me, swirling through my body, coiling around my muscles, making its home among my bones and blood.

But what is it?

Open your eyes and find out, a voice, soft and lethal, murmurs.

I do.

CHAPTER FORTY

My eyes flutter open.

I lie under a soft, downy quilt, my head resting on a thick-padded pillow. Late-evening moonlight trickles in through sparkling glass windowpanes. I blink back a haze of bleariness and catch a glimpse of poetry books scattered over the plain desk.

Rui's room.

A slight noise alerts me to him.

The emperor sits with his head tipped back over the headrest of a plush chair, his eyes closed. His long hair is tangled, and the sash of his fresh hanbok is limp and loose, as if he donned it in a great hurry and couldn't be bothered to knot it.

And although he sleeps, his brows are furrowed tightly, his jaw clenched and fists curled. His chest rises and falls slowly, and the fingers on his right hand twitch, as if he is dreaming. Every so often, his head tilts slightly to the left before straightening, a breath catching between his lips.

I'm clad in only a long-sleeve tunic twice my size, black and silken. He must have replaced my bloodstained clothes with a clean shirt from his own closet.

I try to reach for him, but a splintering ache prevents me from so much as even moving. A groan of pain nearly escapes my lips.

My entire body is taut with agony. I cannot move, cannot so much as breathe, without feeling as if I am splitting apart from the inside out. My chest seems to be heavily bound with bandages underneath the tunic, and underneath those, I am in complete pain.

Frantic, I search through my memories. I do not know, not really, why I'm here. What's happened. My memories are blurred and fuzzy, clouded by an impenetrable mist.

"Promise me that if you do choose to go back, you will let yourself live."

The ambush in the forest.

The sword in my abdomen, dripping with Imugi venom.

Jeoseung. Sang.

And that light...

Panicked, I grip the sheets. How long have I been asleep? Surely the days of our bargain are not yet at an end, for without the enhancer, I will need as long as I can get... But...

Something has gone very, very wrong.

Because I do not want to kill Haneul Rui. And perhaps that will be the death of me.

I flinch from the truth and cannot stop a whimper of pain from slipping past my lips.

"Lina." Immediately, Rui is alert, his eyes wide. "You've awoken."

"How long have I been out?" It hurts to speak, but still I manage, my heart thundering against my chest.

"Only two days," he says, and I choke. The hourglass still hangs on my neck—and the sand at the top has nearly drained to the bottom.

Today is my twelfth day in Gyeulcheon.

The horror of it must show on my face, because Rui's eyes widen. "Lina—"

I utter a swear so vile that it practically burns my tongue. I'm only vaguely aware of Rui saying my name as my vision swims—and only when he curls his fingers around the hourglass and gently rips the godsdamned thing from my neck am I able to collect myself.

The emperor holds the broken chain, and the sandglass, in the palm of his hand. As I watch, he crushes it into shards of glass and lets them fall to the floor, where they glitter among the sparkling silver sand and broken pieces of obsidian. "Surely you've realized by now that I won't kill you, little thief," he whispers. "After all the trouble we went through to save you, I find I'm not in the mood for a beheading."

I can't fully make sense of his words through my stupor of exhaustion and pain. They disorient me, dizzy me. The room begins to spin. I fumble to understand what he means, and utterly fail. My thoughts are clouded, foggy. "What…" I croak through an aching throat before my voice cracks, shattering my words with it. The pain in my tone is audible, and Rui immediately reaches into his pocket, procuring a vial of dried flower petals. He uncorks it with lithe hands and shakes two golden petals into his palm.

"This will relieve some of your pain," he says, pressing one against my bottom lip. "It is from the flower god's garden. Hallakkungi's garden of Seocheonkkotbat."

"Hallakkungi?" I rasp. "Seocheonkkotbat still exists?"

"Overrun with weeds, yes, but it still stands within the Wyusan Wilderness of your own realm." Rui attempts a sly half smile and utterly fails. "Incidentally, the Keep Out sign has rusted over enough that it's illegible if you don't look too hard."

Hallakkungi.

These flowers, they belong to a god.

I am filled with wonder, with eagerness to taste them. I part my lips, allowing Rui to place the first petal on my tongue. It tastes like berries, tart with a tinge of sweetness. I swallow it and open my mouth for the next one.

Rui places it on my tongue. "How bad is the pain?" he asks quietly.

Already, it is numbing, receding to a dull throbbing. I suppress a noise of surprise as I swallow and find that I'm now able to sit up halfway, although my limbs tremble violently. Never have I been this weak. "It's becoming better," I manage to say.

Rui's mouth tightens. "Lina..." He tucks the vial of flowers back into his robes. "What do you remember?"

I swallow the remaining taste of berries to stall for time. I don't know what to tell Rui and what to omit from my account. The Revolution...and the collateral they attempted to collect.

He watches me carefully, his eyes darkening to a storm-cloud gray. "If you are unwilling to speak, little thief, then I will tell you what I have learned during the two days that you have been asleep.

"I know that you fell into the company of Wang Jiwoon and the Revolution. I know, Lina, that you were planning on taking the wongun enhancer and killing me. Chan's spies are thorough—and Kang noticed one of his Imugi scales was missing.

"I also know that Wang Jiwoon saw us at the Black Sea. Enraged by your betrayal to his cause, he sent assassins after you. Against all odds, you made your way back to the palace.

"Strength enhancers are liable to fall into the wrong hands, so as a countermeasure, I commissioned Kang to brew a set of our own for our soldiers. We used one to save your life." Each word is sharp and bitter. Angry. No, more than angry. He is furious. But not at me.

"Soon after, Chan arrested two Revolutionaries," Rui continues. "Chi Misook. Kim Hangyeol. They were found lurking in the woods, looking for a body. We may have them, but Jiwoon has spies everywhere. He knows that you have taken an enhancer. He is coming for both of us, and it is likely that he has taken the enhancer himself." Rui's jaw works as he falls silent, his knuckles white as he clasps them together and props his hands under his chin. "This is what I know."

I gape at him, my mind swimming. Words cluster on my tongue, but all I can say is, "You..." The word sticks in my throat, and I try again. "You gave me the enhancer," I whisper, remembering the scene within Kang's study.

A muscle in Rui's jaw pulses. "It was the only way to save you. And it worked."

"But I don't feel..." The concoction was supposed to multiply the taker's strength, yet my limbs are as limp as a rag doll's. Perhaps I never had any strength to begin with. I swallow the knot of shame in my throat. "I feel weak. Weaker than I ever have."

"The enhancer did its job well enough in saving your life. Kang was able to remove the sword from your body, to stop the wound from bleeding. It's possible that, since you took it when you were so close to death, you will never feel its full effects. But you're alive, and I promise that you will remain so. I grow weary of this game," Rui murmurs as he brushes a strand of hair away from my face and rests his palm against my cheek. Unconsciously, I lean into it. "And I suspect that you do, too."

"You won't behead me," I whisper, and he shakes his head, looking vaguely amused—but the expression quickly fades. "Or shoot an arrow into my heart."

"No. I wanted to end the game the moment we kissed," he says quietly. "Perhaps even long before that. I don't—I don't quite know. All I do know is that somewhere along the line, the thought of killing you…wasn't as entertaining as it used to be. I came to your rooms to tell you that, the day after our kiss." With a start, I remember the words I didn't allow myself to hear.

"Lina. Lina, I wish to speak with you about something."

I should have listened. How easily I could have prevented a blade to my body. My hands are shaking as Rui continues.

"But you looked at me with such…hatred," he murmurs. "I wouldn't have killed you if you lost the game, which I believed you would. I underestimated you, your goals. Who you were working with." Rui shakes his head.

"That wasn't hatred." The words are quiet. Hesitant. I swallow hard. "It wasn't hatred for you. It was for what I felt."

"For what you felt." His response is barely audible. Breathless. We hold each other's gaze, dozens of unspoken emotions passing through his silver eyes to my brown ones. Hope. Doubt. Fear. And something else, something stronger. I drop my eyes first, heart pounding.

Rui is silent for a long moment before he says, "You can have what you came for, Lina. You may take the scarlet-haired back to your city. Resume life as it was."

I close my eyes, hiding the way that happiness and relief crash upon me in pounding waves. Asina's thirty-day deadline has not yet passed. Eunbi is safe. Eunbi is *safe*.

And this…

Neither of us wishes to kill the other. I suppose it's a start, at least.

"Whatever it is that you have with him…chase it."

But then—

Life as it was.

My mouth suddenly fills with the taste of dread, and I open my eyes. "I…" *I don't want to leave you*, I want to whisper. *Not yet. I thought of you, in the world of the dead. I wanted you. I still do.*

But he has not offered me sanctuary. He has only offered me a return. I do not know if I can summon the courage to ask for more, for more of *him*. Perhaps he does not want me here, and his refusal would break whatever tentative bond we've forged— and shatter something within myself that I cannot afford to lose.

Eunbi will live, and that is more than I could ever ask for.

"Truce," I whisper, hardly daring to believe him.

"Truce." Rui gives me a small nod that is infinitely sad yet holds a sort of warmth... A sort of comfort. "And," he adds gently, "Kang, Chan, and Hana would like an audience with you. Now that you're awake, it has to happen as soon as possible. We must hear all it is you know about the Revolution, even if it is nothing we have not heard before. Their greatest desire is to return to Iseung. The Revolutionaries are power-hungry and starved for wealth. Your world and its resources appeal to them. They are dangerous, Lina. They will take Iseung if they can." He brings my hand into his. Our fingers interlock, and I cannot help the warmth that blossoms in my traitorous heart at his tender touch even as my blood goes cold at his words, the same words Jiwoon spat at me in the forest.

The truth.

"They told me..." I rasp weakly. "They told me they wished only to improve this realm. That your taxes were too high, that they wanted a realm of fairness, a rule by the people..." I trail off, hating how foolish I sound, how naive. I should have known better, should have been suspicious from the start.

"They lied."

"About the taxes, too?"

"No." Rui's mouth tightens, and he's silent for a moment before saying, "We would value your help, your information, greatly. It would be momentous in our actions moving forward." His posture is stiff, his eyes searching—hoping, wondering, if I'll aid him. My former enemy, my opponent.

But my answer is immediate. "I know. And I'll help you." For revenge—and for my world. The thought of Jiwoon ruling over Sunpo as emperor makes me ill. "I'll kill him myself." The words come out as a furious snarl. Rui looks amused, but the look quickly fades. "But I want something in return," I add quietly, steeling myself. "Not for me—but for others."

The emperor blinks warily.

"The humans you take from my kingdom," I say. "The men and women you kidnap for servants." I watch as his shoulders stiffen, as he raises his head. His mouth has become a tight line. "Stop stealing them away. They are not yours to take."

Rui swallows hard, and I see his throat bob. "Lina—"

I narrow my eyes at him. "And the ones already here," I demand as sharply as I can, but I feel myself growing weary. The effort of negotiating has begun to take its toll. "They don't belong in this realm. They don't belong to you. Return them. Break their compulsion."

The Pied Piper takes a shallow breath. "I cannot agree to that."

I nearly choke on my indignation. "Then I *will not help you.*"

His face stiffens, and he passes a hand through his hair. The silence between us is heavy with tension. It drags on for one minute, then two—both of us glowering at each other. I stand my ground, even though the exertion of staring down a Dokkaebi emperor is beyond tiring in my enfeebled condition. Finally, I see a shift in his eyes—so small I almost missed it, but still, it is there.

"I will offer you this," Rui says, and I think his voice is the slightest bit hoarse. "I will cease the kidnappings of humans if I must. But I cannot return those I have already taken." As I open my mouth in outrage, he holds up a slender hand. "This is all I can give you, Lina. This is my only bargain."

"Why?" I whisper, but he shakes his head. "Why? They're

only servants to you. Employ your own kind, let the mortals return—"

His jaw tightens. "Take my offer, Lina, or deny it. It is my only one." His words are resolute, stubborn, cold as ice. I seethe, furiously thinking over his jest of an offer, turning the words around and around in my mind until my temples begin to ache.

"Rui—"

"I can't—" He cuts himself off abruptly as my eyes widen at his words.

I can't, he said. *I can't.*

Not won't. *Can't.*

That one word changes my entire perspective.

Liars often have difficulty fooling other liars—and I am one myself. The notion that Rui steals humans merely out of his desire for more servants is a cleverly placed guise to hide something, some other motive—I am nearly certain of it. No longer do I think that it is mere servitude he wants from these humans.

But what is it?

This bargain is a steppingstone, I finally conclude. *If I agree to it now, I can persuade him to modify it later. I can uncover whatever secret he's hiding.*

And if I can stop more men and women from being stolen from Sunpo, I would be a fool to not take this offer.

"Fine," I finally say flatly. Rui's expression doesn't change, but I get the distinct impression that he's relieved. Wearily, I extend my hand. "I'll help you."

His hand clasps mine and he shakes it gently. "A bargain sealed," he murmurs.

"When do we start?" I ask, returning my thoughts to the Revolution—particularly Jiwoon—and imagining with some pleasure their demise.

"First you must recover, Lina," Rui replies. "I thought…" He shakes his head. "I thought that you would die."

There is no humor in his voice, no trace of that perpetual sarcasm. Only hollow fatigue.

I remember his face, wracked with sorrow, as he held my limp hand in Kang's study. I blink rapidly. "I'm here."

"Yes. You are." A small smile that doesn't quite meet his eyes. They are a dull shade of silver, like rusted coins left too long in the rain.

Too weak to walk on my own, I am pushed through the halls of the palace on a contraption of sorts—a wooden chair with a set of wheels.

We are heavily under guard. Chan walks in front of us, and we are flanked by eight other guards. Their boots thud on the marble floor as they guide us toward the plaza. Behind me, Rui laughs softly under his breath.

"This is truly the grimmest parade I have ever been a part of," he announces.

Chan's shoulders stiffen. "This is no joking matter," he mutters over his shoulder to his emperor.

I can feel Rui's sliver of a smile, sharp and sly. "Isn't it?"

The general bristles but says nothing.

We are led into the throne room, where a glossy obsidian table rests underneath the scarlet dragons coiled on the ceiling.

Hana and Kang sit on high-backed chairs, their faces stony as we enter. The guards line against the looming onyx columns as the doors to the room shut with a thud that reverberates through the entire palace. Chan takes a seat next to Hana, and Rui wheels me so I sit at the head of the table, before sliding into the seat to my left, next to Kang.

"Lina," Kang says gently, inclining his head in a small nod. "It is a pleasure to see you awake once more." He cuts a glance toward Hana, who is twirling a strand of hair around her finger, and looking very much as if she'd like to send me right back to Jeoseung. Her eyes are narrowed, her mouth tight. "Isn't that right, Hana?" Kang prompts pointedly.

Scowling, Hana leans forward, toward me. My eyes snap warily to the sword strapped to the back of the emerald and white hanbok she wears. "I hope you realize the distress you've brought upon this palace," she snarls through bared teeth. Her eyes burn with hatred. "Between your part in creating the wongun enhancer and you leading trouble to our doorstep, I have come to realize that mortals truly are the most foolish species of all."

"You have something in your teeth," I retort flatly. I cannot summon the strength to think of a wittier reply. But my lie does its job—Hana snaps her mouth shut and sneers through thin-pressed lips.

"Hana," Rui says calmly, leaning back in his chair and crossing one leg over the other, "Lina and I are the very best of friends now. You'll treat her accordingly." His tone is light, but there's no mistaking the gleam of displeasure in his gaze.

Hana folds her arms, looking completely unconcerned at her emperor's disdain. "Or you'll punish me?" she demands indignantly. "Truly, Rui?" Next to her, Chan looks as if he has a headache.

"No," Rui drawls, his tone holding icy fire, "but I'm sure that she will." He glances toward me with a small smirk. "Isn't that right?"

"Quite," I reply flatly, having summoned enough strength to still be frowning at Hana. She huffs and glances away, muttering something unsavory under her breath to Chan.

Kang clears his throat. "Rui," he murmurs, "we called Lina

out of bed for a reason. Let us not keep her long."

"Indeed." Rui's smirk grows, and he winks at me. "So, little thief. I beg you, enlighten us with your side of the story."

Four pairs of eyes fix on me.

And taking a deep breath, I do.

I leave out my interactions with Sang, my trip into Jeoseung, and the Imugi before the odd white light. Those memories are not for them. They are deeply and uncomfortably personal in a way that the attack is not. So instead, I keep my recap short and simple.

When I finish, the throne room is unbearably silent. Kang's brows are pinched; Chan and Hana are scowling. Rui, however, is remarkably calm. He even looks somewhat…bored.

"Well." He cocks his head. "This is quite the anticlimax."

His friends gape at him. *I* gape at him.

Underneath our gapes, Rui chuckles. "Wang Jiwoon," he explains laconically, "is in possession of only one enhancer. Two doses would require more than the twelve berries that you stole, and it's clear he was unable to obtain more without you." Rui's head is still tilted, and in these moments, I note that he resembles a cruel fox—sly, cunning, and utterly predatory. "This is better than I'd expected," he continues, a smug smile tugging at his lips. "Kill Jiwoon, and the rest of the Revolution will be weakened. Two rather ugly birds with one stone, one might say. Once we kill him, it will be easy to hunt down the others and put this all to rest."

"They want to rule my realm," I whisper, knotting my hands in the blanket draped across my lap. "They want to rule Iseung. To be worshipped again." The words taste like ash in my mouth. To know that I have played a part in this… The guilt is insurmountable. "They want the Three Kingdoms."

Rui goes very, very still. "That will not happen," he says, and his voice is as quietly furious as I've ever heard. He exchanges a look with his circle, who have also stilled, their eyes wide. "That *cannot h*appen, never again. Gyeulcheon is the only realm of the Dokkaebi, and it always will be. It always must be." His tone carries an undercurrent of an emotion I cannot quite place. Warning? Resentment?

Fear?

Surely not.

But before I can open my mouth to ask, Rui is speaking once more. "Wang Jiwoon is coming for us, that much is glaringly obvious. As strong as he may be, the bastard loses points for subtlety. His motives are simple enough. Chan," he says, cutting a look toward the general, "you will interrogate the two Revolutionaries in the dungeon. They are his two most-trusted."

Misook and Hangyeol. I clench my jaw. I do not feel any sympathy for them, not after taking a blade to the abdomen.

"What do you want to know?" Chan fingers the hilt of the sword strapped to his hip, his expression grim.

"Where Wang Jiwoon currently is. When he plans to strike, and where. If he plans to strike alone. We can assume that Jiwoon will be the one to ingest the wongun enhancer, but I want clear-cut confirmation, and I want it now. If they refuse to speak under your methods, others will be used," he murmurs. "They will speak."

"Other methods," I say. "Do you mean Manpasikjeok?"

Rui smiles grimly. "Yes."

I furrow my brows. "Then why not use it in the first place?" I remember the compulsion of his music, my inability to fight off his orders, but also how he said the law forbade him from using it on his own kind. "Surely they've committed a grievous enough offense for you to wield it, even if you don't like to use it on Dokkaebi. Time could be saved."

Rui draws Manpasikjeok out of the folds of his robes, and

rolls the long, dark flute idly between his fingers. "Because," he says quietly, looking down at it, "this is a lenient method, too lenient. I want them to suffer as they speak. I want them to know that they are betraying their cause, their ideology, with every word. I want their consciences screaming as they talk, I want them hating themselves, and I want to savor it. Don't you?" He tilts his head, and I can't stop the corners of my lips from tugging upward in cruel agreement.

"I do," I whisper.

Rui nods and turns to Chan. "Do you understand that, General?"

"Understood." Chan nods briskly. "I will be tripling your guards as well, Rui."

Rui tucks Manpasikjeok away, raising his eyebrows. "That's hardly necessary. I can handle myself quite well."

I happen to agree, recalling how he pulled a dagger from his chest.

"Bullshit," Hana snaps. "Wang Jiwoon will match your strength. No chances can be taken."

"I agree with Hana and Chan," Kang says gingerly. "You are our emperor, and our friend. We take no chances, not with you."

Rui scowls, even as his voice warms. "Mother hens, all of you. Truly. Very well. But I want her"—he glances at me—"to be given an equal amount of security."

The way his voice softens as he looks at me heats my cheeks. Chan grimaces, and I narrow my eyes at him as Rui continues.

"As I said, our bargain has been called off. She poses no threat to me—"

"Doesn't she?" Hana mutters sourly, and I cut a sharp look toward her.

"And I will see that my ally is protected. Am I understood?" His words are now frigid, as unyielding as a winter storm. It is the voice of a king. He pins down Chan with a violent glower.

"I said, *am I understood*?"

"Yes," Chan grits out. "Yes. Fine. As you wish."

Kang frowns at him, but I am too tired to summon outward resentment at his reluctant tone, and instead nestle back into the chair. This meeting has been long, and I am tired.

So tired.

The pain has begun to return, has begun to gnaw again at my bones, sink its teeth into my muscles. I close my eyes, clenching my jaw.

I feel Rui's attention turn to me, feel his taut expression soften.

"This council is dismissed."

CHAPTER FORTY-ONE

A few hours later, rain drums on the circular windowpanes of the palace library, fat droplets running down the glass in blurry rivulets. Tendrils of fog swirl through the sky, heavy and gray.

It is clear that the realm's weather is a reflection of its maker's mood.

As the library's massive fireplace pops and crackles, its flames flicker across the tense planes of Rui's visage. His hands are braced on his knees where he sits on the armchair, next to where I lean back on a chaise with a thick-knitted blanket draped around my shoulders and a cup of steaming gyepi-cha tea clutched between my unsteady hands.

The library is a labyrinth of towering wooden shelves brimming with yellowed scrolls and thick volumes, a slightly uneven floor that creaks underneath one's weight, and a small elderly Dokkaebi who scuttles through the maze of literature, guiding books back into their shelves with a wizened hand. At the very heart of the library is the fireplace, which warms the surrounding overstuffed armchairs pleasantly against the athenaeum's chilly draft. Guards line the shelves behind us, where they can see us but we cannot see them.

It is an illusion of privacy, but one that I do not mind so much.

Rui has been broodingly silent ever since the meeting between his circle and me ended. I wonder what he is thinking, what he is feeling. If the pounding storm outside is any indication, the Pied Piper is just as overwhelmed as I am.

No doubt he is wondering, as I am, why Jiwoon is waiting to strike. *"Time is of the essence,"* Jiwoon said in the forest. My lips twist in anxious displeasure.

No doubt he is plotting, waiting for the perfect moment to launch his attack. But when is that?

Sensing my stare, Rui turns to me, his lips tilting upward in the sharp, wicked way that I know so well. "Are you watching me?"

"You're brooding," I say. My voice is still hoarse and jagged. Rui ordered the gyepi-cha to be drenched in honey for my throat, which is ruined from my screams of agony brought on by the attack. "It's entertaining to watch."

Rui's smile falters. "Drink your tea," he orders, gesturing to the cup.

I don't make a move to raise it to my lips. My hands tremble far too much to even attempt it. Instead, I watch as Rui strolls to one of the towering shelves surrounding us and as he runs his fingers over the length of a few books' spines.

"Ah," he murmurs after a few moments. "Here we are." He tugs a dusty volume out of its place and makes his way back to the armchair next to me, sending me a small, mischievous smile that doesn't quite reach his eyes. "Do you enjoy reading, little thief?"

"I've never had the time for it," I reply hoarsely. It's true. Between working the barley farm when I was younger and then later reaping the souls of Sunpo, reading books has never been a priority for me.

"I think you'll enjoy this one," he says, flipping open the volume to reveal thick yellow pages brimming with a slanted hand written in midnight black ink. "It is about your gods."

I look up from where I have been staring at the dregs of my tea. I cannot prevent my eyes from widening in interest. "The gods?" I whisper. As a child, I always longed for holy books, where the gods lived on paper, if nowhere else in our realm. But they were always too expensive, nothing the price that a household living on a small barley farm could pay.

Rui inclines his head. "There are many stories in this volume," he says, smoothing down the parchment page. "I will let you choose which one I read aloud to you. There is the story of creation, to start—"

"I know that one well," I say, finding strength and solace in the story. "The earth and sky were one realm in their own before Mireuk separated them and created the wonders of our earth. And then Seokga arrived, challenging Mireuk for sovereignty over the world. Through deceit, Seokga won. Enraged, Mireuk created the world's wicked elements."

The words are comforting on my tongue. My father used to speak the same ones, as we huddled in our chogajip with only ratty blankets for warmth. Sang's words come back to me. *Peace of the living.*

I think, perhaps, that those moments were the few times I've ever felt some semblance of what Sang described. And sitting here with Rui, my lips telling the same story, I feel something akin to what I felt those nights in our small house. Something soothing and steady, something that lightens my heart, if only infinitesimally.

"Seokga was eventually overthrown once more," I continue, "but Mireuk's dark creations remained."

"Like thievery?" Rui asks idly, and paper rustles as he leafs through the book.

"Like thievery," I confirm, "and murder."

"Your two favorites." He chuckles, and I think that perhaps the storm outside may be lessening, if only slightly. "Well then. I could tell you the story of the Battle of the Gods, from which my kind was born."

I tilt my head hesitantly. "I'd…I'd like that."

Sitting with Rui, with rain drumming on the windowpanes and a fire crackling merrily is…odd, considering I've been so intent on murdering him.

But it is not entirely unenjoyable.

No, it's not unenjoyable at all.

It's strange how fate works, sometimes. It is strange to think that perhaps I've found peace after all.

Rui's gaze softens, lingering on me for a moment more, before he averts his eyes to the book in his hands. "Long ago," he says quietly, his eyes following the scribbled characters, "there was a great battle of bloodshed between the holy pantheon and the creatures of darkness. For seven hundred years and seven days, the gods and goddesses fought against those who wished to claim the world as their own. Imugi, horrifying serpents with scales as glittering as stars in the night sky, who wished for the destruction of divinity, and a world of darkness. They had, ironically, been created by a god himself—Mireuk, the Creator, who took no part in the war. The Imugi, he said, were his children as much as the gods were. But the Imugi were monsters."

Imugi. The same serpent I encountered in Jeoseung. A strange feeling creeps up my spine. Fear?

No. Anticipation.

My skin tingles with it, and I glance back down at my tea. "Monsters?" I murmur. "How can you be so sure?" With that same morbid longing I felt in Jeoseung, and no trace of fear, I think of the Imugi I encountered.

Rui draws his flute from the folds of his hanbok. "Manpasikjeok does not work on monsters. It is something I learned during the war, fighting against Imugi—my music holds no sway over those with consciences corrupt enough. Had I been able to, the war would have ended in a blink. But such was not the case."

I make a small, noncommittal noise as Rui tucks away Manpasikjeok. I am still thinking of the Imugi, with its sparkling scales, but slowly come back to attention as Rui returns to his story.

"Emperor Hwanin, the heavenly leader of the gods and Emperor of the Sky Kingdom, led the army of the gods with enough strength that the world shook and the sky bled. The swords of the gods and goddesses ran golden and green with both the blood of the divinities and the blood of the monsters. As the rivulets ran down the length of the blades and dripped onto the carnage-soaked ground, the first Dokkaebi were thus created."

Curiosity blooms upon my tongue. "Which one...which god are you descended from?" I have wondered ever since Jiwoon claimed to be of Hwanung's blood.

The emperor's lips crook into a wry smile that doesn't quite meet his eyes. "Guess," he says softly.

"Seokga," I say immediately, but Rui shakes his head, tracing the book's page indolently.

"Sly I may be, but my family does not claim the trickster's bloodline," he murmurs. "Guess again, little thief."

"Yeomra—"

Something like a laugh, but not quite, escapes his lips. It is a huff of amusement, tinged with exhaustion. "No. The answer may surprise you."

I run through the remaining pantheon in my head. Mireuk,

perhaps, for Rui holds the gift of realm creation. I open my mouth to say his name, but Rui arches a brow and shakes his head.

"Jacheongbi." My guesses are random by now.

"I do not possess the agricultural talent you suspect I do."

"Hwanin."

"If I were descended from the Emperor of the Gods, I assure you that I would be much more vain."

"Teojusin."

"I have very little to do with Iseung, Lina. Rest assured that I am not of the Earth Goddess."

"A Japgwijapsin." I say, naming the lower gods. "Cheuksin. Munsin—"

"I resent the notion that I am descended from a lower god," he replies, laughing. The sound is soft and amused, with a tinge of dismay. "Especially the Goddess of the Toilet and the God of Doors."

"Oh?" I grin, unable to smother a laugh of my own. "I think it would suit you."

"I have no use for doors," Rui points out.

"So I've noticed," I say wryly, and he shakes his head, still smiling.

"Do you yield?"

"Fine," I say reluctantly. I am at a loss. I do not know his ancestor and at this rate, I'm unlikely to guess. I watch as he points to the window.

"Look at the sky," Rui whispers, and I do. The dark, furious clouds block the many moons, but I know that they are there, as elegant and glowing as ever, slivers and orbs of pale argon light. *Oh*, I think, and meet his eyes, his eyes that are the color of a midnight moon, a glittering silver ore.

"Dalnim," I whisper. "The Moon Goddess." How could I have believed it to be anybody else? I remember the way that

Rui changed the sky in the observatory, turning the moons from silver to gold with the flick of a wrist and a stroke of magic.

Those eyes lose their tension for a moment—just a moment—and dance with pride. "Yes," Rui replies softly. "It was her blood that created my family line."

I swallow. My throat has tightened with some strange, strong emotion that has brought prickling tears to my eyes. For I am as close to Dalnim as I will ever be—it is her eyes, the eyes of a goddess, that watch me carefully as I try to regain control over myself. Eyes that I imagined watching over Eunbi and me as we fought to survive, watchful in the endless night sky. Eyes that have seen me kill below them—kill and steal and lie. Eyes that have seen me, truly *seen me*.

"Oh," I manage to whisper, and Rui bows his head slightly in...understanding. He turns back to the book. When he speaks again, his voice is even gentler.

"Created from the blood of the holy gods and the blood of the wicked Imugi, Dokkaebi were fickle and sly—with capricious morals, as ever-changing as the seasons. Yet the undiluted bloodlust of the Imugi did not appeal to them. With the help of the newly born Dokkaebi, the divine pantheon defeated the creatures. Yet where one war ended, another began, and soon the pantheon grew weary. Weary of battling the serpents. Weary of the mortal realm. It fell upon the Dokkaebi to continue the fight." A strange glint enters Rui's eyes as he turns to me. "But the war between the Dokkaebi and the Imugi never truly ended—"

"Until the Imugi retreated to Jeoseung of their own accord, long after the gods were gone," I finish quietly, remembering the flash of teal in the dark mist and pounding rain. "Nobody knows why." But when I fix my gaze on his, the question in it is clear.

Do you?

Rui opens his mouth as if to say something—but abruptly

shuts it, returning his attention to the volume as he riffles through the pages. "After the Imugi retreated," he begins again, "the Dokkaebi, rulers of mortals, soon followed. Humankind was able to flourish, unrestrained by terror. The Three Kingdoms became more than villages huddled in fear of the serpents; they became centers of culture and new creations. Trade and economy in Bonseyo expanded as the other continents longed for the native fruits growing in their many orchards; the sweet apple pears, sun-ripened persimmons, and the white melon. Wyusan thrived on the acquisition of new knowledge, birthing sharp-minded scholars and philosophies, as well as fierce hunters who engaged in the global pelt trade. And Sunpo..." Rui's mouth twists. "The only territory still belonging to the Dokkaebi emperor, Sunpo transformed from a sparse village of chogajips to a cramped city, wherein a culture of crime festered in response to a lenient ruling system."

"An *absent* ruling system," I correct, and Rui shrugs.

"Semantics."

"Sunpo," I say, "also became victim to the Pied Piper's kidnappings. Sons and daughters, mothers and fathers...stolen away in the dead of night, following the sound of a flute." I watch Rui closely as he stiffens in his seat and looks toward the rain-smudged window. "Why did you do it, Rui?" I press quietly. "Why did you take them? What purpose do the ones you refuse to release have here?"

And there was that moment, in his bedroom. *"I can't,"* he began to say, but he cut himself off.

He is hiding something. I knew it then, and I know it now.

I say softly, "You can tell me. I, too, have kidnapped; there was always a deeper reason than just the ransom we could get — and the true reason was always dark. Dangerous. What is yours?"

In the distance, there is a crack of thunder, louder than any before. The storm is once again raging, wind slamming against the windows. Rui turns back to me, and I see that his mouth is tight. "They do not suffer here."

"But are they even aware of where they are?" I ask quietly. "They are mindless, knowing only your bidding."

Lightning illuminates the library in a shock of white. Rui runs a hand down his face. He suddenly seems weary beyond words. His shoulders slump, his head bows. "They are well treated here," he says quietly. "Chambers such as yours, meals to eat, and a light workload. They are neither touched nor harmed by my kind."

"But you *have* harmed them...by taking them..." The effort of interrogating him has begun to tire me. I focus all my attention on the Dokkaebi emperor, but I can already feel my grip slipping. "By stealing their will."

"Lina, I treat them well here. It is the most I can do," he whispers. "I tell the truth. You took my bargain, little thief. Remember that it is the only one I will offer. I will not return the ones I have stolen."

His voice is hoarse, but it's more than just that. Rui is...sad. Each syllable is coated in regret, guilt. And shame. My groggy mind fumbles to snatch up the loose threads of my thoughts. "But *why* did you take them?" Fatigue makes my tongue feel leaden. Try as I might to keep them open, my eyelids are already heavy. "Why, Rui? Did you...not want to?" The notion is disorienting. But why would he take them, if not for his own agenda? "Did...somebody make you?"

For a long time, there is no answer. Rain pounds against the windows. The fire crackles. Pops.

But then he lifts his face from his hands, and I see that his perpetual smirk is back in place, that his brows are lifted in gentle question. Although it should, the transformation barely even startles me through my fog of exhaustion. "What would you like to hear of now?" he asks. "*The Sun, the Moon, and the*

Tiger? Habaek the River God and the Deception of Haemosu?"

I am too tired to argue against his abrupt change of subject, and let my suspicions recede, harboring them for later when I can interrogate him with my usual fervor.

"All of them," I murmur, my eyelids heavy. "Tell me all of them."

And so he does.

As the storm ravages Gyeulcheon, Rui speaks to me of how two young siblings clambered up into the sky to escape a hungry tiger and transformed into divinities of the moon and sun — Dalnim, his ancestor, and Haemosu, her brother. He speaks to me of how later, the boy who became the God of Sun attempted to steal away the River God's daughter.

His voice is gentle as he tells stories of dragon lords and mountain gods, his voice weaving a tale of magic and mischief. I fall asleep to these tales, sinking into the sea of sleep, picturing hungry tigers and furious rivers.

CHAPTER FORTY-TWO

Four days pass, and there is still no sign of Wang Jiwoon. With every day that passes, my anxiety grows sharper. What is he waiting for?

I suppose I should be grateful, but all I feel is a buzzing apprehension. Hangyeol and Misook have given little away, even under the compulsion of Manpasikjeok. It is likely that Jiwoon has shared his plans with nobody.

I do not know what will become of Misook, of Hangyeol.

I do not care.

The pain has begun to recede thanks to Kang's healing brews brought to me each mealtime, as well as the flower petals, but I am still weakened. It is my sixteenth day in Gyeulcheon. Asina's thirty-day deadline, which I once scoffed at, now looms large, and I must be healed enough to take whatever beating she or Kalmin give me when I return. I can feel the time ticking, can feel Eunbi's life hanging in the balance, but I cannot yet return. I cannot even walk on my own, much less dodge a punch or survive off the Blackbloods' table scraps.

I have seen little of Rui since the library. His energy is

devoted to hunting down Jiwoon and devising plans of attack and defense with Chan. I don't know whether this is a relief or a disappointment.

I simply know that my heart quickens when he is near, and that I do not want his to still by my hand.

But no matter my changed emotions, Haneul Rui is still the Pied Piper. I cannot forget that.

I lie in my bed, staring up at the ceiling, my mind heavy as it sifts through possibility after possibility. It is likely that Rui takes mortals for his own fickle amusement, to staff his palace, but...I cannot help but suspect, now, that his motives stem far deeper than that. I think of Kalmin, working in the forge, glassy-eyed and blank. My stomach twists.

I will return him to Sunpo as soon as I am healed, no later than the thirtieth day. I will deliver him into the hands of Asina, watching as her fishlike eyes bulge with shock. She will call off the men on the mountaintops, leaving Eunbi out of immediate danger. And I will be put back to work. Beaten, abused. A Talon in a kingdom of Blackbloods.

Ask Rui for his help, a little voice in my head urges me. *He will help you, he will aid you in taking down the Blackbloods.*

But would he? As much as I want to believe it, he has offered me only safe passage into Sunpo, with Kalmin in tow. I rub my eyes wearily, wincing as my fingers brush over the long cut Jiwoon carved into my skin just underneath my right eye. It is long and pink, resembling a streaking, bloodied teardrop.

It's fitting, I suppose.

"There. An eternal tear."

I close my eyes as my throat knots with a potent mixture of hatred, rage, and...fear. Soon that mixture dissolves, turning into a familiar itch. My handmade cigarettes are stored underneath my mattress. My chest aches where my wound rests, but I know I can do it—push myself until my hands close around a roll.

It is an effort to stand, and I lean against the wall, trembling like a newborn fawn. I grit my teeth as I slip my hand under the mattress and pull out the last three cigarettes. My mouth burns. My tongue bleeds. There is nothing I crave more than a smoke.

I make to put it to my lips, but…

No.

No.

With a forceful, spiteful movement, I throw the cigarettes to the ground. My blood roars as I grind them into the floor with the heel of my foot until they are nothing more than harmless pulp, beyond the point of reparation.

"Promise me that if you do choose to go back, you will let yourself live."

A funny feeling tightens my throat. It isn't regret. It is…relief.

Although my body still longs for that inhale of ash — and will, for many days to come — my mind has accepted, at least for now, that not another cigarette will sit between my lips.

Not another coil of smoke will circle my lungs. Not today. Tomorrow, perhaps, I will struggle with my decision. But today, this is a small victory I do not shirk from celebrating.

I close my eyes as I collapse back into my bed.

Sang would be proud, I think. I can almost see his face — gentle and joyous, his lips parted in a smile of utter relief.

"He is coming."

The next day, I sit once again in the throne room, surrounded by grim-faced guards, in my wheeled chair next to Rui. It is Chan who has spoken, his mouth tight, his jaw set. "My spies have received word that Jiwoon plans to strike tonight." I stiffen as he braces his forearms on the table. "He's taken the wongun enhancer. His strength rivals our own. He comes alone, but make no mistake—the danger we are in is notable."

Hana mutters something unsavory under her breath. I ignore her, digging my nails into the palm of my hand.

"We've decided," Chan continues, glancing my way, "that the best course of action is to lure him into an attack of our own. My men were subtle; he does not know that we expect him."

"Mouse Trap," I mutter. The irony of this situation is not lost on me.

Chan ignores me. "I've tripled the guards at all points of entry. I suspect he knows of this—it will be obvious that we have devised a plan if I let those guards go. Our trap must seem natural. Innocuous. Everything remaining as it is."

Rui smiles, sharp and sly, as he laces his fingers. "I do love a good ruse," he says, wicked delight dancing across his face. "How very delightful."

Kang pinches the bridge of his nose, exasperated. "Rui—"

"In fact," Rui continues, "I have a good many ideas for our little trick." He cuts a glance my way, his grin growing. I narrow my eyes at him.

This is no time for jokes, I snap at him through my expression.

He chuckles. *Isn't it?* Turning back to his circle, he says, "What better way to lure Jiwoon out than by the promise of two birds with one stone?"

I frown. "You mean—"

"A stroll in the gardens, tonight," Rui says smoothly. "Eight o'clock, the two of us." He flicks his eyes toward Chan before I can respond. "You may position your men to stand watch, on guard for the attack. Line the garden with them, out of sight. Jiwoon is aware of the—" He hesitates, just for a split second. "The change in relations between Lina and me."

Hana rolls her eyes in clear distaste. Chan looks exasperated and exhausted at once. Kang smiles, but it is a tight smile, and his eyes are contemplative as he scans his emperor's face.

Rui ignores them. "He will not blink at a seemingly secluded dinner, nor a stroll. And then…" Rui grins, holding his right hand out before him. I watch as a blue flame dances in his palm, crackling with coldness. "Either I, or the guards, will take care of the rest."

Ignoring the way my cheeks have heated by his mention of our *changed relations*, my gaze rests warily on the Dokkaebi fire. "Have you ever fought a Dokkaebi with the enhancer in their system?" I ask, gripping the armrests of my chair.

Chan, Hana, and Kang all exchange quick glances I cannot decipher. Rui shrugs. "As a matter of fact, no." The flame disappears. "But there is only one of him and many of us. It will be over before it begins."

"It's a fine enough plan," Chan says gruffly. "I'll have my spies spread gossip of your dinner and stroll through the palace."

Rui grins. "Many thanks, General."

"I don't like this." Hana is rigid in her seat. "You're too confident by far, Rui."

The emperor pins his cold focus on her. "Let me remind you, Hana, that we have all fought and killed adversaries much larger than this cocky Dokkaebi."

Kang slides a glance toward me nervously, as if wary of what I might overhear. But Rui is still speaking, each word dripping icicles.

"We have fought a war against monstrous foes," he continues brusquely, "with far greater stakes. And we won—"

"Through your silver tongue. Not by strength. And it is suspicious that your bargain was accepted—"

"My bargains happen to be a popular commodity," Rui replies glacially.

"Do not pretend that there was no price to pay," Hana snaps breathlessly. "Do not suggest that *you* have not paid."

I blink in confusion, feeling as if I've missed a crucial part of the conversation. I open my mouth to ask if they're referring to the war between the Dokkaebi and the Imugi, but Kang speaks first.

"Enough." he barks sharply, tearing his gaze away from me and focusing one of warning on his friends before I can fully sort through their veiled allusions. "We have no time for this. Hana, we must trust Rui and Chan. Jiwoon strikes tonight regardless; the most that any of us can do is to fight on our own terms."

Rui seems to take a moment to compose himself. "Thank you, Kang." He rises from his seat, fluid and graceful, and places his palms on the handles of my wheeled chair. "Lina will be tired by now. I will return to finish this conversation with you, Hana, and to lay the finer foundations of our plan."

He begins to guide me out of the throne room, walking briskly, even as I crank my neck to send him a dirty look.

"I'd like to stay," I snap.

"Some conversations are not meant for human ears," he retorts, intolerably glib, as we traverse the plaza. I roll my eyes. "And it didn't escape my notice that you yawned six times in the past four minutes."

Immortal asshole.

"What war did you speak of back there?" I demand, still peeved at being so rudely escorted away. "What did Hana mean, that your silver tongue won a war?"

"Hana likes to hear herself talk," Rui mutters. "Much of what she says is of small importance."

"You—"

"Me," he replies with an insufferable smile. "And I do look forward to our romantic evening together, little thief. It's only fitting that both of our dinners together have revolved around the possibility of death. It adds a certain fun to the event, don't you think?" We are outside my door; Rui pushes it open and guides me inside.

"I don't particularly feel like dying," I retort as Rui offers me his arm. I stand with difficulty, on trembling legs, a hand on Rui's forearm.

I can feel his skin through the flowing silk of his robe, and a furious blush spreads up my cheek. I turn away, but I am sure he can see it, sure that he knows I'm thinking of the beach, of his lips on mine, the feeling of his mouth pressed against my neck as his hands slid downward…

But if he is, he doesn't reveal anything as he guides me to my bed, his lips in a nonchalant curve. As I lie down on the mattress, tugging the blanket up to my chin, I remember my last words to him after fleeing from him in the plaza and before venturing into the forest that night.

"Leave me. Please."

It occurs to me now that perhaps I have seen so little of Rui recently because he doesn't know that I don't regret our time on the beach. I regret being stabbed for it, yes. But…not the kiss itself.

Yet how could he know?

I said nothing of it to him when I awoke, nor when we found time together in the library. Any hints I may have dropped have been vague, brief.

Rui is looking down at me, his expression inscrutable.

I swallow hard as we hold each other's gaze for a too-long moment. The air seems to thicken around us as it does in the calm before the storm, moments before lightning strikes. My chest rises and falls unevenly, and I watch as color tinges Rui's cheeks, as his long lashes flutter, his eyes becoming heavy-lidded with want.

"I'll leave you to rest," he says abruptly, tearing his gaze from mine. "You're still recovering, and with the night ahead of us—"

He turns away, but he does not get far.

My hand shoots out from underneath the sheets, grabbing his.

His eyes widen in slight confusion and humor. "Yes?"

"Stay." The word tumbles from my mouth, clumsy and uncertain. "Stay with me."

Rui inhales sharply, lips parting. "Lina—" My name is mixed with guilty longing, with hope, and with reluctance.

I know what he will say.

But I do not care.

"Please," I whisper before I can stop myself. His hand is icy against the heat of mine, and I tug him closer to the bed. He allows it. "Just for a few moments."

It's clear that he is at war with himself.

For a few long moments, he doesn't move. Until— "As you wish," he murmurs, and then he is sliding into bed next to me, his dark hair stark against the white pillows, his silver eyes glittering with some unspoken sentiment.

I am drawn to him like a moth to a flame.

I rest my head on his shoulder and a hand on his chest, curling toward him, unable to resist the pull between us. I feel him tense underneath me in surprise, but then a hand is resting on the small of my back, and his lips are curling into a slight smile. But then the light in them dims, and he takes a shuddering breath.

"Lina," he says quietly, tucking a strand of hair behind my ear, "you must know that I am so deeply, sincerely sorry."

The words catch me unprepared, and I blink in dismay, looking up into the swirling silver depths that shine with regret.

"Had we not…" Rui's hand falls back to his side. "I did not know we were being watched; I did not know that the consequences would be so dire. You must believe that." The pain in his voice is potent and ragged, but I can tell, somehow, that his pain does not pertain only to the attack in the forest. I cannot help but to think of a name, a name different than my own, a name belonging to another whom I know little about.

Shuo Achara.

As if sensing the direction of my thoughts, Rui's eyes leave mine, fixing instead on a point past my shoulder. His mouth is tight with guilt. "I am sorry, little thief," he finishes haltingly, lacking his usual smooth slyness. "I am so very sorry. And whatever tonight brings, I promise you that you shall remain unscathed."

My throat tightens. Looking at him, at the way his eyes have dimmed, the way his brows have lowered in sorrow, I know that what we have is not mere attraction. It is something else, something altogether different.

I do not shrink from this realization as I once might have. My world has changed, and so have we. It is inexplicable, it is unexpected, and yet... And yet it feels so completely right.

"I do not blame you," I say, and it is the truth. Rui's eyes find mine once more as I cup his face in my hand. "I swear it on the gods. We're even now," I add drolly, remembering how I plunged a dagger into his chest.

Rui grimaces. "Perhaps." A moment later, his expression of sorrow is gone, replaced by the dark amusement I have grown to know so well. "You've invited me to your bed, little thief. One does wonder what comes next." He looks at me through his lashes, his voice suddenly hoarse. "So kiss me or kill me, Shin Lina. You'll find that I'll enjoy either equally."

My breath catches in my throat.

Rui smiles, wry and a little hesitant. The look is so unsure, so soft, that I find myself choosing the first option.

A low noise of surprise rumbles deep in his throat, but then he is kissing me, his hands running down the length of my back. But his lips are gentle, too gentle, as if afraid he might break me. It isn't gentleness that I want now, despite my frail state, and a noise of irritation escapes my throat.

"Kiss me," I snap, pulling away, "like you mean it." *Like how you kissed me on the shore of the Black Sea.*

"But do *you*?" His voice is husky, his breathing uneven. "After the beach...I thought..."

"Kiss me," I demand, bunching the fabric of his robes in my fists.

His eyes darken to thunderclouds. Azure fire flickers like lightning in the storm. As if released by an invisible tether, Rui's arms fervently encircle and gather my body against his. I gasp as he knots his hands in my hair and his lips crush against mine with a ravenous need. He tastes of dark winter nights whipped with icy winds and yet feels like fire and flame against my skin. I moan softly as he runs his hands down my bare legs.

And pauses.

Rui sucks in a sharp breath, and I feel his body stiffen. His fingers are slowly tracing the deeply puckered scar that Asina's dagger left so long ago. They linger, pausing over the ruined flesh. I pull back, my heart hammering as I look down at him, taking in the way his chest rises and falls unevenly. I fight the urge to push his hand away. *I am not ashamed of my scars.*

"Does it hurt?" His voice is quiet.

"Sometimes," I admit. My lips feel red and swollen. Shakily, I tuck a strand of hair behind my ear. "When I run, mostly. Or fight."

"Did he do this to you?" It takes me a moment to realize that he is referring to Kalmin. I tense, just barely, but Rui notices. A storm broods in his eyes. Lightning flashes as his face tightens.

"His second in command," I mutter. "She took a knife..." At the memory, pain snakes up my left thigh. "Her name is Asina."

"Was it retribution?" Rui asks quietly. "For the fall through the window?"

I freeze. Surely, he cannot mean Unima Hisao's window.

"How do you know that?"

Sadness flashes across that beautiful face. "You talk in your sleep."

Oh. *Oh.*

I relived that night as I'd fought the wound to my abdomen, the Imugi venom tearing through my body. And he'd heard. Listened to all of it.

He knows.

Shame has me swallowing hard. "You must think—" *That I'm a fool. That I brought upon my friends' deaths.* I cut myself off.

Despite Sang's words to me, I have yet to shake the guilt that clings to my skin, grimy and soiled. Despite knowing that there is beauty in death, that there is a world with the fragrance of cherry blossoms, I still wish my friends were here with me.

I always will.

And I will never be rid of the guilt, nor the Thought.

But I will do my best to accept it.

To live.

And to love.

And maybe that…starts here.

So instead, I begin anew. There is a light that shines within Rui's face, a light that hadn't been there before, as if he anticipates the words about to spill from my lips, carrying with them my story.

"Let me tell you about them," I say. "Let me tell you about the Talons."

And he does.

I whisper of Chara and Chryse, with their coy smiles and quick minds, the way they snorted when they laughed their true laugh—a laugh that they would never reveal to those outside their immediate circle, a laugh they had to learn to replace with one of sultry suggestion. I tell him about Yoonho, about how he saved Eunbi and me from the streets, how he was the one to introduce me to the art of survival.

And I speak of Sang. Sang, with his gentle, scarred hands and unruly head of chestnut curls. Sang, who sat with me on the rooftops underneath the moon, his words floating into the cold air with wisps of hazy smoke. I speak until my mouth is dry and my throat raw, the words tumbling from my tongue, tasting so bittersweet.

Rui listens, silent, his hand finding mine. And when I finish, my eyes glimmering with tears, it is impossible to miss the same sheen within his gaze as well.

CHAPTER FORTY-THREE

The gardens are quiet and dark, lit only by the soft glow of the moons in the velvet-rich sky. Hedges, tall and a deep emerald, wind about the grassy path, and the night air is cool and heavy with a deep floral fragrance.

Small fireflies dance through patches of shadowed flowers, now curled up for the night. Guards stand hidden within the labyrinth of flora, silent and unseen. For this is no ordinary stroll. This is a trap.

Jiwoon will strike at any moment. My heart pounds in anticipation. In hatred. He betrayed me, and now he will suffer.

Rui pushes me through the gardens, every step slow and measured. It's clear that he is on high alert. I hold my whip in my hand, the lash coiled delicately around my arm.

As we round a corner, a jade fountain comes into view, burbling softly as azure water spills from the mouths of gape-mouthed fish into the pool below. Rui takes a seat on the edge, every inch the elegant, unconcerned emperor.

I am a different story. My stomach is tight with nerves. My skin is slick with a panicked sweat. His name runs through my mind: *Wang Jiwoon. Wang Jiwoon. He is coming for you...*

"The gardens look different in the day," Rui says, gesturing to the shadowed plants. "The flowers are vibrant. Beautiful. The daylight shines across every petal, every stem. You might recognize this place, then."

The words tug at my chest with a sharp yank. I force myself to speak past my dry mouth. "This is the garden from the tapestry." I see it now, even in the dark. The tall grass, the bountifulness of the flowers. A strange ache fills my throat as I remember how my hands bled as I tore the tapestry apart. "The one...the one that Achara made. Isn't it?" I wait, watching his reaction. He is gazing at the stars with his face tilted to the sky. *Tell me*, I silently urge him. *Tell me about her, the one who painted you, who you read poetry to.*

"This garden was where I met her," Rui replies softly, even as he tears his gaze away from the sky and scans the gardens for any sign of an impending attack. "She was an artist in one of the nearby villages. I'd commissioned her to create a tapestry of this garden for the palace."

There is a note to his voice that I've never heard before. A deeply raw grief mixed with the bitter ache of regret. I know such a voice well. Have heard it emerge from my own throat more times than I can count. Slowly, I place my hand atop his. Rui's gaze remains on the stars, but his thumb brushes over mine.

"We fell in love," Rui continues, each word halting. "I brought her to live at the palace. I made her a studio, created her a gallery. My court adored her. We were happy. And I...I proposed." A rueful smile twists his lips. "Most Dokkaebi do not marry. There are lovers, and couples, but marriage binds two souls together for eternity. Many of my people prefer not to settle due to their immortality. But with Achara, I wanted to."

"Did she say yes?"

Rui's smile turns bitter as he scours the shadows for Jiwoon.

"She wasn't keen on the idea of marriage. Nor was she keen on the idea of becoming an empress. Achara was the type to prefer cottages to castles. Living in the palace had already been a change for her—and a disorienting one at that. She told me as much and refused my hand. Her words were as sharp as knives. She called me foolish, a Dokkaebi who lives in dreams and delusions. For months after the proposal, our relationship... suffered. We fought often, and over the smallest of matters.

"I understood the rejection, of course, but a selfish, wicked part of me wished to hurt her as she'd hurt me. During one of our disagreements, words came to my lips that I would later regret. We fought, and I vanished to your realm to lick my wounds. And when I came back..." He trails off. The sky seems to dim, the stars flickering uncertainly in the sky. Even the light of the moons pales. "When I came back, I was told that there had been an accident."

The pain on his face is open and bare, and it sends an ache through me. Rui, too, left his loved one, and came back to something awful. Something terrible.

"What happened?"

"As long as Dokkaebi lives are meant to be, we are not immune to death altogether. Illness or injuries can take us to an early grave. My family, they passed in one of the many battles against the Imugi when I was but fifteen. My eomma, my appa. Slain in battle."

I squeeze his hand gently, remembering his story of the empress and the pond in which they played.

Rui squeezes back. His throat bobs. "But it does not always take as much as that. And Achara...she was always delicate. Clumsy. It is not a good combination." Rui's eyes move to the ground, and he bows his head, his shoulders falling. "They told me she fell down the stairs. Her neck snapped."

"Rui…" I falter, searching for words. "It wasn't your fault." Those four words had been all I needed to hear for a year. But Rui shakes his head. His long hair hides the pain in his eyes.

"After Achara died, I fell into darkness. I neglected my realm and, with it, my people. I raised taxes, for irrationally, I blamed them, too—why hadn't they helped her? Why hadn't they saved her? I was quick to anger. I spent hours in this garden, demanding to be left alone.

"Reminders of Achara were everywhere—the tapestry the worst of all. It struck a pain in me so deep that I tore it from our bedroom wall, from this realm. I left it in Sunpo, tucked away in that abandoned temple. I told myself that one day, when I could…I would hang it again. Years passed, and still, I was not ready." Rui laughs under his breath. Every chuckle is forced and tight, hoarse with bitterness. "Until I was alerted that a human girl had stolen what I held most dear.

"Enraged by the theft, I stole Konrarnd Kalmin away. I assumed you would seek him out, and I appeared on the rooftop to taunt you." Rui lifts his head, and I am surprised to see the barest hint of a curve to his lips. "You hurled a couple of pastries into the sky. Despite myself, I found you intriguing. There was a fury radiating from you, a challenge. And even though I hated you, I found myself looking forward to our next meeting.

"My original plan had been to lure you to my realm and kill you. But I found that I couldn't bring myself to cut your life short so soon. Later, perhaps, but…not quite yet. You were covered in fresh bruises, signaling a recent beating. Radiating pain and fear and hate, but still, that underlying dare. So I proposed our game. Perhaps it was that darkness speaking, pushing me toward a game that could end fatally on my part. But underneath all of it…I think that, perhaps, I wanted to know you.

"Kang noticed the change before I did. My quickness to anger slowed. From the moment you arrived, I ceased lurking in these gardens. Your presence changed me. And the irony of it all was that you despised me. Wanted me dead. And at times I despised you, too, for stealing from me. But our game drew me in, and I found myself thinking less and less about whether to behead or shoot you." I pull in a soft breath as he cups my cheek, his words no longer grieving but rich with a deep, passionate emotion. "Our first dinner together," he murmurs, and I remember my red lips, my sultry smiles. "I had not been able to feel that way in near a century."

"I tried to kill you," I whisper, leaning into his touch.

"It added to the excitement." His thumb strokes my jawline with a featherlight touch. "And the beach…" I swallow hard at his reverent tone. "When I saw you later that night, barely able to stand, choking on your own blood…" Rui's jaw tightens, his skin paling. "Every hour was torture. Every minute seemed like a century as you fought the poison. I thought I had lost you. And…I don't want to lose you," Rui whispers. "I don't pretend to know what we are. But I do know that your company brings me happiness, Shin Lina. You could stay here. By my side."

My lips part in surprise. "Rui."

"But I understand that you must leave. Although a visit certainly would do you no harm." His lips tug upward. "Would it?"

"No," I say quietly. What he has just told me… We are more alike than I ever realized. "It wouldn't."

And it is joy—real joy that flashes in those eyes like forks of lightning. It isn't the bright, pure joy I'd seen in the gallery's painting, rather edged with a slight shadow, a reminder of what he has been through. But it is still delight as he tugs me closer, and when his lips meet mine, they are soft. Gentle.

Perhaps our foolish infatuation with each other is why we

do not hear the screams until it is too late.

A shriek of pain, muffled and muted through the shrubbery of the garden, reaches my ears. Heart lurching, I pull away from Rui. The air is thick with a horrible foreboding. The shadows are darker, the moons dimmer.

He's here.

CHAPTER FORTY-FOUR

Rui stands with an abrupt motion, drawing Manpasikjeok. Deep within the garden, there is another scream. And another.

"The guards," I breathe, clenching my whip tight. I can barely summon the strength to stand from my chair, but I'll fight in it if I have to, godsdamn it.

Rui's face is hard. I know what he is thinking. By now, Chan should have appeared to whisk me away. But he has not yet come.

Another scream, this one closer.

And another.

Rui turns to me, eyes blazing, reaching for me like he means to teleport me to safety. But before his fingers can even so much as graze my arm, another scream rings in the air, jagged with pain and horror before it cuts off into dead silence, a silence that hangs thick and impenetrable over the gardens.

One second passes.

Two.

Three—

A shadowed figure bursts from the hedges with a reverberating snarl. Moonlight shifts, its glowing light revealing Jiwoon.

But he is not the Jiwoon I thought I knew. Gone are his wire spectacles and the laugh lines that crinkled his amber eyes. This Jiwoon wears a black chainmail shirt that wraps around hard, toned muscle. His jaw is clenched with fury, and his face burns with undiluted hatred.

There is something different, too, about the way he stands… Almost as if it is a struggle for him to remain still. As if power churns and writhes within him, begging to be released. In his hands, he holds a large, gleaming ax. I tighten my grip on the hilt of my whip. I recognize that ax, forged from the stolen metals. I last saw it underneath Misook's bakery. My mouth twists sourly as I remember how I admired it.

Jiwoon's eyes find mine. A slow smile creeps across his face, even as his gaze remains cold with fury and hatred. I grit my teeth as he turns to Rui, tilting his head this way and that. Mirthless laughter, sharp and brittle, emerges from his throat. "Your Majesty," he says through his teeth, still laughing that terrible laugh. "At last we meet."

"I assume," Rui drawls, "that you're the infamous Wang Jiwoon." His hand finally meets my arm as the air begins to undulate behind us, opening up to the corridor of shadows. "I would say it has been a pleasure—"

Jiwoon notes the rippling air, the darkness behind us. "There's no use." Jiwoon's lips twist into a smug sneer. "Anywhere you take her… Well. I can follow." The air behind him matches Rui's. Abruptly, Rui lets go of my arm. His mouth is very tight. "And your guards won't be coming to help you," Jiwoon adds, clearly enjoying himself. "Not tonight."

I grit my teeth. Godsdamned enhancer.

"Lina," he whispers, "you must run. You are in no condition to fight."

But Jiwoon hears, and his smirk grows. "I suppose that

Aecha should have aimed that sword higher," he says. "I would have liked to carve out your heart, to see it bleed. But that was second to my desire to see your corpse picked apart by grubs and vultures, you filthy traitor." He licks his lips, and another one of those laughs bubbles up in his throat. "I underestimated you, I admit that much. But I won't make that mistake again."

"You bastard," I spit. "You'll never rule Iseung. You'll die here, by our hands, and I'll savor every godsdamned moment of it."

Jiwoon's laughter dies. His mouth curls into a snarl. "I will do as Hwanung guides me."

"Hwanung would not call this *justice*. You are a liar to say that the God of Laws stands behind you—"

"Lina," Rui says quietly, never taking his eyes from Jiwoon. The temperature in the gardens has turned frigid. His eyes are completely blue now, crackling with flames that I know are on the brink of being unleashed. "Run now, little thief, and run far." His voice is urgent, heavy with demand.

But I do not want to leave him. "No. No, I won't go."

"Lina, now," he hisses, and there's fear—genuine fear—in his voice.

"I won't," I retort a moment before music, golden and honeyed, sweeps through the night.

Rui has drawn Manpasikjeok.

And too late—with my stomach sinking with despair and fury—I realize what he's doing.

Lina, the music sings, *Lina, little thief. You cannot stay here; you will die, he will kill you. Run, Lina, run and hide. I'm sorry for this broken promise, so very sorry. But run, Lina, run and hide...*

I nod slowly, deeply, everything but the sweet music fading away into oblivion. *Run and hide*, my mind hums slowly. I must run and hide, for the song has told me to.

As quickly as I am able in my feeble condition, I stand from my chair and move toward the shrubbery in a burst of speed, even though my body is weak and threatens to buckle. *Run and hide*, the beautiful notes sing mournfully, and I throw myself to the ground, rolling until I'm concealed within the wall of greenery. Branches scrape my face, knees bruise from the impact, and my chest heaves, lungs winded.

I'm hidden, I tell the song sweetly as I stare up at the bramble, longing for its approval. Its sugared notes brush my skin, as gentle as a butterfly's touch.

I'm sorry, the song whispers. *I'm sorry.*

A moment later, the music vanishes, but the notes linger in my ears. *Stay hidden, stay hidden, stay hidden, stay hidden…* I obey, hunkering down as I watch Rui take a deep breath.

In the moonlight, his face is drawn tight with regret and resolution as he raises Manpasikjeok to his lips once more.

Wang Jiwoon, Manpasikjeok sings, *lay down your arms. You are not so foolish as to think this a fight you can win. Lay down your arms, surrender yourself. Lay down your arms, Wang Jiwoon, surrender yourself…*

Jiwoon just tilts his head and tightens his grip on his ax. Blinking slowly with dawning horror, I realize that he is unaffected.

Stay hidden, stay hidden.

The music meant for Jiwoon disappears. Stonily, Rui holds Jiwoon's glare as he tucks away the flute. "Only monsters are immune to this flute," he says quietly. "And I cannot say that I am overly fond of such creatures." A promise of death caresses his every word.

Stay hidden, the song echoes in my ears. *Stay hidden, stay hidden, stay hidden.*

"I'm no monster," Jiwoon snarls. "I'm your ruin. And I have waited for this day," the rebel continues. "Oh, how I've waited.

I have paid and paid in this damned realm. And now, it's your turn." He tenses, as if that power within him is about to be released—

Beyond the thorns, I watch as the night shakes, as the stars and moons blaze up above. From my hiding place where I must remain, I do not have a clear vantage point, but it is enough to see when Rui *moves*.

It occurs to me that I have never seen the Dokkaebi emperor truly fight.

He launches through the air with eerie grace, ducking as the ax is swung toward him. Five columns of glimmering Dokkaebi fire, vicious and sapphire, erupt from the ground in Rui's wake. Even from here, goose bumps rise on my skin as the night becomes frigid.

Splitting into ten separate flames that lick upward into the sky, they crackle and burn as they roar toward Jiwoon, who nimbly avoids them. Rui lands a blow on the weak point behind Jiwoon's knee, an attack that sends him stumbling—ever so slightly.

But Jiwoon lands a blow on Rui's nose, fist meeting bone with a sickening *crunch*. The speed at which the rebel moves is disorienting. Faster than a hummingbird. Rui manages to block another uppercut, ichor-like blood from his nose trickling into his mouth and down his chin.

The shock of that blood jerks me out of my reverie, leaving me cold and hollow and *furious*. I shake off the remnants of Manpasikjeok's orders as if they're bugs clinging to my skin.

"Gaesaekki," I spit, leaning on my elbows and peering out of the nettle. A broken promise. He *swore* he wouldn't do this, wouldn't use Manpasikjeok against me. But he did.

I grind my teeth and shake with rage, even as a part of me admits that he was right—I am not at my full strength. Not even close. Although my years of training might keep me on my feet longer than the average mortal, Jiwoon could easily kill me. Frustrated, I bite my lip hard enough to taste coppery blood.

But still, we will have words about this.

After Jiwoon is dead.

Rui is on the defensive, his fire encasing him in a shield as he struggles to avoid Jiwoon and his wildly swinging ax. For a terrible moment, he's left my line of sight.

Hurriedly and with no small amount of effort, I drag myself through the bramble and briar of the shrubbery, attempting to find a better vantage point as Rui and Jiwoon move farther away from me.

They circle each other, both nothing more than a blur of motion as they fight.

Gold trickles from Rui's mouth as he twists away from Jiwoon's attacks, his teeth flashing in a snarl as he counters. The night is alive with power, the air heavy with it. The moons sway from where they hang nestled between rattling stars. The two Dokkaebi seem like quarreling gods as their dance quickens into a lethal routine, reaching its crescendo…

My breath catches in horror as Jiwoon's ax bites into Rui's side, bites *deep*.

My eyes are wide as Rui falls, streaming blood, his face contorted in pain as a roar escapes his lips. The sound cuts deep into my heart, strangling me in terror.

Please, I think to the absent gods. *Please don't let me lose him as well.*

Even when they don't answer, I get the distinct feeling that they're laughing at me.

I watch as Rui rolls away from Jiwoon's next assault and manages to crawl to his feet, his flames swirling around him like blazing snakes. The ground shakes as they fight, their attacks as loud as thunderclaps. But Rui is slow. Too slow.

I blink dirt from my eyes. *Help him.* I have to help him.

My whip is clutched tightly in my hand. I could do it—could stagger into their battle, could try to aid Rui. But I can barely even walk on my own.

And if I die, Eunbi dies.

So I swallow bile and force myself to remain still, hating myself more and more with each passing second.

But Rui has fallen again.

This time, he has not risen. Jiwoon stands above him, his ax raised high, glinting in the moonlight, preparing to strike.

Rui is still, but his gaze slides to where I lie hidden. Blood runs from his side, his nose, and one of his eyes is swollen shut. He is not healing.

And for a moment, I'm back there, back in that bloodied palace, a scream bubbling up in my throat because I had not been there with them, had not fought alongside them. For a moment, my shoes are damp with their blood, the smell of it thick in my nose.

I wasn't there then—but I'm here now.

Our eyes meet.

Run, his seem to say. *Run, Lina. Please.*

And the ax is glowing in the moonlight.

I have already lost my family.

I will not lose him.

So as Jiwoon raises that ax higher, a malicious grin on his face, I crawl from the shrubbery, my whip in hand. Rui makes a noise low in his throat, a noise of protest that I ignore. Trembling violently, I drag myself to my feet. My legs nearly buckle, but I force myself to remain upright even as I shake like a leaf in the wind.

It is a relief that my voice comes out low and even, cutting through the night like a blade. "Jiwoon."

He pauses, slowly turning toward me.

Lina. Rui's open eye is wide with shock and horror. *Don't.*

Don't do this, he seems to say.

Jiwoon tilts his head, and I force myself to hold his gaze as he steps over Rui, his eyes glittering with repugnant mirth. "Perfect." He chuckles. "I think," he muses, glancing down at Rui with notable disgust, "that I will kill her first, and make you watch."

"Lina—" Rui is struggling to rise.

Jiwoon kicks him back down. The emperor groans, blood streaming from a new gash in his forehead into his eyes. He is limp, broken.

Defeated.

Jiwoon grins.

And then the Revolutionary focuses all his attention on me.

CHAPTER FORTY-FIVE

Jiwoon snorts as I scrabble for purchase in the dirt, struggling to find the strength to stand once again. My left leg buckles underneath me as I finally find my feet, and I sink to my knees, breathing hard past the pain.

"Pathetic," he spits, circling me, leveling the edge of the ax toward me. "Absolutely pathetic." He glances to where Rui lies, limp and semiconscious, and laughs.

I wipe my mouth, clearing away dirt and blood, as I struggle to my feet and snap my whip. With as much speed as I can summon, I lash it toward him.

The weapon sings through the night, and I pray for it to coil across Jiwoon's arm, for it to force him into dropping the ax. I know I cannot beat him, not like this—but perhaps I can disarm him, perhaps I can buy Rui some time to heal.

That is all he needs, I tell myself. *Just some more time.*

But Jiwoon grabs the ribbon with his other hand with a speed that should not exist and, with a sharp yank, sends me flying toward him. He lets go at the last moment, and my body shudders at the impact. My whip skids underneath the wall of the hedge, gone.

But I force myself up, tears of pain streaming down my cheeks, mingling with dirt and dust. Jiwoon stands six feet away from me, grinning again. "It's really too easy."

"You have a weapon," I spit out, white-hot pain licking at my bones. "And an enhancer coursing through your veins. It's hardly a fair fight, and you know it. *Hwanung* knows it."

"On the contrary," Jiwoon says icily. "I feel Hwanung looking down upon me tonight. For this *is* fair, Lina. This is justice in its truest form." I flinch as he turns in a sharp movement, and hurls his ax toward the fountain, where it embeds itself in the stone. "There." He turns back to me, face shining with a sick sort of triumph. "I'll enjoy this even more."

I swallow hard.

Even without his ax, I am no match for him. And he knows that.

But still, I will try.

On wobbling legs, I stagger toward him, throwing a punch. It's a pathetic, feeble thing, and I fight back the nausea that rises with the motion.

His fist flies through the air with so much speed that I cannot fully avoid its impact on my shoulder and stumble backward. I feel like I've been hit by a block of iron.

Jiwoon stands over me as I struggle to my knees. I choke for air, wheezing as I clamber to my feet, only to be met with a bone-shattering pain as his knuckles bash into the side of my face. I cry out, hitting the ground, unable to breathe or see past the pain.

But still, I try again to rise. I'm sobbing, sobbing through my split lip, as red-hot agony shoots up every muscle in my body, and blood, sticky and thick, trickles into my eyes from what must be a gash on my forehead.

Jiwoon laughs in sickening delight as his hands grab my

shoulders, his fingers bruising my flesh. He slams me back into the ground, hard, and places his knees on either side of my hips as he kneels over me. His face is contorted with rage. I hear Rui cry out my name in horror as Jiwoon rears his fists back, knuckles already wet with my blood.

He brings one fist down onto the right side of my face. I scream, raw with agony, my hands clenching the blades of grass around me as I wish, desperately, for a true blade.

Out of the corner of my eye, I see Rui trying to rise—and failing.

My head snaps to the other side as Jiwoon lands another blow. My face is wet with blood and swollen with welts. I struggle to push him off me, but he lands another blow.

This is it.

Another.

Jiwoon is going to kill me.

My head snaps from side to side as he rains down the attacks, merciless as blood wets the flame-scorched ground below me. The garden drinks it in greedily.

This is how it will end.

Copper fills my mouth.

This is how I die.

I choke on blood, again and again.

"You're the last of us, Lina." Sang's voice is a ghostly whisper in my mind—there, but barely there at all.

Pounding pain.

"The last of the Talons."

Fracturing bones.

"If you remember one thing from this conversation, Lina, remember…"

Shredding skin.

"Death does not die, and neither will you, Shin Lina."

A stranger feeling now, deep down, past the pain. Something

slithers through my blood, cold and ancient and cruel and cunning.

"Remember that."

And I do.

As Jiwoon stands, stalking away from me to retrieve his ax, I remember.

And as I cling to that memory, that identity, something unravels from deep within my soul. It awakens from a slumber, cracking open hungry eyes.

It feels familiar, so very familiar.

Here I am, it seems to whisper as it hums through my bloodstream, warming my skin, knitting together flesh and bone. *Here I am*.

It surges through my body, a blaze of life, of *power*.

I feel myself strengthening. I feel myself *changing*.

Here I am, the strange power whispers again and again. *Here I am, here I am, here I am.*

I buzz with it, burn with it.

Now what will you do with me? the power inquires softly. Lethally. *What wonders will we perform together? What will you do with me?*

Jiwoon is returning now, his ax hefted in his hands, the blade brilliant under the stars. He smiles down at me as he raises the weapon above his head. So he is planning a beheading. How fitting.

Despite my newfound strength, I lie limply on the grass, broken and bruised and battered.

A simple deception. And Jiwoon falls for it, laughing that horrible laugh.

What will you do with me?

This, I reply to the power inside me.

As that ax swings down, down, down, I lift my hands against it, fueled by a powerful, irrefutable instinct.

I watch as it happens in slow motion. My hands, crusted in dirt and blood, lift into the air, toward the approaching blade. They burn as they rise, burn fiercely, as if plunged into the hottest fire, the hottest flames.

And when that ax is only a half an inch away from my palms, my hands *change*.

Small scales, sharp and teal and glittering, unfold across the skin of my hands.

When they meet the ax, a metallic *clang* echoes through the gardens.

My fingers curl around the blade as Jiwoon's eyes widen in shock. He strains against me, pushing down, but it is futile. My hands, my changed hands, are strong. They are completely and totally unharmed by Jiwoon's weapon, even as they press against it.

I grin wildly with pure unadulterated glee.

For the first time in a year, I am powerful. Ferocious. Something to fear.

How I've missed it.

A surge of triumph sweeps through me as I grit my teeth and, with a grunt, shove the ax away. With it, Jiwoon stumbles backward, panting in hatred and disbelief.

I gape at my hands for only a few moments. The scales are fading, disappearing, yet somehow, I know that when I need them, they will return.

I fight back dizziness. Fight back astonishment. Did the concoction work after all? Is this a gift from the gods? Have they finally, *finally* answered my prayers?

What is *this?*

The power does not answer me. It is once again silent. Yet my wounds feel like nothing more than bruises. I am ready to fight.

And I shall.

"You're the last of us, Lina."

I plant one fist on the ground as Sang's words again dance through my mind, louder this time, as clear and ringing as a bell.

"The last of the Talons."

I do the same with the other, digging my fist into the dirt.

"If you remember one thing from this conversation, Lina, remember…"

As I push myself up, my eyes burn as they meet Jiwoon's.

"Dead," he hisses. "You're supposed to be dead."

"Remember…"

"Death does not die." I hold my head high, shoulders back, refusing to yield. I am Shin Lina. The Reaper of Sunpo. Death incarnate. "And *neither will I.*"

And then I strike.

I whip through the night, as fast as a star shooting across the expanse of the sky. The gardens rush by in a blur of green and black. In only the blink of an eye, I am in front of Jiwoon, that smile still on my face as I summon the scales to my hands with little more than a thought. An order, to whatever rests inside me.

Guided by pure instinct, I flick my wrist, and from the back of my hands, two long scales—half a foot long—emerge. They are sharp, the same rich teal as the others, tapering into blades worthy of the finest daggers.

"What the fuck," Jiwoon pants, eyes wide. *"What the fuck—"*

He launches, the ax aimed at my neck. I twist away, feeling as scales emerge there as well, hard and sharp. The ax scrapes against them, but I feel nothing except a slight pressure.

I twist around, cocking my head. *Interesting.*

In truth, I do not know what's happened to me.

And also in truth, I do not particularly care, not in the moment.

As long as I win.

And I will.

I walk toward Jiwoon, and every step is like gliding across ice on razor-sharp blades. I can almost swear that I feel the God of Death standing behind me, smiling coldly at Jiwoon.

The Revolutionary swings again, wild and undisciplined. I watch as the ax moves through the air, and dodge it with agile ease. He swings again. I reach up, grabbing the blade with my hands. As he chokes in surprise, I send a well-placed kick to his abdomen. The air *whooshes* as my leg moves in a blur of speed.

Jiwoon drops the ax.

There is fear in his eyes now.

Real fear. True fear.

Good.

I kick the ax aside as I stalk toward him again. He throws a punch, but I snatch his fist in the air. He gasps, straining away, but I hold still. I imagine Yeomra behind me, smiling. And I smile, too.

"What are you?" he hisses, face red and contorted as I smirk. "What the fuck did they do to you—" He cuts off as I flip him to the ground, straddling him at the waist as he did to me, holding him down. "Lina." His eyes are so wide now. "Listen to me, hear my reasoning. Please. Lina. *Lina.*"

I say nothing, angling the blade protruding from my hand toward his heart. He writhes, desperate to escape, but it is impossible.

His strength is no match for mine. He has worn himself out already; he is weakened.

And I am fresh. I am young.

I am born anew.

"Wait." Jiwoon is attempting a smile. "Come now. You won't, not really. After all, didn't we once share the same goal? Didn't we work together? Laugh together? Dance together?"

I smile, and with a flick, I break the chainmail covering the spot underneath where his heart rests. I trace it lovingly with my scaled blade, cocking my head. "We did," I murmur. "But then you betrayed me."

Revenge will taste so very, very sweet.

"You wished to cut out my heart? You wished to see it bleed?" I whisper.

Jiwoon abandons all pretenses of regret. *"You fucking bitch!"* he roars, straining underneath me. *"Filthy fucking traitor!"*

I find this hilarious. From sly to furious in a matter of moments—and he once told me that *my* tears were fit for a playhouse. I laugh, scarcely recognizing the sound of it. It is dark, laced with a deadly velvet. "You shouldn't have come here, Jiwoon," I say very quietly once I've stopped laughing. "You shouldn't have hurt him." I glance to where Rui lies limp on the ground, one bloodied hand stretched out toward me even as his eyes remain closed.

Something inside me shatters at the sight of how he reaches for me, even in his oblivion.

Jiwoon spits in my face.

And I carve out his heart.

CHAPTER FORTY-SIX

"Lina," somebody rasps as I hold it in my hands. It pulsates weakly as I admire the golden blood coating it, dripping down the sides. Below me, Jiwoon is silent and still. Dead.

A pity, that.

I would have liked for him to see this, his heart in my hand. My victory.

Rui has somehow awoken, crawled toward me, his silver eyes bright with horror. "Lina," he repeats in scarcely more than a rasp. "Lina…"

I tilt my head this way and that, unable to look at anything but the heart in my hand. I do adore an ironic twist.

"Your hand," Rui whispers, and I follow his stare to skin glittering with diamond-hard scales.

Shock slashes through me as I see, truly see, the scales coating my hands. The scaled blades dripping blood.

I drop the heart. It rolls across the garden, trailing gore, before pausing near a cluster of scarlet flowers.

My astonishment is enough to send the scales retreating, melting back into copper-colored flesh, invisible once more. I gape, and whatever victory I felt is quickly replaced by horror as I clamber from Jiwoon, breathing rapidly.

I blink at my hands, suddenly feeling nauseated. Feeling sick beyond all measure, sick from shock. I look to Rui, hoping for an explanation. He has finally, albeit slowly, begun to heal. His eye is already half open, the deep gash in his side knitting itself together.

"Are you—" I ask breathlessly, and he nods, wincing as he pushes himself onto his knees. His eyes are still on my hands.

"Your hands," he breathes. His face is taut with shock. "The scales."

I hide them behind my back, trembling and feeling absurdly guilty. "The wongun enhancer," I say quickly, hating the shame that brings flames to my cheeks. "It must have worked after all, it must have done this to me, I don't know what this is—" My mind returns to Jeoseung, to the glittering snakeskin cutting through the dark mist. My eyes return to the heart on the ground, seeping blood. "I didn't mean to—"

I cut myself off, trying to silence the roar of shock within my head.

Because I *did* mean to—and I enjoyed every single moment of it. But the alarm on Rui's face…

He grimaces, dropping his eyes as he clutches his healing wound. A part of me is shamefully thankful for the distraction of his pain as I hurry to his side and place a hand on his shoulder.

"Can you stand? Can you walk?" There is still the matter of the guards, of Chan. There is no telling what massacre waits for us within the garden.

"I'll manage," Rui says, and he forces a wry half smile to his lips as he stands, leaning on my shoulder. My newfound strength allows me to support him easily. "That certainly wasn't the way I'd imagined our night ending. I'd expected something much more pleasant." His words are light enough, but his tone lacks any amusement, and no wicked delight dances across his bloody face. Instead, only remorse lives there. Remorse and fury. "I broke my promise. Please, Lina, know that I thought I had no choice." The emperor's voice begins to tremble. He's shaken. "But I also swore you an oath that no harm would come to you—I tried to fulfill it the only way I could. But I'm sorry. I swear to you, Lina, upon my kingdom, upon my crown, never again."

"Rui," I whisper, touching his face gently. My fingertips leave prints of golden blood upon his skin. He places a quivering hand atop mine. "Rui, it's all right. I understand why you did it. I do." He did not want to lose me, just as I did not want to lose him. We protected each other in the only way we knew how, no matter the cost.

Rui closes his eyes briefly, shoulders loosening in relief. "You do not despise me?"

"No," I whisper. "I don't." And it is true—I do not. But I cannot deny that a small shard of wariness lodged inside my heart. Trust is something I cannot give easily, not anymore. And after tonight, I do not know if I can give it to him fully. Not yet.

Morning moonlight has begun to peek through the darkness, bathing the gardens in a warm glow. I try not to think of what lurks beneath my skin, coiled around my blood and bones, humming with power.

We have survived, and that is enough for now.

As if he is thinking the same thing, Rui abruptly folds me into his arms. The emperor holds me tight, crushing me against him. "Lina," he whispers onto the top of my head. "Lina, Lina, Lina."

A prayer, a plea, a promise.

As the moons warm to a shimmering gold, our lips meet, tasting of blood and sweat and tears.

CHAPTER FORTY-SEVEN

They do not know what I am.

I do not, either.

On the surface, at least, not much has changed. The teardrop scar running down the length of the right side of my face still exists, shining a bone-marrow white. The one on the back of my left leg is still there, too, cratered and forever pink, the skin ravaged and rough. The pain from that particular wound still exists as well, despite my new…abilities.

I do not know why.

I do not know anything.

All I do know is that below my skin, something ancient, something cruel and cold and wickedly wonderful, has made a home among my bones and my blood.

We're gathered in a new room this time, a room secluded and hidden from the rest of the palace. The gray stone walls are bare and rough, the room lit by the flickering flames of the stubby candles lining the walls. The door, thick and wooden, has been locked and bolted shut. Only Rui, his inner circle, and I gather around the worn round table, our faces pale and grim with exhaustion.

Chan, at least, is the only one of the inner circle severely injured. His right arm is now bound in a sling, and his left leg demanded gauze as well, after a more extensive treatment from Kang. The bone, shining and white, was peeking out of the mess of gore produced by Jiwoon. Hana was the one who had screamed when she saw him, a scream of raw fear that shattered the night.

Her lover is lucky, though.

The other guards... Most of them are dead. Jiwoon struck, and he struck hard. They'd underestimated him—as had Rui.

In the two hours since the attack, Rui has begun to recover fully, and the gash in his side is now little more than a small cut. My injuries, my wounds, have disappeared—save for the pain in my leg. I sit stiffly, unable to mask my discomfort. My senses have...changed. I am a stranger in my own body.

In my own skin.

I can feel every inch of the tattered clothes that I am clad in. Every scrape of cloth, every stitch of thread. I take a shaky inhale of air. Each breath, every inhale I can *taste*. Can taste on my tongue the sweetness of the moisture humidifying the air.

I stare fixedly at a splinter of wood as Kang speaks. My ears twitch. I can pick up every single cadence within his words.

Next to me, I feel Rui's gaze, heavy with concern, lingering on my hands.

I hastily place them below the table.

"...owe you a great debt, Lina," Kang is saying—slowly. Cautiously. As if speaking to a wild animal. And I suppose I do look like one, smeared with dirt and blood, my nails crusted with gore. "We have said so many times already, but it feels only fair to let you know the full extent of our gratitude. Losing Rui... would have had immeasurable consequences."

I glance up at him.

Kang's eyes do not swirl with that infinite knowledge as he leans against his staff, standing before the table rather than sitting. Instead, they are wary. Confused. Misted over with an emotion that I cannot decipher.

"You have my deepest gratitude," Chan says thickly. "Where I...failed, you succeeded. Thank you." His guilt is palpable as he bows his head, white locks of hair shining under the candlelight. Hana's mouth is tight and trembling, one of her hands resting on Chan's shoulder. She looks my way and inclines her head in a small nod of thanks before hastily averting her eyes.

"I understand that you have questions," Kang continues, "and I admit that I do not have all the answers. But I can tell you, Lina, what I suspect has occurred. This opinion has been formulated without much research, merely with strong suspicion. It offers little in terms of explanation. But I hope that you will hear it."

"I will," I whisper.

"When we administered you the wongun enhancer, I gave no thought to how the venom existing within your body at that time may have altered its composition. We simply wanted you to live, to survive. It was a dangerous gamble. The enhancer was never meant to be consumed by a mortal. All reason led me to believe that a human could not survive the effects. But we had to try—to see if it could help you, for you were dying regardless."

Next to me, Rui stiffens.

"But it worked. You lived. Yet when you ingested the concoction, I strongly suspect that the Imugi venom in your body altered the effects of the enhancer. You see, Lina, we have unintentionally mixed the venom of an Imugi with its scales, along with a myriad of other ingredients. This has never been done before." He pauses, and I can almost hear his thought. *Nor should it have been.*

When Rui described the transformation of my skin, Kang

went so very, very pale. I thought I saw disgust—or something worse—flash across his face, if only for a moment.

But Kang keeps his face composed now as he continues. "Your body was subject to a concoction that had never before been created. This is why you have been...changed so. This is why you possess...traits of the Imugi. I assume that this mixture had a longer transition time than the original enhancer, explaining why these qualities were dormant within you for so long. Remember that this is all speculation," he adds quickly. "It is still far too early to tell. I ask you, though, to show me the... the metamorphosis that Rui has described. I should like to see it myself, to be able to tell."

I take in his words numbly. *The Imugi venom in your body altered the effects of the enhancer.* My mind travels to the creature that circled me so curiously, hidden entirely save for that one glittering scale.

Remembering how I longed to step forward, to greet it, to speak to it. Remembering the bright white light that followed— life, but changed, tinged with a cruel, ancient coldness.

Rebirth of an unknown sort.

I barely feel myself raise my right hand. With a half thought, the cold scales are creeping up from my forearm to the tips of my fingers, glittering underneath the dim light.

Once upon a time, perhaps I would have feared the Imugi features I now possess. Once upon a time, my phobia would have writhed at the sight of snakeskin upon my flesh. But all I feel is a faint surprise that this is not a dream, that I have truly become serpentine. I turn my hand this way and that, watching how the scales catch the candlelight.

Chan chokes.

Hana sucks in a sharp breath.

And Rui's mouth tightens. "Enough with the dramatics, both of you," he snaps at his friends. I swallow hard as he takes my hand in his, locking his fingers with mine, despite their unnaturalness. If the iciness of the scales bothers him, he does not let on. "Refrain from jumping to conclusions," he adds to Kang in a lethal undertone. "There is much you do not yet know." Every word drips with warning.

The adviser is staring at my hand. "Thank you, Lina," he says almost mechanically.

I allow the scales to melt back into flesh. Rui grips my fingers tighter, squeezing once, twice. I find solace in the coolness of his hand.

"And you can summon them anywhere on your body?"

I remember how they appeared on my neck as Jiwoon swung his ax. *Possibly*, I want to say, but something holds me back. Perhaps it is the caution in Kang's voice. Perhaps it is the barely concealed revulsion etched across Hana's face. But either way, I say instead, "I… I don't know. I don't think so. Just my hands so far." I swallow the taste of burnt sugar.

"I see." Kang's jaw tightens, as if he detects my lie.

Desperate to change the subject, I grasp for another, settling on the matter of my leg. "My leg," I say, tracing the puckered skin on the back of my thigh, "and the scar on my face. The injuries from Jiwoon's attack have—have healed, but these remain. The pain in my leg, it also remains. I don't understand why." I wait for Kang to reply, but it is Rui who answers, his voice gentle.

"The pain in your leg, the scar on your face, their existence stems from emotion as much as they stem from your physical wounds. The two of them, they are interlinked." He squeezes my hand again. *I am here, I am with you.*

I blanch. Rui is correct, I realize, as I flinch from the memory of Asina's cruel smile as she sank her dagger into the back of my leg. The memory of Jiwoon tracing a tear onto my bloodied face. The pain, the scar, the eternal tear.

They are a reminder of all that has happened. A reminder of who I lost the night my leg was so irreversibly wounded. A reminder of the horror I felt within the woods.

"So...they will never heal?" The words taste of bitter disappointment on my tongue.

"I'm afraid that they won't," the adviser replies quietly. "There are salves, of course—tinctures and concoctions that may succeed in numbing some of the pain. But I am sorry to say that the pain in your left leg is one that you will carry with you forevermore as you embark on your new life."

"My new life as a..." I falter. "What... What am I?"

Nobody answers.

The room is suffocatingly silent. "What am I?" I whisper again, and this time I feel fear.

Finally, Rui responds, low and quiet. "You are Shin Lina. You are the Reaper of Sunpo. You are the girl who traveled to Gyeulcheon, the girl who cut out a Dokkaebi's heart."

The words sink into me.

I am Shin Lina. The Reaper of Sunpo.

I am the girl who traveled to Gyeulcheon.

I am the girl who cut out a Dokkaebi's heart.

Rui grins, a wicked light dancing in his eyes. "We don't know what else you are yet, Lina. But something tells me that it will be so very, very fun to find out."

CHAPTER FORTY-EIGHT

I stand on the soft green grass of the Gyeulcheon hill lands. A sweet afternoon breeze ruffles my hair, coiling around my skin, nuzzling against my cheeks. The air is ripe, overwhelmingly ripe with the smell of vibrant flowers. My keen nose picks up every hint of nectar, every scent of ambrosia that wafts from the colorful petals. In the distance, I see the pond, glittering under the azure sky. My heart races with anticipation.

Any moment now.

Any moment.

I'm dressed in a lavender hanbok and have dabbed cosmetics over the scar on my face. My hair has been washed of dirt and blood and combed back into a neat braid, at the end of which I have knotted a daenggi, the ribbon an innocent shade of pink. I must look calm, serene. Kind.

I must look like an older sister.

Not like an assassin. Not like…whatever I am.

When the air finally begins to shimmer and ripple twelve feet in front of me, I hold my breath.

And when Rui emerges, holding the hand of a wide-eyed

eight-year-old girl, I fall to my knees, clutching at my chest. Tears spill from my eyes and I can barely breathe, can barely force the sweet country air down my tightening throat. My heart is pounding faster and faster in relief and love, for the little girl is my baby sister.

It is Eunbi.

Her curly hair is windswept from the journey. My newfound vision allows me to see every freckle dotting her cheeks, the joy shining across her face as she locates me, every movement of her yellow hanbok as she lets go of Rui's hand and runs toward me, arms outstretched. She is taller now, I realize with a small gasp. At least by two entire inches.

She has grown while I was away.

"Lili!" Eunbi cries, her voice ringing through the hills as she crashes into me, wrapping her arms around my shoulders and burying her face in the crook of my neck.

"Eunbi," I whisper. She's so warm against me, so warm and small. My baby sister still smells like lavender and lilies—but under that, there's the distinct scent of fried mandu, and I can't help but wonder if she's been sneaking into the kitchens the way I taught her. If she's been ducking into broom closets to polish off the savory treats and thinking of me as often as I've been thinking of her. I hold her tightly, marveling at the softness of her body, the smoothness of her hands. *I've succeeded*, I think as tears slip down my cheeks. *I have protected her from a life like mine.*

Eunbi is safe. She is in my arms.

I meet Rui's eyes over Eunbi's shoulder. *Thank you*, I mouth, holding my baby sister tight. *Thank you.*

When I asked the emperor to bring her to me today, a mere ten days from Asina's deadline, it was with trembling hands. While the threat of Jiwoon was finally gone, Asina's warning was still hanging over my head.

Gyeulcheon, I realized, was now the safest place for Eunbi—at least for a while, until I sorted out what to do next. I was nervous, so nervous that Rui would refuse me.

Yet I should not have worried. Mine was a wish easily granted.

Now, Rui smiles a small smile, his eyes misted with emotion as I clutch Eunbi to me, so tightly that she laughs and squirms.

She is safe, she is alive, she is out of Asina's clutches.

Oh gods. Oh gods.

If you played a hand in this, I thank you. I squeeze my eyes shut against hot tears as I silently speak to Gameunjang. Such luck is clearly her doing, no matter how absent she may be. *Thank you, my lady. Thank you, thank you, thank you.*

I want to hold my sister forever, crush her in my embrace, assuring myself over and over that she is safe.

But she pulls away, frowning. "Don't cry, Lili!" There is no sadness on her face, just bright, childish joy. "I missed you! And now we're together again. And you're best friends with an *emperor*!" she adds in an awed whisper, peeking over her shoulder at Rui, who arches a brow at me with a shrug. "A magical emperor who is so, *so* handsome and who's your very, very, *very* best friend!"

Rui smirks, looking down at the ground and steadily avoiding my piercing look. I snort through my tears. "I assume he told you that?"

"After he asked if I wanted to come and see you, I asked how he knew you. And *he* said that you two are the very, very, very best of friends," Eunbi repeats, smiling widely down at me. She's missing her two front teeth, the adult ones just starting to peek through, and as a result, has a lisp. "So I said yes! Also, are you going to be an empress?" She eyes me suspiciously.

"Absolutely not." I glare at Rui, whose amusement grows tenfold.

Eunbi kisses my cheek before stepping back to admire the hill lands. "A magical kingdom," she whispers in awe. "A magical kingdom with magical kings and magic!"

She's clearly unaware that Rui is the Pied Piper. I watch as she twirls, her arms out, staring up at the moons. Her face is bright with wonder as she turns back to me. "Are Chara and Chryse here, too? Sang, Yoonho?" she asks eagerly. "Can I see them? It's been so long! Do they live here, too? Why did you all move?"

I cannot stop myself from flinching.

She does not know—I have not told her my story. And a part of me never, ever wants to.

But I take a deep breath, hating the excitement in her eyes. "Eunbi—" I cut myself off as she parts her lips in a little circle, attentive.

There will be a time for explanations later. Now is the time for reunion. For joy, for love.

"Promise me that you will let yourself live. Truly live."

So instead, I push down my grief and smile. "Come, Eunbi. Rui and I have something to show you."

As Eunbi splashes in the shallow, lazuline waters of the pond that Rui pointed out to me during our first trip to the hill lands, I sit with the emperor on the shore.

Eunbi's laughter is bright and tinkling as she jumps and spins, spraying water in her wake. In the middle of the lake, a couple of swans glance toward her with what I can almost swear are indulgent smiles. I cannot wipe the matching grin from my face as she looks back at me every five seconds and waves, like she cannot believe that we are once again reunited.

I cannot believe it, either.

"She thinks you a fairy-tale emperor," I say to Rui, who grins at me.

"Am I not?"

"No," I retort sharply, arching a brow. "You're the Pied Piper."

His smile falters slightly, his expression going taut. "Can one not be both?" he asks slyly, but the mischief in his words does not meet his eyes at all.

"Tell me," I press, watching as Eunbi twirls in the water. "Tell me why you steal them." There is no question as to who *them* are. I have been waiting to resume my questioning, and I do so now with a steely fervor.

But Rui has grown quiet. "There are some stories, little thief, that cannot be told." His jaw is tight, his attention set firmly on the waters before us.

"Cannot be told?" I cut a sharp look to him. "Or *will not* be told?"

He doesn't answer me.

"Rui."

The emperor gestures to Eunbi. His eyes are somber, his brows pinched. I remember the mourning in his tone in the library, as he spoke of the humans in his kingdom. *I treat them well here. It is the most I can do.* "You have yet to tell your sister your story," he says softly, but not without an underlying steel. "You have chosen to wait until the time is right. I ask only for the same luxury."

I hold his gaze for a moment more. But I cannot argue that, and he knows it.

"Will you stay here?" Rui murmurs a few moments later. "With her?"

I run a hand through my hair, watching as Eunbi trips over her own feet and lands on her bottom in the water, cackling. "For a while," I reply slowly. "But then…" *You know I must go.*

To my kingdom.

To my revenge.

To destroy those who destroyed me.

It has always been my destiny to do so. Ever since that night of blood and betrayal. And now, I am free. Now, I can fight.

"I see," says Rui quietly. "And after?"

"After?" I smile as Eunbi trips again, and shake my head fondly. "After," I say quietly, "I think I'll want to find some peace."

A moment of silence passes between us—fragile, hesitant with hope.

"She will be safe here," the emperor gently says, and I turn to him. His hair ripples in a stray wind, his flowing dark robes shimmering under the moonlight. "And you must promise me, Lina, that you will remain safe as well. In Sunpo."

In Sunpo.

Fire ignites in my blood. Hope, pure and burning.

Hope, the most dangerous emotion of all.

"Sunpo," I repeat, the word flying out of me in a gasp. "My kingdom. I can truly reclaim it." The realization nearly knocks me over.

Because I am strong. Fast.

Wicked and wild.

And although I was all of those things before, the wongun enhancer has turned me into something else entirely.

I raise a hand, letting the teal scales emerge on my skin. I admire them as I rotate my hand this way and that, and smile.

It has turned me into something that can avenge the Talons.

That can avenge my family.

"Rui." My blood sings with pure, undiluted joy. "Tonight, release Kalmin. Return him to the Blackbloods. Let them think that I died here in Gyeulcheon."

It isn't far from the truth, after all. I *have* died. I simply haven't stayed dead.

"Let the Blackbloods rejoice. Let them drink themselves into delirium, let them parade in the streets."

A mirror smile is slowly spreading across Rui's lips. He says nothing, knowing more is to come.

In the pond, Eunbi laughs, bright and joyful—as if she can sense the justice that is coming.

"Let him rule Sunpo. Let him think himself a victor, an emperor." My eyes glint dangerously. "Let that bastard bathe in riches, in women, in wealth. Let Kalmin Konrarnd have everything he's ever dreamed of."

And although I have turned back to Eunbi as she smiles and splashes, I still sense the dark half-moon that curves Rui's lips. Sense the power that hums within him, lifting its ancient head in interest at the prospect of such a game. "Your wish is my command, Shin Lina," he murmurs, taking my hand in his.

My breath catches in my throat as joy strangles me in its chokehold.

The war did not end that fateful night in the mansion.

No, it has only just begun.

And with Eunbi tucked away safely in Gyeulcheon, I will be free to unleash the full extent of my fury.

I look to the sky, at the glowing moons that flicker almost as if in laughter—as if we share a secret, a dirty little joke. A cruel smile twists my lips as I squeeze Rui's hand tighter.

For even a realm away, I can feel it. A tug in my gut. A spark in my chest. A humming in my blood. I am the last of the Talons. My kingdom calls to me.

And when I arrive…

The Blackbloods will feel my wrath.

ACKNOWLEDGMENTS

During the long and winding road from inception to publication, *Last of the Talons* encountered a plethora of individuals, all of whom supported and encouraged Shin Lina's story with more enthusiasm than I ever could have hoped for.

To Mom and Dad, my very first beta readers and biggest supporters. I am beyond grateful to you both for fostering my love of writing and supporting my dreams unconditionally from the very beginning. To Harry and Jesse, my little brothers: "I made a book!" I love you all so very, very much.

The one and only Serena Nettleton, for listening to me ramble about *Last of the Talons* for hours on end…but also for being my best friend and my soul sister. Words simply cannot describe how much I appreciate and adore you, so these two sentences will have to do. To Penelope Kopa Kim, who is the absolute cutest labradoodle in existence. You can't read, but I think you'd like this book.

To Grandma and Grandpa, who I love dearly (Grandpa—I'll see that the short story we wrote together gets published one day, gerbil characters and all). Halmeoni and Haraboji—for cheering me on and stuffing me with the most delicious Korean food at every opportunity. 사랑해요, 할아버지! 사랑해요, 할머니! And thanks also to my aunt Alice, who relentlessly requested this novel in various bookstores long before its release—your enthusiasm brought a smile to my face.

To the amazing Emily Forney, for being a kick-ass literary agent (with bonus points for being a fellow Stefan Salvatore supporter). Manifesting that goat farm for you. To my brilliant group of agent siblings, for your support and constant kindness. And to my friend Kamilah Cole—your steadfast mentorship and encouragement has been a highlight of my days.

To the people at Entangled Teen, starting with my editors Stacy Abrams and Jen Bouvier—thank you for believing in the assassin and the Dokkaebi as much as I do. I also send my gratitude to Liz Pelletier, Jessica Turner, Curtis Svehlak, Elizabeth Turner Stokes, Toni Kerr, Riki Cleveland, and Angela Melamud—all of whom contributed an immense amount of time and dedication to *Last of the Talons*. Thank you also to Valerie Esposito at Macmillan, for distributing this book into the hands of readers. And, of course, a heartfelt thanks to the brilliant cover artist, Ashley Mackenzie.

And finally, I thank you—the reader. I hope you enjoyed sharing this world and this story with Lina, and that you'll join her on her next adventure soon.

Last of the Talons is an epic, pulse-pounding adventure romance. However, the story includes elements that may not be suitable for all readers. Death of a loved one, violence, indentured servitude, physical and emotional abuse, smoking/addiction/withdrawal, orphanhood, drinking alcohol/hangovers, and PTSD all appear in the novel. Readers who may be sensitive to these elements, please take note.

Let's be friends!

🐦 @EntangledTeen

📷 @EntangledTeen

f @EntangledTeen

♪ @EntangledTeen

📰 bit.ly/TeenNewsletter

entangled teen

an imprint of Entangled Publishing LLC